Spinner's Island
Spinner's Lake
End Haven Regional Airport
Greifenberg Manor
Old Mill Historical Site
Old Mill Road
Birmingham Road
12
End Haven Mall
The Moon Woods
The Place with No Name
Fairfax Community Center
H
End Haven
Main Street
Hunter Avenue
Zobel Compound
Lemon Avenue Library
The Knoll
Lindsay Thorsen's House
Lowell Grendel's House
Finger Lake

# IDLE COUNTY

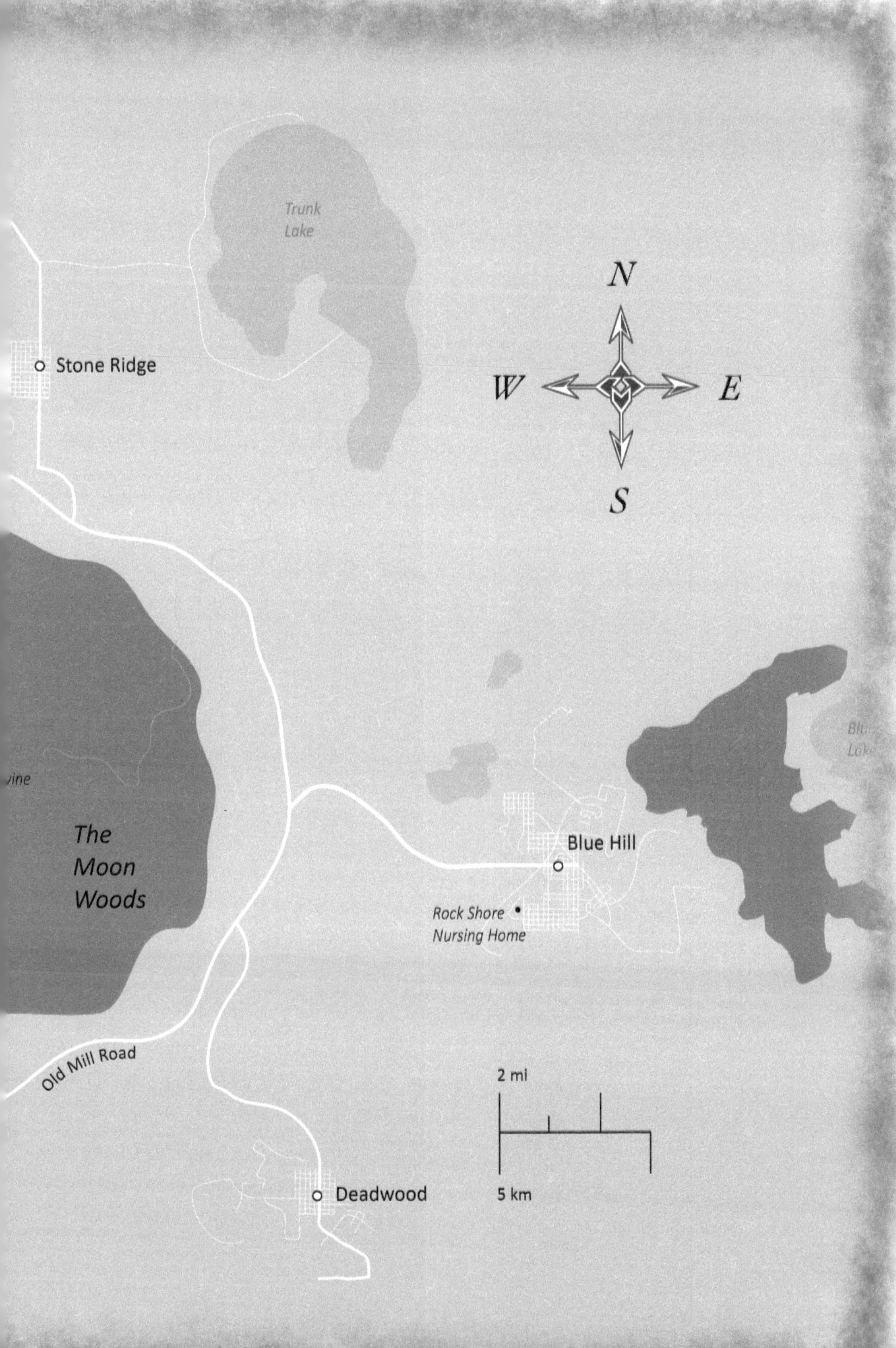

Trunk Lake
Stone Ridge
N
W
E
S
The Moon Woods
vine
Blue Lake
Blue Hill
Rock Shore Nursing Home
Old Mill Road
Deadwood
2 mi
5 km

# THE RISE

## OF

## JONATHAN FLITE

# THE RISE OF JONATHAN FLITE

BY MATTHEW J. BEIER

AN EPICALITY BOOK • EPICALITY BOOKS

*San Francisco*

For my old college friend and dorm neighbor, Lindsay Thorsen, who lent me her name for this book. Fifteen years later, it's finally here.

| 1910 | May 9, 1910 - *Father Benedict Wise discovers the cave anomaly under Idle County's Moon Woods.* |

*May 9, 1910 - Father Benedict Wise discovers the cave anomaly under Idle County's Moon Woods.*

*March 9, 1916 - Elizabeth Parker notices Simon Villard serving on the altar at Saint Andrew's Church in End Haven.*

**1920**

*May 6, 1924 - Elizabeth Parker escapes a house fire at her home by jumping out a third-floor window. Her parents and siblings are killed.*

*February 2, 1929 - Father Benedict Wise dies and leaves his journals to Elizabeth Parker.*

**1930**

*February 16, 1934 - Elizabeth Parker and Simon Villard begin their love affair.*

**1940**

*January 7, 1944 - Earl Zobel signs first weapons manufacturing contract for the United States government under a subsidiary of his family business, Zobel Enterprises.*

*October 2, 1947 - Simon Villard murders Joshua Grime.*

**1950**

*September 26, 1959 - Rose Margaret Layton dies in Jackson Taconite Mine.*

**1960**

*March 2, 1964 - Victor Zobel is born.*

*January 31, 1966 - Max Pope is born.*

*September 1, 1969 - Elizabeth Grime begins teaching at Benedict Wise University.*

**1970**

August 31, 1987 - *Max Pope starts his MD/PhD medical scientist training program at Stanford University.*

May 14, 1988 - *Victor Zobel meets Max Pope and Cassandra Byrne at Stanford University.*

1980

1990

December 1, 1998 - *Victoria and Revis Zobel are born.*

November 26, 2006 - *Lindsay Thorsen joins Molly Butler and Elijah Bryce's Saturday meeting at the Lemon Avenue Library for the first time.*

November 12–13, 2007 - *Natalie Pent sees Jillian Pope arguing with Raphael Dumont; Rebecca Sparks escapes the gas explosion that kills her family.*

July 4, 2010 - *The Idle County Seven vanish without a trace; Victor Zobel organizes search of the Moon Woods.*

September 19, 2012 - *David Thorsen and Natalie Pent meet at Saint Andrew's Grotto.*

2000

2010

September 3, 2018 - *Clovia Bell is born.*

May 30, 2020 - *Jonathan Flite is born.*

2020

May 4, 2034 - *Rebecca Sparks predicts Jonathan Flite's involvement in* WorldLine *in first interview with Alice Winterblume.*

July 20, 2037 - *Clovia Bell starts working full-time at* WorldLine.

August 2, 2038 - *Winifred Flite, Lydia Clark, and others are hospitalized following Weston Carrow's suicide bombing.*

2030

2040

PART 1

# MISSING

ALWAYS THE QUIET, PECULIAR STORIES left tingles on the backs of people's necks. It was impossible to say which ones left the deepest psychological marks, but often, they were those shared most cautiously, sometimes as whispers in the dark.

Rose Margaret Layton had become one of those stories, an inspirer of those shared whispers. And what had her pathetic life even amounted to, when all was said and done? Not much, though she still didn't want to admit it.

She had lived all of her days in Arrowhead Hills, Minnesota, a mining town, and been married twice. Her first husband fled Arrowhead Hills for California; her second husband had drunk himself to death. Both abused her. Neither had given her a child.

During her first penniless winter as a widow—1952, it had been—she had sold herself to local townsmen to get by.

Nine months later had come the first miracle of her life: Samuel, her only son. Oh, how that little boy had been a welcome surprise, even in the face of her destitution! He was the one perfect thing she had ever done. Contrary to the judgmental whispers around town, Samuel hadn't been an added burden. Instead, he had cured her loneliness. He had inspired her to find steady, honorable work as a waitress. He had brought her joy every day.

Then just five days before his seventh birthday in 1959, he disappeared.

Rose had unraveled in front of the whole town. She searched frantically for Samuel and solicited assistance from anyone who would help: the county sheriff, her hesitant neighbors, and even Arrowhead Hills's condemnatory churchgoers, who, despite their moral superiority over Rose's not-so-virtuous past, couldn't ignore the plight of a missing child.

Rumors soon surfaced that a local miner named Carter Van Ness had taken young Samuel to visit Jackson Taconite Mine outside normal work hours, and on more than one occasion—always under the pretense that he was preparing the boy to one day join the mining crew. After questioning both Mr. Van Ness and several other miners, however, the sheriff had deemed the rumors a dead end. There was no solid evidence against Mr. Van Ness, and any old mine shafts from before the open-pit-mining days were simply too dangerous to search.

Desperate, Rose had gone to inspect the old shafts herself, entering through one of the mine's abandoned entrances on the south side of town. About six hundred feet in, she screamed her son's name, and a portion of the mine collapsed on her. Everything went black.

SOON, SHE WAS STANDING outside her own body.

Then outside the collapsed mine.

Then outside Samuel's and her old home—the studio apartment

above Miner's Diner, where she had waited tables nightly after the establishment's owner took pity on her following Samuel's conception.

She now seemed distant from this old world, detached from time, as the world carried on just beyond her reach.

Within six weeks, a new waitress moved into the apartment above the diner. Her occupancy and job didn't last long, however; the business slowly disintegrated in the years that followed, as Jackson Taconite Mine began shutting down.

Soon, the entire town of Arrowhead Hills—once populated almost entirely by miners and their families—became not much more than a ghost town.

THIS WAS DEATH; IT HAD TO BE. Yet Rose was stuck inside her own emotions, feeling constantly drawn to keep searching—not just for her son and others similarly lost but also for the evil people responsible for such crimes. Emotions, both her own and those of others, were magnetic and powerful in ways she had barely begun to glimpse.

She listened, watched, and waited. Understanding of life would come later, when she was ready to let go of it. But here and now, there was a problem: a girl named Lindsay Thorsen, trapped in a collapsed stretch of the now-fully-abandoned Jackson Taconite Mine. She had been taken there by a man who—

*A man who was searching for ghosts. For* me.

Rose's emotions were always a hurricane. Always in turmoil. Always attracting her to the nearest physical events that aligned with her mission to search, to save, to usher innocent victims to safety. She could barely control the whos, whats, and whens, but with some focus, she could see and understand the physical time frames she was affecting.

This was 2006.

February.

Cold, with only a shallow layer of snow.

This man—this *horrible* man—was the camera-toting murderer Rose had seen during snippets of focus, when the emotional pull toward her old world was strong. The first time had been a few months before, on Halloween. He had been luring a young costumed boy named Drew into a jeep, similar to the ones certain miners had driven around Arrowhead Hills in the 1950s. Not even three hours later, he had killed the boy and disposed of his body in a most unthinkable way, as Rose watched with rage.

She had begun following the man, tormenting him, allowing him to see her—and even photograph her—when her ability to physically manifest was strong enough.

This girl now trapped with him in Jackson Taconite Mine—Lindsay— was the murdered boy's sister. She had discovered the truth about her brother's killer, so the man had taken her, too. And the girl's future—a set of probabilities Rose could sense only vaguely—was still somehow projecting the possibility of even more grief.

Even so, it wasn't Lindsay's time. She didn't deserve to die in this mine, as Rose had.

"*Get up,*" Rose said to her.

Lindsay lay under the edge of the collapse's debris. Her captor was farther in, crushed and blocked, which meant she had a chance to escape. To continue her life. To—

"*I'm not sure I can,*" she thought back at Rose.

Suddenly, they were both standing next to each other. Lindsay was outside her own body now, operating as an energetic imprint, just as Rose had done after the mine collapsed on her in 1959.

"*You always have a choice,*" Rose continued.

"*My brother, Drew, didn't.*"

On a level just past Rose's ability to understand, however, she sensed the girl's statement wasn't completely true. Yes, the man trapped deeper into the mine had killed her brother, but life and death were balanced secrets, both hiding their own particular angles of reality.

"*There's more for you to do,*" Rose insisted. "*Find a way out. Do it for Drew.*"

And suddenly Lindsay was gone.

Rose was alone again—listening, watching, waiting. This was her existence now, the one she preferred. Moving on would mean she'd never find out what happened to her son. It would also mean she wouldn't be around to help other people who had lost loved ones, including people like Lindsay Thorsen, who—

2005

—WAS TALKING ON THE PHONE in her upstairs bedroom on October 31, 2005, less than fifty feet away from the backyard below, where her younger brother, Drew, was being kidnapped. It was Halloween night, a blustery one hinting at an early winter.

"No, I'm eating soon, and then I have kickboxing at six," Lindsay told her friend Natalie Pent while maneuvering her long dark hair into a tight ponytail. Just as she tucked the cell phone between her shoulder and ear, Natalie buzzed with garbled gibberish through the other end. Lindsay tied off her ponytail, then repositioned the phone properly. "Say that again. I didn't hear you."

"I said: Can't you just skip kickboxing for one night and come to the party? It's Halloween, for God's sake."

Lindsay scoffed and looked herself up and down in the mirror. There was no way she'd let herself be caught dead in some slutty bunny costume, like the one Natalie was planning to wear. "I told you a million times, I'm not going to that party! I don't have a costume, and

Karly's dad gives me the creeps. I always feel weird when I'm over there."

"Well, you're the only one," Natalie replied. "Everyone thinks he's funny. And seriously, he looks hot in his biking shorts."

"Yeah, and he should know we're all in seventh grade."

"You should be all into him since you like guy sports so much. It's so weird you haven't gotten sick of kickboxing yet."

"It's fun," Lindsay said. There: her gym bag was ready.

Downstairs, the doorbell rang. Lindsay reached the first floor just in time to see her dazed-looking mother, Sandra, paying the young delivery man. It was Brian, their usual one. His parents had recently moved to Idle County from Des Moines and opened End Haven's only Thai restaurant. It was a taste Lindsay had grown up loving in Chicago, and she was glad this rural corner of Minnesota now had at least one option for it. It didn't have much else.

Sandra took the bag of food toward the kitchen, calling back to Lindsay as Natalie Pent continued chattering through the phone about the Halloween party. Lindsay held the device away from her ear while throwing her duffel bag next to the banister. "One sec, Natalie—wait. What, Mom?"

"Go find your brother," Sandra said. "Tell him I got his wonton soup." For the second time that week, Lindsay smelled marijuana on her mother's clothing—covered up by perfume. The trend was continuing.

"Is he still out in the sandbox?" she asked.

"Getting his costume all dirty, I'm sure. He's been wearing that damned mask all day. Probably a snotty mess inside it."

Lindsay scrunched her face. "That's disgusting."

"What's disgusting?" Natalie Pent asked through the phone.

"Drew," Lindsay said. "My mom's dropping me off at the community center and then taking him trick-or-treating. He's dressed up like Doctor Deadlock from *Mousepants*."

"Like every other four year old," Natalie replied.

Lindsay crossed through the kitchen, toward the back patio doors, and stepped outside. A gust of wintry wind blew a loose strand of hair across her eyes.

The afternoon's setting sun shone gold on the picnic table. Beyond the patio, a landscaped brick stairway led up to the main yard, which stretched about eighty feet back to where the sandbox and swing set lay. To the right, a grove of cedar trees formed a barrier to the next yard. Their branches played into the wind's fury like dancing, faceless mimes.

Lindsay squinted in the approaching dusk. The sandbox was empty. With a sigh, she stepped back inside, put on a pair of flip-flops that had been sitting next to the patio doors since summer, and trudged across the cold grass, toward the swing set. She walked around it and glanced into the tree-house cubby above the slide. Drew often hid inside it and played with his action figures. But not today.

"You still there?" came Natalie's voice through the cell phone.

"Yeah, sorry. I'm trying to find Drew. I really should go." She held the phone away from her mouth for a moment. "Mom! Drew's not out here!" Then back into the phone: "Okay, Natalie, looks like Drew's being stupid. I have to go find him."

"Okay, well, if you change your mind—"

"I'm going to kickboxing."

"There'll be Sammy's Pizza."

"As if you'd let yourself eat any of it."

"Shut up. I'll see you tomorrow."

"Yep. Bye." Lindsay flipped her cell phone shut, then stepped back through the patio doors. Her mother was unloading the takeout dinner from a paper bag. "Hey, I forgot you started getting the panang curry," she said. "Totally spaced. Is pad thai good enough?"

"You remembered Drew's wonton soup," Lindsay said with a scowl. "PS: He's totally not outside. Did he go upstairs?"

"Probably," Sandra replied. "I didn't see him come in, though."

She opened the container of wonton soup. "Drew! Dinner!" When the boy's usual rush of footsteps failed to pound the ceiling, she turned to Lindsay. "Honey, can you go up and find him?"

"I just came *down* the stairs," Lindsay grumbled, turning back toward them just the same. Such was life for the only big sister. As she ascended to the second floor, she called over her shoulder, "Is Dad taking Drew trick-or-treating with you?"

Sandra's voice, always layered with stress even though she never did anything but shuttle Lindsay and Drew around town, floated out from the kitchen. "No, he's got a presentation tomorrow, so he's working late. He'll be picking you up from kickboxing, though."

"As long as he's not half an hour late again," Lindsay said.

Upstairs: no Drew. Not even behind the desk in their father's study.

"He's not up here!" Lindsay yelled, sauntering back downstairs.

"I bet he's out front," Sandra said. She crossed through the kitchen, hallway, dining room, and main living room to open the front door. "Drew! Dinner! Wonton soup!"

No footsteps. Wonton soup usually did the trick.

After the neighbors told Sandra they hadn't seen Drew all afternoon, the stress in her voice turned into worry. Strangely, it was the first time in years Lindsay had seen her mother show any real emotion. Usually, she spoke either with her "cocktail party" voice or her "busy" voice. This was neither.

"When was the last time you saw him?" Lindsay asked, trying to hide the hint of worry in her own voice. It wasn't like Drew to disappear right before dinner.

"I was lying on the couch for about half an hour after I called Tickle Me Thai," her mother said. "He was out back playing in the sandbox. Unless he went wandering through the trees over to Provell Street?" Sandra turned toward the door that led to the garage. "Honey, can you stay here and keep an eye out for him while I go look? He's not in the house. Actually, can you also call the Johnsons and the Fitzgibbons to see if he's there? The numbers are on that list by the phone."

"Sure," Lindsay said. "If he shows up, I'll call your cell."

"Yes. Do that."

He would be out there somewhere. This had happened once before, last summer on a Saturday morning, when their father had gone in to work for an emergency meeting. When nobody was looking, Drew had left the house all by himself and walked to the end of Dollywyn Drive. Even so, Sandra had been able to see him from the front sidewalk right away. When scolded, he had said, "I was just going to see Daddy!"

Their father, David, was the chief financial officer of Steelhead Printing, the only nonagricultural company in Idle County that had any national scope. All Lindsay knew was that he was a CPA and had his MBA and that—like his own father, who'd been very poor as a child after moving to Chicago from a Potawatomi reservation—he worked extra hard so he could provide his family with a good life. Two years ago, Steelhead Printing had lured him to End Haven from his previous vice president of finance job in Chicago, with a great title and salary to help sell the "almost rural" location. Lindsay equated this new life with prairies, lakes, rolling hills, and wooded areas—including the oddly circular Moon Woods, which lay directly east of End Haven. It was all generally tolerable, but she missed the hustle and bustle of the city.

Neither the Johnsons nor the Fitzgibbons had seen Drew. Both families promised to keep an eye out.

Lindsay sat at the kitchen table and opened her pad thai. It was still steaming hot, and she ate it right out of the plastic container while listening to the grandfather clock in the living room tick the seconds away.

An hour later, her mother still hadn't returned.

"Drew, if you're hiding in the house, you better get your butt down here!" Lindsay yelled into the air. "Mom's worried, and it's getting serious!"

Only the old clock ticked back in response.

The tangle of worry in her gut was now undeniable. Drew was only four.

*It'll be fine*, she told herself. *Stuff like this always is.*

She searched the entire house again, but the only visible sign of Drew was a pile of *Mousepants* action figures on his bedroom floor.

At ten to seven, Lindsay heard her mother's Chevy Tahoe curl into the driveway and the garage door open. Almost a minute passed before she heard one of the Tahoe's doors slam. She waited to hear another slam—Drew's side of the car—but it never came.

Sandra Thorsen opened the door from the garage and stepped into the house's rear foyer. She was moving slowly, with unusually delicate gracefulness. When she switched on the hallway light, her face was pale.

"No Drew," Lindsay said. It wasn't a question. Something was pounding deep in her chest, a vibration of dread more powerful than any she had ever experienced.

"I looked on every street and called every friend," Sandra said, leaning against the kitchen counter. "He didn't come back? You're sure he didn't come back?"

"I checked the house again about twenty minutes ago. He's not here."

"God. Okay. I called your dad, and he's coming home to help me look."

"Did you call the police?"

"I did. Just in case. They have a couple squad cars out looking. He'll turn up. It's only been an hour."

"Over two," Lindsay corrected.

A dreamlike bubble formed around them, swirling with all the potential outcomes of Drew's disappearance. Maybe he would show up in ten minutes. Maybe he had wandered off toward the center of town. Maybe somebody had—

The doorbell rang.

"Oh my God," Sandra said, jumping away from the counter. She ran through the living room with Lindsay close in tow, toward their house's front door. She pulled it open with enough force to cause a flutter in Lindsay's ponytail.

"*Trick or treat!*" a pile of monsters screamed.

Sandra skipped backward in shock. "Oh, Jesus. I thought—"

Lindsay's gaze dashed from face to face. All were masked—and one of them was Doctor Deadlock from *Mousepants*. She lunged forward and reached through the crowd of kids. "Drew, is that you? Kid, take your mask off!" She tried to grab the neck of the mask, but the little rascal ducked from her grasp.

"Mommy!" Doctor Deadlock yelped in a voice that wasn't Drew's. He ran off the porch, and the other kids followed in a panic, as if Lindsay herself were the Halloween boogeyman.

"Damn it," she whispered.

Instead of batting an eyelash at Lindsay's swear word, Sandra simply hung on the door, looking out at the neighborhood. After a moment, she said, "I'm going to go search again."

"Mom, there are going to be a hundred Doctor Deadlocks out there—"

But Sandra was already moving back toward the garage. "I don't care. I'm going back out. Stay here and wait for Drew. Call me when he comes back. Tell your dad to come and find me. The police have my cell phone number, and they know what Drew's costume is. I'll . . . I'll call you if I find anything."

Dread dripped down her face like wax as she rushed back through the door, into the garage.

Lindsay's stomach turned over and over. It would be fine. Drew would come home. All this hoopla would be for nothing, because it was just a silly child's mistake. He would have no idea how much panic he had caused.

But it was dark outside now.

Dark outside, and no Drew.

No Drew.

Sandra Thorsen was a poster parent for child loss. She had lived it, burned in it, and been reborn from its ashes. When people tried to tell her she was simply fooling herself by believing she had found a way to be happy—and they often did—she would smile politely and remind them that she had lost not one child in life but two, her entire brood.

Yet she had still come out alive.

Still overcome her drive to self-medicate.

Still fought tooth and nail to feel guiltless in the fact that she was somehow alive, and Lindsay and Drew were not.

After living for twenty-one years in the dazzling hills of Sausalito, California, just north of San Francisco, Sandra knew her purpose as a late-blooming psychotherapist was to be a beacon of hope for grieving parents. Because life went on. Life could be good again. The love people had for their lost children could be channeled into positive forward momentum. It wasn't about forgetting a lost child or repressing the grief; it was about assimilating the memories and pain to form a new sense of self. If the alternative was to be miserable forever by focusing on what was no longer there and what could never be, why continue to live at all?

No matter that her patients quietly judged her facelift. Or her nose job. Or the tiny strip of neon pink hair that graced her dyed, strawberry-blond short crop. Sure, their shifty eyes sometimes jumped to conclusions, but Sandra was the one with a three-book deal and a house on the San Francisco Fucking Bay—*let them fucking judge.*

When her phone rang midmorning on February 23, 2034, she was sitting on her patio, sipping coffee and trying to read the most recent draft of her third book. It was garbage—the new ghostwriter just wasn't vibing with the material at all. When the phone's Zen-chime ringtone reached her ears, she immediately assumed it was Zoltan Books, calling to apologize for delivering this horrendous doorstop of words.

But the number was unknown—from Santa Cruz, a city two hours south of her.

*Probably someone from the university calling about a guest lecture.*

She answered without hesitation, despite limiting it to an anonymous "Hello?"

A woman cleared her throat on the other end of the line, then said, "Hi, is this Sandra Thorsen?"

Sandra cleared her own throat. "It is."

"My name is Zoe Caldiero, and I'm the medical assistant to a physicist named Dorothy Garland, down in Santa Cruz. She knew your daughter, Lindsay, back in Idle County, before she disappeared—you might remember her by the name Rebecca Sparks?"

Sandra's aging knuckles turned white. For a moment, she simply breathed into the phone.

Rebecca Sparks was the only part of those dreadful Minnesota years that Sandra had not yet been able to compartmentalize. The wheelchair-driving girl had been proof positive of things Sandra still didn't want to believe in and still felt uncomfortable discussing.

The woman on the other end of the call—Zoe, had she said?—continued as if Sandra's silence were her only window to talk. "I'm calling because Dorothy—or Rebecca, as it were—was almost attacked three nights ago here at her home in Santa Cruz."

Taking three short breaths, Sandra fought the urge to end the call. Then: "Is she okay?"

"She is. We've got added security here, but someone snuck in through the driveway gate after a food delivery, of all things. They tried crawling through her bedroom window and tripped the house alarm. She wanted me to call you, seeing as you were the only Idle County Seven parent who had public contact information available. She's adamantly claiming that the person who attacked her was connected to the disappearance of your daughter, Lindsay, back in 2010."

Now Sandra could barely breathe.

Memories of Idle County—shaded by images of her long-lost daughter—began flooding her mind once again. Rebecca Sparks was the sister of Alan Sparks, Lindsay's first and only boyfriend; she had also been the sole survivor of a gas explosion that killed Alan and the rest of the Sparks family in 2007. Her peculiar psychic abilities had been well documented among Lindsay, her friends, and even Sandra's husband, David. Hell, they were the reason David had found out about Sandra's first extramarital affair to begin with—Rebecca had somehow told him about it at a New Year's Eve gathering, breaking their marriage before inspiring them to redefine it.

"You have my attention," Sandra said to Zoe Caldiero, almost in a whisper.

"I'm wondering if you'd be willing to meet today, as I'd rather not discuss all this over the phone," Zoe replied. "There are things happening here that could start affecting you soon, and I'd love to present you with the facts. If your schedule is open, we can be in Marin County in two hours."

"We?"

"Rebecca and myself."

Sandra looked out at the glistening San Francisco Bay. Today, it was alive with sailboats glowing in the sun. Idle County and everything related to it were far away and had no place here. Not in California. Not in this better, later stretch of life.

"I've already found a spot," Zoe continued. "Would lunch at Rustic Bakery near the Larkspur Ferry landing work for you? It's very public, at Marin Country Mart. If you feel at all uncomfortable, you can leave."

Before Sandra could muster the gumption to comment on the presumptuous nature of the proposal—not to mention the oddness of a total stranger calling out of the blue to lure her back into the muddy psychological waters of the deep past—she found herself accepting the invitation.

Rustic Bakery for lunch? *Yes.*

Would she be concerned if Rebecca Sparks joined them? *No, not at all.*

Could she agree to keep the meeting under wraps? *Why, of course she could—except with her husband, David; he would want to know.*

When Zoe ended the call, Sandra's body was alive with a sort of anxiety she hadn't felt in almost three decades.


SANDRA WAS TEN MINUTES LATE to Larkspur on purpose. She had met strangers on a whim before, usually younger men from "cougar" dating apps, but this was different. More nerve-wracking.

Her white flats scraped the outdoor mall's brick pathway as she approached Rustic Bakery, holding her new ActoPhone to her ear. One ring, two rings, three rings. And then came her husband's voice:

*"Hi, you've reached David Thorsen. I'm not available right now, so please leave me a message, and I'll call you right back."*

*Fuck.* Of all the days to get his voice mail.

David was currently at the Potawatomi reservation in Oklahoma, likely philandering with Hannah, the "not-quite-girlfriend" he had met on his first visit there four years ago. Such was Sandra's and his redefined marriage now. Sandra was thankful David had girlfriends. It meant she could have boyfriends—something she continued to revel in, even at her age. But damn it if she didn't want him to answer his phone right this very moment.

She settled for a message. "Hi, it's me. Something happened this morning. I got a call from a woman who says she's Rebecca Sparks's medical assistant. As in *Rebecca Sparks* Rebecca Sparks, the girl who ratted me out about that first affair back in End Haven."

A rare burst of gratitude surged through Sandra. For a second, she marveled over the fact that her marriage to David—despite its evolution over time and the raised eyebrows he sometimes got when visiting Hannah on the reservation—had somehow survived all these years. They had married in 1992, shortly after conceiving Lindsay, under society's expectations of what marriage should be. Now they had discarded those silly parameters and were true partners. When life threw punches, they were there for each other, and Sandra now had the sense that another punch—a heavy one—was winding up.

As she approached Rustic Bakery's crowded patio, she lowered her voice and recapped for David everything Zoe Caldiero had told her. "This assistant said Rebecca was almost attacked a few nights ago at her house in Santa Cruz. Apparently she's a physicist now, going by the name Dorothy Garland. I Googled her, and it turns out she went to UC Santa Cruz back in the day, under that new name. No public record of a name change, though."

A pause. What else was there to say?

*So much.*

"Anyway, I'm meeting both women for lunch at Rustic Bakery. If anything happens, I wanted you to know. Call me back. Bye."

Sandra ended the call and turned toward the patio. Almost all the tables were full; the Thursday afternoon sun and unexpected February warmth had brought all the Marin County mothers and their babies out for the day.

But there was no sign of Rebecca Sparks. She would be unmistakable, unless medical advances had somehow worked a miracle in thirty years. The girl—or woman now, Sandra reminded herself—had a brain condition called agenesis of the corpus callosum, which made it difficult for her to walk and speak. Back in Idle County, she had communicated by slowly typing on a small computer keyboard and screen connected to her wheelchair. Now, Sandra assumed, she would have a neural chip that dictated her words.

Sandra craned her neck. She didn't see any—

"Ms. Thorsen?"

She nearly jumped out of her skin.

Trying to shield her surprise, Sandra turned around with her usual, well-practiced air of nonchalance. Standing six feet away was a muscular woman in her early thirties. A warm, mustard-colored dress complemented her striking green eyes, and something about her looked sharp. Maybe even ruthless. She held a paperback book but seemed to be shielding the cover from Sandra.

"I'm Zoe," the woman said briskly, extending a hand. Sandra shook it without saying a word. Zoe quickly sidestepped Sandra's gaze to reveal someone sitting behind her—a blond-haired, middle-aged woman in a wheelchair. "This here is Dorothy. But again, you might remember her as Rebecca."

Rebecca Sparks sat in her chair, watching Sandra carefully. They had never met face-to-face, but Sandra had heard things. Oh yes. Like how Rebecca could read minds. How she talked about reincarnation, angel-like "spirit guides," and other New Agey ideas as if they were real things. How she had been unusually friendly with Max Pope, the neurologist who had lost his medical license after experimenting on dying Alzheimer's patients in Idle County. The very memory of Lindsay and her friends volunteering at Max's research facility sent goosebumps up Sandra's spine.

Words suddenly appeared on the tablet connected to Rebecca's wheelchair.

*You should know Maximilian Pope never hurt anyone during his research in Blue Hill. He also never hurt your daughter, Lindsay.*

And there it was. Rebecca Sparks had invaded her mind as casually as one might chat about the weather—were one able to speak. It was like being caught out in public without any clothes on.

"Do I even need to talk out loud if she can just read my mind without consent?" Sandra asked Zoe, unable to hide the bite in her voice.

"It's courteous to speak normally, yes," Zoe said. "And she usually respects boundaries. I'm sorry. I think she was set on proving herself to you today."

Sandra was about to reply when Rebecca's tablet lit up with more text.

*I intend to tell Alice Winterblume at WorldLine about your daughter Lindsay's flashlight incident. The one in Jackson Taconite Mine in 2006. It will matter once this Rhode Island situation becomes more well known.*

Sandra stiffened.
*The flashlight.*

She hadn't wanted to think about it ever again. She couldn't, lest it open Pandora's box.

To deflect the hysteria building in her heart, she focused on the last line Rebecca's neural chip had typed. "What Rhode Island situation? What the hell are you talking about?"

Zoe furrowed her eyebrows and looked at Sandra carefully. "You haven't heard?"

"About?"

"About the boy in Newport who killed his nurse?"

"No. Should I have?"

Zoe grimaced, then pulled out an ActoPhone from her back pocket. After a few clicks, she handed it to Sandra with a news headline facing up.

### *Nurse Killer, 13, Blames Deadly Outburst on "Past-Life Memories" of 7 Teens Who Vanished in 2010*

It was a headline from just last week.

Sandra's heart rate rose as she skimmed the article. It was about a boy named Jonathan Flite who had strangled his nurse last August, after being hospitalized following a suicide attempt. The nurse's husband had since gone public with details of the juvenile case and caused a small uproar in their small, East Coast community. When Sandra reached a statement from the boy's lawyer, her reading slowed.

> *Jonathan accidentally killed Ellen Graber in a burst of momentary insanity. It was fueled by a lifetime of frustration over the fact that nobody believed his claims that the Idle County Seven, a group of Minnesota teens who famously went missing in 2010, vanished in a large forest near their homes, rather than in Dallas, as many believed.*

"'A large forest.' Is he talking about the Moon Woods?" Sandra asked aloud, shaking her head as she continued reading. The forest in question was a circular woodland whose thirty-mile perimeter road linked Idle County's four towns—End Haven, Stone Ridge, Blue Hill, and Deadwood.

"The Moon Woods—yeah. That's where he says they went missing," Zoe said. "He apparently used to draw pictures of them standing under the trees when he was a kid."

Something about this felt oh-so-possible, oh-so-simple—yet Sandra couldn't immediately pinpoint the reason why.

Anxiety bubbled in her chest as she looked again at Rebecca Sparks. The woman had single-handedly been responsible for putting New Agey ideas into Lindsay's head back in the day. Sandra had always blamed her for the way Lindsay changed during that first year after Drew's disappearance.

Rage—deep, secret, and quiet—began seeping from the most private corner of Sandra's heart. She did everything possible to will it away.

More words appeared on Rebecca's tablet.

> *This is all messy. More than you ever knew. Your daughter and her friends did not drive to Dallas. They went to the Moon Woods to save their friend Molly. Victor Zobel killed them there.*

The statement bit into Sandra like a bear trap. Molly Butler, one of Lindsay's best friends, had been dying of a brain tumor the year they disappeared. And Victor Zobel? He was one of the most famous men in the world—a neurosurgeon, businessman, and *New York Times* bestselling author, famous for his radical atheistic movement, New Naturalism. He had also been the stepfather of Jillian Pope, the neurologist Max Pope's biological daughter—also one of the missing. And hadn't that been why Victor kept coming back to Idle County to begin with? To check up on Jillian after she moved in with Max following the death of her mother, Cassandra, in Switzerland?

Yet Victor had purchased the Moon Woods land in January 2011, just six months after the Idle County Seven vanished. Even Sandra's husband, David, had found this overtly suspicious—enough to go on a wild goose chase to Europe in hopes of gathering further information. And now this Jonathan Flite boy was saying that the kids disappeared right there, in southern Minnesota?

*Oh-so-simple. Oh-so-possible.*

More words on Rebecca's tablet.

*Zoe, give her the book.*

Sandra glanced between the tablet and the paperback in Zoe's hands. The medical assistant sighed, then handed the book to Sandra. Sandra glanced at the cover.

*Our Many Lives.*

She recognized the title—and the author.

*Dr. Cora Crowe.*

David had read this book—and many others by this woman— multiple times. Cora Crowe was a psychiatrist in Boulder, Colorado, who had accidentally stumbled into "past-life regression therapy" while using hypnosis to treat patients. She was a nobody in legitimate scientific circles, but for people who had questions about life and death, she was a major somebody. Enough to have sold over a million books. For ten plus years, Sandra had refused to read a single one of them.

"Rebecca said this would help prepare you," Zoe continued.

Sandra looked up from the book's cover. "For what?"

A final statement zipped onto Rebecca's screen.

*For what's coming.*

As Sandra clutched the copy of *Our Many Lives*, a shudder ran through her, like a rock starting an avalanche.

"Shall we eat?" Zoe asked.

Against her burning desire to run back to the hills of Sausalito and never see these two women again, Sandra nodded. Then she followed them toward Rustic Bakery, preparing herself for the very worst.

From the introduction to the memoir *Our Many Lives* by Dr. Cora Noreen Crowe, published on July 15, 2024:

*This isn't a book about religion. Or a book about faith. Or a book about believing blindly in things for the sake of giving life a sense of meaning. What I've come to realize in the past few years is that—for me—life isn't about having some belief about what will or will not happen after we die and sticking to it with guns blazing. It's about living, growing, and looking back: discovering what worked, what didn't, and what I could have done differently.*

*I'm a medical doctor raised as a casual Baptist. For many years, particularly during my tenure as medical director of the psychiatric unit at Boulder Hospital in Boulder, Colorado, I was a staunch atheist and liked to think I knew everything I reasonably could about the world.*

*Now I suppose you could say I'm an agnostic. Like many people, I've had what I would call a spiritual awakening; I've also assigned value to it in a way that now affects how I approach my life. You could say this places me in a particular "camp" of thought, much like people with religious beliefs.*

*One difference I've noticed, observed, and analyzed, however, is that I'm coming to my beliefs from a standpoint of trying to understand what I don't know. With rational thought, this has to come first. Most religions I've heard of today are now based on hearsay, a long game of "Telephone" passed through the ages, following significant events that very clearly caught the attention of people at the times they occurred. But one must also consider history, human psychology, and the slow-burn proliferation of science and information. Under these lenses, it becomes clear that religions were products of their times and places, often stemming from small geographical locations long before the spread of our modern, globalized context.*

*Yet the events that sparked them were influential enough to touch something deeply rooted in the human experience.*

*The Bible; the Qur'an; the Tipitaka; the Torah, Tanakh, and Talmud; the Vedas and Upanishads, and so many more—all of these sacred texts differ in the so-called truths they purport. They can't all be 100 percent correct, yet many who consider them sacred would defend their validities to the death.*

*Consider the power, then, of belief.*

*Belief is the least common denominator in all organized religions. Today, these belief structures are generally based on blind faith—often without critical analysis. During the times in history when they formed, what we now consider knowledge—the science that powers the cars we drive, the phones and computers we use, the airplanes we fly in—didn't yet exist. There was nothing to check and balance the mass beliefs that spread throughout human societies.*

*A thousand years ago, a person who believed in angels and demons but who wasn't aware of magnetism might have seen metal move "on its own" and attributed it to spiritual activity from the beyond. Slightly more recently, people who believed the world was flat found they could circle the globe. Less than 150 years ago, people were unaware that the visible objects in front of them— tables, cups, chairs, and all others—were made of tiny particles governed by four fundamental forces that scientists now call the strong force, the weak force, gravity, and electromagnetism.*

*As our knowledge progresses, so do beliefs. And I think humanity is now on the cusp of a new frontier of both.*

*Today, we're in the process of learning that our entire physical experience is created by electrical impulses in our brains. This includes our ability to measure the subatomic particles—and resulting molecules—that hit the receptors of our five senses, which create that experience to begin with.*

*The sensation of this book in your hands.*

*The sight of its words.*

*The pressure of its cover on your fingers.*

*The smell of its pages, if you're reading on paper.*

*The sound of its pages turning.*

*All of it is created in your mind. So are the thoughts, images, and ideas the experience of reading inspires.*

*Still following me? Good, because now it gets weird.*

*We know these brain impulses result from our perception of the particles that create the illusion of our physical world, but we have no idea what these particles—and this illusion—actually are. It's presumed they've existed for billions of years as a result of the Big Bang, but they continue to be mysterious in many ways. Here are just a few:*

- *Subatomic particles can seemingly take multiple routes from point A to point B at the same time.*
- *Two individuals can consciously measure different versions of the "same" reality.*
- *Particles take physical form only after they're measured. Before that, they exist only in a nebulous wave of probability.*
- *And finally, the award for weirdest: human choice can change the way particles behave— even millions of years after those particles' behaviors should have been decided.*

*Conscious perception, then, can legitimately be said to underscore "everything," yet many scientists think consciousness is a meaningless byproduct of the brain's physical processes. So, what comes first? Physical reality, or this thing we call the mind? Science quietly seems to be erring on the side of the mind.*

*So, I ask: What don't we yet know about life and the universe? In what ways will our context for belief shift next? Might there actually be experiences of consciousness beyond the physical world we perceive? Might the world religions all have common ground in this "beyond," this realm of what many consider to be "spiritual"?*

*The holy grail in modern science—physics in particular—is a Theory of Everything, a testable way to accurately explain all physical processes in the universe. But if consciousness somehow plays a role in how this physical universe operates, must it not also be accounted for? Despite the kicking and screaming of many scientists, experiments are currently giving us some incredibly odd hints that yes, it must be. And for the purposes of this book, it matters.*

*In my opinion, it's foolish to think we currently have all the necessary knowledge for everything that will ever be relevant to us. If I have one unshakable belief, it's that having an open mind is the only sensible way to approach life's questions. It's also often the key to recognizing that those questions exist at all.*

*Dr. Cora Noreen Crowe*
*Boulder, Colorado*
*April 24, 2024*

"Okay, Lindsay, we're going to ask you some questions, and please think about your answers as best you can," Special Agent Kim Forester said. "Try to remember details you might not otherwise care about. Anything can help."

Agent Forester was part of the FBI's North Central Child Abduction Rapid Deployment team. She was sitting in a chair alongside Detective Brian Rhymes from the Idle County Sheriff's Department, in the Thorsens' second living room—the decorative one on the east side of the house that nobody liked to use. Lindsay's parents, who had already gone through multiple rounds of questioning, were in the kitchen with another special agent and two deputies.

It was Tuesday. Drew had been missing all night, and the sheriff's department hadn't turned up any sign of him.

"I'll do my best to answer," Lindsay said. Despite the comfortable temperature in the room, she was fighting shivers. They seemed to be coming from the knot in her chest, as if all her nerves were caged there, frozen and unable to burst free.

"Are you close to your brother, Drew?" Agent Forester asked. "I know he's only four, but do you get along well? Are you his nice big sister?"

What hurt Lindsay most was that she barely had to think before answering. "I don't think I've been as good a sister as I should have. We play together sometimes, but mostly I try to just do my own thing. Even when it makes him cry."

"How do you mean, 'do your own thing'?"

Not wanting to let on how alone she felt at home on a daily basis, Lindsay deflected by telling Agent Forester and Detective Rhymes about kickboxing—about how she'd do it all day, every day if she could, and about Natalie Pent quitting class after three sessions, because she was nervous about having all the boys there, watching her.

"And Natalie Pent? She lives here in End Haven?"

"Yeah, over on Windsong Road. On the south end."

Detective Rhymes scratched something onto his notepad as Agent Forester continued. "Now, I'm sure you're aware that we're asking your parents similar questions. I know some of this might seem pointless, but it all helps. It'll give us ideas about possible paths to take. With disappearances like this, it's difficult to know where to start. It's okay to be nervous, though. We just need to know who you and your family interact with on a regular basis, and maybe on a not-so-regular basis."

"You mean you think Natalie Pent or somebody in her family might have kidnapped Drew?"

"No, no—nothing like that," Agent Forester replied, but she didn't elaborate further.

Lindsay's legs felt like dead weights hanging off the couch. She tried crossing them. It was even less comfortable.

"But you've known Natalie Pent for how long?" the agent continued.

"About two years," Lindsay said. "Her dad was already one of my dad's company's clients when we moved here. He's a marketing manager at some ethanol company. Dad met him during a meeting, and they decided we should be friends, because we were all in the same fourth grade class."

"You all?"

"Oh. I mean me, Natalie, and her brother, Alec. They're twins."

"And are you friends with Alec Pent as well?"

Lindsay blushed. "We went out for a couple months."

Agent Forester smiled. Lindsay wondered with a pang of embarrassment if it was because the term "going out" seemed so silly, considering they were seventh graders and couldn't even drive anywhere. Agent Forester seemed to pick up on Lindsay's feelings, however, and she phrased her next question in a way that made "going out" seem no less important for seventh graders than it was for adults. "Did you and Alec Pent date recently?"

"Well, it was before summer," Lindsay answered. "I . . ." She paused, unsure which details might be necessary. Did they need to know about Alan Sparks, the eighth grader who had caught her eye instead of Alec Pent? Alan had black hair. He was mysterious. He never treated her differently at kickboxing just because she was a girl.

". . . you?" Agent Forester pressed.

"I'm sorry. I mean Alec Pent and I dated before summer, but I wasn't really into him. Plus my aunt in Washington DC invited me out there for a kickboxing camp. It was a month long, so it was a good excuse to dump Alec, because I wouldn't see him much. I didn't really want a boyfriend anyway."

"DC is one of my favorite cities," Agent Forester said, offering what seemed like another genuine smile.

"It was the best five weeks of my life." The words tumbled out of Lindsay's mouth with an inapt chuckle she couldn't control. As her face turned bright red, she searched the room for anything else to look at. Her gaze fell upon the Potawatomi medicine wheel hanging in the living room's darkest corner. Her father had inherited it from his father; it was the only decoration in the house that hinted at her own Indigenous lineage.

"I know this might seem like prying," Agent Forester continued, yanking Lindsay back into the moment, "but why was DC the best five weeks of your life? Is there something you don't like about here, in comparison? School? Friends? Family? What don't you like?"

"I never said I didn't *like* End Haven," Lindsay answered, perhaps a bit too forcefully. "It's just . . ."

She had never tried to articulate the truth now bubbling up in her heart. Drew was too young to understand it, and Natalie and Alec Pent always seemed too happy with their parents to truly commiserate. But might it actually help Drew to tell the police?

"The problem isn't so much with *me*," Lindsay finally continued. "Like, it's more my parents. My dad is always gone at work, because that's how his dad used to be, and my mom drinks and smokes pot and takes pills. Like, all the time. She thinks I don't notice."

Detective Rhymes donned the slightest of frowns, but Agent Forester jumped back in before he could speak. Her tone was somehow both sensitive and matter-of-fact. "Do you mean your mother's drinking and drug use seem excessive?"

The guilt of betrayal tightened Lindsay's throat. "If by 'excessive' you mean cocktails in the middle of the day and red eyes every day when I get home from school, then yes," Lindsay said. "I think it usually happens when Drew is napping. He still does that at two o'clock."

*Or did*, Lindsay thought.

Agent Forester paused before asking, "Is this something that affects how happy you are here?"

Lindsay thought before answering. Yes, it affected how happy she was, because it made her feel that everything her family projected—wealth, a

Western-colonial version of success, the average two-kid household—was a farce. She wasn't sure what had come first: her mother's drinking or her father's work addiction. Perhaps both problems fed off each other.

"It makes me feel alone," she admitted. "Drew's too little to really know that Mom is self-medicating, and my dad is always at work, probably because that's how *his* dad was. Basically, my grandpa grew up super poor after his mom moved him to Chicago during that Volunteer Relocation Program thing in the 1950s."

Both Agent Forester and Detective Rhymes stared at Lindsay blankly. They had no idea what she was talking about.

"I just mean that my grandpa worked like crazy his whole life so he could be just as rich as all the White guys," Lindsay continued. "My dad grew up with that same mentality, more or less, but it's always been kind of overboard. The last time we did anything as a family was last Christmas."

Agent Forester gave her a sympathetic nod. "And how long has your mother been, as you said, self-medicating?"

"I started noticing her being drunk or high when I was about nine. I'd sometimes see joints or Percocet on the kitchen counter, or her blue bottle of Bombay Sapphire. That was back in Illinois. Dad was busy all the time, and Drew was a new baby."

Agent Forester grimaced. "She was drinking when Drew was a newborn?"

"She always used formula to feed him," Lindsay replied.

"And was your mother drinking yesterday?"

"I got home at three, and yeah, she was a little bit drunk. Not a lot, though. Kind of how it usually is. Drew was outside playing."

"She was drunk when he was outside alone?"

Lindsay caught herself. "Wait. I don't know, because I got home at three-fifteen. She said Drew was too hyper to nap since it was Halloween, and he was super excited to go trick-or-treating in his Doctor Deadlock costume. I saw him outside my bedroom window at four o'clock, though. He was in the sandbox. I think my mom had fallen asleep on the couch by then."

"But you were upstairs when Drew disappeared, and you can't one hundred percent account for where your mother was?"

Lindsay's stomach clawed at her throat. "No, I can't."

Detective Rhymes scratched down more notes.

"And the time," Agent Forester continued. "You said you saw Drew at four o'clock. How do you remember so specifically?"

"I have that kind of memory. I remember looking at my nightstand clock right after I saw Drew out the window. I was on the phone with Natalie Pent, and she was giving me crap for not going to a Halloween party at our friend Karly's house. It said 4:02, and I remember thinking that the party started in two hours."

"Why weren't you going to the party?"

"I was supposed to go to kickboxing," Lindsay replied.

"And back to your mother's marijuana use for a second. Do you know where she gets it? And if anyone selling it to her might have ever met Drew?"

"No idea. But kids at school get it easily, so it can't be that hard."

Agent Forester nodded, as if satisfied. She continued on, asking more questions, getting every ounce of information she could about the previous night. No, Lindsay had not seen Drew again after looking out the window. No, she had not gone downstairs to notice when her mother fell asleep, but it had surely been after she ordered takeout from Tickle Me Thai. No, the Tickle Me Thai delivery boy had never shown any extra curiosity in their particular household. No, Lindsay had never made it to kickboxing, because Drew had disappeared.

"And your kickboxing team and instructors—have they met Drew before?" Agent Forester asked.

"Maybe a little bit. He was with my mom when she first took me to the classes. They watched a few times after I started."

"Can you think of anyone who might have been hanging around your neighborhood lately? Maybe someone new you've started seeing regularly? A neighbor, a mailman, a meter man?"

Lindsay filtered the question through her memory, mentally picking through it with a fine-tooth comb. Meter man? No, she hadn't seen one of those since living in Illinois. There were new neighbors who had moved to Dollywyn Drive earlier in the year, but they were just a normal family. Other than that, her own family was the newest on the block.

"But wait," she said. "There was a new mailman when I came back from Washington, DC."

More notes on Detective Rhymes's notepad. Lindsay saw him make two solid lines under something he had written.

"We'll definitely look into that. Your mother didn't seem to notice," he said. "Anything else? Anyone you can think of who's been out of the ordinary?"

Lindsay thought for a long time, trying to remember every day that might have stuck out in her mind.

Suddenly, another memory tugged at her. "Spinner's Lake," she said. "It was the day of the tornadoes, back in August, when that Damon Jacoby kid died."

Agent Forester furrowed her eyebrows and glanced at Detective Rhymes, who sat up straighter and cleared his throat. "Damon Jacoby was a local boy who got into some trouble," he explained to the agent. "There was an accident with a couple other kids out on Spinner's Lake on August ninth."

Lindsay thought back on that day. It had been a Tuesday, because she had been at kickboxing the night before—a training night. On Mondays, she and the boys trained; on Wednesdays, they sparred. At kickboxing the night after the accident, all the boys had been discussing Damon Jacoby and those two other kids—Molly Butler and Elijah Bryce, whom everyone at school now called "the Murderers."

"It was windy that day, before the storms came in," Lindsay said, "but it was still sunny when we were out at the lake. Mom took us out there for a picnic with Mrs. Johnson and her three kids, right in that grassy area by the big parking lot."

"And you saw somebody there?" Agent Forester asked.

"Yeah. A guy. He was sitting alone with a camera at the next picnic table, and I saw him watching us. Our plates blew away, and when Drew chased after them, the guy ran out to help pick them up. He brought back the plates, then ruffled Drew on the head. I remember feeling kind of anxious, even though he seemed nice."

"Why anxious?"

"I'm not sure," Lindsay said. "Like . . . he was watching Drew in this weird way when he was picking up the paper plates, and then the way he smiled at my mom was a little weird. Like, too friendly. But he seemed fine otherwise. I guess I'm not sure."

"Have you seen this man anywhere else?"

"I don't think so," Lindsay replied. "He was tallish, and I think his hair was dark with some white streaks—kind of long for a guy. But now that I think about it, I remember his face looking too young for him to have white hair. That stuck out to me."

"Did you see him leave?"

"He sat down at his picnic table after we sat down at ours, but he left before we did. I didn't think to look if he had a car there. He probably did, since the lake isn't walking distance from anywhere."

"Great, Lindsay, that really helps. All of this helps." Agent Forester looked at Detective Rhymes, and a million things seemed to pass between them silently. As they stood up and made forced idle banter with each other, Lindsay leaned backward onto the hard couch, worrying she'd said either too much or nothing of importance at all.

THE BOY HAD LIGHTS surrounding him. Souls.

Lowell Grendel had been watching him since August.

He had first seen the child at Spinner's Lake—on "the day of the tornadoes," as people in Idle County now referred to it. It had been Lowell's second official day in town. The barista at the Bean & Leaf had suggested Spinner's Lake as a "place to go" in the summer, so Lowell went. It was basic. A lake.

August 9 had been sunny at first. Breezy, then windy. Lowell had taken his camera there for fun, in the off chance he might see something interesting to photograph. There hadn't been much, save for a small island on the right side of the lake rising from the haze.

Upon arriving at the grassy picnic area preceding the beach, however, Lowell had noticed the boy. Three orbs had been floating near his young head and torso, two hued gold and one tinged blue.

At the time, Lowell had been questioning his move to Minnesota, especially given that it was feeding the appetite of his greatest burden—that terrible drive to study the things he saw. But here he was, already seeing more than ever before.

The man in Laguna Beach had been correct. Idle County really *was* special.

Lowell had been able to sneak sixteen photos of the boy and his orbs while sitting at the next picnic table over. The boy's party, consisting of his mother, sister, and another woman and her three kids, seemed oblivious to Lowell's fascination.

Before their party left, a stack of paper plates from their table alighted with the wind. Lowell caught two and gathered ten more from the grass as the enlivened boy chased them, catching none. He handed the stack back to the boy with a smile and a ruffle of his hair, intending to be jovial. Unthreatening. Uninterested in the orbs, or the strong presence they must be guarding.

The boy's sister, who wore her dark hair in a long ponytail, also had two orbs winking in and out of Lowell's perception. But they weren't as strong as her brother's. No sirree.

He left the park before they did, but he waited inside his Jeep until they departed. That's when he followed them back to Dollywyn Drive.

THE PHOTOS OF THE BOY came out beautifully. In two of them, the orbs around him had faint outlines of form—if not human, then of something similar. To get this lucky in Idle County so soon? It was as if the universe were giving him a sign that it had pulled him here at just the right time. That perhaps he was *meant* to satisfy his inner burden even further.

AS HE BEGAN BUILDING his real estate photography business in the weeks that followed—some markets never dried up—Lowell began to feel the pull. He had to see that child again. To study the orbs. To photograph them and try to see the shapes beyond.

The boy would be his fourth murder. Lowell had known it the day of the tornadoes.


ON SEPTEMBER 14, 2005, Lowell drove for the first time the full loop of Old Mill Road, which ran a circular perimeter around a forest locals called the Moon Woods.

Upon hearing the road's name, Lowell had wanted to find its namesake: the Old Mill. Was it a proper noun? Was it real?

He had asked around town. This time, he got answers from an old woman named Barbara, who was selling her condo.

"There *was* an old working mill, once upon a time," she said. "It's halfway between here and Stone Ridge."

"That's the town on the north side of the Moon Woods?"

"A rundown place," Barbara said, as if it were an agreement. "The mill itself is in ruins, but the river still runs, until it falls into some underground cave nobody's ever explored. It's worth seeing just for that."

Lowell immediately pictured a romantic old mill preceding a grand waterfall, whose torrents careened into a vast chasm cut into the earth. But he didn't let on the extent of his curiosity. Instead, he finished up the photos of Barbara's condo, thanked her, and continued on his way.


IN REALITY, THE CHASM at the Old Mill Historical Site didn't live up to Lowell's imagination. It was perhaps ten feet in its rocky, irregularly shaped diameter. Barbara hadn't been lying about the old mill preceding it, however; the building was indeed falling apart. Its spinning water wheel was broken at all its spokes; its roof was caved in; and portions of its weathered siding seemed to be sprouting trees, as if time and the elements had forced it to surrender in some long-past battle of the wills.

The water rushed past it, coming from the north. Instead of overflowing into the dirt lot where Lowell had parked his Jeep, however, it splashed over some rocks before tumbling straight into the earth. The tall grass, boulders, and trees around the chasm made it invisible from the parking lot. One had to approach it to really see it.

But the depth of the waterfall—and the rocky blackness into which it fell—did verge on impressive. A few pieces of old litter were strewn around its outer edge, clearly from immature visitors who had tried to toss their trash into the black abyss and missed. Otherwise, the sheer crevasse was clean, and the water was powerful, cleansing everything in its path.

It was the perfect place to make something disappear.

LOWELL RETURNED TO DOLLYWYN DRIVE fourteen times between late August and mid-October, twice in the early evening and twelve times during the night.

On one of the evenings, a Wednesday, he followed the young boy's mother and sister to Fairfax Community Center. The sister was toting boxing gloves—for a class, possibly? He made a note to search the organization's website for a boxing-class schedule, in case it might someday matter.

On his night visits to Dollywyn Drive, Lowell explored the family's backyard. Took note of the layout. Walked from the wooden swing set to the patio, imagining the family sleeping inside.

During these nights, he saw no orbs.

Perhaps when the boy slept, so did his bright guardians.

Because that's what they were. Guardians. Everyone had them, but not everyone could see them. Lowell himself rarely saw these beings; it was always a privilege when it happened, for reasons obvious to anyone who believed in realms beyond the dimensions people could typically perceive.

AND THEN SERENDIPITY brought him his chance. On October 31, Halloween, Lowell scheduled a last-minute real estate photography job at a house on Provell Street. The location was directly behind the boy's backyard, separated only by a grove of cedar trees. Straight through them was the wooden swing set, complete with the boy's play alcove above the slide, the home of his toys. Lowell knew this spot didn't belong to the sister—she was older, in middle school at least.

Jenna, the real estate agent managing the Provell Street house's listing, was new to the business and handling the sale for her parents' friends, who had already relocated to Florida. Because she was time-crunched not to miss her hair appointment on that cold, crisp Monday, she left Lowell alone to photograph the house's exterior immediately after he was finished with the inside.

"Just get all the necessary shots from the yard—front and back," she told him in a rush.

After she left, Lowell did just that. First the front. Then the back.

But then he stayed in the back, hiding in the trees.

When the boy came out to play, the orbs around him were fierce in their intensity, almost blinding. But it was easy for Lowell to cast the lure. Once the boy heard the clicking of the Nikon's shutter, all Lowell had to do was promise him he could snap photos all by himself with the camera, if only he'd come back to play in the cedar grove.

2005

"AN IDLE COUNTY BOY has gone missing, and authorities are doing everything in their power to find him," came Alice Winterblume's WCMP news report from Lindsay Thorsen's family room television.

The photo Sanda Thorsen had given the police yesterday morning overtook the screen.

"Four-year-old Andrew Nikan Thorsen was last seen playing in his backyard on Dollywyn Drive in End Haven, Minnesota, dressed in a red Halloween costume of Doctor Deadlock from the popular children's cartoon *Mousepants*. He has brown hair and—"

Lindsay clicked the television off.

The bubble of speculation had popped. It was real. Drew had been missing for almost three days. Cities even farther away than Wind Prairie were reporting the disappearance—Minneapolis, Des Moines, Madison. Searches had begun, and today, Lindsay faced the impossible choice of sitting in the house with her unhinged parents or going back to school.

She chose school.

No sooner had she reached the building's doors, however, than Natalie Pent and their shared social pod were upon her. As usual, Natalie was in the lead.

"Oh my God, Lindsay, how are you doing?"

The other girls in the group—Tessa Silverman, Candace Dickson, Karly Lillefeld, and Sarah Brownie—jumped in and began raining down on Lindsay like little drops of forced hope.

"It's going to be okay, Linds. Just keep your chin up . . ."

"I'm sure they'll find him . . ."

"Do the police have any clues yet?"

"Seriously, just think positive!"

"Is Mr. Sandberg actually making you take the geography test?"

Lindsay now wondered if her decision to come and take today's test—and escape her dazed, grief-stricken parents—had been a mistake. She remained stiff as her friends hugged her. It was almost a relief when Sophie Higgins and Pauline Gilbert, two quiet girls on the fringes of their group, simply offered compassionate bobs of their heads.

All eight girls stood in the school's foyer, surrounded by a hundred other kids who were watching Lindsay with almost shameful curiosity. Noticing what a scene Natalie and the other girls were making, Pauline Gilbert offered Lindsay an understanding roll of the eyes.

The first of the day's class bells rang: five minutes until her geography test. It was a relief when most of the girls scattered.

Natalie Pent remained and walked with Lindsay toward Mr. Sandberg's classroom.

"They made a school announcement during Ms. Olson's class yesterday," Natalie said. "It seems like everyone's on the lookout for Drew, so . . . God, I really just hope he's okay."

Lindsay grappled for something else to talk about, some remaining nibble of the ordinary. Natalie couldn't possibly know how it felt to have a sibling disappear or to have the television blaring the dismal news all over the state. The worst thing she had ever endured was a sprained ankle from figure skating, the year Lindsay moved to End Haven.

"I just need to pass this geography test," Lindsay finally replied. "Mr. Sandberg made us memorize every single capital city in Europe, but I didn't really get a chance to study."

"More like Mr. Sand*balls*," Natalie said, scoffing. "He makes every test hard, I've heard."

Lindsay had nothing else to add as her friend clip-clopped next to her in what appeared to be new shoes.

After about a hundred feet, Natalie stopped at her open classroom door. Most of her classmates were already in their seats. She looked at them, then back at Lindsay, and suddenly continued their conversation out of nowhere, even louder than before. "Yeah, the police came to talk to me last night, because they wanted to ask if we were really on the phone when Drew disappeared."

Out of the corner of her eye, Lindsay saw Natalie's entire class perk up and turn toward the door. Looking distressed—perhaps overly distressed—Natalie sighed.

"It was so weird and sad. I told them the truth, at least. I've been trying to think back to anybody creepy who's been hanging around End Haven lately. I thought maybe that new guy who moved in down the street from me? I mean, I've seen him wandering the neighborhood, but maybe he's just, like, making himself at home."

Lindsay, having never met Natalie's new neighbor, simply stood there, blushing, as Natalie's classmates stared. Natalie, for one, seemed perfectly willing to absorb their attention.

"I'll see you at lunch," Lindsay whispered. Without waiting for her friend to respond, she rushed toward Mr. Sandberg's classroom at the end of the hall.

SHE FINISHED HER GEOGRAPHY TEST in twenty-three minutes. Unlike last time, it had been easier than she feared. When the class bell signaled the quick hiatus between first and second hour, Lindsay rushed to her locker, sighing with relief when Natalie and the others weren't already waiting there, ready to shower her with further condolences. She entered her lock combination and swung the door open with more force than was necessary.

Just as the locker door bounced off the closed adjacent one, she heard a surprised male voice say, "Yikes! Almost got too close on that one."

"Oh gosh, sorry!" Lindsay yanked the door back, afraid she had hit the person. She tried to focus on the floor to avoid the boy's stare.

"No, my fault for sneaking up on you—Hey," he said. His voice was familiar. Noticing that he also had black hair and a muscular build, Lindsay looked up.

It was Alan Sparks, the eighth grader she could never beat at kickboxing. His hair was perfectly ungroomed, and dark stubble covered his squared jawline. He had nodded to her once or twice at school since the beginning of the year, but they had never talked face-to-face outside of kickboxing. Even there, it was only ever about athletics.

"Hi," Lindsay said, surrendering to his gaze. How had he known where her locker was?

"Missed you at kickboxing the other night—" he started, then seemed to reconsider his words. "I mean, obviously other stuff was going on, but . . . yeah."

Lindsay took a deep breath. Somehow, Alan's quick and thoughtful comfort over Drew's disappearance seemed infinitely more real than Natalie Pent's dramatic eulogy. "It's been kind of crazy," she admitted.

"Well, let me know if there's anything I can do," Alan said. "I really hope you find your brother. I just wanted to say that."

Against Lindsay's will, a butterfly fluttered in her heart.

"Okay, gotta get to History," Alan continued. "Coach Martinez'll get on your ass if you don't make it back to kickboxing, so I better see you soon." He flashed her a hopeful grin. It was more than just an awkward attempt to lighten the mood, however, because it filled Lindsay with a sense of calm she hadn't felt in months.

"I'll try to come tonight," she replied.

Alan smiled, then turned to run back down the hall.

Lindsay stood alone, watching him scamper off to history class. As usual, her kickboxing brain told her Alan was an enemy to be conquered while her heart let loose a hundred more butterflies.

But on their wings came guilt, because dreaming about boys was a girly waste of time. Especially now.


At lunch, Lindsay could only pick at her chicken sandwich. It was her favorite: thinly sliced chicken lunch meat with spinach, tomatoes, and a light Dijon mustard. It was also Drew's favorite—probably because it was hers. Only now did she realize just how thoroughly she had taken his four-year-old admiration for granted. Today, it felt like the only real thing in a daze of normal-life fluff that didn't matter anymore.

"Did you see Emily McMillan this morning?" Natalie Pent said as she grazed from her bag of carrot sticks. "She was totally crying but didn't want to talk to me."

"Phil Battles dumped her last night," Sarah Brownie replied.

"No, no, no," Tessa Silverman chimed in. "He didn't dump her.

It was just, like, a 'we might not be the best couple' conversation, but they're still totally going out for now."

Lindsay tried to swallow a piece of chicken.

Natalie, wearing a wry smile, opened her mouth to respond to Tessa but then eyed Lindsay. The smile disappeared, and she shook her bangs out of her eyes. "You guys, I doubt Lindsay really wants to talk about this."

The group went silent. Now everyone picked at their lunches.

Blushing, Lindsay forced herself to take another bite. With a full mouth, she said, "You guys can talk about whatever you want." The girls looked at each other, each mentally begging the others to start a new conversation. It was a full thirty seconds before a solution walked up to them.

"Hey, Lindsay," came a boy's voice from behind her, along with a tap on the shoulder.

It was Alec Pent, her ex-boyfriend—and Natalie's twin brother. Natalie glanced at the half-eaten cheeseburger in his hand, then gave him a warning look, as if she'd claw his eyes out if he brought up Drew. But Lindsay knew Alec was too kind not to say something.

"I'm sorry about your brother," he indeed said the second she acknowledged him. "I guess everyone's probably bringing it up, but I just wanted to say so. Let me know if you need anything."

"Thanks," Lindsay replied. "I'll be all right. We're going to find him."

Alec grimaced, probably unaware of how hopeless the expression looked. He then ran off to finish his cheeseburger.

"You know, I wish everyone would stop staring at you," Natalie said with a huffy sigh. Narrowing her eyes, she gestured to Lindsay's right. "The Murderers have been looking at you over and over since lunch started."

Pauline Gilbert quickly turned to follow Natalie's gesture. Lindsay and the other girls turned as well.

Elijah Bryce, blond haired and about six inches taller than last year, was talking to Molly Butler, a quiet dark-haired girl who had transferred this year from Saint Andrew's Catholic School. As usual, they were sitting alone at an empty table in the front-right corner of the cafeteria.

Molly, who also sat in the back corner of Lindsay and Natalie's Advanced English class, was already one of the weird kids in school. She and Elijah Bryce had been involved in the accident at Spinner's Lake that killed Damon Jacoby three months ago, and since the start of the school year, nobody knew how to approach them. News stations all around southern Minnesota had dubbed Elijah a "hero" for supposedly carrying Damon's body away from the lake after he fell off a rock, but since the sweeping gesture had tainted the scene of the accident, a lot of kids in school were whispering that the two oddballs had somehow caused the accident on purpose.

"They're so weird," Natalie said with a scoff. "I don't get why they think they can just stare at you."

Pauline Gilbert gritted her teeth. "They're probably just concerned."

"What, you're suddenly friends with Elijah again or something?"

"I was never *not* friends with him," Pauline said. "And stop calling them 'the Murderers.' They didn't kill Damon Jacoby."

Lindsay watched Elijah and Molly. They were whispering closely to each other, intermittently looking over in her direction. The dark-haired girl seemed agitated for some reason.

"Molly Butler is so weird, though," Natalie said. "I don't even know why Elijah is friends with her."

"Um, maybe because you told everyone that he's gay, and he got too embarrassed to talk with any of us ever again?" Pauline said, simmering with anger. It had been clear for weeks now that she was losing patience with Natalie's popularity act: the beauty, the boys, the making fun of "inferior" people.

"Look, I was just telling you what Alec told my parents at the dinner table," Natalie hissed. "It's not my fault people overheard."

Pauline shook her head in frustration. "Yeah, well, Damon Jacoby almost killed Elijah because of it. Take some damned credit."

"Maybe those two Murderers made it all up," Natalie snapped back. "I mean, they were crazy enough to be out on Spinner's Island, looking for a dead body in the first place, weren't they?" She bit into her next carrot with a forceful crunch of satisfaction.

Lindsay couldn't exactly argue with her. The news had raced across town with lightning speed back in August, the day after those three tornadoes ripped through the area. Elijah Bryce—who lived on the same street as Natalie, Alec, and Pauline—had apparently found in the Moon Woods a buried human jawbone that ended up belonging to a man who vanished without a trace in the 1940s. Following a new set of clues, he and Molly had tracked the rest of the man's remains down to a small island accessible from the shore of Spinner's Lake via a naturally built rock bridge. Damon Jacoby, who had been on house arrest after assaulting Elijah with a knife, somehow found out they had ridden their bikes there and followed them in his uncle's truck. According to Elijah and Molly, he tried to kill them on the rock bridge and ended up tumbling off one of the crags. Both claimed he had leaned backward off the rock on purpose, to commit suicide.

*Well, it worked*, Lindsay thought. *Death and Tragedy: the Real Idle County*. It sounded like the title of a *60 Minutes* special.

Tessa, Sarah, Karly, and Candace all seemed to have taken Natalie's side in thinking the Murderers were freaks. Pauline and Sophie, however, didn't seem convinced. Either way, apart from the obvious Drew situation, it didn't explain the Murderers' sudden interest in Lindsay.

Pauline took a deep breath, then said to Natalie, "Well, please don't forget whose fault it was that Damon went after Elijah in the first place."

Natalie's eyes, aimed at Pauline, grew cold and narrow. "Maybe *you* should remember that Alec was the one who told us about Elijah drooling all over him when he took his shirt off in that tent. It's technically

Elijah's fault. If he wasn't gay, Damon wouldn't have made fun of him for it."

Blood rushed into Pauline's face. "So, you think it's okay that Damon almost killed Elijah because he's gay, or might be? Made all the bullying just fine, huh?" She stood up from the table and eyed Sophie for support. Sophie only shrank into her sandwich. Lindsay, who had never really known Elijah, tried to do the same.

Natalie only glared at Pauline, then said, "I love gay people!"

Lindsay closed her eyes. All she could see was Drew, alone in the cold.

*Kickboxing tonight*, she reminded herself. *I can just kick ass there, and nobody will care.*

Pauline grabbed her empty lunch bag and left the table without another glance at any of them.

"You know, Pauline has turned into a total bitch ever since she started telling everyone she's *Black*," Natalie said, settling back into her lunch.

"*Half*-Black," Karly Lillefeld corrected.

"Whatever. Isn't it basically racist to suddenly start caring about skin color?"

Lindsay, who was never sure whether her one-fourth Indigenous heritage gave her the credibility to identify with non-White people in southern Minnosota's vast Caucasian sea, remained silent. Natalie, who looked full-on White, had probably never considered what *not* being White might mean for some people.

To cover her discomfort, Lindsay took the last bite of her sandwich.

"Anyway, you'd think she'd be looking at the bigger picture and realizing there's actually legit stuff going on," Natalie said, glancing at Lindsay. With a sorry droop of her eyes, she ate a french fry.

Lindsay gritted her teeth, then glanced again at the Murderers, who for some reason were carefully folding up their paper lunch bags.

Elijah Bryce was frowning, nodding to whatever Molly Butler was saying. He looked up, met Lindsay's gaze, and then looked away quickly.

Taking a leaf out of Pauline's book, Lindsay gathered her trash and left the lunch table without a word. As she made for the lunchroom garbage cans, she noticed Molly arguing with Elijah and pointing in her direction yet again. Upon turning and catching Lindsay's gaze, however, the dark-haired girl grew rigid. There was more than just compassion in her expression; there was also fear.

At that very moment, a freezing cold tingle ran like a finger down the back of Lindsay's neck.

*What the—*

She tilted her head to shake off the icy chill just as Molly turned back toward Elijah. They descended into whispers.

*Even the Murderers are feeling sorry for me now*, Lindsay thought, knowing she must have looked half-crazy while shaking off the strange sensation.

She chucked her crumpled lunch bag into a nearby garbage can, left the cafeteria, and turned right, toward the nearest girls' restroom. When she entered, it was empty. She sat down in the farthest stall with her pants still up.

As she buried her face in her arms, counting down the five hours left until kickboxing, she couldn't shake the image of Molly Butler staring at her in the cafeteria. There had been a strange look in her dark eyes, more than just concern.

It had almost felt mutual. Like recognition.

THIS WAS WHAT CLOVIA BELL HAD KNOWN the day she walked into her first meeting with Jonathan Flite: that he was a murderer, that he was rich, and that he claimed to have memories of other lives—ones he had even made crayon drawings of as a child. What she hadn't anticipated was that he would be hypnotizing. Almost alarmingly so.

It had happened in a single instant last August, the day they met at the Renaissance Providence Hotel for his initial recorded interview with Alice Winterblume, the preeminent host of CBS's popular docuseries *WorldLine.* As Clovia shook the nurse killer's hand, something in his steely hazel eyes had felt instantly familiar to her, as if he were an old friend.

Now, eight months later, they were walking together through Storer Park in Newport, Rhode Island, followed closely by Jonathan's bodyguard, Sounder, and a small production crew. It was April 5, 2039, and Clovia had spent the last few months strictly liaising with the production team as they documented Jonathan's daily life here. This week, however, Alice had tasked her with directing an unexpected run of pick-up footage—all under the watchful eyes of at least ten police officers, some of whom were in unmarked vehicles.

"Okay, so just, like, sit here?" Jonathan said, taking his position on the bench.

Clovia nodded. "Yeah. Ponder your life. Look out at the water. Maybe imagine the first day you were enrolled at Crescent. Remember what that felt like."

She checked the camera-monitor feed through her ActoLenses, then turned to make sure the small crowd of reporters following them were still keeping their distance. One in particular, a local blogger named Lydia Clark, had now tried to get past the police twice.

Clovia glanced at her sound mixer, Gemma, who was sitting about thirty feet away, adjusting the input levels of the young man's hidden lavalier microphone. They weren't doing any official interviews today (unlike yesterday, when they had joined Jonathan at Crescent's day program), so Gemma's sound was simply reinforcement, in case they captured some spontaneous gem of dialogue from Jonathan.

"Gemma, we good?"

Gemma gave her a thumbs-up.

Clovia ushered Terrance, her camera operator, closer, then whispered, "Okay, let's get the close-up, then a medium shot in profile, and then a few different frames from this diagonal angle." She stepped in front of Jonathan but slightly to the right, gesturing toward his face. Jonathan, surprisingly professional, simply sat there, looking as mysterious as ever.

If Clovia weren't already familiar with the mature nineteen-yea-old's hesitant yet piercing sense of humor—and his reluctant yet slow-to-melt smile—she might still have been afraid of him. He was, after all, Newport's famous nurse killer.

But she wasn't afraid. Some days, she had to remind herself how dangerous this could potentially be.

They got one shot, then another, and then another. Clovia ran a hand over her short, close-cropped hair, as was her habit when pondering how to execute a particular task. "Okay, let's do one that feels a bit more optimistic. Imagine the happiest day of your life, and keep looking out at the water."

"I haven't had a lot of happy," Jonathan told her.

"Well, you're under contract," she joked. "Think of something."

Jonathan looked into her eyes with an exaggerated sigh, and she saw it: that slow-to-melt smile. "Okay. Got it," he said. "Let's go."

Clovia watched the recorded video stream from Terrance's camera through her ActoLenses. It was a perfect shot—the late morning sun backlighting what remained of Jonathan's dirty-blond hair, which had been trimmed yesterday. Jonathan kept a hint of his smile, and as Terrance caught it from all the necessary angles, a rush of satisfaction ran through Clovia.

Lately, she remembered having dreams about being trapped in a fire. On days like this, she felt like a phoenix rising from the ashes. She wondered if Jonathan ever felt similarly, now that he had managed to start a life for himself here in Newport.

While their liaising and logistics planning had started as professionally as possible through Jonathan's friend and personal assistant, Jimmy Barber (who was currently in Boca Raton for a family function), Jonathan had quickly become the one to take over communication with Clovia about everything *WorldLine*-related: his shooting schedules, fact checking for the show's story editor, and of course next month's location shoots in Boulder, Colorado, and southern Minnesota. He had even been comfortable enough with her to share just how nervous he was about both trips—particularly Boulder, where he would undergo multiple hypnotic past-life regressions with a psychiatrist named Dr. Cora Crowe. He knew the regressions would be a litmus test of sorts—at least to some—for the validity of his peculiar past-life-memory claims.

Apart from sharing *WorldLine*'s healthy skepticism about the legitimacy of regression hypnosis, Jonathan had never been guided into a hypnotized state before, let alone instructed to remember backward through time, to the beginning of his life—and to whatever might have come before.

Even Rebecca Sparks, the disabled physicist from Idle County, had been purposefully silent on the topic. In her words, this upcoming journey "*was for Jonathan to experience first, and him alone.*"

Reading between the lines, Clovia now surmised that Jonathan was afraid of finding answers he didn't want to know—particularly about an eighth figure with a scribbled-out face he had included in one of his childhood crayon drawings of the Idle County Seven "disappearing." Upon seeing the drawing, Alice Winterblume had theorized that perhaps the figure was meant to be Max Pope, a troubled neurologist who had figured prominently in the Idle County Seven's lives before vanishing himself in 2009. Yet there was no evidence for this. How could there be, in a realm where evidence was circumstantial at best? And what did it say about Clovia that she cared more about Jonathan's psychological well-being than about pushing him to give *WorldLine* the juiciest story possible?

Still, the production had to remain her priority. The eight-episode season was already scheduled to premiere on May 30, 2040—Jonathan's twentieth birthday. While it was still over a year away, the story's scope was getting bigger by the day, and Clovia knew the deadline would creep up fast.

As of late, the heightened energy throughout *WorldLine*'s New York production office had been almost palpable. Clovia had been working there for just two years, but she could already tell that this new season was different. Some people were nervous about audience reception; some were excited; others were downright scared, and not just because they were aligning themselves with Jonathan Flite, the famous nurse killer. All of it was coming on the heels of frightening events that were, more and more, starting to show their underlying, tangled threads:

The nuclear terrorist attack in Geneva, Switzerland, two years ago.

The rumors about celebrity atheist Victor Zobel being personally associated with Jean-Claude Apostol, the Catholic cardinal responsible for detonating the bomb.

The triple homicide—and attempted murder of Jonathan—mere weeks after the FBI had reluctantly questioned him about his supposed "memories" involving Zobel. The alleged recollections primarily related to Zobel's time in Geneva, when he was a stepfather to Jillian Pope, the neurologist Max Pope's biological daughter, who later became one of the vanished Idle County Seven.

Now everyone's biggest concern was the surge of violent backlash against Jonathan and his loved ones following his release from Crescent Rehabilitation Center last summer. Much like the Geneva bombing, it all seemed to be fueled by religion-based fears of change—in this case, concern that Jonathan's "New Agey" past-life-memory claims might prove to be legitimate and lure the masses away from Christianity's "one true God."

Of course, the reemergence of Rebecca Sparks, the physicist who also went by the name Dorothy Garland, seemed to be the icing on the cake.

The woman had first approached *WorldLine* back in 2034, shortly after Jonathan's story had gone public. Apart from demonstrating her uncanny mind-reading abilities during the first of four secret interviews recorded that year, she had also made a startling prediction that Jonathan would one day be the subject of a major, socially upheaving season of *WorldLine*—one whose success would hinge on a tiny detail he would eventually mention about a mysterious "flashlight incident" that once occurred with Lindsay Thorsen, one of the Idle County Seven.

For four years, Alice Winterblume had mulled over Rebecca's tantalizing prediction, waiting to see if it might validate the woman's alleged psychic abilities. Then, last summer, Jonathan had quietly mentioned Lindsay Thorsen's 2006 abduction—and the flashlight that had helped her escape—during his first on-camera interview in Providence. Tingles ran up Clovia's spine every time she remembered it, because it had proven the legitimacy of Rebecca's clairvoyance, which in itself was proof of things most people didn't even want to think about.

Today, under the blue skies of Newport, *WorldLine*'s looming story felt electric. Perhaps even alive.

"Hey, Clovia, are we good on this?" Terrence asked. "Any other angles you want?"

"How about a shot from behind me, facing the water?" Jonathan suggested. "Look how it's sparkling."

Clovia eyed the shimmering water and wondered: Was Jonathan truly sensitive enough to appreciate such beauty? If his hands had strangled his nurse, so had his mind—on some level, at least.

"Awesome. Yes. Get those sparkles." As Clovia moved out of Terrence's way, Jonathan's gaze fleetingly crossed hers. He smiled again in the morning sun—almost imperceptibly, the way he always did when they stole clandestine glances at each other.

As if on cue, Clovia's ActoPhone rang.

"Excuse me for a second," she whispered, walking north, away from Jonathan and the crew. White sailboats bobbed in Newport's Atlantic inlet as she pulled her phone out, expecting to see Alice Winterblume's personal line or *WorldLine*'s main office number on the caller ID. But no. It was from an 845 area code—Nyack, New York, her hometown.

"Hello?" Clovia answered, trying to ignore the instinctive pang of claustrophobia that came whenever she thought about the small Hudson River village.

"Hello," came a woman's voice. "Is this Clovia Bell? Daughter of Patrick and Jana Bell?"

"This is she."

"This is Officer Carrie-Anne Golding with the South Nyack Police Department up in Rockland County, New York. I'm wondering: Are you anywhere near Nyack right now?"

"No, I'm in Rhode Island for work." The tremor of intuition returned to Clovia, this time more clearly. It wasn't just her usual claustrophobia about Nyack. "Is this about my dad?"

"I'm afraid it is," Officer Golding continued after a moment's hesitation. "I hate to tell you this over the phone, as it's our usual protocol to wait until family can receive news like this in person, but we found your father pulled over in the bus lane on the Tappan Zee Bridge earlier today. He was unconscious and sitting in his car just outside South Nyack, about a block onto the bridge. By the time paramedics made it to the site, he was no longer breathing."

*Was no longer breathing.*

Clovia's bright and promising morning dissolved in that horrendous euphemism. Her immediate reaction was to glance over her shoulder at Jonathan, who was still sitting on the bench. He must have already noticed her stiffened posture, because he was looking at her, concerned, and ignoring Terrance's camera. Clovia turned back toward the water. To her right, in the distance, was the Newport bridge. The cars driving over it shone as a few sunlit sparkles moving east. She wondered if anyone had ever been found unconscious on its sidelines.

"He's dead?" Clovia said in her lowest possible voice. In her head, she was thinking: *I'm an orphan.*

"I'm so sorry," Officer Golding confirmed. "He wasn't carrying a wallet, but he was driving a car registered to a recently deceased woman named Jennifer Corino. A nurse at Nyack Hospital named Leiken Smith was able to identify him and give us your name."

*Leiken Smith. Jesus.*

The odds of that young woman being on duty at Nyack Hospital for her father's death seemed astronomical. Leiken had been a high-school senior when Clovia was a freshman, and after the death of Clovia's mother, Jana, in 2031, Leiken's then-boyfriend had become a heroin supplier for her father, Patrick. It was as if life were telling Clovia a joke, and the punchline was a figurative slap to the face. And who the hell was this recently deceased Jennifer Corino?

The rest of Clovia's conversation with the officer passed in a blur, the same way it had with the hospital chaplain when her mother died.

Though this time would be different, of course. She was the only surviving family member now, and she had to listen to the officer give instructions about contacting a hospital social worker to help her figure out how to manage her father's minimal estate and the possible process of probate in Surrogate's Court. There were other people Clovia could talk with about the investigation into his death, and while it was surely a difficult time, the police and Nyack Hospital staff would be there to help in any way they could. Did Clovia have any questions, and was she all right?

She hung up with a lie—yes, she was all right (but no, of course she wasn't)—and turned back to Jonathan and Terrance.

Static.

The world around her had suddenly stopped.

No matter how prepared she thought she'd been for this news—and considering her father's addiction issues, she had seen it coming—it still felt as though a gaping pit had opened up before her, along with an irrevocable risk of falling into it.

Terrance was still shooting, watching his camera monitor, but Jonathan was eyeing Clovia carefully, seemingly aware that the phone call hadn't been one of routine nature.

"Everything okay?" he asked.

"I guess it has to be," Clovia said, doing her best to stay professional. She had a job to do. Her dream job. One her father had always discouraged her from pursuing. "Let's keep shooting," she said. "We'll have you walk through the park a bit, and then we'll head toward city hall for some shots at the bombing site, if that's okay."

Except it was Clovia who had to shake away inklings of death as they approached Newport City Hall, where the suicide bomber Weston Carrow had killed six people last August, during a press conference given by Jonathan's mother, Winifred. Newport had been abuzz during Jonathan's release from Crescent Rehabilitation Center, calling for his further incarceration or for him to leave the city altogether.

That night, just as Winifred Flite had stepped in front of cameras for the first time ever to defend Jonathan—

*Boom.*

Clovia had seen the footage over and over. She never wanted to see anything like it again. Being at the site today—especially with Jonathan, whose mother had experienced the blast firsthand—felt like walking through someone's ghost.

Everyone died.

It was so inescapable.

Life was beautiful and cruel.

Her father's face, as she last remembered it, rose in her mind. The mental picture of it hovered between his old self, from the good parts of her childhood, and his more recent self, gaunt from the chemicals he hadn't been able to outrun.

*I hate that I miss him.*

Yet Clovia forced herself to look forward as they continued filming at cafés, along the waterfront, and finally amid some of Newport's residential areas, where they received a mix of scornful and curious glances.

Jonathan's gaze lingered on her all day, as though he were seeing right through her meager attempts to ignore the life-altering phone call she had received that morning. Looking at him, Clovia hoped he would someday find a way to escape his fame and live a satisfying life. There was more to think about regarding her father, Patrick, than she currently had time to process—much more. But as the shooting day wound down and the sun began to set, she reflected on one basic truth she hoped her father had, by his end, finally discovered: that life's quality never had to be dictated by outside circumstances; that it was, at any given moment, the sum total of what one chose to make of it.

ONE STEP. TWO STEPS. THREE. The same old thing.

Winifred Flite needed only to consider her current circumstances to realize that the universe had a very twisted sense of humor. She was balancing like an invalid between two bars, knowing her intent to walk should cause her legs to move normally—but instead of moving, all they did was shake. Everything inside her head moved too fast; everything outside her head moved too slowly; all goals she might have had before last year were officially dissolved.

Yet there was something she still hadn't admitted to anyone, even after being in a coma for eight weeks and in daily physical therapy for the sixth months since:

She was, for the first time in her life, a believer in meaning.

Last August 2, after slowly clip-clopping down the hallway of Newport City Hall in her stilettos to face a yard full of reporters, cameras, and flashing lights (not to mention a goddamned suicide bomb), Winifred had experienced what she could only call a near-death experience. It had been beautiful; it had been timeless; it had continued to happen over the course of weeks, when her EEG reading, according to her doctors, showed no corresponding activity in her cerebral cortex at all. By current medical standards, this shouldn't have been possible, yet during her eight-week coma, she had observed people and events from outside her body. Later, she confirmed things that had happened—things she shouldn't have been able to see.

She had witnessed the doctors describe her blast injuries as "primary" and "secondary" and "quaternary," throwing around willy-nilly terms like "acoustic barotrauma," "diffuse axonal injury," and "subdural hematoma."

She had listened to conversations between nurses outside her room, sometimes on other floors of the hospital.

She had also visited other people and places: Jonathan crying in their living room on Columbus Avenue in Newport, having just watched Weston Carrow's bomb explode on live television; his friend Jimmy Barber leaning against a balcony railing in Providence Place Mall, where the FBI had just captured Nicolas Rim, the perpetrator of the 2037 murders at Crescent Rehabilitation Center; and Jonathan's biological father, Dominic Bock, who had, unbeknownst to her, been aware of his relation to Jonathan for almost thirteen years. She had also visited her mother, Julietta; her father, Stanley; and her brother, Michael—all of whom arrived in Newport from separate locations within forty-eight hours, ready (as usual) to fight.

Their most egregious exchange occurred on October 1, the day before Winifred woke up from her coma. The spark? Her father's callous speculation over the status of her investments and who would inherit them in the event she progressed toward brain death and the termination of life support.

"Jonathan would get her assets, obviously," Michael had hissed at his father.

"Maybe not," Julietta had suggested, claiming Jonathan's status with the Family Court might prevent him from being considered a worthy heir.

"Maybe we should have legal look into it proactively," Stanley had confirmed.

This of course had resulted in her brother exploding on both their parents, their mother trying to mediate the situation, and their father storming out of the room, saying he didn't consider Jonathan a grandson at all—and that he'd rather be hung than see the boy inherit a single cent of Winifred's money, which had obviously started out as his. The hospital's trauma social worker had been tasked with calming all three of them down.

It was the type of Flite family drama Winifred had been relieved to escape since Jonathan's childhood, after they had stopped visiting following the onset of his psychological problems. These days, she had more than enough life challenges to contend with—not the least of which were brain damage and Jonathan's progression toward becoming a world-renowned, terrorist-attracting, supernatural wonder boy.

On the bright side, she was able to worry about it all at New Dawn Recovery Center on Cape Cod, the most peaceful place she could think of for such a task.

"You're smiling," her muscular physical therapist, Matías, said with his usual, jokingly snarky tone as she forced herself along the parallel support bars. "What's so funny?"

*My life*, Winifred thought and tried to say.

It came out broken, in shambles:

"M-my . . . lyyy . . . *life.*"

She couldn't even speak normally.

"I wouldn't say it's *funny*," Matías said with his ever-so-handsome grin. "Unless we're now considering traumatic brain injury something to make fun of. I mean, between us, I'm okay with making fun of it if you are."

Winifred smiled again. Her snappy wit might be a thing of the past—temporarily, she kept telling herself—but she had control of her thoughts and her face. Not to mention she could still write with her burn-scarred hands, which was another plus. Perhaps they'd fit her with one of those brain-connected typing devices, like Jonathan's new physicist friend, Rebecca Sparks, had. So many possibilities, now that she was one of earth's cripples. Except . . .

*Would you believe I'm happy to be alive?*

It took her almost fifteen seconds to ask the question aloud.

"I should hope you're happy to be alive," Matías said. "I'd be worried if you said otherwise."

"I . . . haav . . . haven't always enjoyed living."

Matías's eyes widened, and he grinned. "Dude, four words in a row. You're getting better. Except for that whole quasi-suicidal statement."

Winifred pursed her lips and pushed forward. If she had to spend this much time in physical therapy, she was glad it was with someone who could keep up with her. With a sniffy sigh, she said, "I only tolerate you because . . . yyyou're good look . . . *looking.*"

Matías, who always smelled good and always ate up Winifred's jocose flirtation, shrugged and smiled. "I get that a lot," he said. "Except I also get called a 'bro' a lot. Not sure that's a good thing. Okay, now, let's turn around and walk back."

Balancing her weight on the parallel bars, happy to feel strength in her arms, Winifred turned around and began hobbling back. Seeing how slowly the carpeted floor passed under her, she looked up and forward to defy her newfangled disability.

What she saw made her want to turn back around and have Matías whisk her into the sunset.

Her mother, Julietta, was standing in the doorway, fifty feet away, clad in a chic designer pantsuit and wearing her gray hair styled in a new glossy bob. She was chewing gum and leaning against the doorframe, probably reading yet another gossip column about Jonathan on her ActoPhone.

*Figures that she isn't even watching me,* Winifred thought with a familiar deflated sense of self-worth.

Yet this feeling was a vestige of her old life; almost all the negative feelings that had dragged her down before the bombing were lighter now. While she hadn't yet assimilated all aspects of her near-death experience, one particular notion had followed her back into consciousness: that life was a test in one of the most difficult schools imaginable, and everyone succeeded at his or her own pace.

Sweating, Winifred made her way to the end of the parallel bars, where Matías had walked around to meet her with her wheelchair. "Great job, and good enough for today," he said. "Looks like you have a visitor, anyhow."

Hearing a reference to herself, Julietta Flite looked up. Her gaze flickered back to her ActoPhone as she walked nimbly into the physical therapy room, showcasing a new color of lipstick—valentine pink. It didn't suit her, especially with her mouth repeatedly contorting around that wad of gum.

"The new front desk lady said I should come back here, because you were the only one doing PT at the moment," Julietta said. "What's her name again? Laura?"

"It's *Lena*," Winifred managed to say without any problem whatsoever.

Julietta stopped in front of Winifred, dangling the wrist of the hand holding her phone. "Well, listen to you!" she said. "You might look like a nightmare, but you sound a hundred times better than last month."

*You should have heard me earlier,* Winifred thought but didn't say. Her mother didn't need to know about her slurred, choppy conversation with Matías.

"She's doing absolutely awesome," the beautiful physical therapist said. "One of the most determined patients I've ever had."

"Yeah, well, she always knew how to pick her battles." Julietta stepped behind Winifred's wheelchair. "Here, let me take her."

Matías stepped to Winifred's left and looked her in the eyes. She gestured with her neck toward her mother, then rolled her eyes in an exaggerated manner. Matías laughed, but not without an eyebrow furrow. "I'll leave you to it, then. You know where her room is, Ms. Flite?"

"Yes, yes, I know." In an unnecessary huff, Julietta pushed Winifred past the young man, toward the double doors leading into the main hallway of the posh single-floor facility. "I'll save you the trouble of trying to talk, though it *does* seem like you're doing better," Julietta continued. "Anyway, I'm sure you know your father and I have been bombarded with phone calls and press and a million other things lately—which is only getting worse now that Jonathan is out on the loose. Did you know he was seen in Newport today being filmed with a camera crew? Why on *earth* would he be doing that? That desperate Lydia Clark woman who was next to you in the ICU just posted a bunch of photos to her blog."

Winifred, who possessed only vague recollections of Lydia Clark's questions prior to Weston Carrow's bomb going off last summer, had no desire to tell her mother what Jonathan was doing in Newport. Explaining the contract with *WorldLine* was his prerogative, and seeing as Julietta still hadn't earned his trust, Winifred didn't blame him for being secretive. Not to mention he had signed a nondisclosure agreement about the project with CBS.

"That Lyyyydia Clark woman is smaaaaall potatoes," Winifred told her mother.

"Whatever. The real reason I'm here, apart from normal motherly visits," Julietta said, as if she had visited regularly at all in the last fifteen years, "is to tell you that I've also been getting calls from Dominic Bock, that navy boyfriend you used to have—the one we never met. He first called last August, wanting to involve himself in all the drama, but I thought he'd stop."

For the first time today, Winifred found herself both pleasantly surprised and upset. She had visited Dominic Bock during her out-of-body experience, even sensed that he knew the truth about his relation to Jonathan and wanted to reach out. And her mother had been keeping his contact attempts secret for eight months?

"He lives in Texas now," Julietta continued.

"I know," Winifred said.

A sharp pause, then: "You're in touch?"

"No. But I juuus . . . *just know.*"

"Well, he's left about a million voice mails claiming he's Jonathan's biological father and that he hasn't been able to reach anyone due to all the fame and security and such. I guess everyone is crawling out of the woodwork now to get a piece of us. But it obviously raises some questions."

"Give me his n-num . . . *number.*"

"You can't be serious."

"*Give me his goddamned number,*" Winifred repeated.

Julietta Flite stopped pushing the wheelchair in the middle of the hallway. She stepped around it and leaned in, toward Winifred's face. With their gazes locked and her face quivering with rage, she asked, "Were you lying about Jonathan's father being a sperm donor?"

Winifred, both unable and unwilling to verbalize the true story of Jonathan's conception and birth, simply narrowed her eyes.

Julietta, with one of the grandest scoffs Winifred had ever seen, stepped back behind the wheelchair and jerked it onward down the hall. There would be little talking for the rest of the afternoon; Winifred would see to it. Whatever goodwill Julietta Flite actually had in prancing back into her daughter's life, it could sit and steep a little while longer.

2040

ALL THESE SOULS, *bouncing off each other*, Dominic Bock thought as he stood behind his wife, Carolyn, who was transfixed at the window of their Marriott Extended Stay suite in San Antonio, Texas. Like many of the thoughts crossing his mind as of late, this notion was a symptom of the ideas his son, Jonathan—and Jonathan's friends at *WorldLine*—had recently introduced to the world.

Outside, at least a hundred reporters lined the hotel's main driveway. It seemed someone had tipped them off to Dominic's location yet again. Over the last year, it had almost become routine.

"Don't they have anything better to do?" Carolyn whispered.

Dominic put a hand on her shoulder. She shrugged it off.

On the other side of the room, their daughters—Anna, Edith, and Jessa—were getting ready to go down to the pool.

Dominic whispered into his wife's ear. "I know this is all my fault. I wish . . ."

Carolyn turned to him, suppressing tears. "Don't even start."

"Are you going to help me on this, or am I just—"

"I said *wait* until the girls are swimming, Dom."

As they waited, he wondered whether he could have—or *should* have—prevented their shared family life from derailing so thoroughly.

Two Augusts ago, on the same night Dominic saw Winifred Flite's televised press conference literally explode in her face, he had told Carolyn something he had kept from her for almost fifteen years: that he was almost 100 percent sure he had a son—and that this son was Rhode Island's famous nurse killer.

He had found out about Jonathan in 2026 while visiting Newport's navy base for department head school. When parking his rental car on Thames Street before meeting his friend Burt for drinks, Dominic had seen a most unexpected sight: his ex-girlfriend Winifred dragging a young boy into Benjamin's Restaurant. The boy's eyes, nose, hair, and general demeanor had immediately struck Dominic as would a mirror peering back into his own childhood.

Seven years later, after young Jonathan began making news headlines for killing his nurse, Dominic had been sure of his relation. Their resemblance had become even more striking over time; the only physical trait that resembled Winifred was the boy's taut, ropy build.

Now, in the week and a half since *WorldLine*'s full-season exposé had premiered to the world and all but proven the legitimacy of Jonathan's mysterious connection to the Idle County Seven, the true scope of Dominic's blunder in keeping the boy a secret from his wife had finally become apparent. The first downhill tumble had occurred last July, when Lydia Clark, the crazy Rhode Island blogger, had leaked his identity and relation to Jonathan to the press. Reporters from all over the country immediately began hounding Dominic and his family at their home in Corpus Christi, throwing everything onto shaky ground: his familial relationships; his marriage; and even his new job as director of engineering at WaveForm Electric, one of Corpus Christi's premiere renewable energy ventures.

To date, Dominic was seemingly the only one in his family who didn't want to take his relationship with Jonathan back. The fame was terrible, but was he glad to know his son? Yes, of course. It wasn't even a question.

When Anna, Edith, and Jessa flip-flopped out of the hotel room, Dominic glanced at Carolyn, who immediately took three long steps away from him and shook her head. As always now, it was a shattered sense of security—and perhaps a newly changed perception of place in his life—that emanated from her face.

"The media won't let up until they find him," she said.

*Him.* She never allowed herself to say Jonathan's name.

"Which is why I have to go," Dominic replied. "I can't let him make some crazy, reckless decision just to satisfy some burning curiosity."

"If he's so obsessed with his precious Idle County Seven that he takes a lure from that snake Victor Zobel, then yes, you can. He's a grown man now."

"Of *twenty.* Not to mention one who hasn't even had a life."

"Oh, he's had a life all right. He was born rich and is famous as hell. He can do anything he wants."

Dominic gestured out the window, at the reporters. "Would you let *your* kids go fight that zoo all alone?"

"He's not alone. He has that Clovia Bell girl. And that psychiatrist friend. And, hell, even that gay kid."

"I think Jimmy Barber is bisexual," Dominic corrected, hoping Carolyn might lighten at his minuscule attempt at humor.

Instead, she looked at him in disbelief.

Dominic stepped toward her, resting his hands on her shoulders. "Okay. For real, though. It's summer. You and the girls are safe here, and Jonathan's paying for both hotel rooms. It's almost like a free vacation, right?"

Carolyn raised her hands in front of her chest and pushed Dominic away with more force than he would have expected. She clenched her mouth shut without finding words; all that came out was tension, followed by a sigh. Finally, she walked toward their hotel suite's bathroom—maybe to get ready for the pool, maybe to escape his pleading glances.

The vise grip on Dominic's heart tightened further. Such irony it was that the one aspect of his life in which he could have done better (and been braver) hinged on the son he had never meant to have, the one he couldn't now abandon.

Jonathan wasn't exactly missing, but after CBS had posted its cataclysmic new season of *WorldLine*, the young man's story—and its implications about Victor Zobel's involvement in both the 2010 disappearances of the Idle County Seven and the 2037 bombing in Geneva, Switzerland—had transfixed the world. Underscoring it was the physicist Rebecca Spark's now-famous Theory of Everything, which posed not just a testable unification of quantum mechanics and general relativity but also a mathematical means to prove that physical reality was simply an illusion created by so-called higher consciousness. That her own psychic abilities—and Jonathan's past-life memories—offered compelling evidence for the more sensational aspects of the theory had officially rattled the scientific community, enough for people in mainstream society to start asking questions.

Since *WorldLine*'s season premiere eleven days ago, Victor Zobel had issued just one public statement about the show's controversial allegations, neither confirming nor denying criminal involvement in either the disappearances of the Idle County Seven or the Geneva bombing. He had ended his video stream by dangling in front of Jonathan a personal invitation to Star Island, his orbiting space hotel, promising a much-sought-after prize directly linked to the unsolved disappearances from 2010.

By that point, Jonathan had already been off the grid for almost a month with his girlfriend, Clovia Bell. His mother, Winifred, had thus far refused to share their location with Dominic, even though Jonathan was surely now considering Zobel's offer to pay for a shuttle flight up to Star Island.

Dominic glanced out the window again and saw a blond female reporter preparing her stance in front of a tripod-supported camera—no doubt about to spout some speculative, fantastical sound bite to the world about his son having legitimized the concept of reincarnation and the afterlife.

He pulled out his old black ActoPhone and brought up Jonathan's phone number. Fearing Carolyn's reaction were she to know he was making the call, he pressed the Call button instead of using the voice command feature.

One ring.

Two rings.

Five rings.

And then came a recorded message saying the number was no longer in service.

Next, Dominic pulled up Clovia Bell's number—also no answer—and then that of Sounder, Jonathan's paid bodyguard. Same result. And hell, even Jonathan's assistant, Jimmy Barber, wasn't answering, which was odd, considering he was mildly obsessed with Dominic.

Dominic doubted Winifred's brother, Michael, or parents, Julietta and Stanley, would give him the time of day, so the last person he could think of who might know Jonathan's whereabouts—and actually share them, unlike Winifred—was Dr. Thomas Lumen, Winifred's closest friend.

A second later, Dominic's call to the man was ringing.

His heart lifted with relief when the psychiatrist answered. "This is Dr. Lumen."

"Hey, Tom, it's Dominic Bock, Jonathan Flite's dad. I got your number from Jimmy Barber last year?"

Against Dominic's expectations, the psychiatrist's tone went from clinical to friendly—though not without inflections of fatigue. "Dominic, hello. I'm sorry if I sounded short. I didn't have your number saved, and I thought you might be a patient. Or a reporter."

"You still treating people long distance, then?"

"Not as much lately. Crazy year so far. But I did come back to Cape Cod two weeks ago, so I could be here with You-Know-Who when *WorldLine* hit."

Winifred's unspoken name silenced them for a moment.

"I assume you're calling about Jonathan?" Dr. Lumen continued.

Dominic lowered his voice to a whisper. "Yeah. I'm worried. He hasn't returned any of my calls, and last I heard from Jimmy Barber, he was off the grid somewhere, considering Victor Zobel's offer."

"Same worries on my end," Dr. Lumen said. "Winifred knows where he is but won't say a word. And I'm honestly not sure what to expect. I think *WorldLine* hit the jackpot with that Lindsay-Thorsen-flashlight story, especially since the Idle County Sheriff's Department confirmed it was all true. It's really making people stop and think."

The damned flashlight. It had burrowed deep into Dominic's mind, as had the related questions about reality that Rebecca Spark's new physics theory had posed.

"I need to find Jonathan," he finally said. "Someone has to at least try to communicate with him before he goes up and visits Victor Zobel. I'm scared he might—"

"See it as a suicide mission?" Dr. Lumen cut in, perfectly filling in the words Dominic didn't want to say.

In the hotel suite's bathroom, the toilet flushed. Carolyn's pleading face rose in Dominic's mind.

*Please leave this alone. Please let us be a family. Please let your son go live his life without destroying ours.*

For the first time, Dominic wondered if his marriage was strong enough to weather the storm.

"I know he wants answers, but this isn't the way to get them," he said to Dr. Lumen. "Especially up on Victor Zobel's damned space yacht. Anything could go wrong, no matter how safe they say those shuttles are."

"Jonathan's probationary period is done," Dr. Lumen replied. "He's free to do whatever he wants."

Behind Dominic, the bathroom sink shut off. Carolyn would be out any second.

"I should go—but do you think it would help if we both go talk to Winifred in person?" Dominic said. "Like, maybe she'd see how worried we actually are?"

For a moment, Dr. Lumen was silent. It was clear he was choosing his words carefully. "Honestly, I'd welcome another voice of reason out here. It's getting muddled now, even for me. Could you fly out any time soon?"

"I have a few ends to tie up here, but yes. I could likely be there in a few days."

"Okay. Let's plan on it. Let me check a few things on this end, and then I'll reach out. Good?"

"Yes. Thanks, Tom."

They hung up just as Carolyn exited the bathroom. She opened the door slowly, as if taking care to avoid the marital glass she was about to step on. Stress heated Dominic's body. His breaths shortened.

"You were talking to that psychiatrist?" Carolyn said.

Dominic turned toward her and firmed his stance. "Dr. Lumen? Yes."

"You're not letting this go, then."

"No, I'm not."

Sweat broke out under Dominic's arms, on his hands, and on the back of his neck as Carolyn, holding a white hotel bath towel, strode toward him. Her footsteps were too calm to be genuine.

"And what about our family?" she asked, her voice like a razor.

"What do you mean? We're going to be fine."

"Are we?" She inched toward him in a way he had seen only a few times before, when she was at her most vulnerable—and when her defense mechanisms were preparing to strike first. "You've done a total one-eighty since you went out to visit your son last summer, and it's only getting worse now that his New Agey bullshit is smeared all over the TV," she said. "But I'm a Christian, Dom. I'm not giving that up. Or turning my back on everything we believe."

"*We* believe? That's an assumption."

Sorrow and anger played a tug-of-war on Carolyn's face. "An assumption?" she said. "So, now you're just throwing in the towel on everything we've built together, all because of your fucked-up son?"

Dominic's entire body grew numb. He had known his wife was uncomfortable with the very idea of Jonathan, not to mention the young man's disturbed past, but she had never said anything so outright cutting about him. She wasn't that person. But had she changed? Had everything changed?

"You hear one silly story about a stupid flashlight, probably made up by that Lindsay Thorsen girl way back when, and suddenly you're all 'spiritually woke' like one of those damned left coast hippies. Great. Just great."

Dominic considered the hotel room they were standing in. Then the city outside. Then Earth. Space. The universe. How had it all come to be?

"Doesn't it ever bug you how much you don't know?" he asked in a trembling voice. "Do you actually think our little Texas bubble is all there is? Christ, Carolyn. I feel like you don't even want me to wonder about things."

Carolyn spun away from him to face the hotel door and shook her head. "Damn it, Dom. You sound like one of those 'energy of the universe' lunatics!"

"And do you have a better explanation for why Jonathan was born with other people's memories in his head? People who died ten years before his birth, no less? If so, I'm all ears. Seriously."

"He could have made it all up."

"What about that flashlight incident with Lindsay Thorsen? The police records were cut-and-dry about how she survived that night. How could Jonathan possibly have known what was engraved on the flashlight handle if it was locked in evidence for thirty-plus years?"

Carolyn shifted on uneven feet. "You know those *WorldLine* editors can fabricate anything to make their stories play a certain way, Dom."

"And Rebecca Sparks? How could she have predicted everything about Jonathan's first interview with *WorldLine* six years before she ever met him?"

"It's TV! They can make it look like anything!"

"She can literally *read minds*, Carolyn. She's already proven it on a hundred other news shows across the country. Do you honestly think all those reporters would put their credibility on the line?"

Carolyn opened her mouth to respond, but no words came out. She simply stood there, staring at Dominic with her hands on her hips.

A key card suddenly unlocked their hotel room door.

Anna, Edith, and Jessa rushed in. They hadn't even been at the pool fifteen minutes, yet all three of them were out of breath. Their faces, usually glowing under their brown hair, were pale.

"What's wrong?" Carolyn asked before Dominic could even register just how off-kilter the three girls seemed.

Edith, their middle daughter of twelve, spoke first. "There was some guy down there asking what room we were in."

Carolyn's gaze cut to Dominic, then shifted back to the girls. "A reporter?"

Anna, their oldest, shook her head. "I don't think so. He was dressed in black with slicked-back hair, and he sounded European. I think he—"

"He had a weird little ponytail and smelled nasty, like cigarettes," ten-year-old Jessa interrupted.

"And he talked to you?"

All three girls nodded, but it was Anna, their most thoughtful daughter, who was shaking most. "He said we should be careful."

Carolyn took three quick steps toward Anna. "Careful? Why careful?"

Just as Anna took a breath to continue, Edith spoke over her with a shadow of the same disappointment currently dimming her mother's face. "He said something about *WorldLine*, but he made it about us." She looked at Dominic. "He said your other kid, Jonathan, is trying to be a 'bright and shining light' for people, but that it was going to cause problems if we weren't careful."

*A bright and shining light.*

Alice Winterblume had used those exact words when equating the now-famous story of Lindsay Thorsen's 2006 flashlight incident with the effect Jonathan's rising influence was having on the world.

"He actually said it would 'cause problems'?" Carolyn pressed. "What kind of problems?"

"He was watching us before we even walked by him, like he knew who we were," Anna said, now with tears in her eyes. "And I think I know who *he* was. His shirt collar was high, but I saw a tattoo on his neck. Of a snake. Just like that guy from the *New York Times*."

A ponytail. A smoker. A snake tattoo.

Dominic's heart froze in his chest.

The description indeed matched only one man he had ever heard of—just twelve days ago, to be exact, in a *New York Times* op-ed written by a middle-aged personal trainer from Idle County named Natalie Pent. In it, she had called out *WorldLine* for egregiously omitting important facts about a man named Raphael Dumont, whom she had long suspected of being involved in the Idle County Seven cold case.

As Carolyn pulled all three girls further into the hotel suite, Dominic rushed to the door and opened it. He looked down both sides of the hallway. It was empty, save for a hotel maid's cart.

*Raphael Dumont.*

What on earth had Victor Zobel's estranged friend been doing in San Antonio, let alone at the hotel Dominic and his family were staying at? Given everything that had happened to Jonathan's close associates over the last year, the question could only have alarming answers.

*Screw Lindsay Thorsen and screw her fucking flashlight*, Dominic thought. Then he pulled out his ActoPhone to call the police.

R EVIS ZOBEL SAT STIFFLY in his rented helicopter as it landed on the giant **X** outside his father's Minnesota estate, which lay at the center of Idle County's fabled Moon Woods. It was April 6, 2039, and he was forty-one years old—a far cry from the age he had been the last time he visited this place.

*And somehow I let myself come back,* he thought, wondering what the notorious Jonathan Flite would think if he knew what was on today's agenda.

If the young man really did have Jillian Pope's memories in his head, however that might be possible, Revis wanted to erase them. To prove he wasn't the same person from his half sister's frozen past—the battered boy who cried and cried, often seeking refuge under her king-size bed.

Because Revis was strong now. A person all his own.

Yet he shuddered when he glanced out the helicopter window. Jillian's disappearance from Idle County was the reason he had visited this place just three times since childhood. Avoidance was best, always, because why remind himself of Jillian and their shared mother, whom he had lost one after the other? Some would say boo-hoo, that he was rich, that he had more money than God (if God actually existed), and that he could handle a bit of tragedy. But no matter how much money one had, it didn't make up for the—

*STOP.*

There it was, his psychological coping mechanism.

His racing mind immediately calmed.

Revis basked in the mental quiet for a moment before glancing out the window again. The mansion outside was larger than any of his father's other houses. There was the tennis court, the pool, the golf course, the twenty-foot-tall cement perimeter. All in their usual order, he supposed.

Would his sister Victoria react adversely to his visit today? Would she see right through him, as usual?

"*Je serai aussi rapide que possible,*" Revis told his pilot, Thérèse, through the helicopter's intercom system once she had gracefully landed them on the X.

"No problem—take your time," she replied in English.

The helicopter doors opened, and Revis jumped out onto the landing pad. The first thing to hit him was the slightly off-kilter feeling he had always experienced whenever visiting this place: a desire to scream subdued by a sense of total serenity. It was the only place on Earth he had ever felt such a thing.

Of course, the sensation was always followed by the not-quite-inviting aroma of southern Minnesota: grass, trees, and dirt—the smell of boredom. Revis wondered how his sister could stand living here, all cooped up, locked away from the world.

Victoria had always been the family favorite, and save for her recent outright refusals to visit their father up on Star Island—the man's crowning, orbiting space hotel—she never seemed to question his bidding.

Today, Revis aimed to test her.

He turned around, glanced at Thérèse through the cockpit window, and gave her a thumbs-up.

DESPITE THE MORNING's early March chill, Victoria stepped onto the back patio before Revis could even reach it. The mansion's security team would have alerted her to the helicopter's approach, of course, but he had hoped to surprise her, at least a little.

"You better have a good fucking reason for being here," were her first words. She was wearing a sports bra and spandex, and her blond short crop was threaded with sweat.

"Hello to you, too," Revis replied, doing everything he could to maintain his composure. He had always been the one to suffer verbal and physical beatings from their father while Victoria chose the route of daughterly deference. And yes, she had adopted some of the man's repulsive behavior herself—but only as a defense mechanism. Taking their father's side had been her only way to stay safe. Revis couldn't blame her for it.

But didn't it still show her character? Hadn't it been a slap to the face to leave him alone during their formative years, with the solo task of building a protective framework to defend himself against their father, both physically and mentally? Clearly, Revis had yet to overcome the complexities of his relationship with Victoria. They were tandem. Tethered. Two sides of the same scratched coin.

"I'm in the middle of a workout," she said. "My trainer's here."

"Well, take a damned break."

"You don't talk to me for eight months and then decide to just show up unannounced? Please don't talk to *me* about taking a break."

"Well, we need to talk."

Victoria narrowed her eyes.

"And I need some coffee," Revis added. "Let's go inside. Please?"

With a scowl, Victoria followed him across the patio, into the gargantuan house.


"I'M SURE YOU KNOW why I'm here," Revis said once coffee was in hand and they were finished with feigned pleasantries. He sauntered from the kitchen back down the hall, toward the patio doors he had entered through. Opposite them was the glassed-in gym, where Victoria's fitness trainer was waiting—and staying politely out of the way.

*Not to mention looking hot as hell*, Revis thought. The trainer appeared to be in her late forties and fit as a fucking fiddle.

For some reason, she also looked familiar.

He stepped toward the door to get a closer look.

"No, you stay the hell away from her. I don't want her mixing with family," Victoria said, approaching him from behind and pulling on his sweater. "Let's go to the library."

Revis surrendered to his sister, hating the fact that she still held sway, even when he was pretending to be in control.


"OKAY. TALK."

They sat amid their father's wall of books, behind closed mahogany doors.

"I know you're not here to make amends," Victoria continued. "You never do shit like that."

"Honestly, there's nothing to amend on my end," Revis replied. "You're on your track. I'm on mine."

"Have you ever really had a track?"

There it was. The deep cut. Always undermining his very worth.

Was it because the question implied a truth he hated to examine? Maybe. He spent his time partying, sailing boats, and philandering with countless women while Victoria ran companies, starred in television shows, and kept their modern monarch of a father publicly in line. Sure, Revis had two university degrees in psychology, but he never used them, except to navigate his alarming family dynamics. What *did* that say about him?

He cleared his throat. "I visited Dad last August, after we left New York," he said. "Did I tell you that?"

Victoria froze while raising an energy drink to her mouth. "Like, up on Star Island? Jesus."

"I called him on his bullshit. Right before he attacked me with a letter opener."

Now came raised eyebrows. A genuine reaction from Victoria.

"I asked him about all the shit you and I talked about. He wouldn't give me anything. Nothing about Jonathan Flite. Nothing about those 'consciousness studies' in Estonia we weren't supposed to know about. Nothing about the Geneva bombing or the threatening letters you said that physicist Dorothy Garland was sending him. But his silence on that pretty much answered all my questions."

"You don't know that for sure."

"No, but . . ." Revis glanced up at one of the library's bookshelves. There sat a hundred old copies of his father's classic atheistic treatise, *In God We're Dust*, along with an equal number of ancient shrink-wrapped DVDs of the book's many follow-up television documentaries—each now collecting its own dust. "There's something I didn't tell you last summer in New York," he continued.

Victoria waited. Revis took a deep breath.

"I'm back in touch with Nicolas Rim, from Geneva. Remember him? His dad, Jonas, built that addition onto our house in Gland a few years before Mom died."

Victoria's knuckles turned white as she clutched her metal drink shaker. Surely she was remembering the day they'd been playing near the construction site, how Revis had stepped on the nail, and how their father had stood there screaming reprimands at his son instead of taking him to the hospital.

"Haven't actually seen Nick since he and his parents moved to the States," Revis continued, "but we've talked a few times in the past couple years. Did you know his dad, Jonas, built this place, too?" Revis gestured toward the library books, the walls, the entire compound. "That's why they came to the US back in the day. Except Nick says his dad died here, a few days after having some type of blackout episode while digging an elevator shaft. Did you ever know about that?"

"I was twelve fucking years old," Victoria said.

"I've never seen an elevator here."

"That's because you don't spend any time here."

There. She was budging an inch. Maybe two. The other side of his coin.

"Nick also told me his boss at Carey Developments hired him to do a hit on that Jonathan Flite kid in Rhode Island. And that Dad gave the directive, because of what Jonathan was saying about the Idle County Seven disappearing here."

Victoria's facade tightened. "He actually said that?"

"He did. Now I'm asking: Do you know anything about Dad giving that order?"

"Do you actually think I'd tell you if I did?"

"Yes, I do," Revis said. "Because—"

*Here it goes—*

"—I'm starting to wonder about Mom."

And there it was.

Victoria's facade grew brittle, then cracked. And just like that, Revis ensnared her.

IN THE LIBRARY, they continued to talk.

"Did you see the article in *Physical Review Today* last year? The one about Dorothy Garland?" Revis asked.

Victoria smirked. "I'm sorry, no. I don't have time for crackpot physicists."

"She went public last year with some big Theory of Everything that unifies quantum mechanics and classical physics, among other things."

"You're talking gibberish to me."

"Okay, well, put it this way: she's done something that's never been done before in science. She basically aligned airtight physics with a bunch of crazy-deep concepts that apparently explain not just what the universe is but also *why* it is. And unlike other theories of this sort—all those ones Mom used to talk about—this one is potentially testable."

"And that has anything to do with us *why*?"

"Because she's directly, publicly challenging Dad by using science to discredit him. And I've been reading up on her. Apart from all the new math in her theory, she's included a bunch of stuff about how our conscious energy apparently 'forms the particles we perceive.' She says she can prove all of it, just like she was threatening to do in those letters."

"Revis, she's a nutjob. A nobody. Dad doesn't even—"

"Did you know she was supposed to be in Geneva the day Dad's Catholic terrorist friend set off that fucking nuke? Along with about two hundred other physicists who were planning to back her new theory? Except she never boarded her flight from California. Were you even aware of that?"

Now Victoria said nothing.

"The group was supposed to meet that afternoon at CERN, in that big sphere auditorium thing Mom used to give talks in. Which, by the way, was less than half a kilometer from where Jean-Claude Apostol detonated his bomb. And considering Dad was going crazy over this crippled Dorothy Garland chick's letters and all the shit she was say-ing in them—not to mention that *he fucking knew Jean-Claude Apostol when he was a kid*—it really fucking matters."

"Not again, Revis—*Jesus!*" Victoria's entire face quivered. "Dad barely knew that cardinal. I don't know what you're hoping to—"

"I got another letter from Dorothy Garland last week," Revis inter-rupted. "This one came directly to the house in Salerno instead of going to the law firm. I have no idea how she got my Italy address."

Victoria waited for five seconds before saying, "And?"

"It told me to ask one of Dad's old friends about his obsession with poisons."

Victoria's face suddenly tensed, even though Revis hadn't yet said Raphael Dumont's name.

"You look like you've seen a ghost," he continued.

"Are you talking about Raph?"

*Raph.*

So, Victoria was still on a nickname basis with their father's tat-tooed, slithery ex-friend. "You're not still in touch with him, are you?" Revis asked.

After a moment of hesitation, Victoria said, "No. Of course not."

She was lying; Revis could tell. But why? Their father had de-manded they both sever all ties with Raphael four years ago, after the man was accused of murder in Croatia—a potential PR nightmare that Zobel Enterprises had somehow managed to keep quiet. And hadn't Victoria seemed relieved when Raphael was out of their lives? Hadn't the man, with his leering eyes and that frightful snake tattoo coiling around his neck, always repulsed her?

Or maybe she had been faking her revulsion. Maybe she and Raphael were—

*STOP.*

Revis forced himself to breathe.

*Keep it to-fucking-gether, or you'll blow this whole thing.*

When he continued, it was with a low, controlled voice. "My letter from Dorothy Garland also said to ask Raphael what really happened to Mom."

Victoria's face was clammy. She shook her head furiously, stood up, and began pacing. "If you talk to Raphael, Dad will set the fucking dogs on you. Don't think he won't."

"Do you know something I don't?"

"Mom had heart problems. That's all it was."

"Some poisons cause heart problems."

"And you think Dad was poisoning Mom? *Christ*, Revis!"

Revis took a breath. "Do you remember back in Geneva, when he freaked out at her and that physicist friend from CERN who was over for dinner? We were, like, five."

"I barely remember back that far," Victoria said.

"I never understood why dad would have exploded on them until I started reading about Dorothy Garland's new theory. It's presenting solutions to some major arguments going on in the physics community about consciousness and what it actually is—basically because there are multiple experiments out there that lend credibility to certain meta-physical ideas Dad would hate. At least publicly."

Victoria quickened her pacing and raised her voice. "And you think he started feeding Mom poison because she was talking to some friend about a bunch of woo-woo concepts? *Come on*, Revis. Do you realize how ridiculous that—"

"If you think it's ridiculous, why are you getting so upset?"

"I'm not upset!"

"Oh please, Vic. Self-awareness. Jesus." With a cynical chuckle, Revis realized he was coming out on top. Finally. "And you know our dad. You fucking know him. And maybe since you also know why he built a goddamned house here—"

"You're just jealous that he—"

"And why Jonas Rim died after an accident in some elevator shaft without anybody ever really questioning it—"

"Nobody's died because of this place, Revis—"

"Oh really? Are you actually certain of that? Because Nick Rim also said—"

"Said what? That Dad's the boogeyman? That he helped a Catholic mental case blow up a bunch of physicists in Geneva just to preserve his precious reputation? Do you realize how insanely far-fetched that sounds?"

Revis didn't reply. He didn't need to.

"Jesus *Fucking* Christ, Revis. If you're going to walk around accusing Dad of being some obsessive psychopath, start with your own damned childhood. Then maybe—just *maybe*—you can work your way up to telling people he's the worst terrorist in human history."

"What are you saying?"

"I'm saying that Dad's an asshole, but *you* need to watch yourself. I'm only going to tell you once."

"And what about Jillian? She was our sister, Vic."

"You mean *half* sister."

The cruelty embedded in Victoria's dig officially severed her from Revis for the millionth time in their intertwined lives. But he couldn't give up. Not today.

"What if they really did die here, like this Jonathan Flite kid says?" he pressed. "What if Dad—"

"I told you in New York: Jonathan Flite is a joke. Dad hasn't even given him a second thought."

"Is that why he attacked me with a letter opener?"

"How should I know? I'm a button pusher, Revis. I watch over this place. I push buttons. I do what Dad says. I try to travel as much as I can so I don't go crazy here. But I *don't* ask questions I shouldn't be asking. We both know what that would lead to."

With a tremor of rage in his heart, Revis said, "One more time: Do you think Dad knows what happened to the Idle County Seven? Or what happened in Geneva?"

Victoria paused her pacing and stared at him for a long moment, shielding all hints of emotion. Then she took two steps toward the library door. "We're done here. Have a nice life."

She waited for him to leave the library first.

As Revis stepped off the patio, onto the cement pathway leading back to the helicopter landing pad, he spoke into the microphone planted under his shirt. "Did you get all that?"

Into his earpiece came the voice of Heather Mousseau, the FBI special agent he'd spoken with two months ago in New York. "Yep, we got it. Not sure what it all means, but it was good. It was really good."

"Do you think she knows something I don't?" Revis asked.

"She was squirming. I could tell that much."

"Good. I'm getting back on the helicopter now and heading to the Twin Cities airport. I should be back on the East Coast by five o'clock."

"Great," Agent Mousseau said. "And thanks, Revis. This was a big deal. I'll let you know next steps as soon as we—"

But Revis lost the agent's last words when he heard the patio door slide open behind him.

"One second," he whispered as quietly as he could.

As he turned to face Victoria, he prepared one last effort to make his case—and to solicit something incriminating.

Except it wasn't Victoria standing on the deck. It was her personal trainer, the bombshell cougar who had looked familiar when he entered the house. In her bare feet, she crossed the patio with determined eyes and a light step.

"Why aren't you with Victoria?" Revis asked, noticing only after the words were out that he had spoken them with a tone of Zobel family superiority he hated.

"I don't have much time—Victoria's in the shower, and her assistant, Greta, is about to get back from the grocery store," the woman said in a pleasantly authoritative voice. "Anyway, my name is Natalie Pent. I knew your sister Jillian. And Lindsay Thorsen. And some of the others who disappeared back in 2010."

Revis stared at her for a moment, muzzling his lust. He glanced toward the house. Nobody was watching from the windows.

"And?"

"And I heard what you and Victoria were talking about in the library." Natalie held out a matte-gray business card. "I'd love to talk to you—here's my number. I also might have some relevant information about your dad's friend Raphael Dumont."

"What the hell are you talking about?"

"There was some stuff, back in the day. The police knew about it but never did anything, because there was never any real evidence."

Knowing Agent Mousseau might be interested in hearing what Natalie had to say about Raphael Dumont, Revis thought for a split-second before saying, "Yes. Let's talk tonight."

"I'll be around," Natalie said. "And one more thing. I think your sister is still in touch with Raphael. And that he told her what happened to my friends."

"And what exactly would that be?"

"I think they found out what happens after we die, and your dad killed them for it." Without waiting for a response, Natalie Pent turned on her bare feet and ran back toward the house in silence, leaving Revis standing alone under the chopping whir of his rented helicopter.

2005



"WATCH HIS LEG KICKS, THORSEN! He's faking you out going into that punch. Try to see them coming!"

Coach Bill Martinez, a Fairfax Community Center staple, paced about ten feet to Lindsay's left as she sparred with Pete Sanchez, the smallest boy in her kickboxing class. It was evening on Wednesday, November 2, and—as always—Coach Martinez was not-quite-yelling his instructions and encouragement. Twenty other boys, including Alan Sparks, stood alongside the floor mat, watching the fight.

"Sanchez, good punch," Coach Martinez continued. "Thorsen, push kicks'll only keep him away!"

Pete, an eighth grade boy, threw another jab at Lindsay's face. She ducked and spun away. From the corner of her eye, she saw Alan Sparks whisper something to Jeff Miles.

*Concentrate, concentrate—*

Pete's fist hit her temple. Her skull rattled in her helmet.

*Come on, kick his ass. Focus focus focus—*

She swung into an uppercut, hit Pete's fist, then turned the opposite way, into a hook. He blocked it with little effort.

"Come on, Thorsen!" Coach Martinez yelled. "One more minute. Get in his space, and don't let up! Give me an early Thanksgiving present! Come on! Give him hell!"

Lindsay, who had been conditioned by her Grandma Thorsen not to embrace America's whitewashed version of Thanksgiving, only grunted in response.

Leg kick, hook, jab, jab—Pete was dodging it all, coming back with his own attacks, each one looking easy and spontaneous. Lindsay could barely breathe. Her lungs were now emptying faster than she could fill them.

"Five seconds!"

Blushing, Lindsay stopped and let her fists down. It took her a second to realize nobody was laughing or giving her grief for losing to Pete. Was her inner daze over Drew's disappearance that obvious? Contrary to what she had hoped at school earlier today, kickboxing hadn't offered much relief from it.

"That's it for tonight, guys and girl," Coach Martinez said. "Lindsay, you weren't focusing at all tonight. He was on the attack, and you just let him at it. Gotta get in there on the offensive."

Lindsay popped out her slimy mouth guard, blushing, and turned her back to the boys. Just as she aimed to rush for the locker room, however, Coach Martinez's familiar, heavy hand rested on her shoulder.

"Good job tonight either way. I know you're having a tough week."

Lindsay turned and glanced at Coach Martinez. He was a short but powerful man of fifty-two. Despite being physically fit, time had softened his muscles a bit, and a slight belly protruded from his gut. The man was divorced and single; Lindsay always guessed that he passed his womanless free time by working out and drinking beer.

"Good job?" Lindsay said, still panting. "I screwed that whole fight. I should have seen his moves coming." She pressed the left boxing glove between her knees, yanked her hand free, and then pulled the right glove off. "He wasn't even trying. None of them do."

"Alan Sparks does. You still haven't beaten him, have you?"

"Yeah, well, I only beat the others because they're afraid to hit a girl."

"Not sure what kind of guy that makes Alan, then," Coach Martinez said with a wink.

Lindsay couldn't even muster a shrug. She bid a frustrated farewell to Coach Martinez, then walked across the sparring mat, toward the locker rooms. Through a large pane of glass lining the upper floor, she eyed a few women chugging away on the gym's ellipticals. She upped her pace, hoping she might beat them to the showers. Lindsay hated rinsing off in front of others, but she hated worse walking outside on a freezing cold night covered in sweat.

She wound her way into the locker room through its U-shaped corridor and found her locker at the far end. To her dismay, water was pounding the floor inside the shower chamber just beyond.

*Damn it.*

She wasn't alone.

Huddling in the corner and rushing as fast as she could, Lindsay took off her top and stood in her sports bra, trying to gauge how many people she might have to share the shower chamber with.

But the spouting water was making a smooth and constant sound against the floor tile.

*Maybe somebody left it on.*

Lindsay grabbed a towel from the rack, ripped her clothes off, and wrapped herself up. Her breasts, which had started developing late last year (earlier than all the other girls she knew), pressed against each other and formed a small mound of cleavage. She had been self-conscious about them at first, but now, furtively, she enjoyed looking at them in the mirror.

*"You'll grow into them,"* her mother always said. Lindsay never knew whether to take it as an insult or a compliment.

She crept into the shower chamber and peered right, through the steam. In the far corner, one of the twelve showers was indeed running at full blast over nothing but hot, humid air. The stream of water hitting the floor made the only sound in the whole locker room.

Lindsay unwrapped herself, walked toward the shower spout, and extended a hand into the hissing water.

*Damn!*

She pulled it back with a sudden jerk. The water was burning hot.

After reaching behind the torrent and turning the handle left, toward a cooler setting, Lindsay tested the water, found it tolerable, and stepped back in.

On any other night, she would have been all business—get in the shower, hurry to wash up before anybody else joined, and run out. Tonight, however, on the most difficult Wednesday of her life, she stood in the water and let it beat down on her head. Her ponytail fanned against her back before she turned and let the water rush over her face.

She thought back over her day: the news report about Drew she had watched over breakfast, the way Natalie Pent had seemed to enjoy talking about his disappearance, the conversation with Alan Sparks by her locker.

As Lindsay turned around again under the water, Elijah Bryce's and Molly Butler's faces rose in her mind. Why had they been acting so weird in the cafeteria during lunch?

Behind her, the shower handle suddenly squeaked. The water on her back grew scalding hot.

Lindsay jumped out of it, shocked back into the moment with surreal bewilderment. "What the hell—?" she said aloud, her gaze jumping to the shower handle. Sure enough, it was turned all the way to the right, to the red zone marked **"HOT."**

The handle had moved all by itself.

Lindsay stared at it, still standing outside the rush. The shower chamber once again filled with steam.

Keenly aware of her nakedness, Lindsay looked around the empty, tiled room. She was still alone.

*Must be a weird handle*, she thought. *Maybe the water pressure did it.*

She reached behind the hot downpour and adjusted the temperature again. This time, she was quick to start soaping up. If there was any more funny business, she'd jump out and go to a different shower spout.

But no. This time, the water turned off completely, right when Lindsay was in the middle of washing her face. She screamed, scrunching her eyes shut. But the remaining soap had already crept beneath her eyelids and was starting to sting. "Is someone in here?" she asked, feeling around for the shower handle.

From across the shower chamber came a child's giggle.

Lindsay froze.

*That's his voice. That's—*

She found the shower handle and turned the water back on as fast as she could. It jetted back out, steaming hot but not burning. She plunged her face into it, wiping like mad to get the soap off.

Another giggle sounded from the shower entrance, near the locker room.

This time, she was sure.

"Drew?" Lindsay said, opening her eyes and turning the shower handle off. She spun around to face the exit. The steam was thicker now, making the light from the locker room beyond glow like some kind of heavenly doorway.

A small figure stood in the mist. He was a mere shadow blocking the light.

*Oh my God, that's him. It's—*

Lindsay ran toward her brother, then slipped. She swore as her ankle twisted and she went sailing for the floor. Her right knee scraped along the wet tile.

More giggling. It was the same eruptive laugh Drew used when they played hide-and-seek.

"Drew! Wait!"

Lindsay jumped up, her ankle barely offering support. Her lost brother was still standing at the steamy shower exit, but she could see more than just his shadow now. It was clearly him, and he was wearing his red Halloween costume—Doctor Deadlock from *Mousepants*.

"Drew! Get back here! How did you—?"

Gaining secure footing, Lindsay lunged forward—

—and ran right through him.

She hit the shower chamber's entryway wall with her hands, then immediately looked left, into the locker room. It was empty.

And something was squeaking again behind her. Metal on metal.

It was the shower handle she had turned off just moments before. On the far side of the chamber, it was moving to the right, on its own, toward the "**HOT**" label.

*This can't be happening.*

Water shot out of the shower spout at full force as an icy chill ran down Lindsay's neck. It spread through her body but hovered on her back, along the new burn from the previous burst of scalding water.

It was the same chill she had felt in the cafeteria earlier that day, during that moment of eye contact with Molly Butler.

Lindsay grabbed her towel from the wall hook, wrapped herself, and stepped off the tile, onto the main locker room floor. She checked the third row of lockers, then the second, then the first.

All empty.

Two minutes later, she rushed out of the locker room with her hair still wet. At the far end of the gymnastics and kickboxing atrium, Coach Martinez was standing with Alan and a few other freshly showered boys, miming an upper cut with perfect form.

"Hey, guys, did you just see my brother?" Lindsay called out without thinking.

The words immediately sounded absurd. Coach Martinez, Alan, and the other boys glanced at her across the tumbling mat, frowning as if they weren't quite sure she knew what she was asking.

As they ran toward her, Lindsay's head and heart spun in a horrible dance. Could she have imagined it? Could the stress from the past two days have caught up with her enough to make her see things?

Except her back still burned. Something—or someone—had turned the water handle to "**HOT**." *Twice.*

"I saw my brother, Drew, in the locker room," she finally said, knowing she wouldn't be able to take the statement back.

Coach Martinez reached her first. "What? What do you mean?"

Lindsay shook her head. "He was just in there. I heard him laughing. He turned my shower handle. Did he come out here?"

Coach Martinez thrust a hand into his pocket and grabbed a cell phone. He flipped it open and was ready to dial. "You're sure it was him? Should I call the police?"

Alan was already rushing toward the community center's childcare area. "I'll go search," he said. "What was he wearing?"

"His red Doctor Deadlock costume," Lindsay said, growing more and more certain with each passing second that there had been some sort of mistake. Yet even if her mind *had* played a terrible trick on her, it might not matter; judging by Coach Martinez's conversation with the 9-1-1 dispatcher, the police were already on their way.

# ROUND AND ROUND

2010

ANDLES. A SEA OF FLAMES. FEELING. Even though Natalie Pent did everything she could to put a face on for the crowd in Heart Park, there was something about vigils like this—the solemnity, the grief, the dots of light in darkness—that pulled her toward something she didn't want to acknowledge. A sense of peace she longed for but couldn't name.

It was September 10, 2010. The so-called Idle County Seven had now been missing for three months.

Natalie stood with Sarah Brownie, watching End Haven's concerned citizenry listen to the missing kids' parents talk to the news cameras. Sarah had been hesitant to come with Natalie tonight—just as she'd been hesitant to hang out at all as of late—but Natalie had solicited reluctant agreement after reminding her that Victor Zobel was going to be here. It might be their only chance to ask him questions.

Not to mention that they had been horrible to Lindsay Thorsen, Pauline Gilbert, and the others over the years. They owed them this vigil.

*"You were horrible to them,"* Sarah had reminded Natalie with a tense voice earlier that day.

*"Yeah, well,* you *followed along,"* Natalie retorted.

Tonight was a big deal for Idle County—even bigger than when Drew Thorsen disappeared. That his older sister had also now vanished was sending Idle County over the edge. The reporters' cameras and microphones had logos from a slew of different networks, and not just from local affiliates. Some were national. Natalie had even seen CNN.

As she stood next to Sarah, it felt like their younger days—like they were still a team. But Sarah had recently started doing what all of Natalie's friends had been doing over the last two years:

Fighting back at her.

Slowly drifting off.

Hanging out with other people.

It had been almost three months since they'd discussed their missing classmates in Natalie's bedroom in a confused daze, debriefing over their statements to the police and breaking out every possible theory about why the seven kids might have disappeared.

Their biggest outstanding question related to one person in particular: the man with the ponytail and snake tattoo who had been arguing with Jillian Pope back in 2007, the afternoon before Alan Sparks's house exploded. That had been almost three years ago now, during all the nursing home drama with Jillian's dad—her *real* dad, Max; not her famous stepdad, Victor Zobel.

Tonight, it seemed Natalie and Sarah had gotten lucky.

"Keep looking," Sarah whispered to Natalie as they peered through the crowd. "I swear he's here. It's the same guy."

"I don't see anyone with a ponytail."

"Trust me, it's him. He has the same tattoo of a snake on his neck. It coils around, remember?"

Natalie simmered, clutching her candle. Jillian Pope's argument with the tattooed stranger had stuck out to her over the last three years, especially because the two had been speaking in French, and Jillian had seemed irate. The argument only became more relevant the next day, after the tragic gas explosion, when Natalie had walked in on Jillian and a sobbing Lindsay in the school bathroom. Just as Natalie entered, she'd heard Jillian say to Lindsay, in a low and terrorized voice, *"Victor wanted her gone, and* this *is how he tries to do it?"*

When both girls had seen Natalie, they immediately stopped talking. Making only fleeting eye contact with her, they had rushed out of the bathroom.

Natalie knew it wasn't her job to solve the case, but every day the police failed to find the Idle County Seven, each detail she had witnessed over the years burrowed further into her mind.

The only "her" in the gas-explosion equation Jillian could have been talking about was Rebecca Sparks, Alan's disabled older sister. Oddly, Rebecca had been the only one in their family to survive that night, because she had been visiting with Jillian's crazy real dad, Max. And yes, the rumors about Rebecca's psychic abilities were true—Natalie had witnessed them firsthand at Alan's sixth-grade birthday party—so it made sense why Max might have been obsessed with her. He had lost his medical license for illegally studying life, death, and consciousness, hadn't he?

Yet the person who had most to lose were people to find out about Rebecca was Victor Zobel. His New Naturalism brand relied on squashing anything that lent credence to such concepts of higher consciousness.

*"But to think he tried to kill her?"* Sarah had said back in July. *"That's a fucking stretch."*

Maybe so, but so was the fact that Jillian, Lindsay, and the others hadn't yet been found. It made Natalie wonder about other people's secrets. She herself had plenty of her own.

"Did you see Jillian's step-siblings?" Sarah whispered. "Looks like they came with Victor. For some reason, I thought they'd still be younger."

Natalie craned her neck. "Where?"

"There. Look. The blond twins." Sarah gestured. "What are their names again?"

"Victoria and Revis," Natalie whispered. "Rich-people names."

She stood on her tiptoes to look over the shoulder of the man in front of her, then saw them: two blond kids, probably ten or eleven, standing up on the stage next to Victor Zobel, their celebrity father. Their clothes were stylish. European.

God, it was surreal to have someone as famous as Victor Zobel standing in the middle of Heart Park. Natalie wondered if that was why the majority of these candle holders had come out tonight.

"Look at their faces," she continued. "Revis looks nervous as hell. Do you think he's—"

Somebody tapped Natalie's shoulder from behind. She turned to see a middle-aged woman with three kids draped around her. "Shhhh! Will you please be quiet?" the woman hissed.

Natalie recognized her. It was Melissa Johnson, one of Lindsay Thorsen's family friends. Natalie had met her a few times in passing, back in the day.

*Before life got weird.*

But Natalie didn't like to think about that. It wouldn't help anyone.

Either way, Mrs. Johnson didn't seem to recognize her. Natalie turned toward the stage again, holding her candle as the Idle County Seven parents eulogized their missing teenagers. Wax dripped into its clear plastic cup holder, warming her fingers.

There was Claire Gilbert, the only parent in Pauline's life, taking the microphone in tears. With her basic brown hair still styled like the '90s, she talked about how "Pauline was a good girl, always kind and always innocent."

*Clearly she never found out about the abortion*, Natalie thought. She had mentioned Pauline's rumored pregnancy to the police two months ago, after the girl disappeared with the others, but as of today, it seemed to be just another random tidbit in a gaping silence of questions.

Next on stage came Andrew Butler, Molly's dad, with his black hair and awkward grief. He had apparently lost his wife in a car accident in 2004, and judging by the way he now stared at the ground as he talked, this unexpected loss of his only daughter—who had already been dying of a brain tumor—looked as if it might become the nail in his goddamned coffin.

The next person to speak was Shelly Bryce, Elijah Bryce's divorced, adoptive mother. She choked out loving words about her son—somehow sounding fake about it—and then made some contemptuous comment about Elijah's biological mother, Cynthia Foster, who for some reason wasn't at tonight's vigil. Natalie had heard bits and pieces of Elijah's adoption story over the years, but she had never met his birth mother. He had stopped being Natalie's friend by the time he finally met the woman, just before that incident with Damon Jacoby at Spinner's Lake.

David Thorsen—Lindsay Thorsen's dad—took the stage after Shelly Bryce. As always, he was handsome enough to make Natalie's body buzz. His wife, Sandra, who had always looked at Natalie with narrow eyes, was nowhere to be seen.

*I wonder if they're still together*, Natalie thought.

The very idea of David being single made her want to go up to him and—

"Jesus, look at Victor Zobel's spray tan," Sarah whispered.

Natalie let her fantasy dissipate. She refocused on the stage, where the celebrity author, neurosurgeon, and businessman extraordinaire had just taken the microphone. As always, he looked rehearsed—too ready for the cameras, considering the somber occasion. His face was handsome on his tall frame, but he looked better on television. Less shiny in his complexion.

"Do you really think Jillian hated him?" Natalie whispered back to Sarah.

Mrs. Johnson shushed the young women again.

Sarah gave Natalie a nervous glance. Together, they looked toward the stage once again.

With tight lips and a smirk to hide a sense of grief she couldn't quite articulate, Natalie listened as Victor Zobel said nothing about his stepdaughter's disappearance that he hadn't already said on the news.

She glanced across the stage, taking note of the other parents who were missing. Javier Graff, Clayton Graff's dad, wasn't present. Neither was Abigail Creed, Gabriel Creed's gargantuan mother. Considering she had recently told reporters that her son and his six depraved friends had disappeared to hell to take up residence with Satan, it was probably for the best that her lanky husband, Hank, had brought their remaining children on his own. Gabriel's six siblings, shockingly varied in age, all stood next to their father. Like Hank's threadbare jeans and flannel, all their clothes were faded and worn.

The last missing parent was Max Pope, Jillian's father. According to the news, he hadn't been seen by anyone—not even his new neighbors up in Alaska—since late 2009. Still, it wouldn't make sense for Max to return to the public sphere, let alone to Idle County. Considering those secret tests he did on his dying drug-study patients, people would run him right out of town.

Natalie scanned the crowd again. She still couldn't pick out Victor Zobel's friend, the European man with the snake tattoo.


Until just after the vigil's end.

Natalie finally saw him as she was leading Sarah through the crowd, toward David Thorsen, who was standing amid the other Idle County parents, greeting fellow grievers as if they were guests in a deathly wedding line.

The foreigner suddenly disappeared from her sight as David stepped out of the line to talk with Alice Winterblume, the reporter from WCMP news in Wind Prairie.

A few seconds later, however, the man reappeared just behind Alice. His dark, ponytailed hair; distinct, angular features; and spiraling snake tattoo looked the same as they did in 2007. Tonight, he was also wearing an earpiece, like a Secret Service agent.

"Yep, that's him," she said.

Sarah looked clammy. "You're seriously going to try talking with him?"

"And see if he has anything to say about the day Alan Sparks died?" Natalie said. "You're damned right I am."

Anxiety colored Sarah's face as Natalie grabbed her hand and struck forward, toward Victor Zobel and his posse—four other men besides the one with the snake tattoo and ponytail.

They were all wearing earpieces. Victor whispered something to the tattooed man a moment after David Thorsen, still mid-conversation with Alice Winterblume, gestured graciously toward him.

It was a clear shot. Now or never.

Natalie's heart raced as she approached Victor Zobel. She had never spoken to a famous person before—there was something otherworldly about the very idea of it, now that it was staring her in the face. She charged forward, barely noticing an immediate tension stiffen Sarah's arm.

"Victor," Natalie called out. "I was friends with your stepdaughter, Jillian. And the others. I was wondering if we could talk?"

Three of the men in Victor's posse—bodyguards, Natalie now realized—formed a swift, silent blockade around him. They left just enough room for him to turn, notice Natalie, and respond.

"Oh yes?" he said. "Then I'm sorry for your loss as well. So sorry."

Saccharine. Too saccharine. Everything he said tonight sounded like a performance.

Natalie thought back to Jillian's argument in 2007. And then to what the girl had said in the bathroom the following day, after the gas explosion.

*"Victor wanted her gone, and* this *is how he tries to do it?"*

"I'm wondering—" Natalie started, but then she stopped to gather her thoughts and reframe her words. She had reached the blockade of bodyguards, who now parted just enough to allow direct communication with Victor. Instead, Natalie looked at the man next to him—the foreigner with the snake tattoo. In a split-second decision, she refocused on him, drawing his eyes. "You—I'm sorry as well. I know you and Jillian were close."

It was almost imperceptible, the flicker of confusion on the man's face. "Yes," he said. "Thank you." He had a European accent. Definitely French, like in the movies.

"I didn't get to meet you officially last time you were here," Natalie said. She extended a hand through her own bluff, hoping he'd take the bait. "I'm Natalie Pent."

"Raphael Dumont," he said, reaching past his comrades to shake her hand.

From behind, Sarah pulled quietly on Natalie's shirt. *Be careful.*

"I'm not sure *we* ever got the chance to meet," Victor said, suddenly rotating fully toward Natalie and overtaking the conversation. "I'm sure I've heard your name come up."

"And this is Sarah Brownie," Natalie said, turning to acknowledge her friend, whose pale face was now perspiring.

Sarah shook Victor's hand. Then Raphael's. For a moment, nobody spoke. Victor switched back to his camera-ready smile with a polite head nod. "It was nice of you girls to come pay your—"

"We're wondering what you and Jillian were arguing about the day of that gas explosion," Natalie said to the tattooed man—Raphael. "We saw you after school."

Natalie looked at Sarah, nodded assuredly, and then glanced back at Victor and Raphael.

Victor's smile crimped. "Excuse me?"

"The day our friend Alan Sparks's house had the gas leak," Natalie reiterated. "You were in town, right?"

"That was around the time Jillian's father decided to move to Alaska, wasn't it?" Victor said to Raphael.

Raphael's eyes were piercing blue. As he took a breath to speak, he glanced at Natalie. Saw her watching. "I think, yes, it was that day," he said, looking back at Victor. "You sent me to pick her up from school."

"But Jillian never wanted to go back to Switzerland with you," Natalie pressed Victor. "Why would you send someone to pick her up from school?"

With the finesse only a celebrity could manage, Victor smiled and began turning away from them. "Excuse me, but I—"

"What about a journal?" Sarah cut in. "Did Jillian ever mention a journal that her dad, Max, was trying to find?"

Victor Zobel froze in his tracks. With his back to them, he cocked his head. His leathery neck wrinkled as he showed them the side of his face. "A journal? I don't know what you mean."

Natalie also stared at Sarah. What the hell was she talking about? What journal?

Sarah's breaths were fast, and she glanced fleetingly at Natalie as if her impending words were a betrayal. "I walked by Jillian at the Bean & Leaf a few weeks before they disappeared. She was sitting on the patio with Pauline Gilbert and Clayton Graf, and Clayton was showing them some old book. It had a leather cover. Jillian said something about having no idea if it was the journal her dad was looking for. I heard it when I walked by."

Natalie could only stare at Sarah. She had never mentioned this.

"I didn't ever hear of any journal," Victor said. He looked at Raphael, who shrugged blankly. "But perhaps you'd be better off letting me worry about this. I'll ask the police if they've heard anything else like that. Now, if you please, my dears, I need to find my—"

A young girl's voice cut through their awkward circle.

"God, Revis! I'm telling Dad."

Victor's blond daughter, Victoria, was pushing through the crowd, looking more ornery than she did in the tabloids. When she reached Natalie and Sarah's small audience with her father, she stopped short. Made herself taller.

"—children," Victor finished.

"Revis stole my phone," Victoria whined.

Her sulking twin brother approached the circle. "Whatever she's saying, it's a lying sack of crap."

"No, it's not! He threw my phone in that stupid duck pond!"

Victor looked down at his son, Revis, with an eerie sense of calm that set Natalie's heart on edge. "Revis, remember what I told you earlier," he said. Then he turned to Natalie and Sarah with a polite smile. "If you'll excuse me."

The three men blockading Victor closed the gap, but Natalie stood there, watching Victor, who bent down, into Revis's face. He was still smiling, but in a warning sort of way. "If what your sister said is true—and it usually is—you're not going to be a happy camper."

"I want to go back to Genève," the boy moaned.

Just before the bodyguards cut off Natalie's view of the exchange completely, Victor's smile disappeared, and his eyes took on a deadened look that Natalie couldn't have described even if she wanted to. He lowered his voice to young Revis, speaking words too low to hear.

Natalie caught Raphael Dumont's eye over the three bodyguards' shoulders. He was staring at her—just like grown men always stared at her. But he was sharp and handsome, possibly in his early thirties. She let his gaze linger.

Sarah was staring at Natalie, too. "I'm sorry," she said. "I didn't say anything about the journal because—"

"Not now," Natalie said. She tugged on Sarah's arm, and they started back the way they came, passing the reporters and other Idle County Seven parents. Natalie turned her face away from Pauline Gilbert's mother as she and Sarah passed.

Yet Claire Gilbert looked dazed. She was talking with Elijah Bryce's mother, Shelly, and didn't even glance their way.

They neared the edge of the crowd just as David Thorsen ended his conversation with Alice Winterblume. He was looking at the ground as if he were focused on leaving, and leaving quickly. But then he looked up. For a split second, he and Natalie locked eyes.

She saw nothing in them. No recognition. No feeling. Lindsay Thorsen's handsome, rich dad looked like an empty shell.

Then he was back. The same as ever. He knew her.

"Natalie Pent."

"David Thorsen," she replied with her usual flirtatious smirk. For some reason, it felt comforting to say his name.

Nevertheless, he just stood there as if processing her very presence. "I'm sorry, I . . . thank you for coming," he finally said. "Lindsay would have appreciated it."

"I'm so sorry about what happened. I never got a chance to tell you. Or Lindsay's mom."

"Sandra is . . . well, she wasn't able to make it tonight. It's been hard on both of us."

"Yeah, I bet."

Next to Natalie, Sarah was balancing on one foot, then the other, watching the crowd dissipate. Natalie was about to reintroduce her when David abruptly continued on his way without saying goodbye. His facade, it seemed, had lost steam.

An untethered sense of emptiness crept back into Natalie, fusing itself into the facade that she, too, wore in crowds.

She turned to Sarah. "Okay, *now*. What the hell was that journal thing all about?"

"I'm sorry, I just—I had to ask Victor when I had the chance," Sarah said. "It's been bugging me since July. I really did walk by Jillian and Clayton and Pauline back in June, before they disappeared."

"Okay. Did you tell the police?"

"Yeah," Sarah replied.

"Then why keep it a secret?"

"Because I—" Sarah stopped, took a deep breath, then shook her head. Natalie saw tears in her eyes. Then a grimace. Then a glare. "I was with Alec."

Static. Natalie let the name rattle in her mind. She raced around the implications. "You mean my fucking *brother*?"

Sarah's face contorted in the worst type of fear—the kind that made a person pathetic, ugly. In it, Natalie saw her own new truth. She had just lost the two closest people in her life—the *only* two people in her life—to each other.

"You're together?"

Sarah nodded vigorously, as though aware of the truth's potency. Just like that, Natalie knew it would never be the same between them. *Could* never be the same. And her twin brother? He was the only person who seemed to love Natalie unconditionally. He had driven them both to Heart Park tonight before scampering off with Jacob Jenkins, but he hadn't said anything about being in a relationship with Sarah.

He hadn't trusted his own sister.

"I'm going to walk home," Natalie said. "You can go with Alec. I'm sure he's looking for you."

"Wait, Nat—"

"I said I need to think."

"Okay, but I—"

"Bye."

Natalie left Sarah Brownie standing next to Heart Park's heart-shaped duck pond. Upon reaching the sidewalk, she turned south and began walking toward Hunter Avenue. All the while, she ignored the piercing sorrow bubbling up in her chest, choosing instead to wonder why Victor Zobel had frozen in his tracks upon Sarah's mention of a journal Max Pope had been trying to find.

2005

TWO HOURS AFTER SEEING her lost brother, Drew, in the women's locker room at Fairfax Community Center, Lindsay Thorsen sat alone on her bed, lit only by the open PC laptop she and her mother shared. In her mind, she replayed the incident over and over, beat by beat.

The shower.

The moving water handle.

The figure in the steam.

Police had searched the community center high and low, as well as every street in a five-mile radius. There had been no sign of Drew.

Lindsay considered the implications for almost ten minutes. Finally, she said aloud to herself in the silence of her dim bedroom: "Ghosts aren't real."

Nobody answered.

She glanced at her AOL Instant Messenger buddy list. Nearly twenty of her friends were signed on, probably chatting about nothing of substance. Tonight, their screen names seemed to float there, in some other world. In the *normal* world.

Lindsay sat back, against her pillow.

The so-called afterlife was something churchgoers in Idle County believed in, but such convictions had never been a priority for the Thorsen family. Her father, apart from never having learned any Potawatomi traditions, flat-out didn't have time for spirituality, and her mother had always been very vocal in her disdain for organized belief systems. Last year, after reading some book called *In God We're Dust*, the woman had also begun to lament that religion was "for poor people who can't afford a good education." According to Sandra Thorsen, these people simply weren't wordly and didn't know how to think critically.

But Lindsay was thinking critically now, and the facts flew in the face of everything she believed.

She opened YouTube, a new video site Alec Pent had told her about, and typed "ghosts" into the search bar.

It brought up hundreds of results. Some were cartoon clips—including one from *Mousepants*, which immediately reminded her of Drew—and others were clips from television shows or movies. Still others were homemade videos of varying sorts.

She clicked on one titled "Why Ghosts Aren't Real."

"I'm here to talk about ghosts," a twenty-something hunter in camouflage said into his camera. "I'm making this video because three of my friends say they've seen ghosts, but what they don't know is that the Bible is very clear about what happens to a person after death! It's heaven or hell, folks. There's no in between. Satan has the power to appear to us as *anything*, and he'll lure you with promises of—"

Lindsay chose another video from the "Related Videos" column titled "Evidence of Ghosts? Korea Hotel 9-24-04."

It was a surveillance video showing an orb of light floating behind two male elevator passengers. When the passengers stepped out of the elevator, a hunched old woman appeared in the orb's place and then drifted after them.

Tingles ran up Lindsay's back and shoulders. The video looked real, not altogether different than the figure she had seen through the shower steam. When she looked at the video comments, however, she saw an array of opinions.

*Doctored footage!!!!!!!!*

*WOW! I'm a believer, that is the scariest freakin thing EVER!!!!!!! What a gross old hag.*

*Creepy, yes. But real? The problem here is that videos nowadays are not a way to prove anything due to CGI. Where's the real, hard science?*

*I CANT BELEIvE ANy OF YOU BELEIVE THIS. IN THIS DAY AND AGE OF SPESHAL AFFECTS, PEOPLE CAN MAKE ANYyTHING. UR ALL STUPID!*

Below the fourth person's egregiously spelled comment, there were dozens of others. There seemed to be no shortage of people who believed in ghosts and people who didn't.

*What does that say about how much we actually know?* Lindsay thought. She watched at least twenty more videos of supposed ghostly activity. Some were more convincing than others, and all of them had people commenting on either side of the fence.

*Ghosts. Spirits. Life after death.*

According to kids at school, a lot of people in Idle County believed in ghosts. Some even claimed to have had strange experiences. Then there was the whole Moon Woods cult from 2004; the men involved had supposedly been idolizing the ghost of some serial-killer priest from the 1940s who had "studied death" by murdering over fifty people. The cult members had even mimicked the priest twice, forcing two people to kill themselves in the Moon Woods while they watched and analyzed the process. One of the victims, a young woman named Mary Lumen, had lived in the nearby town of Stone Ridge. According to the FBI, her own father had been one of the perpetrators, along with most of the Idle County Sheriff's Department.

Lindsay navigated back to Google and typed "Idle County" and "ghosts." It brought up twenty pages of results, most of which related to the 2004 cult incident.

On page six of the results, however, Lindsay clicked on the home page of something called the Gateway Project. She came to a gray and white home page decorated with a simple lone tree standing in the middle of a dome-shaped open field. Below it was white space filled with three blocks of black lettering.

### *THIS PAGE IS UNDER CONSTRUCTION.*

*Thank you for your interest in the Gateway Project. As our Midwest operations in Idle County are only just getting underway, we invite you to contact Maximilian Pope in our West Coast medical office at:*

*825 Dale Ghost Road*
*Laguna Beach, California*
*92651*
*(949) 304-2990*

Five menu buttons lined the top of the home page. Lindsay clicked the one labeled "About." It brought up an identical page. Upon further inspection, she found that every page on the site was the same.

She shrugged and clicked back to her Google search. The next two results looked like PDF scans of old books, but the fourth one looked interesting. It was an online essay published just four months ago by a magazine called *The Renegade*.

Lindsay skimmed the essay, which appeared to have been written by the biological grandson of the serial-killer priest from the 1940s—an Idle County resident named Thomas Lumen. It took her a few paragraphs to realize the young man was also the twin brother of Mary Lumen, the young woman who had been forced to kill herself by the Moon Woods cult.

According to the essay, his sister's death had been the result of people's beliefs in the unseen. Even so, he didn't attribute such beliefs only to crazy people; it seemed he attributed most of them—at least the local ones—to Idle County itself.

One paragraph in particular caught Lindsay's eye.

> *There are many ghostly legends around Idle County. One is about a white-eyed soldier haunting the long empty stretches of Old Mill Road, which circles the now-infamous Moon Woods. Then there's Taconite Rose, "the woman in the dress," who disappeared in Jackson Taconite Mine north of Idle County in 1959 while searching for her missing son; she's said to haunt towns as far south as Wind Prairie. There's also the famous Greifenberg Manor, site of at least two grisly murders, where unexplainable occurrences have been well documented, often by ghost hunters who visit from all corners of the country. For whatever reason, this peculiar region seems to be a hotbed for ghostly or otherwise unexplainable activity. Does this give it a particularly dark brand of charm, or is it a place to be avoided altogether?*

Despite having lived in Idle County for just three years, Lindsay was now among those residents who had a ghost story. Seeing Drew tonight had peeled back a layer of security around her perception of the world.

She clicked back to her Google search and selected the next website link. It was a blog, sparsely decorated, called *Butterfly & Lightning*. Lindsay skimmed the most recent post, only the third of three, which was dated mid-October—just over two weeks ago. No real names were attached to the writing, but it appeared to be written by two different people. The first post's author was marked by a code name "Butterfly." It was dated September 23, 2005.

*Welcome to our blog!!! We are Butterfly and Lightning, and we've seen dead people. Have YOU? Tell us about it!*

The second blog entry, dated a week after the first, read:

*Well Butterfly says it's my turn to write in the New Blog. I don't really know what to say except that it's sort of fun to have a little Weirdo Group thing, like we talked about last summer, even before everything happened. I don't really have anything to say though. It's time to go to bed. At least Butterfly will be happy. These code names are actually kind of fun, even if people would make fun of us for it.*

Something about the closing phrase made Lindsay stop. She read it a second time.

*Even if people would make fun of us for it.*

She immediately thought of the two Murderers—Pauline Gilbert's old friend Elijah Bryce, and the dark-haired, mysterious Molly Butler.

Could this blog belong to them?

With sudden voracious interest, Lindsay looked again at the third entry by "Butterfly," dated the first of October.

> *Today we decided to start a club at the Lemon Avenue Library. It's our favorite place. For some reason it's peaceful here. It's also full of books about ghosts and other things. I've read most of them completely. Lightning hasn't read them all yet, but he's working on it. They're on the second floor by my favorite stained glass window (which Lightning likes too). We're doing an experiment with the blog now to see if anybody will read it and actually show up for our meetings. We're basically calling out for everyone who has seen ghosts here in Idle County (or wherever) to come meet us! We know we're not the only ones!!!*
>
> *Today, Lightning saw his fifth ghost. We'd been wondering since summer if the first one he saw was a weird thing in his head. Now it's kind of like how it was with me. He started with one and now has seen a few more. We're starting to wonder why. None of the ghost books in the library really tell us anything. So basically, we're wondering what you think, Dear Reader (if you're even out there)!! Lightning thinks nobody will see this. But we've already had nine blog visitors, so yay!!!! That's that. We'll be at the Lemon Avenue Library on Saturdays at noon (upstairs under the stained glass window, like usual, haha).*

There were no comments on any of the entries. According to the ticker at the bottom of the web page, Lindsay was the fourteenth unique blog visitor. Yet somehow it presented a glimmer of hope. If "Butterfly" and "Lightning" actually were Molly Butler and Elijah Bryce, and if they really did see ghosts, they might understand what happened tonight in the shower.

Lindsay suddenly remembered the icy chill that had run down her neck in the cafeteria, right when Molly looked at her in alarm. It had been identical to the chill in the shower.

*Was she seeing you, Drew?*

Lindsay read each blog entry again. All the kids in her class talked about the Lemon Avenue Library with fawning eyes, even though the larger library in the main part of town was the first stop for most people. Lindsay had never visited the older one, but she had seen it when driving to Natalie Pent's house. It was an aged castle-like building on the corner of Lemon Avenue and Main Street—probably only two and a half miles from Lindsay's house as the crow flew. To walk there would be much farther, however, because a large marshland separated her neighborhood from central End Haven.

*You're not actually thinking of going there to join the Murderers,* an inner voice chided. It sounded mysteriously like Natalie's.

Yet wouldn't it be worth visiting even if "Butterfly" and "Lightning" weren't the Murderers? According to the blog, they would be there this coming Saturday—just three days away.

Now all Lindsay needed was a bit of courage.

She was still arguing about it back and forth with herself when a message notification popped up from AOL Instant Messenger. She had forgotten the program was still running.

*"Would you like to accept a message from SparkMe244?"* the notification read.

Lindsay had never seen the screen name, but her heart fluttered. "SparkMe244" could only be one person she knew. She clicked "Accept."

An AOL Instant Messenger conversation between Lindsay Jean Thorsen and Alan Edward Sparks on November 2, 2005; recovered by the Idle County Sheriff's Department on July 9, 2010:

**SparkMe244**: *is this lindsay? alan sparks here. got your screen name from tessa silverman.*

**LinnyT63**: *Hello. Yah it's Lindsay*

**SparkMe244**: *u all right? was worried after kickboxing.*

**LinnyT63**: *yah I'm ok*

**SparkMe244**: *got to be weird having ur bro missing.*

**LinnyT63**: *Yah super weird*

**SparkMe244**: *u still coming back to kickboxing?*

**LinnyT63**: *I dunno*

**SparkMe244**: *hope so . . . . . . . . . and I believe that u saw something in there. u looked pretty freaked.*

**LinnyT63**: *Jeez thanks*

**SparkMe244**: *let's just say I have reason to believe there's more to life than all the stuff we can see.*

**LinnyT63**: *What do you mean?*

**SparkMe244**: *remind me to introduce you to my sister rebecca sometime.*

**LinnyT63**: *Ha okay?*

**SparkMe244**: *she knows things.*

**LinnyT63**: *Knows things . . . . . ?*

**SparkMe244**: *i guess i'm not supposed to say.*

**LinnyT63**: *Not sure what you mean*

**SparkMe244**: *if it really was ur brother and he didn't*

*make it, we're all here for u. just really hope you come back to kickboxing.*

**LinnyT63**: *Everyone would make fun of me*

**SparkMe244**: *no they won't . . . a lot of them know idle county is weird with ghosts and stuff. wait till u meet my sister . . . we can talk more about that later.*

**LinnyT63**: *Ha okay*

**SparkMe244**: *I gg to bed now, school tomorrow . . . blah. just wanted to check in. glad tessa had ur sn.*

**LinnyT63**: *Yah same - Glad you said hi*

**SparkMe244**: *one more thing before i say gnight.*

**LinnyT63**: *Yah?*

**LinnyT63**: *You there?*

**SparkMe244**: *i know what you saw was real. someday it'll be normal. that's what my sister says.*

**LinnyT63**: *Normal?*

**SparkMe244**: *someday people won't question it.*

**LinnyT63**: *How so?*

**SparkMe244**: *my sister says people are starting to wake up.*

**LinnyT63**: *Yeah well, I feel sleepy. And alone*

**SparkMe244**: *you're not alone.*

**SparkMe244**: *for real.*

**SparkMe244**: *nobody is alone.*

David Thorsen was half-White, half-Potawatomi, and not at all religious, which was why he felt like an impostor when he parked his car in the empty parking lot of Saint Andrew's Church in End Haven on the evening of September 19, 2012.

He glanced at Saint Andrew's School, which lay adjacent to the church. It was the school Molly Butler had attended before transferring to End Haven Middle School in 2005, if he remembered correctly. That was before she developed her brain tumor, before she disappeared alongside his daughter, Lindsay, and their five shared friends.

Seeing the newer students' art now pasted in the windows was somehow bittersweet; surely their young minds were still under the impression that nothing bad had ever happened in their town, let alone to one of Saint Andrew's past students.

David sat silently with his own breath for ten seconds before grabbing his favorite steel thermos (which was full of lukewarm decaf coffee from his office) and exiting his car. It was late enough for him not to be too conspicuous; the last thing he wanted was for people around town to see him lurking here, to wonder if he was like the people who had taken his own children—those sick, mad individuals he had never known, who could now exist only in his imagination.

And so he walked quickly up a small hill from the parking lot to the school's baseball field, which harkened back to any Midwestern boy's childhood—wilted dandelions, a mussed diamond of brown dirt, and vague hints of old white chalk lines beaten into near-oblivion by hundreds of zealous feet.

Today, it had rained. The baseball diamond's dirt was still damp, pocked by tiny divots where raindrops had pummeled it. Sometimes these simple reminders of the universe's persistence were all that kept David oriented toward his place in it. He thought of the medicine wheel hanging in his living room—that one reminder of his father's lost culture, with its directions and colors that signified the cyclical nature of life, death, and renewal. Part of David longed to identify with that naturally balanced, fearless outlook, but how could he when his children, Lindsay and Drew, were both gone? Searching for explanations now only left him feeling dispirited, untethered, alone.

Behind the baseball field was a long trail leading toward a larger hill of trees. Its path stretched almost five hundred feet before branches obscured its steep ascent, which David followed up to a spacious clearing of well-manicured grass covered by a canopy of maple branches.

At the clearing's center lay a raised brick dais—and atop that, a fabricated stone grotto housing a statue of Saint Andrew. Facing it was a cold marble bench.

Rumor had it that the grotto had been donated to the church in the early 1940s by a woman named Evelyn Morrow, who later killed herself by leaping off the rocky cliff lining the clearing's far end. David had investigated the site after hearing the story two months ago, and during his first visit, he had stepped onto the brick dais to look into Saint Andrew's hollow eyes. The statue, staring back at him, had seemed to mock mankind's search for meaning. All those religions, sciences, and cultures trying to give humanity a sense of place in some greater context—they were all climbing the same mountain from different sides, weren't they?

Now that David had lost his children and become paralyzed with questions about the nature of life and death, it was time either to climb that mountain or tumble off it. There could be no more camping out on its side, waiting and hoping for an upward trail to be revealed.

He walked across the grass clearing, crossed through a thin layer of trees, and took his usual seat on the edge of the cliff beyond. He sipped his dwindling coffee while looking out at the rising moon. Below him, the water in Miller's Creek trickled southward.

Tonight, his impulse to jump was stronger than ever.

David had been wavering back and forth for weeks. It was a clean spot. Fast. Easy. The cliff was at least a hundred feet high, and if the fall wasn't enough to ensure a swift, simple end, the jagged rocks along its face probably would be. Somebody would find his body, eventually.

To everyone around town, he was still the ethnically ambiguous businessman. The put-together father of two lost children. Idle County's local face of hope and action and tenacity.

Yet his tenure here had begun to feel like a descent into madness. His chief financial officer job at Steelhead Printing had been his first step into the abyss—a life occupation busy enough for him to unwittingly cast his family into second place, just as his own father, for similar reasons, had done with him.

But then Drew had been kidnapped.

Lindsay had claimed to see his ghost shortly after.

This had led to her befriending Molly Butler and Elijah Bryce, which of course changed everything.

At first, David had simply observed the birth of their unusual friend group, curious about their shared interest in ghosts. He hadn't been prepared for what soon became a spiral into chaos.

Their intertwining with Max Pope.

Lindsay's abduction by Lowell Grendel.

The flashlight that saved her life.

Max Pope's nursing home fiasco.

And finally, the gas explosion at Alan Sparks's home just a year and a half after he and Lindsay started dating. Only Rebecca, Alan's disabled older sister, had survived.

David thought back to the only night he and Rebecca had ever met—New Year's Eve following Drew's disappearance. It had happened while he was dropping off Lindsay, Molly, and Elijah at the Sparks house for a small gathering. Following a round of family introductions and a hot toddy, he'd been buttoning up his jacket to leave when Rebecca took a momentary but intense interest in him. It had taken a few seconds for him to notice she was typing a message on the digital tablet connected to her wheelchair. The font was boring—a dull Courier.

> *Your wife is having an affair with the UPS driver. He lives on Woodbury Street. Her wedding ring fell out of her pocket in his yard. Also, she knows about Mia.*

David had simply stared at the teenage girl, dumbstruck. No sooner had she typed the divinatory text string than she slowly moved a hand to her keyboard's Delete button and backspaced over the entire thing.

How could Rebecca have known about Mia Waltrix, his executive assistant? Or the affair David had, as of three days before, begun contemplating? And what of his own wife, Sandra? Had she truly already taken the leap into unfaithfulness?

Six days later, David had finally asked Sandra where her wedding ring was. She claimed to have lost it while doing the dishes. Both their dalliances had gone on, unaddressed. That was what their marriage had become, even back then.

In the weeks that followed—after David's quiet but tenacious prying—Lindsay had told him that the Sparks family kept Rebecca's gift a secret, partially because they weren't religious, and she often spoke about ghosts, the afterlife, and reincarnation as if they were real things. She claimed that everyone had a soul, and that life was simply a school for growth—a chosen set of circumstances to help people learn how to manipulate physical reality into a desired outcome. She also claimed everyone had spiritual "coaches" quietly guiding them at all times, and core soul groups they incarnated with over and over, to experience life from different angles.

Mother and child.

Child and father.

Friend and friend.

Friend and enemy.

All combinations—different life roles for different life goals.

Tonight, David wondered if it had all been New Agey nonsense. The only thing he was learning from this life, it seemed, was the meaning of misery.

He pulled out his phone and brought up his email app, hoping to see at least one response to his most recent group message to the other Idle County Seven parents. He was particularly curious to hear from Victor Zobel, Jillian Pope's famous stepfather, because the email had involved his old college friend Max Pope, Jillian's real father. Six of the seven missing kids had been closely connected to Max, and David was hard-pressed not to see him as a common link in the case.

Pauline Gilbert had been Max's daughter's best friend.

Lindsay had volunteered at Max's research facility.

So had Molly Butler.

So had Elijah Bryce.

And Gabriel Creed? He had started volunteering with the other kids after they unexpectedly befriended him in 2007. His father had been Max's janitor.

The gas explosion at the Sparks family home later that year was one of the last events in Idle County Max Pope had intersected with. Rebecca had survived only because she'd been visiting with Max late into that night—discussing "theories of the universe," according to news reports. Yet David still couldn't wrap his head around the fact that Nathan and Maureen Sparks had let their disabled eighteen-year-old daughter visit with this death-obsessed man into the wee hours of the morning on a Tuesday. It didn't add up.

The most concrete thing the police and FBI could attribute to Max thus far—albeit indirectly—was the death of Elijah Bryce's biological mother, Cynthia Foster, who had attempted to track Max down in Alaska two years ago, shortly after the kids disappeared. There, she had been killed by a hunter in a fluke accident while hiking with a man named Frank Brennin.

Or maybe it hadn't been a fluke. David had no idea. But the event from 2006 he had just remembered today—the one he had emailed the other Idle County Seven parents about—was something. He was sure of it.

It had occurred in February, the winter after Drew disappeared, at Benedict Wise University's First Annual Ghost Symposium—the same day he, Lindsay, Elijah, and Molly first met Max Pope.

Or so David had assumed.

They had initially seen Max during his opening keynote speech about spirituality and the human brain. In the lecture, he had also discussed the "highly spiritual" journals of Benedict Wise, the Capuchin friar who founded the university. Wise's journals, according to Max, were housed in the university's English department, waiting to be transcribed—all except for one. The friar's first and longest journal, Max had explained, was missing.

Two hours later, after lunch, David had walked past a drinking-fountain alcove and seen Molly Butler standing with Max. The girl had been feeling ill that day, yet she'd been talking with the handsome man, asking him in a quiet voice: *"Is that what Mrs. Grime was hiding in her library? The missing journal?"*

*"I honestly think it was,"* Max had responded.

They had both looked up suddenly as David passed, smiling as if nothing had been the matter at all. Since David had not yet been aware of Max Pope's questionable nature, he had smiled back, barely registering Molly and Max's apparent familiarity with each other. Not one hour earlier, however, Molly had politely shaken Max's hand during lunch and introduced herself as if they were strangers. Max had done the same.

Later, after the symposium's first day had ended, David was donning his jacket next to Molly. He had asked about her exchange with Max.

*"Oh no, I've never met him before,"* Molly replied quickly. *"But he knew my friend Mrs. Grime. She was his English teacher here when he was in college. She died a year and a half ago."*

At the time, David hadn't questioned Molly's response, and it had somehow slipped his mind until now. He had of course told police this morning about the girl's curious conversation with Max Pope, and they had graciously listened before doing whatever they usually did with tangential information.

Now David looked at his phone again. Still no responses to his email. Not even from Andrew Butler, Molly's father.

He suppressed an urge to throw the phone over the cliff. If he didn't make it through tonight—if it was finally the night to give up on everything—he didn't want a tossed phone to confuse police. He wanted his choice to be obvious, blunt, known.

Life could be pitiless and cruel. Despite society's presumptions that children should never die, marriages should stay intact, and tragic murders should be solved, the universe always seemed to force unforeseen hands. What, then, was life's value? If it all really was a random byproduct of the Big Bang, as famous Victor Zobel claimed in his book *In God We're Dust*, why suffer through it at all?

Except there was still Rebecca Sparks to consider. She had been proof positive that consciousness somehow transcended the physical brain. And if it really was part of the fundamental unified force that created the universe—as the young woman had once told Lindsay—was it so much bigger a step to believe that life might have purpose?

To jump would give David one answer or another. All he had to do was muster the courage to stand up, close his eyes, and—

Footsteps crunched over fallen autumn leaves somewhere behind him.

*Fuck.*

David immediately put on his happy face, the normal one everyone knew him by. Nobody ever questioned its lit-by-life tenacity.

The crunching footsteps drew closer.

He braced himself against his arms on the cliff's edge as if he were casually enjoying the view before making the hop, skip, and jump home for the night. When he pushed backward to stand up, he turned to face the approaching person, intending to acknowledge him or her politely before ducking away for the night without further ado.

Instead, he froze.

It was a young woman. He recognized her face.

"David Thorsen?" she said. Her voice sounded hesitant. Vulnerable.

David's face burned red, even as he noticed that the young woman's incredulous expression seemed to be covering for something more: a look of dejection, and the shine of sadness washing down her cheeks.

It was Natalie Pent, Lindsay's old friend from middle school. Her face was glistening with tears.

WHEN REVIS ZOBEL SAW Natalie Pent walk into Prohibition Bar on the twenty-seventh floor of the W Hotel in Minneapolis, he was already drunk—or at least getting there. The middle-aged fitness trainer was dressed in regular clothing, looking neither too casual nor overtly sexy. Her demeanor was authoritative and no-nonsense, just as it had been that morning—only now, she wasn't sneaking around under the nose of his sister, Victoria, and he wasn't recording their conversation for the FBI.

"You actually came," Revis said under a smile, in his most submissive playboy voice.

When he stood up to pull a chair out for Natalie, however, she put a hand firmly on his arm. "Mr. Zobel, I'm perfectly capable of sitting down by myself. But I appreciate the gesture."

Revis took a step back and raised his hands in a conciliatory gesture. "I'm very sorry," he said. "I meant no offense." Yet the woman's forceful dismissal of him made her even more appealing. Not because he wanted to fight her for power but because she already had it all.

"I didn't come here to be wooed," Natalie continued. "I know how men are. I've also seen the tabloids—I know how *you* are."

"Tabloids lie," Revis said, knowing the woman would be shocked if she truly knew him.

"Well, in case they don't, just be prepared to have your pilot fly me back to End Haven."

Revis deflated just enough to see reality for a moment. This random Idle County fitness trainer, however she had managed it, was closer to his family than most people ever got. Now she was sitting with him here, in a bar, unaware that her very act of rejection was feeding his basest sexual instincts.

"Was the flight smooth? Not too bumpy?"

"I hadn't been in a helicopter before," Natalie said. She glanced around the drinking establishment—which was lavish for Minneapolis—then looked back at Revis. "I also couldn't say no to an excuse to ditch End Haven for a night. Why did you want to meet me all the way up here when we could have just met down there?"

"Because people see me when I'm in towns that small. It's easier for Thérèse to hire us a helicopter in Minneapolis—fly down, fly back."

"The life of the rich," Natalie said with a wistful, sarcastic sigh.

Revis blushed again. "When you can't get into your family's house because it's being swamped by reporters who think your dad might be an international terrorist, you sometimes need to fly in. Fame comes with its downsides."

Natalie sat up straighter and nodded. "I'll give you that. The reporters are going crazy. They've been hounding the entrance road to your dad's Idle County place more and more since all this Jonathan Flite stuff started happening," she said. "And sorry—I didn't mean to sound cynical."

Revis spun his gin-and-tonic glass on the marble table. "Would you like a drink?"

"I'd like to talk about what happened to the Idle County Seven, if you don't mind. I overheard you asking Victoria about your dad. I take it you don't actually know if he had anything to do with their disappearance?"

Instead of sharing with Natalie the few hints he had learned from the FBI, Revis said, "If I knew a hundred percent what happened, so would the world."

Natalie smiled. For the first time, it looked real. "That's fair. And I'm glad to hear that."

"What was it you wanted to tell me, Miss Pent?"

"Well, first, that there's something going on at your dad's house in the Moon Woods. I've seen people coming and going from there like it's some sort of business facility or something. Victoria thinks I don't notice."

"And you make the effort to monitor?"

"I've been looking for a way in there ever since your dad built it. I monitor everything."

"You know talking to me right now could cost you that job with my sister?"

"Of course. But again, I didn't take that job because I needed it. I'm the best personal trainer in Idle County. Anyone will tell you that."

"Well, my family is the type to sue over NDA breaches and make your life a living hell. Anyone will tell *you* that."

Natalie shrugged. Revis stared at her. How genuine was her nonchalance, really?

"You looked familiar when I first saw you," he said.

"We met once, when you were a kid." Natalie glanced at Revis's drink, then back up, into his eyes. "At least sort of. It was the September after your half sister and the others disappeared."

Of course. His first trip to Idle County—and the first time his father had outright threatened to kill him. That subtle, deadpan whisper into his frightened ear.

"The candlelight vigil in that creepy duck-pond park?" he asked in a low voice.

"That would be it," Natalie said. "I was there, trying to ask your dad questions."

"What questions?"

Instead of answering, Natalie looked around the bar again. This time, her eyes lingered on all the things that weren't Revis. "I think your dad is doing research on something in the Moon Woods."

"And what would that be?"

"Things are weird there. Haven't you noticed?"

She looked back into Revis's eyes, and he studied her face. Her mannerisms. Her truth. He thought back to the familiar feeling he had experienced that morning, in the helicopter—the serenity mixed with a need to scream.

"It's like I'm outside of my head when I go there," he admitted with a bit of sheepishness. "You've also felt that?"

"*Everyone* has felt that, I think," Natalie said. "Some more than others." Then: "Do you remember Max Pope? Jillian's dad?"

Revis nodded. "He came to visit Jillian once in Geneva. But I don't actually remember him."

"But you know he studied the brains of his dying Alzheimer's patients in Blue Hill, right? That he lost his medical license?"

"I remember hearing something like that. But only because my dad couldn't let it go."

"How do you mean?"

"He kept going back to Idle County, even after Jillian's dad moved to Alaska."

"He was trying to bring Jillian back to Switzerland," Natalie said. "Everyone knew that."

Revis's defenses went up as another wave of alcohol hit him. "No, he hated Jillian. *Hated* her. But he was always nice to her, because he didn't want to get on her bad side. He didn't have any rights over her custody, so he couldn't control her."

Natalie sat back in her chair with furrowed eyebrows.

"He only *told* everyone he was trying to bring her back to Switzerland," Revis said. "But he always came home from his Minnesota trips super pissed off. He'd pace back and forth and get really mad at tiny little things for no reason at all. That's what he does when he's cornered. He acts out. He's a sociopath, you know. All but diagnosed."

Natalie froze in her chair. Revis's heartbeat quickened as he sensed fear in her. He could almost read her thoughts: *Was he the same as his father? Were all the Zobels capable of acting like animals now that Jonathan Flite had them under a social magnifying glass? Was she in danger here?*

No, she wasn't in danger. The worst thing Natalie had to worry about was Revis's fantasy about her tying him up. Blindfolding him. Dominating him.

"You were saying something about Max Pope?" he continued.

Natalie Pent stared at him. Cold. Calculating.

"Do you believe in God, Mr. Zobel?" she finally asked. "Or something bigger than all this?" She gestured toward the bar, the city, the world.

Sipping his drink, Revis felt both heavy and weightless. Judgeless.

"I believe we don't have all the answers," he finally said.

"Well, I think there's something in the Moon Woods making your dad ask questions," Natalie continued. "I also think it's the same thing that caused a priest back in the 1940s to obsess over death and murder sixty goddamned people there. And maybe even the same thing that made Jillian's real dad, Max, study the brains of those Alzheimer's patients at that old nursing home. I've seen enough things in Idle County to make me a hundred percent sure that there's life after death, or some version of it."

"You mean like ghosts?" Revis said, adopting an immature, spooky tone.

"If you want to call them that, sure. But I think your dad has seen them, too."

"That would be his worst fucking nightmare."

"Okay, well, knowing your dad, do you think finding proof of ghosts—or higher consciousness or life after death or whatever—would give him reason enough to kill seven kids? Especially if they found out about it and he wanted to cover it all up?"

Revis didn't even have to think on the answer. "Absolutely."

"And what about influencing some deranged Catholic cardinal to bomb Geneva in the name of Jesus—basically to demonize people who promote those types of ideas even further?"

Revis marveled at Natalie Pent. And at her ability to put together the pieces he had confronted his sister, Victoria, with last summer. "I don't think you're far off base," he said.

Natalie leaned forward. "Okay, then. One more thing: Are you aware that Alice Winterblume is making a full *WorldLine* season about the Idle County Seven mystery? And that the nurse killer, Jonathan Flite, is participating? She's basically planning on exposing a bunch of shit about your dad, including stuff that links him to the Geneva bombing and other crimes."

Revis's drunkenness stopped cold in its meandering tracks. "She's actually pulling the trigger?"

"You know about it, then?"

"I heard *WorldLine's* been contacting my dad and sister like crazy for the past two years."

"Yeah. And Victoria refuses to talk with them. But she doesn't know that *I'm* planning to talk."

Revis began bouncing his knee up and down under the table. The FBI hadn't mentioned this to him. As part of his strategy to exist peacefully under the shadows of his father and sister, he'd also told his reps to deflect all calls from the media in recent years, including any from Alice Winterblume, the reigning queen of television journalism.

Except now he saw the potential. Saw himself on camera, ratting out his father to the world.

He leaned forward to meet Natalie Pent's gaze, then said, "Tell me everything you know."

WORLDLINE'S CACOPHONOUS NEW YORK OFFICE whirled around Clovia Bell like a carousel. It was Friday, April 8, and she was wondering: Was it normal for a young woman not to attend her father's funeral? Was she really going to be that daughter?

*It was his choice to pick drugs over you,* a defensive voice in her mind said.

Ignoring the pang of doubt in her heart, Clovia sifted through her multitude of morning emails, waiting patiently for Alice Winterblume to return from her emergency breakfast meeting. The woman had scheduled it herself at nine o'clock last night, while Clovia was flying back from her unexpected B-roll shoot in Rhode Island. Alice had left a voice mail just ten minutes later, as Clovia's plane landed at JFK airport in New York.

*"Terrence sent over the B-roll you guys shot in Newport,"* she said in the message. *"I don't care what Jeff says—it looks perfect. I think we're going to need a better title for you than 'producer's assistant.'"*

Clovia's reaction was twofold: first, her heart swelled with pride (something she'd never admit to anyone); next, an uncomfortable weight settled on her shoulders. Jeff Clausen, *WorldLine*'s director for all the upcoming Jonathan Flite episodes, had threatened to step down just last Monday due to "disagreements" about the controversial angle Alice wanted to take with the story—that being full support of Jonathan. No sooner had he done that than Alice instructed Clovia, without Jeff's knowledge, to direct this week's run of second-unit footage in Newport.

"*Which brings me to the point of this call,*" her voice mail continued. "*We need to talk about the Jonathan Flite story first thing tomorrow. For multiple reasons. My office at 9:30. Don't be late.*"

But Alice was the one who was late—a rarity, despite her tight sunup to sundown schedule. When she walked in at 9:47, *WorldLine*'s busy office ruffled like bird feathers. As usual, the newsroom employees upped their game out of sheer self-conscious habit. Their media goddess of a boss never actually demanded hard work from them; she commanded it through her very presence—and the respect she gave back to them.

When Alice spotted Clovia at the desk by her frosted-glass office door, her pace lightened. Clovia immediately stood up and handed her a coffee—no sugar, extra cream.

"God, you know me too well," Alice said as she shouldered her purse with one hand and grabbed the drink with the other. She paused to let her office door's security panel scan her face, and then the door opened into her glassy personal oasis. Its decor had an outdoorsy theme: grays, greens, and light blues. A rock fountain ran like a mountain stream in the corner. There was a stone-tiled kitchen. A wood-paneled bathroom. Even the bedroom off Alice's main desk and lounge area would have fit in at a posh mountain resort. Large glass doors led outside to a spacious deck patio with a gas fire pit.

Beyond it all towered the jungle of New York City.

"Am I in trouble?" Clovia asked, closing the door behind them.

Alice set her bag and coffee on her large wooden desk, looking out the window for a moment. Then she turned to Clovia. "Are you a hugger?"

"A hugger?"

"For condolences. Becky told me your dad passed away unexpectedly."

"Oh. I told her not to say anything."

Alice took four long steps toward Clovia and grabbed her in a firm embrace. It wasn't the professional back-tap kind of hug. "Honey, I'm so sorry."

Clovia allowed the hug to linger as she imagined her estranged father pulled over on the Tappan Zee Bridge: high as a kite, heart slowing, light leaving his eyes. Emotions she couldn't yet name—grief of her own particular sort—welled in her chest. Instead of letting it take over, however, she calmly said, "Thanks, Alice. I appreciate it."

"After this meeting, you're taking a week off," Alice said. "That means no work—no show, no emails, no Jonathan Flite, and no poring over the photos that blogger Lydia Clark posted all over the internet. You're going home to Nyack."

"I already told Becky I'm not going to the funeral. My dad was a drug addict. We haven't talked in four years, and—"

"I said a week off. Paid. And yes you are going to the funeral. When is it scheduled for?"

"Tomorrow morning."

"Then I'll call Gerard and have him drive you up to Nyack this afternoon. You'll forever regret not going. I'm telling you this from personal experience. My mom and I hated each other, so I didn't go to her funeral. It was the biggest mistake I ever made."

Clovia forced herself to nod. She knew Alice's multitude of tones. This was one of her serious ones. The *life* kind of serious.

"But we do have other things to discuss before you go," Alice continued in the no-nonsense way she often did after laying down the law. "Something came up."

*Work.*

Clovia jumped at it. "What do you mean?"

With a sigh, Alice walked to the window and peered out at the buildings. "We're in a bit of a pickle. I haven't been a hundred percent honest with you about something, but given how closely we work together, you need to know. Maybe we can call you 'creative producer' now. Especially if Jeff steps down."

Clovia rested her fingertips on Alice's desk and braced herself.

"This is strictly need-to-know, and up until this point, you haven't needed to," Alice said. "But I'm wondering: How much has Jonathan Flite told you about his relationship with the FBI? I know you and he are getting close."

The woman's words exposed Clovia's feelings for the Rhode Island nurse killer like a slick hidden TV camera. The truth rose with a blush on her face.

"He hasn't really mentioned the FBI, beyond what's been in the news," she said, focusing on Alice's paper coffee cup.

The woman's intonation made it clear she was smiling. "You know, Jonathan gets that same look on his face whenever you give him screen directions. I noticed it in the raw footage from Newport. Especially that shot on the bench. Where was that, by the way?"

"Storer Park," Clovia said. Her chest tightened as she looked Alice in the eyes again. "Should I change the way I act around him, then?"

"That might be a conversation we have to have down the line, but you're fine for now," Alice replied. "People are people, and that young man needs good ones in his life. I don't think he's a psychopath."

"Neither do I."

Now it was Alice who stared at the coffee cup. "The thing I haven't told you is that I'm *also* working with the FBI. On this season, primarily.

They've been involved with its development from the get-go. I've been letting them know what information we've been getting on both the Idle County Seven angle and the Geneva angle, what we're planning to include in the show—all that stuff. Though, before I continue, I'm trusting I don't need to remind you that you're under NDA?"

"No, you don't." Clovia lifted her fingertips from the desk.

"Good, because you're the first person I'm telling all this to," Alice replied. "I haven't even told Jeff."

Clovia blushed again.

"Heather Mousseau, the special agent I'm working with here in New York, called me yesterday. She asked to see those test interviews all the Idle County people sent in—particularly the ones from Natalie Pent and Lindsay Thorsen's dad, David."

Clovia furrowed her eyebrows. David Thorsen had been hesitant to participate in the production, but Natalie Pent? She had positively jumped at the chance to be interviewed.

"Why those two?" she asked.

"Because of what they said about Victor Zobel's old friend Raphael Dumont." Alice let out a heavy sigh, then paced back toward the window.

*Raphael Dumont.*

The skulking man's name—to say nothing of the snake tattoo he wore around his neck—always made Clovia shiver.

"The FBI wants us to cut every mention of Raphael from this season due to an ongoing investigation. They want to keep him under the public's radar for as long as possible—and not just because of that alleged attack on Rebecca Sparks five years ago in Santa Cruz. Apparently it's something even bigger. Agent Mousseau wouldn't give me details."

Clovia stood stock-still, considering the implications. Raphael Dumont wasn't just one of Victor Zobel's oldest associates. He had also been present in Idle County (along with his celebrity-billionaire boss) on two of the most significant days in the region's history: the day of the gas explosion that killed the physicist Rebecca Sparks's family, and the day the Idle County Seven vanished. Perhaps even more significant, the man's social media accounts placed his lifelong residence in Saint-Paul de Vence, France, the same town Victor Zobel spent much of his childhood in—and the same town where the Catholic terrorist Jean-Claude Apostol had once resided, two decades prior to detonating the nuclear bomb in Switzerland.

Clovia immediately began re-editing the upcoming *WorldLine* season in her mind. Removing Raphael Dumont's connection to the Idle County Seven's disappearances and the Geneva bombing could flatten much of their angle on Victor Zobel's connection to the two events. Dumont was the story's link.

*Fuck.*

"My thoughts exactly," Alice said. She scowled, walked toward a mini fridge behind her desk, and pulled out a bottle of Grey Goose vodka. She grabbed two glasses from a nearby rack, then filled them to the brim with ice and liquor. "Which brings us to the next project I'm asking you to take on. *Once you get back from Nyack,*" she added, handing Clovia a full glass.

Clovia glanced down at the drink. It wasn't even 10:00 a.m.

"I won't tell if you don't," Alice said. She drank from her glass—more than just a sip. "Again, this all stays between us for now. Nothing I say here leaves this room. Not even Jonathan Flite can hear about this from you, even though he's already aware of some of it. Got it?"

With a nod, Clovia sipped her morning drink.

"So, the FBI's been investigating Victor Zobel for years—even longer than I have," Alice continued. "You know they've interviewed Jonathan, but what you don't know is that they worked with Jimmy Barber and Winifred Flite last summer to flush out the guy who broke into Crescent Rehabilitation Center two years ago—the one who killed Mason Witzel and those two security guards. The sting actually happened during Winifred Flite's press conference, right before everything went haywire. Apparently the whole thing at Newport City Hall was intended to be some sort of diversion while Jimmy Barber lured this guy out into the open, in Providence."

Clovia simply stared at Alice. For all her own communication with Jonathan and his friend Jimmy this past year, she hadn't had the faintest clue that the perpetrator from Crescent had been caught. That was huge. That was *gold*.

"Who is he?" she finally asked.

"His name is Nicolas Leandro Rim. Do you recognize the name?"

Alice watched expectantly as Clovia turned the name over and over in her head. And then—

"Jesus." Clovia suddenly recalled the last ten minutes of their first interview with Jonathan Flite last August. "You mean it's—"

"—that family from Geneva Jonathan talked about. To be specific, the little boy who had a crush on Jillian Pope."

Clovia nodded again. According to Jonathan, this little boy's father, a contractor named Jonas Rim, had been in charge of building an addition onto Victor Zobel's house in Gland, Switzerland, in 2004. Jonas's son, Nicolas—the little boy Jonathan had mentioned in the interview—had been friends with Revis and Victoria Zobel, Victor's two children. He'd also allegedly fostered a childish infatuation with Jillian Pope, who later disappeared in Idle County.

"It turns out the Rim family's employment didn't stop with that house in Geneva," Alice continued. "Victor got them all jobs after that. Jonas Rim, the contractor Jonathan mentioned, actually came to the States to build Zobel's house in Idle County, then apparently died there after experiencing some type of blackout while building an underground elevator shaft."

The story buzzed between Clovia's ears. This could definitely make up for losing Raphael Dumont. Perhaps even more so.

"What you need to know," Alice said, "is that the FBI struck a deal with Nicolas Rim to become an informant. He's been helping them build their case in exchange for immunity. Heather said he admitted to being instructed by one of Victor Zobel's top real estate executives to orchestrate Jonathan Flite's murder two years ago. But of course he killed Mason Witzel and those two guards instead."

"Will they let us interview him?" Clovia asked.

Alice shook her head. "Not yet. But I found out yesterday that they helped get us someone better."

"Who?"

"Revis Fucking Zobel."

Clovia's vodka suddenly tasted sweet. Was it flavored, or just morning?

Revis Zobel, Victor's son, had been turning down Alice's interview requests via his reps for almost two years, just like his father and sister. If he were to participate now, it could change the entire season. Tremors of potential glittered in Clovia's mind.

"Revis went to the FBI on his own volition back in February, after getting multiple phone calls from Nicolas Rim that were rather alarming. He also got one of those blue-envelope letters from Rebecca Sparks—just like the ones Jonathan Flite was getting last year, before we started shooting. I guess Rebecca tipped Revis off to a few things—one of which was that meeting of physicists at CERN in Geneva, scheduled for August 12, 2037, the day of the bombing two years ago. I guess Rebecca told him how she 'purposefully didn't board her flight to Switzerland,' because she 'had a hunch' Victor Zobel would target her there, along with all the other physicists who supported her new theory. We now know most of those scientists ended up dying."

Alice took a sip of her vodka.

"Now, I think we can still mention the CERN factor in the show, but I want to avoid discussing Rebecca's letters—they make her look a bit too manipulative for my taste. The one she sent to Revis was interesting, though. He didn't even know her real name at the time or that she grew up in Idle County. All he knew was that she was the same physicist who was sending his father 'letters in blue envelopes' and harassing him about the nature of reality. I guess his sister, Victoria, told him about that part last year."

With an exhilarated sigh, Alice walked toward her whiteboard and picked up a marker.

"Basically, Rebecca's letter hinted that Raphael Dumont might have evidence of Victor Zobel poisoning Revis's mother, Cassandra, back in the day. Unfortunately, Revis has been kept out of the loop on almost all family affairs for the last decade, so he couldn't give the FBI anything incriminating on Victor. Agent Mousseau did say he wants to see his dad in prison just as much as we do, though, which might work in our favor."

Alice uncapped her marker, made one big circle on the whiteboard, and labeled its center.

*IC / MW*

It was Alice's usual shorthand for "Idle County" and "the Moon Woods." Then she added two more bubbles near the border of the larger one.

*RD - No.*

*RZ - Yes.*

Clovia surmised that "RD" meant Raphael Dumont, and "RZ" meant Revis Zobel. She refrained from asking the swarm of questions in her mind as Alice continued to scribble.

"Now, Agent Mousseau says the bureau got lucky. After they caught Nicolas Rim, they had him make those calls to Revis and drop some lures—mostly about Victor hiring him to set up the assassination attempt on Jonathan Flite. They have the whole conversation recorded."

"And?"

"Apparently, Revis had no idea about any of it. Heather said he allegedly went off his rocker during Nicolas Rim's call, cussing out his dad, saying he didn't want to know if Victor was a criminal, etcetera etcetera. Then, in February, Revis came forward to the FBI. They still don't know if it was to save his own skin ahead of some looming family collapse, or if it's a legitimate attempt to help. He also met with Natalie Pent two days ago, of all people. She's the one who told him about our documentary—completely flouting our NDA, of course—but in this case, it could help us. I guess Revis's reps never even told him about our calls, but now he wants to talk to us. The FBI's totally on board with it, especially if the interview could flush out an incriminating reaction from his father. Or even his sister, Victoria."

Alice added a bubble to her diagram, offshooting from the "RZ - Yes" circle, and wrote in a new phrase.

*Int. X*

"Revis is going to be 'Interviewer X' to our editors and segment producers for the time being, because I need to keep this absolutely silent," she said. "I can't risk employee slip-ups with our NDA or production-team egos getting in the way. I'm coming to you because I trust you, you're great as a one-woman crew, and you know the structure of this season backward and forward. Am I wrong?"

Clovia shrugged. "Not wrong, no."

"Good. Because your new project is to look at our current season plan and take a first pass at a full restructure. Take out Raphael

Dumont, and put Revis Zobel in—but try to keep all the story ties to the Geneva bombing intact. We're going to work closely on our own to plan his interview, shoot it, and then mark the areas in the edit where we'll splice him in. If Jeff ends up leaving the project, I'll step in to direct. Either way, the majority of our office won't know who Revis is until much closer to the air date."

Alice took a step back and stared at her chicken scratch.

"What I'm really saying here is that nobody can know he's involved, or it could have unintended effects on the FBI's investigation. Do you think you can work with me on this? I need to know now."

Answering yes wasn't a choice for Clovia; it was a perfect way to save whatever grief she had over her father's death for another day. She was already starting the work in her mind.

Once she confirmed it aloud, however, Alice nodded and sipped her vodka, then stepped forward to add another bubble to her whiteboard, below the other two. She scribbled another brainstorm equation into it.

$$KB + SB = WTF?$$

"And *this* is going to be our fucking rocket fuel," Alice said, circling the equation three more times. "I don't just want to make a documentary about the crazy-ass tangle that is Jonathan Flite, the Idle County Seven, Victor Zobel, Rebecca Sparks, and the Geneva bombing. I want to make a documentary about *Idle Fucking County*. Like, not just why things go bump in the night there but also the fact that it seems to be ground zero for *all* of this, assuming Victor Zobel really was trying to kill Rebecca Sparks in Geneva two years ago."

*KB + SB.*

Clovia knew those initials.

*Kara Butler and Shelly Bryce.*

Last August, Kara Butler, the younger half sister of Molly Butler, had recorded a bizarre incident while visiting Victor Zobel's Moon Woods compound with Elijah Bryce's aging mother, Shelly. Shelly had experienced a peculiar mental "whiteout" while stepping out of her car, and Kara's ActoLenses had recorded every second of it on video. The footage showed Shelly's figure flickering white, then disappearing from the frame entirely for just over three seconds—to the point where the trees behind her had become visible. Thus far, nobody had a solid explanation for how this could have been possible, unless Kara had for some reason taken the time to meticulously remove Shelly from the high-resolution video—something both she and Shelly vehemently denied. Even so, Alice still wasn't sure whether *WorldLine* would legally be able to use the footage, since it was shot secretly on the Zobel family's private property.

"I want to show Kara Butler's video to Revis Zobel," Alice said, once again reading Clovia's face. "I want to see his reaction on camera."

"Can he get us the private-property release?" Clovia asked. "If we could use the footage in the actual show, it would be—"

"—icing on the damned cake," Alice said, nodding. "And since Shelly Bryce's whiteout experience aligns perfectly with what Jonathan said about that cave under the Moon Woods, I think we could—"

A sudden commotion in *WorldLine*'s main newsroom interrupted Alice's words. She immediately bristled like a cat, turning her neck sharply to the frosted glass window separating her office from the rest of *WorldLine*'s staff.

The clamor hit Clovia's senses slowly, like screams of a shark at the beach. As she and Alice looked at each other with both curiosity and concern, a man in the newsroom suddenly began screaming in a language Clovia couldn't understand. Then came the sound of desk chairs rolling back en masse, and a rush of people—*WorldLine*'s employees—moving in pandemonium.

The excitement in Alice's eyes turned to dread as a choir of shrieks in the newsroom rose like worship in a minor chord. At the exact moment it gave way to an eruption of blinding light and deafening sound, Alice leapt toward Clovia, spun her away from the office's frosted windows, and pulled her to the ground.

The blast was deafening. The windows shattered, and their fragments rained onto Clovia and Alice like burning hail.

*I'm going to see my dad today*, was all Clovia could think as she and Alice fell.

A N EXCERPT FROM ALICE WINTERBLUME'S transcribed video interview with the physicist Rebecca Sparks (a.k.a Dorothy Garland), recorded on May 4, 2034:

*[All responses from Rebecca Sparks generated by her VerboSync neural chip due to a neurological disability.]*

**Alice Winterblume:** *And what can you—*

*[Ms. Sparks's neural chip text begins appearing on-screen behind Ms. Winterblume.]*

**Rebecca Sparks:** *Don't ask me that.*

**Alice Winterblume:** *I didn't even ask the question yet—*

**_Rebecca Sparks:_** _You were going to ask if I can prove my psychic abilities. These aren't the questions you should be asking. You should be asking why psychic abilities can exist at all._

**_Alice Winterblume:_** _But how can I ask that when I don't know for sure that they can?_

**_Rebecca Sparks:_** _You woke up this morning wondering if you should end your marriage, because you feel you've moved past your husband, in terms of drive, ambition, and passion. In the shower, you cried after realizing you look at him more with sad compassion than with love and excitement about who he is. You hate the part of yourself that thinks he's lazy. You cried because you know that you don't want to grow old with him. Do you need further proof that I have psychic abilities?_

_[Silence from Ms. Winterblume for nine seconds]_

**_Rebecca Sparks:_** _The trap of proof is what has separated humanity. Religious people—however peaceful or violent—operate without physical proof that their spiritual experiences and beliefs are valid. Conversely, scientists operate on the assumption that everything needs measurable physical proof to be considered real at all. But the universe doesn't give a damn what humans think. It simply operates the way it was created to._

**_Alice Winterblume:_** _And what created it?_

*Rebecca Sparks: We did. You. Me. Everyone. That river. That rock. It's all conscious energy from a larger main source.*

*Alice Winterblume: I don't understand what that means.*

*Rebecca Sparks: Are you aware that many physicists are in a tizzy over the nature of consciousness—mostly because certain facts presented by quantum mechanics suggest that our observations and choices play a role in the creation of reality as we know it?*

*Alice Winterblume: I read a book on the subject once.*

*Rebecca Sparks: A pop science book like* Our Elegant Universe?

*Alice Winterblume: That was the one.*

*Rebecca Sparks: A lot of theory, though it simplified many of the facts perfectly. Still, it missed one perspective that could fundamentally shift human understanding of the nature of things.*

*Alice Winterblume: Care to elaborate?*

*Rebecca Sparks: The book outlined the crux of quantum mechanics very well: that physical reality doesn't seem to exist concretely until it is measured. This is important, because before being measured, particles only seem to exist in waves of probable locations in space. Experiment after experiment has confirmed this. Probable position can be figured out mathematically, but it's only ever probable. One answer to this conundrum formulated by theoretical physicists is the Many Worlds interpretation, which postulates that all alternate histories and futures are real, in one system or another. The physical matter we measure here, according to that theory, is only one version of all possible realities, which exist with equal validity.*

**Alice Winterblume:** *And what did* Our Elegant Universe *get wrong?*

**Rebecca Sparks:** *Like most physicists, its author pre-supposes that physical reality is external from us and precedes consciousness. But it's the other way around.*

**Alice Winterblume:** *You're saying consciousness pre-cedes the universe?*

**Rebecca Sparks:** *Yes. It is a facet of the unified funda-mental force that started our universe. We're all part of it.*

**Alice Winterblume:** *I don't see how that's possible. What about before we were alive? The Big Bang was billions of years ago.*

**Rebecca Sparks:** *It's possible because time is an illusion. Even the underlying physics of our universe tells us this much. What we call time is simply the way our brains perceive distinct differences between any two possibilities,* *down to the Planck length—the smallest unit of distance possible before the laws of physics completely break down. If you consider consciousness the theater, then the rules of the physical universe are the stage. The big joke on all of us is that we don't even need a dress rehearsal, because on parallel playing fields, we're already experiencing all possible outcomes of any given situation. Each of us, from a level of existence outside this space-time illusion, builds our own theater. We share the same rules as part of the game, but your reality is yours. Mine is mine.*

**Alice Winterblume:** *Okay, so maybe that brings us back to Jonathan Flite, this thirteen-year-old kid making news in Rhode Island. You say he inspired you to contact us three weeks ago. How do all his claims about having past-life memories—about seven different people, no less—fit into all this?*

**Rebecca Sparks:** *Related to what I said a minute ago about the unified fundamental force, there are many structures of consciousness that you can't currently conceive of. I'm aware of only bits and pieces.*

**Alice Winterblume:** *Is there anything you can tell me that I can conceive of?*

**Rebecca Sparks:** *Yes. All things, including us, are off-shoots of the creative fundamental force responsible for existence. This unified force seeks to know itself through growth, development, and experience—in life after life, and form after form. We are it. It is us. It is all that is.*

*Alice Winterblume:* I take it that's where this idea of re-incarnation comes from?

*Rebecca Sparks:* Reincarnation is simply a word to de-scribe a process by which we grow and develop. We choose our bodies, brains, and circumstances before each life, of-ten ones that will assist us in our goals. Say you are born to abusive parents. Perhaps your intent is to use this experi-ence to overcome that challenge and find reason to help others in similar circumstances. All circumstances can be used to spark positive development in some way or another. We all do this. You do it. I do it. The trajectories are cur-rently in place for Jonathan Flite to do it on a mass scale.

*Alice Winterblume:* You say you once knew the kids he claims to remember.

*Rebecca Sparks:* I knew five of them. And you'll know I'm telling the truth about all this when you meet him a few years from now. Your guides are telling me that part of what you came to do in this life is tell his story.

*Alice Winterblume:* That sounds too fatalistic to me.

*Rebecca Sparks:* It's not fatalistic. You always have a choice. But often these choices will line up with agree-ments made with others before entering life, to help you fulfill what you as an entity fragment fundamentally value most.

*Alice Winterblume:* Entity fragment?

**Rebecca Sparks:** *As I said earlier, your individual consciousness is part of a greater whole.*

**Alice Winterblume:** *Okay, well, that brings me back to my original question: How can I know any of what you say is legitimate?*

**Rebecca Sparks:** *If choices and events continue to align, you'll have an interview with Jonathan Flite four years from now. It will be your first of multiple interviews with him, though the road won't be easy. When he mentions Lindsay Thorsen and the flashlight that saved her from an incident in Jackson Taconite Mine, you'll have something new to look into. It will lead to proof—at least for you and WorldLine—that he's legitimate. And that I'm legitimate.*

WINIFRED FLITE KNEW SOMETHING was wrong the moment Jonathan walked into her room at New Dawn Recovery Center. The last time she had seen him like this, he'd been sitting in her living room in Newport, the night Weston Carrow bombed her press conference. She had, of course, been out of her body at the time.

His gait was stiff, self-conscious. "It happened again," he said. "A Muslim guy this time."

For the first time since he was a toddler—back when he hadn't yet mistrusted her enough to know any better—he collapsed onto her bed, then began to cry as he placed his head in her lap.

"Hello t-t-toooo youuuu, too," she said. Then she glanced up at Sounder, Jonathan's bodyguard, who was leaning on the hospital room door.

"It's all over the news," Sounder said.

In her lap, Jonathan sniffed back his tears and said nothing.

As Winifred clicked on her room's television, she decided she'd wait at least a few minutes to tell him that his biological father, Dominic Bock, wanted to meet him.

THE NEWS WAS LIKE DÉJÀ-VU. First it had been Geneva two years ago, then the attack on Jonathan at Crescent Rehabilitation Center, then the shooting at her house on Columbus Avenue last year, followed closely by Weston Carrow's homemade suicide bomb.

Winifred sat in silence, watching news footage of people evacuating from CBS's new Fifth Avenue high-rise in New York City. Jaden Marks, CNN's daytime anchor, took on the gravest of tones as he relayed further information about the office bomber's possible motive.

"We're now getting claims from another anonymous witness," he said into the camera, "that the *WorldLine* employee who detonated the bomb was Muslim—which marks the first time a non-Christian has committed an act of terrorism in response to Jonathan Flite's pseudo-spiritual 'past-life-memory' claims. According to our witness, a native of Egypt, the bomber screamed in Arabic just before the explosion, saying, and I quote the witness, 'something about Allah and blasphemy and needing to save the world from Jonathan Flite's spiritual lies.' He then detonated a bomb that was in his backpack."

Winifred's heart sank, and she wondered: *Will it ever stop?*

These days, it seemed to be another day, another bombing—a new slow-burn status quo for anything and everything connected to her son. Winifred's old ego—that part of her mind ruled by fear, social expectations, and suppression of self—piped up in her mind.

*You'll never be safe around Jonathan. And if you're even remotely considering inviting Dominic Bock into this mess, you're even more cruel than you let on.*

Well, then. It was a good thing her brain injury made it almost impossible to speak.

FOR NEARLY AN HOUR, Jonathan lay on Winifred's bed, listening to the news while exchanging text messages with Jimmy Barber, his only friend. Finally, during a lull in the text conversation, he asked his mother in a near whisper, "What was it you wanted to tell me today?"

Winifred's pulse quickened, and for the first time in weeks, she felt nervous around her son—the way she often used to, before her jaunt through kingdom come.

*Do I dare tell him?*

"Something c-c-aaaame . . . up on Tuuuuesday," she said. "Your graaand . . . grandmotherrr . . . told me somethinggg she's been hiding for the last year."

Jonathan propped himself up on his elbow and looked at Winifred. His hazel eyes were tear-swollen—distraught enough to make her look toward the window. Where was Dr. Lumen when she needed him? In Minnesota, of course, living his life and treating the psychiatry patients he hadn't seen face-to-face in months, due to all the hopping back and forth.

Winifred took a deep breath. First in. Then out.

And just as she was about to confess to Jonathan the true story of his conception—and the truth about Dominic Bock—her own ActoPhone buzzed. It was lying on the bed, next to Jonathan's head. Because she didn't have her ActoLenses in, she couldn't immediately see who was calling.

But of course Jonathan could. When he held up the phone to Winifred, he was staring at the caller's name with curiosity, perhaps even uncertainty. Then, in a most offhand way, he asked the question she had been dreading for almost nineteen years:

"Who's Dominic Bock?"

With pursed her lips, Winifred tried to find words.

Of course, she failed.

FINALLY, LYDIA CLARK had a story to report on. A *real* story—not just the kind her friends and family would laugh off as "a cute attempt at journalism." This one was solid, something that would add to the social conversation about Jonathan Flite rather than detract from it. It could put her independent online journal, *Providence Today*, on the goddamned map.

Thanks to her serendipitous intersection last August with Timothée Boucher, the mysterious Frenchman who was now her twice-a-week lover, she had it: the identity—or supposed identity—of Jonathan Flite's biological father.

*Yes, but do I dare publish it?*

As she lay in bed with Timothée under the buzzing news reports about yesterday's bombing at *WorldLine*'s New York office, she browsed the chain of ActoMessages somehow appearing on his phone. It had to be through some sort of windowing app, because they were looking directly at the phone screen of Jonathan Flite's swishy little friend, Jimmy

Barber, whom Lydia had twice tried to question in Providence last spring—first outside a bookstore called Scripted Corner, then outside the back entrance to Garrahy Judicial Complex the day of Jonathan's release hearing.

Here now were text messages between the two young men—hundreds of them. Some of the more recent ones mentioned Jonathan Flite's romantic feelings for an employee at *WorldLine* named Clovia Bell. Others—sent just today—were focused on Dominic Bock, the father Jonathan had found out about twenty-two hours ago. As most people knew, he'd previously been under the impression that his father was a sperm donor.

"And you're sure these text messages are legit?" Lydia said to Timothée, wondering again for a sudden doubtful moment why the man had taken a liking to her. It wasn't exactly flattering on her part to be both thirty-eight *and* still playing the part of confident, budding reporter, so what was his game?

"I have friends who like to hack into phones, just to see if they can," Timothée replied. "They're what you Americans would call 'nerds.'"

Lydia scoffed and continued scrolling through the messages, certain her face was puffed with shame over invading Jimmy Barber and Jonathan Flite's privacy. But she needed a story. A way to finally make a public splash as a serious reporter. And since she didn't have to name her source to anyone, all she had to do was trot down to Texas, confirm the identity of Dominic Bock, and write a goddamned news article.

People like her sometimes won when they took risks, didn't they? Especially when no other risks were paying off? And hell, this was the first life dream that had ever been served to her on a silver platter.

"Did you hear me?" Timothée said, rolling over in bed and putting an arm around her. He was older than anyone she'd ever slept with by ten years at least, but something about him—maybe it was that greasy, piratelike ponytail; maybe it was that sexy way he looked at her—made her feel rebellious. Made her feel *bad*.

"You really think it won't be wrong for me to just . . . follow up on the stuff they're saying on this chain? I mean, that's what a good reporter would do, right?" She shook her head. "Hell, I could also break the story about this Clovia Bell girl. Who knew someone like Jonathan Flite could even *have* a crush?"

"See? This is why I asked around," Timothée said. "I want you to get your break."

"Or you just want to keep fucking someone who could almost be your granddaughter."

"Maybe it's why we found each other. Right place at the right time. Sometimes life just goes that way."

"Yeah. Maybe it does."

Timothée was gearing the conversation back toward sappy romantic dialogue, as always—but this was how he wanted it, wasn't it? He made a habit of holding back personal information and deflecting any attempts on Lydia's part to get more intimate. But if she was going to get what she wanted, she would have to continue playing along. And maybe that was okay, because the sex with Timothée, despite his age, was some of the best she'd ever had.

Looking back, it all seemed so unlikely, so silly. She had been bedridden at Rhode Island Hospital for almost a month following Weston Carrow's August bombing of Newport City Hall. Before that night turned fateful, she had somehow managed to secure a front-row position amid the legitimate reporters—and even ask Winifred Flite an intensely personal question. Then had come the blast. The fire. The screams.

And then of course Timothée, who had found her in the hospital following a visit to another one of Weston Carrow's victims. He had just so happened to see Jimmy Barber—who'd become somewhat recognizable by that point—stop by Lydia's room after visiting the co-matose Winifred Flite in the ICU.

Jimmy had recognized Lydia's face from the few public exchanges they'd shared during the fervor surrounding Jonathan Flite's release from Crescent Rehabilitation Center. There, at the hospital, the fluttery but listless young man had sat in the chair next to her bed. They had even talked.

*"Why do you care so much about Jonathan Flite?"* he had asked—his most memorable inquiry that day.

*"The same reason you do,"* she had answered. *"Exposure."*

The fact that young Jimmy hadn't negated her proved she had been right about him. He was a gold digger, just like her—but not one for money. He was a gold digger for *status*. For the potential to be *known*.

That night, Timothée Boucher had been standing just outside her hospital room. He had overheard the desperation in her voice as she told Jimmy about her do-or-die need to become a legitimate re-porter after all the years of failure, rejection, and people telling her she couldn't, couldn't, couldn't.

Tonight, as she and Timothée trolled through Jimmy and Jonathan's private messages, she wondered: Was it finally time to snatch up what-ever parts of her dream were left?

"You're quiet," Timothée said, hugging her from behind. "What's wrong?"

She was often right about people. Was she right about this man?

"I almost feel like the sperm-donor-dad story for Jonathan Flite was better. Like, all his weirdness just being the luck of the draw."

"No story is better than the truth," Timothée said. "Go down to Texas. At least check it out."

"I'm just nervous to publish information I got illegally."

"It'll be like you're following up on a rumor."

"Fine, then you pay for the trip," Lydia said, feigning a smile.

"Oh, little budding reporter bird tweeting into my ear about money . . ." Timothée hugged her extra tight. She knew he *would* fork over the cash.

"Do you really believe any of this Jonathan Flite stuff is true?" Lydia pushed, grappling for further authenticity. "I mean, that he could possibly remember those missing kids?"

Timothée held her close—even though her question verged on personal territory. "I think a lot of things are possible."

"Okay, but, like, even if past lives *were* somehow real, how would he be able to remember *seven* sets of memories from one time frame?"

The nurse killer's face rose in Lydia's mind, followed closely by those high school photos of the missing Idle County Seven. She had no desire to believe any of Jonathan's pseudospiritual nonsense was real, but damn it if she didn't want to ride the wave he was creating.

"There's a lot we don't know about life and the universe," Timothée continued, his French accent more pronounced than usual. "People are so quick to say there's nothing beyond this existence, yet here we are, a blip in the universe caused by some mysterious Big Bang. Do you never wonder further?"

Lydia shot Timothée a defensive smirk. "I think we just exist, perceive what we perceive, and then die. Easy as fucking pie."

"But don't you ever wonder what's doing the perceiving?" he asked in return, chuckling with that shameless European air she couldn't get enough of. When he rolled her around to kiss her, however, he tasted like cigarette smoke, so she buried her face in his neck, where she was eye to eye with the spiraling snake tattoo lining his aging shoulder blades.

FROM CHAPTER TWO of the memoir *Our Many Lives* by Dr. Cora Noreen Crowe, published on July 15, 2024:

*On the day my life changed in 2009, I wasn't in a particularly good mood. I had just found out I wasn't pregnant after my twenty-third month in a row of trying; I had a headache; and perhaps worst of all, my secret desk drawer was fresh out of dark chocolate. So, when a patient named Charlotte walked into my office with a doldrum face, I pasted on a smile.*

*She was there for her first session of hypnotic regression therapy, a form of psychological treatment I had studied a few years prior that I'd seen much success with. In theory, it helped patients access suppressed memories from the past—usually traumas from early childhood— that were manifesting later in life as psychiatric symptoms.*

*By the time we had gone over Charlotte's immediate personal history and got around to an initial attempt at hypnotherapy, she was resistant. It took four separate attempts to bring her into a deep suggestive state. Once there, I began the therapy process by asking her to remember the most prominent cause of her eating addiction, and her seemingly related depression. Her answer was immediate and matter-of-fact:*

*"Sex," she said.*

*At first, it was difficult to make the connection. I asked her to clarify what she meant by this.*

*"I make myself fat because I'm trying to be unattractive to men. I want them to find me repulsive, because I don't want them to use me as a plaything . . . But I'm going about it the wrong way, and I know it. I hate myself for that . . . It makes me feel even more worthless."*

*It was obvious to me then that Charlotte had a deeper-rooted issue tying her appearance and confidence to men and sex. Once we had established this, I asked her to go back to any events that may have informed her desire to become unattractive to men. We started at age twenty, then went back to fifteen, ten, and so on. Events from age ten and later were not surprising: instances of physical abuse from her father, a mother who ignored the abuse, and later, after puberty, a string of sexual encounters with older men who used her for pleasure before discarding her.*

*"But I'm allowing it. . . . I'm allowing myself to be trash . . . I want to be trash." Charlotte then described her first independent sexual experience at age thirteen. "I want to know I'm not stupid for thinking I'm only there for boys and men to do whatever they want with me."*

*I directed Charlotte to go backward still, to the point in life where her feelings of worthlessness began. I must admit I wasn't surprised when she began reliving a period of ongoing sexual abuse by her father between the ages of three and four. (She would later confront her father about this and get confirmation that it indeed happened—but that's a story for another day.)*

*"I don't know why it's happening, but I think it's normal and good, because he tells me it's normal and good. He continues touching me.*

*"When I turn five, he stops. Mama is mad at him . . . I hear them fight one night. It's a big fight . . . It's June . . . There are mosquitos in the house. Mama says she hates Daddy. But Daddy throws her against a wall . . . Then he tells her she'll be homeless if she leaves him or tells the police, because he supports her financially. We stay with Daddy even though Mama hates him. None of the neighbors or family friends ever find out. I still love my daddy."*

*At this point, I presumed we had found the root cause of Charlotte's psychological problems. The woman's sexual abuse at a young age was reason enough to explain her desire later in life to shun men. When I asked the hypnotized Charlotte to go even further back, however—simply to see if there were any other reasons for her current psychological state—our session shifted in a most unexpected way.*

*Charlotte sighed, then smiled. She continued in a tone far lighter than the one she usually spoke with. "I'm near the temple again. Oh my . . . how much I loved it here. This was a fun life. I'm bringing gifts with my daughter to Aphaia."*

*I was utterly caught off guard by the shift. My first thought (which I chuckle at now, due to its prescience) was that it seemed she was suddenly talking about some other life altogether.*

*And Aphaia? I had to look the name up later. It turned out she was an obscure Greek goddess worshipped almost exclusively at a single temple on the island of Aegina, in the Saronic Gulf. Nevertheless, Charlotte continued as if she were describing the most basic of life memories.*

*"The hills . . . what a beautiful place. My favorite place. My daughter and I walk together, but today, she's crying because of what I've done to her. I'm very angry, because I believe she's mine to do with what I want. I'm a large and powerful man . . . muscular . . . one of the local elite."*

*Breathing slowly, Charlotte grew silent for nearly six minutes. My attempts to speak inspired her to shake her head. Bouts of anxious, heavy breathing followed.*

*As I braced myself for more of the unexpected, I fought to stay calm. I had no idea what Charlotte was talking about or where the words were coming from. Her subconscious, obviously—but why? Was she fabricating some sort of story to justify the horrors she had experienced at the hand of her father? Some other imaginary existence to paste her pain onto?*

*The audio recording of our session shows that Charlotte's silent pause lasted five minutes and forty-two seconds. When she continued, her tone grew meek.*

*"Oh no . . . Oh, please, no . . . It makes sense to me now. I see . . . I see my daughter . . . Adrasteia. Oh, Adrasteia. I love her very much. Or think I do. But*

*really it's the power over her I enjoy. I'm a bad man. I torture Adrasteia regularly, physically and sexually. She's . . . she's Daddy."*

*I felt a twist in my soul. At first, it was revulsion—a sudden burst of hatred for Charlotte's father, who had untethered his daughter's mind and forced her to create this awful, unnecessary, and damaging justification for his abuse.*

*Except as Charlotte continued to describe her apparent life as this muscular, domineering man in ancient Greece, I couldn't help but see patterns emerge. This man and his daughter, Adrasteia, whose mother had died during the stillbirth of her younger brother, lived on "one of the islands." Because he had some status in their society, nobody dared to challenge him when they saw his daughter walk around with bruises or in tears from the physical and sexual abuse. Charlotte, in her own words, described herself in this apparent life as a "tyrant."*

*She spoke with a matter-of-fact sort of pensiveness about it all, then went still for almost a minute.*

*"I'm outside my body now," she finally continued. "I've been killed by a fallen rock while climbing in the hills. Nobody finds my body."*

*Silent and scared, I waited almost two minutes for Charlotte to keep speaking. I was about to bring her out of hypnosis when she suddenly gasped as if in awe.*

*"Oh my God," Charlotte finally whispered. As tears formed in her eyes, she repeated the phrase six times. "It's so beautiful now that I'm outside my body! I see white. Like a fog, but brighter than anything I ever knew on Earth. It doesn't blind me, though. And . . . oh my.*

*Here is my guide, my old friend Otho. He wasn't incarnating with me in this life—it was my first trip into the world without him by my side. He politely chastises me for the life I just completed, saying that I succumbed to the lure of power and oppressive sexuality. I know he's right, but he isn't judging. There's no judgment here. It's all about choice, experience, and growth. I already know I'll eventually choose to undergo the same type of torment I put Adrasteia through, so I can understand it better."*

*It sounded like the idea of karma. I was about to ask Charlotte whether that was indeed the case, but she beat me to it—with a twist.*

*"It's not as if going back into the victim role will be a punishment. We agree on circumstances ahead of time, so we can grow in new directions and become more aware of ourselves and others. Life is like a big stage production, and we usually come into it with the same groups, taking different roles until we learn certain lessons."*

*"And what did you learn in this life?"*

*"I was a baby soul. It was only my fourteenth incarnation. But it's starting to make sense. I see now that Adrasteia is part of my usual group. We always incarnate together, because we understand each other the best."*

*"And Adrasteia is now your father in this life as Charlotte?"*

*"Yes. It's why I always loved my dad even though he abused me. It's also why I felt guilty and hated myself. I didn't have the full context, and now I do. And now it's time to rest. Please, let me stay here and rest."*

*Charlotte grew quiet once again. Because her session*

*was almost up, I once again began the process of lulling her back, out of hypnosis. But then, on the recording I listened to later, Charlotte's voice suddenly grew low—far more forceful than it had been a few minutes before.*

*"My guide, Otho, wants me to convey a message, and it's this: Your daughter, Flora, died early so that you would use this moment to change your life trajectory."*

*It took me a moment to realize that Charlotte was talking directly to me. She seemed to be referring to my first child, a daughter named Flora, who died of hypoplastic left heart syndrome (HLHS) at just twenty-two days old. I was a Heart Mom, but never publicly and never outwardly to patients. Furthermore, I had been trying for four subsequent years to get pregnant and mitigate that loss, but to no avail. So, when Charlotte said Flora's name, I could only listen in shock. I had no other choice, because the alternative would have been to burst into tears—poor form for any on-the-job physician.*

*"You and Flora both agreed that her death would play out the way it did before coming into your respective lives," Charlotte continued, still directing the words at me. "She chose a body that would develop prenatally with a heart defect on the left side. Otho says Flora's death at twenty-two days was not meant to be a tragedy, but a planned catalyst for you."*

*I couldn't even respond. Tears escaped my own eyes now, no matter how hard I tried to keep them at bay.*

*"The goal was for you to overcome your grief by understanding the eternal nature of life. Are you hearing me, Cora?"*

*"Yes," I whispered.*

*"You can now change your course and study this form of therapy with your patients. It has the potential to help countless people understand their deeper nature and the meaning behind their pains."*

*I forced myself to ask the biggest question pulsing through my mind: "Why me?"*

*"Because your goal in this life is to help the collective human consciousness evolve and move forward, past the young phase it is currently in. Flora came here as a beacon for you, to make sure you would now pay attention."*

*I was crying freely now, flabbergasted by the fact that Charlotte, my socially challenged patient who had no knowledge of my personal life, wasn't just speaking about my dead daughter; she was speaking like a sage.*

*In my rational mind, I knew her words couldn't be true.*

*Yet something in my heart had already shifted. It related to the balance she spoke of—the sense that life's horrors, no matter how bad they might be, could be processed, understood, and valued for the wisdom they might instill in a person.*

*Little did I know that my journey with Charlotte into the mysterious depths we call consciousness and life had only just begun.*

S ANDRA THORSEN'S ANKLES SHOOK as she stood next to her husband, David, outside Dr. Cora Crowe's psychiatry office in Boulder, Colorado. She thought back to the previous February, when she had accepted the paperback copy of Dr. Crowe's book, *Our Many Lives*, from Zoe Caldiero, Rebecca Sparks's medical assistant. Despite having sworn multiple times that she would never read a book of this sort, Sandra had finished it in a single afternoon on her Sausalito deck that overlooked the San Francisco Bay. Against her will, it had rattled loose the first satisfying answers she had ever heard to life's most dire questions.

Today was November 22, 2034, and for the first time in years, Sandra was letting David hold her hand. All the things that had shattered and rebuilt their marriage—the addictions, the extramarital relationships, and of course Lindsay's and Drew's deaths—hung between them like decorations on an unpredictable life.

"How the hell did you ever convince me to come and get a *past-life regression*?" she said. "Jesus. What would my book fans think?"

David chuckled tensely. "It was your idea. Maybe you finally let Lindsay's New Age mumbo jumbo get inside your head."

"I'm starting to wish she'd chosen the Indian beliefs from your dad's side instead. I feel like a fucking loon."

Not to mention that Sandra hated the inner shame brought on by the pseudosciencey phrase "past-life regression." It accompanied an overwhelming panic that her fiercely intellectual, carefully developed facade was cracking. Was she finally one of those people who resorted to a belief in spiritual hokum to explain life's biggest challenges?

"This is silly," she said to her husband, stepping back from the office door. "Let's just go back to the car and—"

David put a hand on her shoulder. "No. You paid fifteen hundred dollars for this. You're not going to cancel."

Sandra turned back to the door with a racing heart. What she hated most about the newfound curiosity *Our Many Lives* had instilled in her was its brightness. It felt warm, like a glowing hearth welcoming her in after a long night out in the cold.

She had to do this. She couldn't let her reservations—which were really just her fears of being seen as a lunatic—threaten to crush this new and luminous sense of understanding. For the first time ever, she felt the desire to assign meaning to life. The feeling was fresh and delicate, as if the slightest breeze might tip it over—or worse, blow it into oblivion.

A young woman with radiant blue eyes and a matching hair weave suddenly appeared next to Sandra, holding what appeared to be a take-out lunch. After waiting a moment before glancing at the door handle, she asked, "Mind if I scoot past you? I just need to—" Suddenly, the woman took a closer look at Sandra. "Hey, are you Sandra Thorsen? Here to see my mom at 1:00? I recognize you from your website."

Sandra's face went red. "You're Cora Crowe's daughter?"

"Yep. Taisha. I'm working here until I figure out what to do with my postcollege life." The young woman extended a hand, first to Sandra and then to David. As the older couple made room for her to enter the building, Taisha added, "Take your time, though. A lot of patients get nervous their first time. I'll see you in a few?"

She smiled warmly, then entered the building. Looking after her, Sandra wondered whether Lindsay would have grown up to be as beautiful, warm, and courteous as Taisha. Or would she have learned from Sandra to lock all genuine warmth behind a hundred different facades?

"Did our little girl really believe in ghosts and spirits and past lives?" Sandra whispered to David. "How did she go from school and friends and kickboxing to *that*?"

"She had her reasons," David said in a low voice.

Sandra fought tears, then shook her head. "I treated her like garbage, David. Like *garbage*. Especially that winter after Drew disappeared."

"You were grieving. We all were."

Sandra wanted to nod and confirm this, but a deep, unmentionable truth was creeping upward from the darkest corner of her heart. She couldn't find words for it. Couldn't even name it.

David squeezed her hand, then opened the door to Dr. Crowe's office. "Your appointment starts in two minutes."

As they walked in, Sandra knew that the nameless truth she had just failed to utter—that obscure, important brick in her rebuilt life with David—had just rattled the scaffolding they were standing on. If it was all about to collapse now, twenty-two years after leaving Idle County behind, perhaps it would be best to tumble down together, with their eyes wide open.

2005

BITING. SINISTER. WITCHY. Over the five days following Drew's disappearance, Lindsay Thorsen watched her mother, Sandra, become all these things. Far from being a hopeful force, Sandra remained inside the house, continuously in her bathrobe, walking like a wraith from the bedroom to the kitchen to the liquor cabinet and back to the bedroom.

Conversely, Lindsay's father, David, had spent six hours yesterday making telephone calls to neighbors, local businesses, and even schools to see if there had been any sign of Drew. He had even taken his wife's usual place as "chief grocery shopper." When he came home without Sandra's favorite Lean Cuisine entrée, the woman screamed, "You know I hate the store brand ones!"

David, showing tremors of despair, drove back to the store and replaced the generic frozen entrées with Lean Cuisines.

During breakfast on Saturday, the fifth of November—the day the blog writers "Butterfly" and "Lightning" were scheduled to meet at the Lemon Avenue Library—Lindsay forced down two whole-wheat waffles and a glass of orange juice, first to make her father happy and second to keep her mother from staring with the spiteful glare that hadn't let up since Lindsay outed her substance abuse to the police on Wednesday. Just seconds after loading her dishes into the dishwasher, however, she heard a guttural scream from the upstairs hallway.

"Lindsay! What the hell did you do to Drew's room?"

In the family room, David looked up from his laptop computer, where he was finally catching up on work that had gone untouched all week.

"What? What do you mean?" Lindsay yelled back to her mother, setting her empty breakfast glass on the kitchen countertop. Leaving the dishwasher open, she walked out of the kitchen, toward the stairs leading to the second floor.

Sandra came storming down them, her nightgown trailing behind her, her entire face more livid than Lindsay had ever seen it. "First you made up those lies at the community center, and now this?" she shrieked. "What, are you just screaming for attention now that your little brother has gobbled it all up? Can't take the pain of being invisible now that his face is smeared all over the goddamned news?"

A defensive heat rushed through Lindsay's body. "What are you talking about? I didn't do anything!"

"Sure you didn't. His room is a mess!"

"What? I—"

"Don't you realize what you've done? This is a crime scene, for God's sake! And now you've gone and messed it all to hell!" Sandra screamed the words in Lindsay's face, waving her arms like a mad woman. Even though the police had already thoroughly examined the room (even taking Drew's bed sheets for their canines to match his scent), the violence in Sandra's eyes left Lindsay numb. It squeezed the woman's face until tears rushed from her eyes. "There could have been clues here! Don't you want Drew to be found?"

"I haven't touched Drew's room!" Lindsay yelled. "Why would I do that?"

"How the hell should I know?"

David rushed toward the hallway just in time to block his wife's arm from hitting Lindsay. Lindsay, her heart racing, cowered against the wall.

"Sandy! Stop!" David wrapped his arms around Sandra, who was thrashing, screaming, sobbing. "Stop it, right now! What the hell is happening?"

"Ask her!" Sandra screamed, almost spitting the words toward her daughter.

Lindsay stared at her father with wide, tearful eyes and shook her head. She didn't need to say anything for him to take her side. No, she hadn't messed up Drew's room. She would have never done such a thing.

David turned back to Sandra and gripped both her shoulders. "Sandy, nobody touched Drew's room! Nobody's been in there all week—not since the police went in to get his sheets for the dog scent. Remember?"

"I just got out of the shower, and his door was wide open!" Sandra screamed. "Everything from his shelves and toy box was all over the floor!"

"Lindsay, I'm going to hold your mom," David said. "You go check Drew's room, okay?"

It took all of Lindsay's courage to move away from the wall under her mother's scathing gaze. Once free, she walked slowly upstairs and down the hall, toward Drew's bedroom. Sure enough, his door was open, casting the morning light from the room's windows into the hallway.

And the mess was incredible. Nothing like it had been the day

Drew disappeared. His entire shelf of children's books was empty. Its contents were scattered across the floor like a textured, multicolored rug. Two toy bins, usually placed neatly against the far wall, were uncovered and overturned. Drew's small bed, stripped bare by the police, was now home to his toy cars. They were lined up at the far end of the bed as if ready to race to the other.

*It was Mom*, Lindsay thought. *She's going crazy. She was the only one up here. Maybe she just—*

The sound of metal spinning on the bedroom's hardwood floor suddenly rolled into her ears. It was coming from across the room.

*Oh, please, no. Not again.*

But Lindsay knew right away what it was: Drew's favorite toy, a red-and-blue aluminum top.

She closed her eyes and turned around.

One breath.

Two breaths.

Three.

She opened her eyes again.

The gyrating top, in its whirl of color, was spinning all by itself in the bedroom's far left corner. As Lindsay's breathing stopped, the toy made the only sound in the entire house.

*Is that you, Drew?*

No sooner had the thought escaped her mind than the top fell on its side and rolled into silence.

Lindsay stood rigid by her brother's bedroom door as fear crawled out of her heart and into her throat. In the silence that followed, tears formed in her eyes, and she knew it for sure: Drew was dead. But he wasn't gone forever.

EATH. It was a spinner of the mind, both impossibly permanent and the only sure bet in life. Clovia Bell had now been invited to its table, and there was no going back.

It was April 15, 2039, and she was sitting in the front pew of First Methodist Church in Nyack, New York, next to her aunt Ivy, the only close relative she had left. To their left was Jimmy Barber, Jonathan Flite's only friend. He was here today in Jonathan's place, since Jonathan himself was still forty-five days short of being able to leave Rhode Island, except to visit his mother on Cape Cod.

At the front of the church was Patrick Bell's casket. It was now closed forever.

Even though Clovia hadn't seen the man in nearly four years, his absence was somehow fresh—coarse and newly torn, like the skin on all those scraped knees from childhood. Was it simply because he was now just one of eight dead people in this month's tally, following the

*WorldLine* office bombing? Or was it punishment, perhaps, for leaving him as good as daughterless, to die alone?

Clovia had doubted her father. Presumed he had somehow overdosed on one of the many drugs he'd been addicted to the last time she saw him. Now, in the week since her decision to postpone his funeral and actually attend it, there were new truths apparent that suggested his death might have been her fault instead.

As far as Clovia was concerned, the last seven days had opened her up to something irrevocable, a life path that was now crumbling behind her.

*EYES OPEN. SMOKE. Gasps. People yelling—mostly men, a few women. There was cold water hitting Clovia's face. Coming from the ceiling? Yes. The sprinkler system.*

*A bomb? It had to have been. The last thing she remembered was someone shouting in another language, then Alice Winterblume spinning around, grabbing hold of her, and pulling both of them to the ground. Oh, and that final thought:* I'm going to see my dad today.

*But Clovia hadn't seen her dead father after the explosion. She had simply awoken to the yells and water droplets and smoke, then to the realization that* WorldLine *and the upcoming season about Jonathan Flite and Idle County might not even exist anymore. People were dead, Jonathan's story might never be told, and now—*

—SHE WAS SAYING GOODBYE to her father the way a good Nyack daughter should: from the front pew of First Methodist Church. Of course, it was the quietest moment of the funeral when Jimmy Barber's phone began buzzing uncontrollably. He slapped it silent as Leiken

Smith, the nurse who had identified her father's body at the hospital (and who had been only three grades ahead of Clovia in high school), stepped off the church's modest sanctuary following a surprisingly heartfelt eulogy.

She flashed both Jimmy and Clovia dirty looks as she passed, seemingly judging their small party and intimating, *"You don't belong here anymore. You abandoned him."*

Yes. Maybe so. But nowhere in the young woman's teary tribute had been a single mention of her ex-boyfriend being Patrick Bell's main drug supplier after his last relapse, back in 2035.

Still, Leiken's eyes weren't the only ones on Clovia today. By now, every funeral attendee surely knew about her job at *WorldLine*, that she was connected to Jonathan Flite, and that, since last week's bombing, *WorldLine*'s new exposé on the famous nurse killer was in shambles. This past Wednesday's exit of the season's director, Jeff Clausen, had made world news headlines—as had the fact that a third of the show's remaining staff had followed him out the door. That didn't even include the seven who had died in the blast.

But Clovia was staying. In the week since the bombing, she hadn't had the peace of mind—not even a second of it—to consider other options. She also wanted to see the season through, not just for Alice's sake but also for Jonathan's. His story, and its unlikely yet increasingly compelling connection to the 2037 Geneva bombing, was too important; she knew it in her bones. Since *WorldLine* still had enough contracted crew members for the upcoming Boulder and Idle County shoots, the show was still set to go on.

Furthermore, while news of Patrick Bell's death had made rounds among *WorldLine*'s remaining staff, new information about its cause now lurked beneath the surface. Thus far, only Clovia, Alice, and a handful of law enforcement officials knew the truth.

"THANKS FOR COMING IN, MISS BELL," *was the first thing Detective Kelly Marshall said at the police station the morning after Clovia finally returned to Nyack.*

*The shock, grief, and questions, questions, questions from the NYPD and FBI had already made an exhausting dent in her week, but here she was again, talking to the police—this time in her hometown.*

*"Your father had no illegal drugs in his system—something I thought you might want to know, given his record," Detective Marshall went on as Clovia took a seat in the comfortable interview room. "But we found something in his tox scan that gave us pause: moderate amounts of aconite. It's a poison. Have you heard of it?"*

Aconite?

*"No," Clovia replied, her heart shaking.*

*"It's not exactly hard to come by if you know what you're doing," Detective Marshall explained. "It's lethal very quickly in high doses—but in smaller doses, it can cause heart problems and often cardiac arrest. Enough to look natural at first glance. I'm wondering—do you have any idea how or why your dad might have had a poison like this in his system?"*

*Clovia simply sat there, flabbergasted, wondering if the detective was interrogating her. The last time she had seen or spoken to her father, he'd been an addict—hopeless and dependent.*

*And now—*


—HE WAS DEAD IN A COFFIN right in front of her eyes, a possible victim of aconite poisoning. And because the FBI knew about her father's death (they had somehow known even before the bombing), all it had taken to understand the situation's true scope was a thirty-minute meeting with the special agent working alongside Alice Winterblume on *WorldLine*'s new season.

*"It makes no sense," Clovia told Special Agent Heather Mousseau when they were speaking face-to-face the day after her visit with the Nyack police department. "I haven't even seen my dad in four years. How could this have anything to do with me?"*

*The agent's close work with Alice Winterblume on the Jonathan Flite documentary slowly became evident as she explained how one of the bureau's "significant active investigations" intersected with certain aspects of the show: first the lingering mysteries of the Idle County Seven case; then Rebecca Sparks's scheduled conference with physicists in Geneva on August 12, 2037; and, finally, Victor Zobel's varying degrees of international separation from known weapons manufacturers, money launderers, and smugglers.*

*Finally, the woman adjusted her posture and said, "Alice also told us you agreed to work on the new Revis Zobel interview, which is why we wanted to warn you about something else."*

*Clovia waited.*

*"There's a strong chance that poisons might come up in his discussion with Alice," Agent Mousseau continued. "Particularly if he tells WorldLine what he told us about his mother's death back in 2006 and the suspicions he still has about his father's role in it."*

*Shock from the last week, already sneaking into the most unsuspecting corners of Clovia's mind, began to shift and sharpen. Then came the facts, enough to make her worry once again for her own life.*


And here they were:

Raphael Dumont, Victor Zobel's best friend and assistant for almost three decades, had been excommunicated from the celebrity billionaire's inner circle four years ago, after being accused of murder in Croatia. The murder charges were later dropped under questionable circumstances, but as of now, he was what Agent Mousseau called a "free radical." She didn't tell Clovia specifically why, but she did share two facts:

First, Revis Zobel had confirmed to the bureau that the physicist Dorothy Garland—known to *WorldLine* as Rebecca Sparks—had recently sent a letter to his home in Salerno, Italy. In it, she had advised him to ask Raphael Dumont directly about his father's interest in poisons and the role they might have played in the 2006 death of Cassandra Pope, Revis's mother.

Second, the FBI, in conjunction with "other government agencies," had just last week identified a malware attack on the cell phone of Jimmy Barber, Jonathan Flite's closest friend. Jimmy had clicked a hyperlink in a random ActoMessage (something he did often), which had funneled all data on his phone to a second phone—albeit one whose location and unique identifiers were hidden behind a logless VPN account. What the FBI did know from reviewing Jimmy's compromised text message chains was that Clovia's name had come up in threads with Jonathan multiple times, enough to make it clear that Jonathan cared about her very much. This association could make Clovia—and those close to her—targets for anyone seeking to punish the young man for sharing his story.

And the presence of aconite in her father's system? It aligned suspiciously with the statement made about poisons in Rebecca Sparks's letter to Revis Zobel.

Thus, Raphael Dumont—and anyone else associated with Victor Zobel—was now a possible suspect in her father's death.

No, they couldn't tell Clovia any more than that.

Yes, Jimmy Barber had now been alerted to the malware detected on his phone and had purchased a new one for personal use.

Did she have any questions?

Yes, Clovia had a million.


In the evening following her father's funeral, she sat alone on the window seat in her childhood bedroom, listening to the clinks and

clanks of dishes in the kitchen downstairs, where Aunt Ivy was cleaning up after the last remaining funeral guests. The sound reminded
her of childhood, of the days before her mother's aneurysm and her
father's renewed drug habit. Back then, life had been simple, if not exactly perfect. No matter how frustrating it got on any given day, Clovia
could always return here, to this bedroom window seat, and ponder the
things she needed to ponder.

She had also experienced death for the first time from this spot,
two weeks after her sixth birthday. The deceased? Her favorite neighbor, Ernie Ducey. Ernie had earned this status five weeks before, in
mid-August, when Clovia had recorded a "news report" on him using
her mother's phone. This, of course, had been her hobby since age four.
Some days, she reported on her stuffed teddy bears. Other days, she
reported on her mother's untouchables—usually tampons, rare china
dishes, or other treasures that were off limits.

When reporting on Ernie Ducey in August 2024, however, it had
been an exposé on his gardening skills. He had been watering his yellow
roses, and because yellow roses had always reminded Clovia of angels
(maybe it was that heavenly smell), she'd decided to make a news segment about them. Using her mother's phone, she had gone outside and
asked Ernie for an interview. He'd happily obliged, smiling warmly as
he told her everything he knew about yellow roses. Clovia had filmed
herself asking Ernie questions, then quickly turned the camera back to
capture his answers. Her camera movements had been calculated, even
back then.

Five weeks later, Ernie died of a heart attack. When the ambulance
came to his house, it was raining—which meant there was no sunset
to usher the day's dwindling light from the sky. Clovia had taken her
mother's phone from the kitchen counter without permission and quietly filmed the paramedics wheeling Ernie's covered body out of his
house, to the ambulance. The video footage, which she had used eleven

years later in her application to New York University, was backed by audio of her six-year-old self trying not to cry.

This window. This house. That not-quite-innocuous childhood.

Tonight, her dad was dead. Seven of her coworkers were dead. Clovia didn't even know if the B-roll footage from her recent shoot with Jonathan Flite would ever see the light of day, but she reviewed it now as an escape. The video played through her ActoLenses, and she wondered: Was *WorldLine* trying to bite off more than it could chew with the full Idle County Seven season? Would its crippled staff really be able to pick up all the pieces, incorporate Revis Zobel's interview, and tell the version of the story (replete with its startling connections to the Geneva bombing) that Alice Winterblume had in mind?

Clovia had already begun reviewing every story asset set to be used this season: each bit of interview, historical news footage, photography, and video footage. If Revis Zobel's interview could corroborate the global web of facts linking his father and the Idle County Seven mystery to the 2037 Geneva bombing, it might just offer them enough story beats to cover for the loss of Raphael Dumont.

And did Clovia feel guilty for work-work-working instead of spending every waking moment of today grieving for her dead father and seven coworkers, who had all been killed because of this story?

Yes. Perhaps.

Perhaps a lot.

AT 8:47 P.M., HER ACTOPHONE VIBRATED on the desk next to her bed, and a call notification showing Jonathan Flite's name dimmed her ActoLenses' viewing area. Her heart immediately raced, and she wiped her tear-filled eyes as if to expunge her grief.

"Answer," she voiced after a few deep breaths. The phone obeyed her. "Hi, this is Clovia," she continued, sounding abysmally professional.

"Hey, it's Jonathan. How's it going?" His voice was careful, quiet.

"Oh, doing fine," Clovia replied, injecting false cheer into her tone despite her nose being clogged from unwanted tears. To cover them up, she immediately added, "So, regarding the date changes for Boulder and Minnesota—it turns out we *are* still carrying on with the shoot, and Cora Crowe was able to adjust her—"

"I'm actually calling to see how you're doing," Jonathan said before Clovia could spiral their conversation into business. "Because of your dad, I mean."

The only follow-up words that came to her were, "Oh. Thank you."

"I hope it's okay that I asked Jimmy to go to the funeral instead of me. I just . . ." He sighed. "I would've gone if I wasn't stuck here. Rhode Island is definitely starting to feel like a prison."

Clovia's heart was pounding. Never before had a boy (or man) reached out to her simply to see how she was doing. And today, it was more than that; she was caught in the whirlpool of death surrounding Jonathan, yet he wasn't letting her fall into it without extending a supportive hand.

More tears formed in Clovia's eyes. "I really appreciate that you called. And yeah, I'm just trying to keep busy. All the *WorldLine* funerals happened this week, too."

"Must've taken a lot of energy," Jonathan said. "Funerals are so hard."

Clovia nodded even though he couldn't see her. "Have you been to many?"

Jonathan took a breath, then let out a vulnerable chuckle. "Just one. My friend Mason. He's the one who got shot during the break-in at . . ."

"At Crescent—I remember." Clovia didn't share that she also now knew the FBI had apprehended Nicolas Rim, the man who had committed the murder. Never had she realized just how much an omission could feel like a lie.

Mattress squeaks sounded through the phone as Jonathan seemed to switch positions on his bed. "I guess if you consider all the stuff in my head, I've experienced a lot of funerals. If that makes any sense."

As always when facing the possible reality—or malarkey—of Jonathan's memories, Clovia struggled to find a response that wouldn't betray the self-consciousness her own acknowledgment of them instilled. Finally, a question she hadn't yet asked came to mind. "Are the memories as strong as your own, if you had to compare?"

"Sometimes," Jonathan said. "The emotions and images all jumble together, kind of like normal memories. But I—" His truncated statement floated in silence for a moment. "Sorry. I didn't mean to make this about me. You get enough of that at work."

"No, please—I love hearing about your memories," Clovia admitted. "It's actually kind of comforting to think there might be more to life than all this. It's just that—"

Screams from the *WorldLine* office bombing suddenly echoed in Clovia's memory. They floated amid the seemingly permanent controversy surrounding Jonathan. Would she ever be able to forget them?

"Sorry," she said. "I shouldn't bug you with all my issues."

"I called so you *could* bug me."

Like Jonathan's endearing smile, Clovia's heart slowly began to melt as words found her mouth. "I guess I feel guilty for some reason," she said. "Like, with everything going on, all I want to do is work. Even after the bombing."

"You like what you do."

"Yes. I love it."

Jonathan let her statement hang. He was inviting her in, except she couldn't cross his threshold, lest she risk losing her *WorldLine* job. But oh, she wanted to cross it. Yes, she did.

"My dad was an addict, and I lost my mom a while ago," Clovia continued, using the life script she was most accustomed to. "I've also always had a clear vision of what I wanted to do with my life. I'm lucky like that." She wiped away two tears that had formed under her ActoLenses. "But after this week . . . I don't know. I think I might need a counselor or something. *WorldLine* is offering it for free."

"Therapy can help a lot," Jonathan said. "And that's coming from someone who's been in it his whole life."

Clovia's throat suddenly tightened. "Oh God—sorry. I didn't even think about that."

"No, it's true. And the good thing about therapy is that you have, like, a 'safe space.' It's probably even more effective if you're not forced into it like I was."

Clovia twirled the window shade's drawstring all the way around her finger, to the point where she couldn't twirl anymore. "And how are you?" she asked. "Pretend for a second that I'm not part of the TV show looking to profit like crazy off you."

"Ha," Jonathan said, sounding as if he might be smiling. But his next words hinted otherwise. "It's my fault, what happened. The bombing."

"No, it's not," Clovia replied automatically.

"Seven more people are dead because of me. It's not just Ellen Graber anymore. Or Mason Witzel. Or the people who died last summer at my mom's press conference."

*And I can't tell you that my dad might also now be on that list*, Clovia thought. The only things she could say in response to Jonathan felt like lies, so she simply let him talk.

"I'm starting to think the whole *WorldLine* thing was a mistake. That it was better for everyone when I was still at Crescent."

"But the story found you there, too," Clovia said.

"Maybe, but now it's finding a bunch of *other* people. I just wonder if Judge Wallace still stands by what he said at my release hearing last year. Like, about me sharing my story. If people actually do believe the truth, what then? Won't it just cause bigger problems?"

A sudden weight descended on Clovia's chest. Thus far, Jonathan wasn't even aware that his offhand comment last summer about Lindsay Thorsen's flashlight incident was shaping up to be *WorldLine*'s biggest "one-two punch" of the new season. The story itself—that Lindsay grabbed a flashlight from Elijah Bryce's bedroom during an out-of-body experience following an altercation with her brother's killer—was fantastic in its own right. But to combine it with Rebecca Sparks's validated 2034 prediction that Jonathan would one day mention the occurrence to Alice Winterblume, just in time for the physicist's new theory to provide a compelling explanation as to how both events might have been possible? That would be a true social curveball, one *WorldLine* was poised and ready to throw.

Yet the most pertinent question—one *WorldLine* was now inquiring about with the Idle County Sheriff's Department—was whether police had indeed retrieved Elijah Bryce's flashlight from Arrowhead Hills, the abandoned town where Lindsay's altercation took place. All case files and evidence involving the Idle County Seven had been locked by cooperating jurisdictions twenty-nine year ago, so *WorldLine* had run into some roadblocks. As of now, Idle County's sheriff, Eli Thropp, refused to reveal any details about Lindsay Thorsen's 2006 abduction until he was sure it wouldn't impact the unsolved Idle County Seven investigation—which, since Jonathan Flite's rise to fame, was being revisited.

"You're quiet," Jonathan said through the phone.

"Yeah, I just . . . there's a lot I want to talk to you about, but I can't."

"The show," he said.

"And more, I guess."

"Should I let you get back to work?"

Clovia looked out the window again, at Ernie Ducey's old house and the dwindling sunset. "No. Not yet. But I'll admit: talking to you sometimes feels *too* comfortable."

"Well, I have my issues, obviously," Jonathan replied with a hesitant chuckle.

"I guess that's part of what makes me nervous," Clovia said. "I have my job to think about, and I don't want to end up like—"

She stopped short, before her next awful words could tumble forth.

Jonathan, however, could seemingly read minds. "Like Ellen Graber, you mean?" he asked. "Or like one of the many other people who are dead because of me?" Dejection trickled from his quiet voice.

Clovia's heart sank. Both on camera and off, Jonathan had discussed his incurable struggle with people's fear of him. They always kept him an arm's length away, forcing him to maintain his own isolation. Now Clovia herself was doing the exact same thing.

"I'm sorry," she said. "I didn't mean to—"

"It's okay. I understand. Really."

Clovia fought the urge to wail out in sudden desperation. No, she didn't want Jonathan to leave her alone. Her heart, bursting in her chest, was screaming the opposite. Jonathan was the only person she had anything in common with now that the tragedies of their lives had begun to intertwine.

"I guess I was under the impression you saw the real me," Jonathan finally added. "I liked the idea of that, but maybe I latched on too quickly. Sorry if I'm being awkward."

At long last, Clovia's feelings broke through her outer barriers. "I *do* see you, Jonathan. I *promise* I see you. If I could snap my fingers and make everything perfect, we'd be drinking tea right now under the stars."

For a moment, all she heard through her ActoPhone was silence. Then came Jonathan's voice. "I get what you're saying. And I'm probably idealizing all this anyway. I can let you go."

"Jonathan, wait—"

But he had already ended their call, leaving Clovia's heart beating faster than it ever had before.

REW'S TOY WAS MOVING *on its own.*
*He really is dead.*
*Mom tried to hit me.*

Under a deceivingly bright sun, Lindsay Thorsen's feet carried her toward the Lemon Avenue Library. Most of the grass around the neighborhood was still green, but winter was in the air. The smell of nature saying goodbye to its season of thriving met her nose with an ironic sense of bittersweet rejuvenation, as if death and loss didn't always have to be crippling. Maybe all she had to do was look at the trees and their falling leaves year after year to see that life always came back around.

She glanced at her watch. It was almost 11:30 a.m. "Butterfly" had written that the Lemon Avenue Library meetings took place at noon on Saturdays. Would they really be there? Was it worth the walk?

The winding roads and cul-de-sacs of her neighborhood gave way to the older, less affluent area of End Haven sooner than she expected. In her three years of living here, Lindsay had seen the "main" part of town only through her parents' speeding car windows. She walked north, crossing the first five avenues in slow succession. The sixth, however, was a welcome surprise: Lemon Avenue. She turned right and kept walking.

Fifteen minutes later, Lindsay finally saw it: the library everyone loved. It was a large building on the left corner, inching out from behind a grove of oak trees. Its tan-brick structure had an irregular shape, as if it were a few curves and corners away from being a church. Tall tapered windows lined the library's ground-level every ten feet while parts of the second floor had smaller diamond-shaped windows. The yard in which the oak trees were scattered was a generous plot, almost large enough to be a park.

As the library's curved front sidewalk grew closer, Lindsay slowed, noticing four bikes parked on the bike rack. Two of them, both differing shades of blue, looked brand new. They were tethered to the rack with the same lock.

Lindsay glanced apprehensively at the library's large mahogany doors. They had dark iron handles and were tapered at the top. Above them, a section of the building's front brick wall towered thirty feet into the air. A bell tower, perhaps?

She pulled open the left door. It was heavier than she expected but opened without a sound, leading into a dark foyer with an ornately tiled floor and heavy wooden benches sitting on either side of her, nestled in the shadows. Ten feet beyond, the floor dropped a step into a much brighter atrium, where lights dangled on long black chains from a thirty-foot ceiling. The center of the library was open all the way up, but solid wooden balcony railings protected what appeared to be a second level on both the west and east sides. To Lindsay's right, an elegant wooden staircase spiraled upward.

It was completely different than any library she had ever seen. Nothing here appeared to be new, save for the computer at the circular front desk under the main atrium. Even so, despite its clanking radiators and plethora of dark and hidden corners, the place felt like a sanctuary.

Lindsay stepped past the spiral stairway and down two steps, to the library's main floor. Fifteen feet ahead of her were two women standing at a "New Releases" table to the right of the front desk. One of them was dressed in a cheap-looking sweater vest and had a toddler grabbing at her legs. The toddler looked at Lindsay and smiled.

Blushing, Lindsay turned back toward the spiral staircase, only to bump into a curvy, thirty-something woman with thick-rimmed glasses and long brown hair pulled back in a clip. "Oh! I'm sorry, I didn't—"

"No, sorry myself," said the woman, who was holding a blue and yellow book called *In God We're Dust*. "I didn't even see you standing there! I was on a mission to find this book for that lovely lady over there—somebody put it in the wrong section." She gestured with her head toward the visitor with the sweater vest before glancing back at Lindsay. "I'll just let you browse. Nice to see some new faces around here, either way! Always looking for a reason to show the city we're worth keeping open, right?" The woman, clearly the librarian, smiled and stepped around Lindsay without further comment.

"I guess so," Lindsay said in a fumbled, belated response. For the first time, she realized just how shy she could be in new places.

She made for the spiral stairway. As she circled up, she looked over her shoulder, first at the atrium below, then at the second-floor book-shelves on the far side. "Butterfly" and "Lightning" had mentioned that their meeting spot was under a large stained glass window on the upper level. Lindsay hoped it was on this side of the library so she wouldn't have to find her way to the other.

The spiral staircase ended at a long aisle stretching into the library's east wing. Bookshelves, all wooden and somehow ominous in their silence, towered upward to her right and left. The floor creaked under Lindsay's feet as she took note of the section labels passing by her eyes.

*History . . .*

*Psychology . . .*

*Self-Help . . .*

And then she saw it: a pinkish glow shining from the third row on her left. When Lindsay passed the row, she looked down it, and two thoughts registered simultaneously—each a variation of the same emotion:

*Great, I found them!*

*Damn it, I found them!*

Set in the wall at the far end of the row, about forty feet down, was a radiant stained glass window. And indeed, sitting below it at a small wooden table were the two Murderers—Molly Butler and Elijah Bryce. Lindsay hopped extra fast across the row, hoping they hadn't already seen her. She turned left, into a section labeled "Law." As she neared the middle of the row, their voices sifted through the bookshelves—and it didn't sound as if they were discussing ghosts. Lindsay stopped to listen.

". . . Well, he took me out to dinner last night instead of tonight," came Molly's voice. "He's definitely changed a bit since last year—it's better, but not amazing. Like, after my mom died, he was really messed up for a while. He kind of just let me do whatever."

"Yeah, well, at least he isn't a religious freak," came Elijah's response. Molly must have given him some sort of look, because he responded a moment later with, "Well, she *is*."

So, Molly Butler's mother was dead, and Elijah Bryce's was a religious freak. Perhaps Lindsay's chemically dependent mother and workaholic father would fit right in.

"I made a MySpace last night," Elijah said next. "Mostly so I could look at profiles of hot guys. My mom would flip out if she knew, but Cynthia would probably say it's fine. Oh well. Kind of nice to have some space now, at least."

"My dad still says no to MySpace," Molly said. "He thinks internet creepers would stalk me, and I'd get kidnapped or something."

*Kidnapped.*

Lindsay's heart lurched. The simple word now rattled her all over. The floor creaked under her as she shifted her weight.

"Yeah, well, can't blame him these days, can you?" Elijah said. Their next words were hushed and mostly inaudible. "Oh!" Elijah interjected suddenly. "Did I tell you that Pauline Gilbert left me a voice mail last night? She asked if I wanted to hang out, but it was kind of weird, because we stopped being friends after the whole Alec Pent thing happened."

Lindsay's ears pricked up. Pauline had stormed from the lunch table just three days ago, right after Natalie had attacked her for defending Elijah.

"Wasn't she all into being popular with Alec Pent's sister?" Molly asked.

"Apparently not anymore. I guess Natalie's a total bitch now or something. Not too surprising. She was always kind of into herself."

"My neighbor Jacob Jenkins asked her out and got turned down," Molly said. "He was telling me about it on the way home from school the other day."

Lindsay marveled at all the secrets these two kids knew. She was vaguely familiar with Jacob Jenkins, mostly because he played soccer with Alec Pent and had eaten lunch at her table a few times. For some reason, Lindsay wouldn't have presumed Molly knew him.

"I guess Jacob thinks Natalie Pent's the hottest girl in the world," Molly continued. "I, on the other hand, think she looks like a zebra."

Elijah burst out laughing. "A zebra? What the hell does that mean?"

"You know how everyone looks like an animal, if you had to pick?" Molly said. "And I think zebras are cute either way—I'm not trying to be mean."

"Yeah, well, she's mean."

"I guess you were right last summer about End Haven Middle School kind of sucking. Like, at least people at Saint Andrew's didn't think I was a freak. I can't even say anything in class without all those girls giving me weird looks."

Lindsay immediately felt defensive, then thought back on all the English classes when their teacher, Ms. Olson, had called on Molly to contribute. More than once, Natalie had flashed Lindsay and a few of the other girls snide grins, no matter what Molly said.

"Last summer didn't help," Elijah said. "I don't think anyone will ever believe us. But whatever. Let them think we're killers. Maybe it'll keep them from bugging us."

Lindsay's body went rigid. Elijah was referring to the accident on Spinner's Lake that had killed Damon Jacoby.

"I still see him," he continued as the library's radiators began clanking again.

"What? Where?" Molly asked.

Once again, Elijah replied in an inaudible voice. Were they talking about ghosts? Damon Jacoby's ghost, maybe? For a moment, Lindsay yearned to be sitting next to them, to be their friend. If they were talking about ghosts, it was something she could relate to—if only the one thing.

"I just can't stop thinking about this week," Molly said after a while, once again loud enough for Lindsay to hear. "Do you think they know? I doubt anybody would believe us if we said anything."

"By 'us' you mean 'you.' I didn't see him," Elijah replied.

"Yeah, but you saw that creepy lady in the raggedy skirt."

Now the boy laughed. "First, I still don't even know if that skirt lady was real, and second, are you sure *you* didn't just see one of the lunch ladies' kids or something? You said yourself you weren't able to see his face clearly enough."

"He was standing *right there*, and his sister didn't even notice," Molly pressed. "He had that weird look, like he wasn't quite there. I've seen it enough now to know it."

Lindsay's heart froze in her chest.

*Drew. They're talking about Drew.*

Somehow, her arrival at the library just in time to hear Molly's comment didn't seem like a coincidence. In some odd corner of her heart, Lindsay wondered if her path had always been leading her here, as if befriending these two might be the reason she'd come to Idle County in the first place.

"I just can't get it out of my head," Molly continued. "I feel so bad for Lindsay—I mean, I want to say something to her, but she'd think I'm a freak."

"Probably already does," Elijah said.

Hiding among the library shelves, Lindsay blushed. Yes, she *was* one of those people who thought they were freaks—or had been until now, at least.

"I just hope they find his body," Molly said. "Whoever did that to him . . . unless it was an accident or something . . . it just makes me so mad and sad. I mean, his little face in that picture on TV, all smiling and stuff? And now he's dead. Life is just . . . so weird."

*They're talking about him like they know he's dead, too,* Lindsay thought. Her heart suddenly felt untethered from her body, and her breaths shortened as she grabbed the side of the bookshelf and looked at the floor. Tears dropped from her eyes like bullets and sank into the row's worn gray carpet. *But if they've also seen other ghosts, maybe it means—*

A hand touched Lindsay's shoulder. She flew around in sudden guilty surprise, sure that one of the Murderers had caught her eavesdropping. But it was the brown-haired librarian with thick glasses. How had she snuck upstairs without the main aisle's wood floor creaking under her?

"Are you all right?" the woman asked. "I noticed you were huddled back here and thought you might be lost."

Two rows over, Elijah Bryce's and Molly Butler's voices hushed.

"I'm fine," Lindsay muttered, wiping her tears.

"Crying in the Legal section? That seems pretty lost to me. Everything okay? Can I help you with anything? Talk?"

Lindsay adopted the most detached expression possible, even though her heart warmed at the librarian's offer to help.

"Nope, I was just leaving," she said. "Thanks, though."

She walked back toward the second floor's main aisle with long steps, trying to keep her round face from scrunching into tears again. It took all her willpower not to run.

When Lindsay passed the row with the stained glass window, she turned her face so that Molly and Elijah wouldn't see it. She rushed down the spiral staircase and toward the library doors, hoping they hadn't seen her ponytail and thick athletic legs—sure giveaways to her identity.

*The first time I venture out on my own, and it's a disaster,* she thought, stepping out into the cold day, which had become overcast. *Now I'll never figure out what I saw.*

And who was this supposed "raggedly dressed" woman Elijah Bryce was seeing? Another ghost wandering the world of the dead with Drew and Damon Jacoby?

Lindsay now realized that to even ask such a question put her very close to the brink of insanity. Perhaps even worse, she now knew that befriending the Murderers would also require her to admit a truth she feared more than any other: that she was just like them, and there was no going back.

Natalie Pent was seeing her again: the woman in rags. For the third time in two weeks, the figure was walking in the shaded strip of yard between the two houses across Windsong Road from Natalie's house, showing only her back as she moved east, toward the trail leading to the Moon Woods.

Except the woman wasn't real. She couldn't be.

Natalie closed her eyes and forced herself to think about the present moment:

*It's Friday, November 12.*

*Two months since the candlelight vigil.*

*I'm a senior at End Haven High.*

She opened her eyes again. The woman in rags was still there.

For the thousandth time since seeing her first ghost—that incident in 2006 she didn't like to think about—Natalie felt her mind falling through its own cracks.

*Does she want me to follow her to the Moon Woods?*

Since Natalie had no last hour of school—and no close friends to spend the free time with—she was home early, alone, feeling crippled by fears about what her lack of extracurricular activities might mean for her university prospects next year. After being cut from the dance squad last spring for smoking a joint on school grounds, all she seemed to have was free time and no future.

So why not waste it following this ghost?

*There. You said it. "Ghost."*

Natalie put on her favorite hot pink jacket and neon yellow running shoes, then stepped outside and began walking.

THE GRASS BETWEEN THE NEIGHBORS' houses across the street was frosted over and crunchy. As Natalie stepped past both houses, into their sprawling and conjoined backyards, a cold wind cut against her cheeks. Yes, the woman in rags was still there, veering south, toward the backyard that used to be Elijah Bryce's. She was indeed heading straight for the mile-long dirt path that led to Old Mill Road and the Moon Woods.

*Am I really doing this?*

Natalie closed her eyes. Breathed.

*Yes. Because I'm losing my mind.*

And where better to do that than alone in nature?

WITHIN FIVE MINUTES, she was on the path to Old Mill Road, surrounded by barren, leafless trees—mostly birches and spruces and small evergreens. Their branches clacked in the cold wind—the only sound apart from her own footsteps.

The woman up ahead of Natalie, still close enough to remain visible, seemed to stride atop a layer of silence. Natalie, in her own silence, followed.

Natalie was warm from the hike when she reached Old Mill Road. The woman in rags was already across the street, passing through the thin layer of trees preceding the Outer Ring, the halo of grassland surrounding the Moon Woods. Its dead straw-colored turf stretched another mile before hitting the forest's wall of massive pines.

Natalie had last ventured to the Moon Woods in July, during the group searches for the Idle County Seven. For the three days she volunteered, her search line had been focused on the east side of the forest, closest to the town of Blue Hill. The search groups, funded by Victor Zobel, Jillian Pope's famous stepfather, had of course uncovered nothing.

Now Natalie crossed Old Mill Road and tramped through the thin wall of trees preceding the Outer Ring. The sky above the expanse beyond was wide and large, offering one last mile of freedom before the forest swallowed the heavens completely.

Fighting the cold, ravaging wind, Natalie started across the long stretch of dead grass, watching it pass beneath her feet. After five minutes, she looked up just in time to see the mysterious, shabbily dressed woman disappear through the Moon Woods' domineering threshold: that wall of great pines.


When Natalie reached the trees, however, the woman was gone. First a hundred feet in, then two hundred, and then—nothing. Not even a hint that the ragged figure was anything more than a figment of her mind.

*Which I've completely lost*, Natalie thought. Yet her eyes were dry. Tearless. Sane.

Three hundred feet into the woods, Natalie reached the vertical slab of rock that Pauline Gilbert had once officially named "the Knoll." Its stone face stood chiseled through a ten-foot mound of earth that fell gracefully around its edges.

Today, it looked smaller than she remembered it. She had camped here with Alec, Pauline, and Elijah in the summer of 2004, mere weeks before a young Stone Ridge resident named Thomas Lumen had exposed a cult of men operating from a ramshackle chapel built deep in the forest. When word got out that the men had forced suicide upon Thomas's twin sister, Mary, and one other man—all in the name of carrying on "death studies" begun by a serial-killer priest from the 1940s—Idle County had suffered its first dark smear across national news headlines.

Natalie's overnight camping trip with her brother and friends also marked the night Alec had caught Elijah shining a flashlight onto his bare chest in their tent—a story Natalie herself had later perpetuated as gossip around school.

The memory was now particularly sad, because Elijah had been proud of that flashlight. It was made of metal and had his initials engraved on it—one of the few birthday gifts his long-gone adoptive father in Florida had sent him over the years.

*And now it's probably just gathering dust somewhere*, Natalie thought as she started climbing the Knoll.

Then she heard footsteps—muffled ones on the dead pine needles covering the forest floor.

*The woman in rags?*

Natalie rushed to the top of the Knoll and looked deeper into the Moon Woods.

There. Through the trees. Was it the ghost?

No. Just a large oddly shaped boulder.

*But maybe—*

"What the hell are you doing out here?" came a young man's voice from behind her.

Natalie's heart knew the voice before her mind did. The stress it induced clamped her chest like a vice grip as she turned to see its source: her twin brother, Alec, approaching through the trees.

"What the hell?" she hissed. "Are you following me?"

"I saw you walking through the backyards on my way home, and yeah, I was concerned. You've been acting weird lately."

"Oh. Sure. '*Concerned.*'"

"Jesus, Natalie. I'm not out to get you."

Alec climbed to the top of the Knoll. He looked around, completely oblivious to the reason Natalie had come here—clearly, he hadn't seen the mysterious woman in rags. The *ghost*.

Natalie scoffed and shook her head. Deflection was her only choice now, lest he think her insane.

Instead of taking the bait, he took a seat on the Knoll's front edge and dangled his feet over its vertical rock face. "God, remember this place? I don't think I've been here since we camped that night with Pauline and Elijah."

"Yeah, along with Elijah's famous flashlight."

Alec sat in silence.

"You always do that," she said.

"Do what?"

"Hold back whatever you're thinking and act all innocent. Like you had no role in any of it."

"Any of what? The Elijah-gay thing?"

"Yes. That. Everything." Memories whirled through Natalie's mind. They were all tinted gray now, like opportunities lost.

"*You* were the one who told everyone at school about that," Alec replied. "God, Natalie. Wake up."

"From what?"

"From the fact that you don't have to make everyone hate you." Alec shook his head, stood up, and started back down the side of the Knoll, talking the entire way. "Like, you've been pushing people away for the past few years now. You're not applying to any good colleges. And—God, I don't even know. It's like you're spiraling. It's not just me and Mom and Dad who've seen it. Your friends have, too."

"Maybe that would mean something if you hadn't started dating the only friend I had left!"

On the ground below her, Alec spun around. "Sarah and I are dating because *we like each other*. And you know what? I actually care about her. I don't just use her to prop myself up, like some sort of—"

"Like some sort of what, Alec? A bitch? Is that all I am now?"

"You said it, not me," he said, throwing up his arms. He turned on his left heel and began marching out of the Moon Woods in the same petulant way he'd always left their arguments, ever since childhood.

Yet so much had changed since then. Not only had she lost the people whose mutual friendship she'd destroyed, but she was also now seeing the dead. It was all related somehow. She was sure of it.

"I'm calling that reporter from Wind Prairie!" Natalie screamed after Alec. "I know Pauline and Elijah and the others didn't just drive to Dallas. The police are ignoring stuff that matters!"

Exasperated, her brother swung back around. "Ignoring *what*, Natalie? You're not a detective. You have *no idea* what happened to them or what the police do or don't know!"

"But Sarah said you saw them reading that—"

"Jesus—stop obsessing over that journal! You weren't even there! All that happened was Sarah and I walked by Clayton and Jillian and Pauline sitting at the Bean & Leaf. They were holding some old leather book. It could've been anything!"

"Yeah, well, Victor Zobel said he was going to bring it up to the police again, but they haven't even followed up."

"So, you think talking to that small-timer Alice Winterblume is going to solve the case? You're just making a fool of yourself. Let the police do their damned job."

"Yeah. Just like they did with that cult six years ago."

Alec shook his head, turned around, and kept marching. But then he stopped again and swung back toward Natalie, even more high and mighty than before. "It's like you *want* to be the center of attention in all this. Our friends are fucking *dead*, Natalie."

"And I want to find them!" she screamed. Frightening truths danced behind her eyes, things she could never admit to him: the ghosts she had seen, her crumbling mind, the possibility that she might be just as crazy as those missing kids.

Now Alec chuckled incredulously. "I'm sure if they were found, they wouldn't want it to be by *you*."

"What's that supposed to mean?" Natalie yelled.

"It means treating them like shit didn't do you any favors. You're not going to connect with anyone new until you grow the fuck up."

With that, he turned and walked back toward the Moon Woods' Outer Ring, leaving Natalie standing alone with her ghosts under the pine trees' swaying, clacking branches.

I N THE BRIEF MOMENT OF SILENCE after Natalie Pent said David Thorsen's name, David wondered: Could she possibly suspect that just moments ago, he had been pondering jumping off Evelyn Morrow's suicide cliff behind Saint Andrew's Grotto?

He felt naked now. Caught.

"Fancy meeting *you* here," Natalie said when he didn't immediately return her greeting. She wiped her tears and leaned against one of the maple trees lining the way back to the statue of Saint Andrew and the church parking lot below.

"Natalie Pent," David finally said. "Fancy meeting you as well." On instinct, he glanced down Natalie's athletic frame. Just a few years ago, she had been alarmingly thin—something Lindsay had once, in passing, attributed to a "quasi eating disorder." Tonight, the young woman looked perfectly able to hold her own in the world—fit and sharply focused, despite the tears in her eyes.

For a moment, they exchanged silence. The evening's deepening darkness defined the world around them.

"Funny place for someone your age to be on a Friday night," David said.

Natalie's gaze flitted toward the cliff. "Oh, you know. Needed to get away from the world. The usual."

"Apparently this is the place people go to do that." David gave her a wry smile. A second later, he reached back for the surface. "Aren't you in school these days? Last time I saw your dad, he said you were at the University of Minnesota."

"I was," Natalie said. "But some shit happened. I'm back here now."

"I'm sorry to hear. Is everything okay?"

Natalie grimaced. "What do *you* think?"

Her bluntness struck David right in the heart. She was grown now. Smart. No nonsense.

"Funny—I haven't seen you since that candlelight vigil," she continued, still leaning against the tree.

David checked his memory, and yes, she was right. He had last seen her—along with another of Lindsay's old friends—in Heart Park on September 10, 2010, after the candlelight memorial service for the Idle County Seven. The teens had been presumed dead at that point, and everyone, even David, had finally given up hope that they might ever be found alive.

"That night was a blur," he said. "I'm sorry I barely talked to you. There were so many people and reporters wanting a piece of us. The parents, I mean."

"Yeah, I saw you on the news afterward."

"Blabbering like an idiot, I'm sure."

"I remember thinking you sounded hopeful."

David chuckled. "I've been dialing the 'hopefulness' notch up for years. To keep other people feeling positive, probably."

For a moment, there was nothing else to say. Natalie shoulder-pushed herself off the tree and shrugged, letting out a somber "Hmm."

She strolled toward David in her unremarkable athletic clothes—black running tights and a hot-pink Northface jacket. Her hair, dyed a darker brown than it used to be (and now decorated with blond streaks), was pulled back in a messy knot behind her head. Despite her puffy eyes, she approached him with a gait that verged on daughterly, as if she were somehow relieved to see him. Gone was the uncomfortably flirtatious air David had always sensed from her. Perhaps it had simply offered her a safe space during those formative years—an emotional wall barricading a lack of self esteem.

*Just like the walls we all build*, he thought.

As if to crash through them, Natalie now took a seat next to David, dangling her feet over the cliff's edge. "You know some woman killed herself up here, right?" She swung her legs with metronome cadence, each a mirror of the other.

"Yeah, I heard that once or twice."

For the first time tonight, Natalie held his gaze. "Is that why you're here?"

David's heart suddenly went from heightened beating to outright pounding. Yet Natalie only chuckled and shook her head.

"Trust me. You're not the only person who thinks about this place more than they should."

David's throat was cottony dry, tightening more and more with every heartbeat. His nose suddenly wasn't giving him enough air, so he opened his mouth for breath. "I've probably been coming here more than I should lately," he said. "I don't really know why. It's complicated, I guess."

Instead of offering him a maudlin gasp or a hand on his shoulder, Natalie squinted her eyes in a half wince, half smile, then looked out over the wooded area below. A few blocks beyond them lay the houses of central End Haven. From up here, they looked miniature in a way that reminded David of his childhood Matchbox cars and cities.

His gaze fell upon the spot where the Lemon Avenue Library used to stand, before the city tore it down. Lindsay had grown to love that place shortly after meeting Molly Butler and Elijah Bryce. That had been around the same time she and Natalie stopped being friends.

"What ever happened between you and my daughter?" he asked. "I was never really able to pry it out of her."

Natalie kept looking out at the woods and neighborhoods beyond but stopped swinging her feet. "There was some stuff that happened. Back after Drew disappeared and all that. I was at the height of my queen-bee-bitch phase, and it all kind of blew up in English class one day."

"English class?"

"With Ms. Olson—the cool lesbian teacher, remember? I heard she moved to Oregon a few years ago, but you probably had conferences with her."

Ms. Olson. Yes. The slightly jowly yet supportive face he had met at a parent-teacher conference the year Drew was murdered. She was the one who'd given Lindsay a brochure advertising the ghost symposium at Benedict Wise University in 2006—the event where Molly Butler seemingly feigned her first meeting with Max Pope.

"I do remember her, actually," David said. "She helped Lindsay get through that first winter after we lost Drew."

"What a crappy-ass year," Natalie replied. "God, I was such an idiot back then."

The moon continued to rise in front of them. They sat silently and watched it until the young woman edged back toward daughterly warmth.

"Funny coincidence you ended up being here," she said.

"I'm not sure I believe in coincidences."

"But were you planning on jumping tonight?"

For a second, David's answer stalled in his throat. Then: "Yes. Maybe."

"Why?"

David suddenly realized he was holding his breath. He purged it now with a massive sigh. "The whole laundry list. No kids. No real life. I don't know why I even bother to pretend I want to be here anymore."

"I was going to say, I'm surprised you're still in Idle County. I'd have thought you and Mrs. Thorsen would've moved by now."

"No, I mean *here* here," David said, waving his hand at the night sky and the universe beyond. "The only thing keeping me alive is all the stuff Lindsay and her friends talked about."

"Ghosts?"

"And the possibility that life might . . . I don't know . . . have some sort of purpose."

"Maybe there's nothing at all after we die," Natalie said. "Maybe it's just relief."

"Ha. But if you're not around to feel it, what's the point?"

Natalie frowned. They sat together for another minute, watching the rising moon, before she continued in a meeker voice than before. "I don't really believe there's nothing."

"I don't either."

"It's this place," Natalie whispered, gesturing with her neck toward the trees and houses below.

A chill touched David's neck. "What do you mean by that?"

Once again, the young woman's eyes began misting over. She brought her feet up to the cliff's edge, then pressed her lips together as if she were about to form some pointed word. Then she scrunched her face into something resembling agony. "It's something here in Idle County. All the death and drama. I don't even know why I came back." Her expression teetered as if she were attempting to out-smile a rush of grief, but a tear dripped down her cheek just the same. "Fuck, who am I kidding? I'll probably never live anywhere else."

"Can I ask what happened at the U of M?"

Natalie's eyes narrowed as she gave David the saddest half smile he'd ever seen. "Quite frankly, Mr. Thorsen, I wouldn't expect any straight male to understand what happened to me at school."

For a second, David simply sat there, confused. Then his mind filled in the details Natalie wasn't explicitly telling him. His heart broke as he immediately glanced back at the trees and houses in the distance.

"I was trying to get a date with this guy for all the usual reasons," Natalie said, wiping her tear. "Star goalie of the Gophers hockey team. Mansion on Lake Minnetonka. All that bullshit." She scoffed and shook her head. "He took me out on his parents' boat, and everything started out normally. But then it got rough. I told him to stop, and he didn't. Men are from Mars, women are from Venus, right? I guess I invited it to happen. I should have known better."

Tears formed in David's eyes. All he wanted was to put an arm around Natalie, to hug her and comfort her and tell her that no, it wasn't her fault, and it never would be. But of course he couldn't offer any uninvited physical contact or opinions.

Trapped in his good intentions, he simply listened. For the first time in years, he no longer felt alone.

Natalie wiped a single tear off her cheek. "My parents think I just got super depressed and needed to come home. My friend Jamie said I should say something to the administration at the U of M, but that seems like more drama than it's worth." Natalie barely even faked her next chuckle. "I guess I should just buck up and realize that I'm not the only person this has happened to. But people on the news who 'come forward' or whatever? They make it look so easy."

David thought of the people who had violated and killed his own children—how simple it had been for them to make Drew's and Lindsay's lives disappear. Now he felt a similar sort of rage for this hockey-goalie rapist. "Nobody should have to go through that, Natalie," he said. "And I'm so sorry. I wish I could—"

"Comfort me?" Natalie said. "I'm not even sure that's possible.

Unless you can, like, download me some self-confidence." The smile that crossed her face now was genuine. "Or find me a Reset button. I have no idea what I'm going to do. My dad is making me get a job if I'm not going back to school."

"I'll check at Steelhead to see if they have any openings," David said, his heart suddenly lighting up with enthusiasm to help. "I know the human resources team was looking to hire a new assistant."

Natalie turned her head and looked him in the eye. "Really?"

"Really. I'll ask tomorrow."

"Well—thanks. I'd like that. But you realize that presupposes you're *not* going to jump off this cliff tonight, right?"

Now David laughed. "You can hold me to it. Maybe this is why people stay alive. To have random, meaningful interactions."

"Mrs. Thorsen doesn't give you any random, meaningful interactions these days?"

There it was again: Natalie's bluntness—and a taste of the flirtatious air she used to display around him. Now, however, it felt like a lens focusing on all the cracks in David's crumbling life.

"Honestly, I don't think she even likes me anymore," he said. "I sometimes think I'd be doing her a favor now by removing myself from the equation." He gestured with his neck toward the cliff.

"But that doesn't fix anything for *you*," Natalie said.

Her chastising tone made him blush. "I never thought in a million years that I'd be stuck wondering what life even *is*, but . . . Christ. It feels crazy."

"It's this place," Natalie said for the second time tonight.

Finally, David sensed what she meant. It was something about *here*.

Fierce intellect blazed in the young woman's eyes. "Like, has anyone really sat down and talked about the fact that *all* the Idle County Seven kids believed in ghosts and psychic stuff, or were somehow connected to people who were obsessed with those ideas?"

"Do *you* believe in ghosts?" David asked, leaning toward her.

Natalie immediately clamped her mouth shut. Realizing his face had moved uncomfortably close to hers, he pulled back.

"No—I mean, not really," Natalie said, blushing. "I've just—I've seen some weird things here and there. Honestly, it's nothing."

"I'm betting it's not. I've seen stuff myself, I think."

The young woman looked into his eyes for a fleeting moment, then said, "Well, the first time for me—it was just something weird I saw. The night Lindsay got taken to that abandoned mine, actually—the February after Drew disappeared."

Natalie clasped her hands together around her knees and slowly began rocking. David waited.

"I know Lindsay and all the others were interested in ghosts or whatever, but this wasn't that." Now shaking, she looked David square in the eyes. "That night she was taken, I woke up around 11:30 and saw her standing at the foot of my bed. Like she was right there, except I knew she wasn't. She was too bright—too *visible*—for how dark the room was. And then later I found out she was kidnapped by that Lowell Grendel creep and almost died." The mist in Natalie's eyes had become heavy again. "I've never told anyone I saw her. I can't believe I'm telling *you* of all people."

As if on cue, David burst into tears. Natalie's hand immediately went to his shoulder, and her own tears—gleaming with both relief and uncertainty—began streaming down her face.

"I saw Lindsay that night, too," David whispered. "She and my wife and the police were the only ones who ever knew about it, because there was something else we all decided to keep under wraps."

Natalie waited for David to find words.

"Did you ever read the news articles about how they found Lindsay?"

"You mean the helicopter pilot? Didn't he see her shining a flashlight up from the woods or whatever?"

David nodded. "The thing we never told anyone was that she didn't have that flashlight with her when she went into the mine. She told us later that when the mine collapsed, she left her body and took it from Elijah Bryce's bedroom."

Natalie stared at him. More tears crept down her face. Between David's and her whispers floated all they had lost in life, along with all they were gaining by confiding in each other on this exact night, at this exact moment. And just as David wondered again if their chance encounter might be more than mere coincidence, Natalie scrunched her face into a new expression as if she had just made some unforeseen connection.

"Okay, this is going to sound weird," she said, "but . . . have you ever seen the woman in rags?"

# PART 3

# TACONITE ROSE

L OWELL GRENDEL LOOKED AT HIS photo print again. Yes, the figure made of light was indeed showing up. It was a woman, he thought—somewhat dumpy and old-fashioned looking, clad in what appeared to be a ragged dress covered by a threadbare jacket. As usual, her face and all but a vague form of her body were obscured by overexposed white as if she were exuding her own luminescence.

He had shot this photo in his bedroom the night he killed Drew Thorsen, while this woman—this *ghost*—was screaming in his face. Now she visited him regularly, flickering in and out of his perception like a huntress, a vampire waiting to feed on his guilt. And her face— my *God*, her face. It was made of rage.

Drew Thorsen's name, now famous around Minnesota from the news, echoed between Lowell's ears every waking second of every single day, tingling like sparkle-dusted guilt. He wondered: Would the Idle County Sheriff's Department and FBI identify him as a suspect? Had he been careful enough? Would he get away with this murder like he had the others? Perhaps it had been stupid for him to take the boy so soon after arriving in Idle County.

But those orbs. The boy had positively glowed under them.

The night of the murder, as Lowell had wrapped himself in blankets to hide from the raggedly dressed woman (who couldn't be hidden from, he found out; she still found her way under the blankets), he remembered a name from the internet—one he had seen while researching Idle County before uprooting himself from California.

*Taconite Rose.*

There were just four online references to Rose Margaret Layton. From what Lowell could gather, she had been a poverty-stricken woman living in Arrowhead Hills, Minnesota—now a ghost town—in the 1950s, and she had disappeared near an abandoned taconite mine while searching for her missing son, Samuel. While the police's official story remained steady—that Rose had never returned to her studio apartment after leaving it on September 26, 1959—they received multiple sighting reports about her as the years passed. Each one shared the same detail: that Rose was always wearing a long faded dress and threadbare jacket—an ensemble other mothers around town had often mocked her for.

As the story went, only three people claimed to have seen Rose's ghostly face. One was Carter Van Ness, the man she'd suspected of kidnapping her son. According to nurses at Wind Prairie Hospital, where Mr. Van Ness died in 1979, he had, on his deathbed, called out over and over that he was seeing Rose and that she was "finally showing him her face."

The next person was Anne McGree-Willis, a deranged housewife who strangled her three children in 1982 in Deadwood, a town on the opposite side of the Moon Woods. Before killing herself, she wrote a note claiming that "Taconite Rose had watched her kill the children."

The third reported sighting of Rose's face had been right here in

End Haven, by a juvenile probation officer named Bob Hudgings. Prior to his suicide in 1993, he adamantly claimed to have seen Taconite Rose's face four times, though nobody ever chronicled how or why.

*And now she's facing me*, Lowell thought, staring at his newest photo print.

He clothespinned it to the drying line in his basement darkroom. The room's red light, as always, rendered the photo's two dimensions even flatter—a series of bloody lights and darks.

Anxiety twirled in the pit of Lowell's stomach. He knew that this woman, despite being dead, had seen him. Had found him out.

He stood back to look at his work: twenty-five photo prints, all shot over the last three days, hanging to dry. And yes, each one showed the same figure: Taconite Rose, the woman in rags.

**2005**

I n the two weeks leading up to Thanksgiving, Lindsay Thorsen saw her brother's ghost three times. The first time, she was exiting the front doors of End Haven Middle School, walking toward her mother's black Chevy Tahoe. Drew was standing right there, in front of it. The second time, she was unscrewing a lid of peanut butter in their kitchen after kickboxing, and Drew was sitting on the granite countertop, watching her. The third time, she woke up in bed at 2:15 a.m., exactly in line with the numbers of Drew's birthday on February 15. He was standing in front of her face at the side of the bed.

"I'm hiding! Come and find me!" he whispered in the darkness, with a giggle.

All three times, Lindsay blinked once, and he was still there. After she blinked twice, he was gone.

THEN CAME THE ISSUE of Molly Butler and Elijah Bryce. If they had recognized her at the Lemon Avenue Library on November 5, they weren't showing it. Lindsay's fear of losing her place in Natalie Pent's friend circle kept her from approaching the Murderers, but every time she failed to laugh at a joke during lunch, make fun of school losers, or gawk at Natalie's stories of "dry humping," the girls noticed.

"Have fun at kickboxing tonight," Natalie said with a sneer on Monday, November 21, three days before Thanksgiving. Lindsay had just defended Pauline Gilbert—without any subtlety—after Natalie had commented on how big the girl's hips were getting. When Natalie walked away without so much as a goodbye, Lindsay surprised herself by not caring at all.

AFTER SCHOOL, Lindsay came home to a sore sight: her grandparents on her mother's side, the insufferable GeeMa and GeePa Mills. Amicably divorced, they had arrived from Palm Springs earlier that afternoon in separate rental cars.

Lindsay, sensing her mother had already told GeeMa and GeePa about her supposed "Drew sightings," hid in her room until 5:45 p.m., when it was time to leave for kickboxing. On her way out the door, GeeMa stopped her while holding a martini.

"Honey, you have got to do something about those thighs of yours! They're getting huge. I'd be careful of doing boy sports if I were you."

Lindsay could have jabbed GeeMa in the nose. How was it that a woman of sixty-seven was still as immature and rude as Natalie Pent?

GeePa, who was in the family room making business-related small talk with David, seemed purposefully to be avoiding discussing Drew's disappearance. David, consequently, was letting his father-in-law do all the talking, as if, for the first time in his life, he would rather be discussing the elephant in the room—or at least the missing one.

When Lindsay asked her father to drive her to the community center, he seemed relieved to escape GeePa's surface banter.

"God, was I one of those people?" David asked as they left the driveway.

"I don't know. Were you?" Lindsay answered with a grin.

David shook his head in a way that mimicked a bird ruffling its feathers. "Maybe it'll be better when Grandma Thorsen gets here."

"I wouldn't be surprised if it gets worse," Lindsay said.

Grandma Thorsen, David's mother, would be arriving tomorrow to even things out. Unlike the grandparents on Sandra's side, Grandma Thorsen was as down to earth as they came. She lived modestly on the generous nest egg left by Lindsay's grandpa Nikan, never rambled on about fabulous material objects, and always wore jewelry that was minimalist and classy—never gaudy.

"Grandma Thorsen's never said it, but I'm pretty sure she can't stand your mother's side of the family," David continued as they crossed into central End Haven.

"Yeah, well, I think they're still mad at her for explaining what the Potawatomi Trail of Death was."

"Ha. True. She did always pride herself on being a White ally."

"Does Mom ever talk about that kind of stuff?"

"You mean White people killing Indians? Or ignorance?"

"Both, I guess."

David sighed. "Oh, you know. Your mom doesn't like talking about serious things."

"Maybe that's why Grandma Thorsen doesn't like her," Lindsay said.

At this, David only scrunched his nose upward, forced a smile as if Lindsay had been joking, and drove on in silence.



KICKBOXING KICKED ASS.

"Good job, Thorsen! Get in there, but watch those uppercuts!"

Lindsay stepped to the side just in time to avoid Clay Mason's punch. There was nothing but her and the fight, and this time, she was winning. She aimed a kick at the side of Clay's leg and hit it square on the side of the knee. He faltered for a moment—just long enough for her to test out her strengthening left hook. Not too bad.

Clay was short but meaty, and just as with all the other boys except Alan Sparks, Lindsay had to work to piss him off and get him to hit her. Once he started trying, she dodged all but two of his attacks. She could tell he was getting tired of missing.

"Ten seconds!" Coach Martinez yelled.

*Concentrate, don't let him get in there, get in when he pulls the punch back—*

She blocked a kick.

*Five seconds.*

Then a punch.

"Four . . . three . . . two . . . one . . . Way to go, Thorsen!"

Lindsay let her arms down, then bent over and watched the blue floor mat whirl as she caught her breath.

"Now, everyone gather around for a second!" Coach Martinez yelled. He checked his watch, then turned to the group with an encouraging smile. "As you know, this is an open class, but seeing as we haven't had too many newbies show up for a while, I've been thinking that we should have a tournament, most likely early next year—February or March."

A wave of intimidation washed over Lindsay while most of the boys around her started laughing and punching each other's shoulders with anticipation. Only when she looked up from the floor did she notice Alan Sparks from the corner of her eye. He was standing very still with his arms crossed, staring right at her.

"Now, all of you are welcome to do this tournament, girl included." Coach Martinez winked at Lindsay. "Can't promise that these boys' competitive natures won't get the best of them, though, so Lindsay, you're welcome to sit this one out if you want."

At this, Lindsay almost growled.

"We'll only do it the last thirty minutes of our Wednesday classes for maybe four weeks. So, yeah. Get ready for that. And Phil, go shower right now. You forgot to wear deodorant, and you stink."

"I did too wear deodorant!" Phil yelled against jeers from the other boys. "But whatever, I'll shower. . . ." As he walked away, he said with a guffaw, "Hope I don't see any ghosts in there!"

Lindsay's heart sank to her stomach as Phil's group of friends laughed and stared at her. Before she could figure out a proper retort, somebody did it for her—and in a deathly serious voice.

"Hey, shut the hell up," Alan Sparks said to Phil. "Don't make fun of her." It was an order, spoken with a level of social authority that put Lindsay's own to shame. Her heart, despite burning in her stomach bile, fluttered.

Alan glanced at her again, then walked ahead of the other boys to the men's locker room. As Lindsay hustled toward the women's, a burst of clarity surged through her. No matter that her little brother was missing, dead, and a ghost. No matter that her parents were manufacturing knife-cuttable tension with every breath they took. No matter that GeeMa Mills and Natalie Pent didn't understand her. Right now, in the glow of Alan's social support, life was good.

When Lindsay walked into English class on the Wednesday before Thanksgiving, she immediately noticed Molly Butler sitting in her usual corner, quietly reading a small paperback. As Lindsay took her own seat next to Natalie Pent, she avoided eye contact with both of them.

"So, we're finally discussing essay structure today," their teacher, Ms. Olson, began as everyone got settled. Ms. Olson was the coolest teacher in school—a funny, out-and-proud lesbian who liked to teach this Advanced English class her own way, regardless of the school's suggested curriculum.

In the three months since school had been in session, Lindsay and her classmates had received homework only four times. Their first assignment had been the most interesting: Ms. Olson had tasked them with making large paper collages that reflected who they were as people. In the weeks since, class hours were spent in discussion, usually starting out relating to English but always digressing into completely unrelated topics, often ones associated with bigger life issues. Lindsay suspected it was Ms. Olson's way of grooming their debate skills.

"Okay, time to calm down," the woman said. "I know our final essays are still a few months off, but you all need to be thinking now about what your topics are going to be. Come January, we're going to start delving into research, which you'll mostly be doing in your spare time. And you thought I was never going to assign homework. Ha!"

Most of the students groaned, but Lindsay smiled.

"You've had an easy year thus far," Ms. Olson said. "But next spring, we're going to be doing persuasive essays—college-level writing, college-level research, and college-level critical thinking. So, your homework tonight is to figure out a topic you'd enjoy persuading somebody else to believe in. You've got two months to come up with something. Should be enough time to finish the assignment, don't you think?" Ms. Olson chuckled.

Lindsay sat in the middle of the classroom. To her immediate left was Natalie, who was giggling and whispering something to Jacob Jenkins. Apart from being good looking, Jacob had quickly become popular for his unmatched soccer skills after transferring from Saint Andrew's School. Everyone now knew he had asked Natalie out and been turned down, and today, he seemed to be doing his best to ignore her.

Ms. Olson butted into Natalie's giggles by stepping right up to her desk and peering downward. "Is something funny, Miss Pent?" The woman's baggy sweater and hole-torn jeans clashed with Natalie's polished fashion sense. "Come on, share it. No secrets in here. Why all the laughs?"

"Nothing. We were just . . . talking about the collages," Natalie said, glancing at the ceiling.

"Which one?" Ms. Olson stuck her hands in her pockets and looked up. Her six regular English classes had taken up all the wall space, so the Advanced English class's art had been relegated to the ceiling.

"The one with the ghosts and butterflies on it," Natalie said.

Ms. Olson's eyes narrowed. She sauntered back to the front of the classroom. "I happen to like that collage a lot," she said. "Who does that one belong to again?" She scanned the room, and her eyes landed on the far right row. "Ahh, that's right. Molly Bubbly Butler. Why the ghosts and butterflies, Molly?"

Jacob, still blushing, turned toward Molly and gave her a sympathetic look. Molly kept looking at Ms. Olson, however. Her quiet presence now drew an unprecedented amount of attention.

"You never did explain that part of the collage," Ms. Olson pressed.

A few chuckles skittered across the classroom, but Molly nodded in fairness. When she spoke, it was matter-of-fact. "It's because my mom died a couple years ago. She liked butterflies."

The chuckles immediately stopped. Lindsay glanced from Molly to Natalie. Behind Natalie, Jacob had turned forward again and was weaving his fingers in and out of each other.

Ms. Olson nodded, then formed a question that could have sounded happy-go-lucky if it didn't come out so serious. "Do you believe in ghosts, then?"

Lindsay's heart raced for Molly. People already hated the girl for having been with Damon Jacoby at the time of his apparent suicide; surely the attention Ms. Olson was now bringing to her would make things worse. At the Lemon Avenue Library, Molly had mentioned knowing Jacob, but Lindsay had never seen them talk, even in English class. The girl was practically alone here.

"Yeah, I believe in ghosts," Molly said after a long pause.

Ms. Olson raised her eyebrows. "Have you ever seen one?"

"I think. Maybe."

"You didn't tell us about your mom when you presented your collage," Ms. Olson said. "I'm sorry to hear she passed away. I'm also sorry we haven't heard more from you over the past three months. I think there are some immature kids in this class who might benefit from getting to know you." In her peripheral vision, Lindsay saw Natalie sink down, into her desk chair. Then Ms. Olson turned toward the rest of the room. "How many of the rest of you believe in ghosts?"

About a third of the students raised their hands, including Jacob Jenkins. Most went up slowly, as if weighed down by embarrassment. Bettina Knoblock, a tall curly-haired girl with freckles, blurted out, "My dad said he saw one in our attic once!"

"My mom saw her dead grandma at the foot of her bed, the night before she gave birth to my little brother," Eric Quigley followed up.

"I think I saw one once," Ariel Hendricks said. "It was some weird guy dressed in black, and he was standing in the corner of a grocery store in Stone Ridge. It was back when my dad still lived there. He just didn't look right, and nobody else was noticing him."

After a mild lull, Ms. Olson asked, "Anyone else?" A spark of excitement had lit up her face. Thankfully, Molly Butler appeared to be off the hook, because all the more popular kids had chimed in their two cents. "Lindsay Thorsen, how about you?"

Hot blood rushed to Lindsay's face. "I'm not sure," she said quietly.

"Come on, you're probably the second quietest person in this class," Ms. Olson pushed. "It's always Bettina or Natalie or those goober boys in the back corner doing all the talking. Please reveal to us your insights."

Lindsay's heart now skirted the edge of panic. All she felt was the black hole of Drew's absence, underscored by the ever-growing sense that she was losing her mind by believing his ghost had visited her.

"Hey, she might not want to talk about this," Natalie piped up. "You know . . . considering . . . ?"

Ms. Olson's eyes widened as she made the connection.

"Oh God, Lindsay. I didn't realize this might have implications on what you're going through. I totally spaced on that. I'm so sorry."

"It's okay," Lindsay replied, somehow more annoyed with Natalie for turning the discussion into an issue.

But Natalie couldn't keep her mouth shut. "No, it's not okay. Lindsay shouldn't have to be put on the spot like this. She needs support right now, not everyone staring at her and talking about depressing things like dead people!"

Before Lindsay could glare at Natalie for once again playing the martyr and good friend, Molly Butler's voice shot out from across the room. "Depressing things like dead people? First off, you're the one who started this conversation, because you were laughing at my collage. And second, have you ever known anybody who died? I mean anybody close to you?"

"I knew *Damon Jacoby*," Natalie said, sneering through the dead boy's name.

Ms. Olson watched the two girls' interaction silently, tending to each word like a shepherd to sheep under an approaching storm.

"Yeah, but were you actually friends with him?" Molly the Murderer asked. Now that Damon Jacoby's name was being thrown around, everyone in the room was staring at her.

"He and my brother played baseball together," Natalie said as if that ended the conversation.

Molly chuckled. "Then you probably didn't know him at all. You probably thought it was too depressing to think about the sad things in life, like the fact that both his parents died of AIDS when he was a kid. And you probably didn't even notice that he had a bunch of psychological issues."

"What's your point?" Natalie snapped.

Molly continued in a respectful tone that elicited pensive gazes from the other students. "My point is that you say we shouldn't talk about 'depressing things like dead people' or Lindsay's brother, Drew, even though that's what everyone's thinking about right now. And I know from experience that it doesn't work to bottle feelings up. When you say that talking about dead people is depressing, you might as well be saying that about my mom. Or Damon Jacoby. Or anybody else people might have loved at some point. I don't think anyone can know how that feels until they've really experienced death."

Everybody stared at Molly except Lindsay and Jacob. The room was quiet enough to hear a pin drop.

Ms. Olson, beaming with pride at Molly, finally took back the conversation's reins. "Molly, I agree with you one hundred percent. My dad died when I was fourteen, and I loved him so much that it still rips me apart every day. The sad thing is, I don't believe in heaven or an afterlife. And yeah, I know this is approaching a discussion about religion in a public school, but you're all old enough to know I'm not trying to preach." Ms. Olson looked around the class, her hands in her jean pockets.

"So, you don't believe in ghosts?" Molly asked.

"I might change my mind if I ever see one," Ms. Olson replied. "But right now, I think that once we're dead, we're gone. There's no evidence to suggest otherwise."

Molly accepted this with a nod. Lindsay, now having seen Drew's ghost, knew this was one area where Ms. Olson didn't have all the answers.

"Okay, back to essay structure," the woman said with a slight smile, obviously having enjoyed seeing Molly peacefully settle the debate with Natalie. "How many of you have ever heard of a thesis statement?"

A discussion of essay terms ensued until class ended forty minutes later. When the bell rang, Natalie stomped out of the room ahead of everyone else. Lindsay stared at the floor as she got up and walked toward the door. Just as she reached it, however, she nearly collided with someone.

It was Molly Butler.

Their eyes met, and for a moment, a type of comfort—or perhaps emotional recognition of some sort—fluttered between them.

"Hi," Molly said first.

"Hi," Lindsay replied.

Students rushed past them on their trajectories to escape school and catch their buses home. For Lindsay and Molly, however, time stopped.

And then they both smiled.

NATALIE PENT STOOD ALONE in the Moon Woods, atop the Knoll where she had once played with her brother, Alec, and their now-missing neighbors, Elijah Bryce and Pauline Gilbert. She inwardly cursed Alec. And Sarah Brownie. And Victor Zobel. And hell, even Victor Zobel's snaky, tattooed friend, Raphael Dumont. They were all letting whatever crime had happened last July slip into the realm of forever-mystery.

*And fuck Idle Goddamned County*, she added, turning on her feet to face the forest's depths once more.

The woman in rags was standing there again, in the trees. As always, she was facing away from Natalie.

*She's not real. She can't be.*

But the ghost was just two hundred feet away, next to the large boulder Natalie had noticed right before Alec had come strutting after her into the Moon Woods, when all she wanted was to be alone, alone, alone.

As Natalie's eyes adjusted once again to the sight of someone who wasn't there, the woman began walking. She was moving deeper into the forest.

*Where are you leading me?* Natalie thought at her.

The response came like a whisper from the slow, ethereal, and overtly false vision.

*To answers, my dear.*

Since Natalie's feet were already carrying her forward, she continued on, past the point where anyone outside the Moon Woods would be able to find her, were she to cry for help.

TODAY, SHE DISCOVERED something new: that the forest had a trail of boulders leading toward its center like bread crumbs. Each new boulder was visible, at least in daylight, if she stood next to the one previous. As the woman in rags began moving faster and Natalie began jogging to keep up, she realized the cloudy day above her was getting darker.

*No hat. No food. No water. What are you doing?*

She ignored the voice. No matter that her hands and ears were freezing or that the sun would be down in three hours or that she'd have to backtrack the same number of miles to her house. If she disappeared, Alec would at least have a clue where to start looking. She also had a compass app on her new iPhone; perhaps in a dire emergency, it would get her out of here.

As she walked, Natalie further learned that silence ruled the Moon Woods. The trees were its only sign of life; there were no birds, squirrels, or autumn creatures of any kind. More than once, she stopped to stand and embrace the total solitude.

Somehow, she was at peace here. The trees blocked much of the afternoon's biting wind, and with each step farther toward the forest's center, the ghost leading her way became more and more real, more and more normal. This was reality. This was the right path.

ONE HOUR PASSED. Then two. From boulder to boulder Natalie walked, following the woman in rags, and with each passing minute, the November sky grew darker and darker.

NEAR WHAT HAD TO BE the Moon Woods' center, the trail of boulders ended at a long rocky ravine. It stretched like a gash through the forest floor, which had gradually transitioned from flat to hilly with each passing mile. Perhaps it made sense: Idle County's terrain generally grew more and more dramatic the closer one got to the blue-spruce-covered bluff on the eastern side of Blue Hill. What struck Natalie now, however, was how strange it was to have spent her whole life next to this vast forest without actually knowing what lay inside it.

*I wonder if that priest's chapel is still standing*, she thought, remembering back to 2004, when news headlines about the serial-killer cleric, Simon Villard, spread across Minnesota. Accompanying the story had been photos of the man's small wooden structure near the center of the Moon Woods. According to police, Villard had paid impoverished men to help him build the chapel in the 1930s, before starting his decade-long murder spree and burying over fifty bodies in a nearby spread of land. Tingles crept down the back of Natalie's neck as she realized it had all happened *right here*. Villard himself had allegedly vanished and never been found, but as recently as 2004, a cult of local townsmen had been following what they believed was his ghost, killing two people in the process.

Now Natalie was following her own apparition. True, she had never kept up with Idle County's local ghost stories, but she wondered:

Had this woman in rags been one of Simon Villard's victims, or was she someone else altogether, unrelated to Idle County's biggest time-buried drama?

The woman stopped at the edge of the rocky ravine, with her back to Natalie.

Panting from thirst and exhaustion, Natalie slowly approached her. Above them, the great pines' branches clacked in the wind sailing across the sky.

One step.

Two steps.

Three. The ghost was almost close enough to touch.

The details of the woman's ragged outfit—a threadbare jacket over a long dirty dress—became more muddled with each passing step, as if close proximity to her were somehow repelling Natalie's sense of sight.

*You're going crazy. Get the hell out of here.*

The woman flickered in Natalie's mind.

*Go go go, get out of here, get—*

But Natalie had to touch the woman's jacket. Or her graying hair. Or her hunched shoulders. Because that would offer proof that—

A rock caught on Natalie's foot.

*Jesus fuck—*

She tumbled forward, over the edge of the ravine. For the half second it took for her reflexes to kick in, she was normal again, sane, and facing the reality that there were jagged rocks in front of her, strewn in a steep decline at least twenty feet into the ravine.

*Oh God, oh God, oh God—*

Three feet down, midtumble, her hands found the only slab within reach that was angled properly to support her. Her left wrist twisted as it slammed into the rock's mossy surface, bracing her just enough to prevent her face from also slamming into it. Pain exploded in her right leg as her shin hit the sharp edge of a smaller rock jutting up from below.

The larger slab moved under Natalie's hands. Without even thinking, she pushed herself off it, lifting her bad leg out just in time to step right, at an angle, onto yet another rock. When it held her weight, she hopped onto it and, panting, righted herself.

*There. Breathe. And don't fucking move.*

Natalie looked left and right. The woman in rags was gone—no hint of her in any direction. A creek cut through the ravine's shallow rocky basin, probably moving east to west. Natalie grabbed her iPhone and opened the compass app.

*Nope. North-south.*

Her ankle suddenly shuddered, and with a whimper, she took another step down, toward the creek, before turning back to make sure the ravine edge was still reachable. Yes—the rocks would be easy enough to climb. But *God*, the pain in her shin shot like a ray through the bone. It throbbed enough to bring on tears.

The sweat on Natalie's ears had begun to freeze in the evening's chill. Above her, the sky was losing light.

*Okay, time to get out of here. If it's too dark to follow the boulders back, then—*

Something up ahead, deeper in the ravine, caught her eye. A glint of blue.

On her bad leg, Natalie balanced her way farther down, toward a muddy spot between two triangular rocks. She looked closer, taking a moment to discern the blue fleck's size and shape.

It was a candy wrapper. Bright aqua blue.

She dug into the dirt and pulled it out. There, on the face of the wrapper, were language symbols she recognized but didn't understand.

หวาน

The wrapper was from one of the small coconut-pineapple candies in the host-podium bowl at Tickle Me Thai, End Haven's only Thai restaurant. These had been Natalie's favorite candies ever since the restaurant opened—partly because she associated them with those special nights when her parents splurged on takeout. She had often been jealous of Lindsay Thorsen, whose lazy mother, Sandra, ordered takeout from the restaurant at least twice a week.

*Lindsay Thorsen.*

Hadn't Lindsay once grabbed a secret handful of these candies when she and Natalie accompanied Sandra Thorsen to Tickle Me Thai on their way back to Lindsay's house for a sleepover?

*"So we can eat them all night,"* Lindsay had said with a snarky grin.

Natalie's pulse quickened.

Yet to presume this Thai candy wrapper had been Lindsay's would only prove her brother, Alec, correct: that her amateurish sleuthing inclinations were both presumptuous and absurd. Surely other people who liked these candies had been to this ravine. Hell, the wind could have blown the wrapper here.

Natalie pocketed it, noting suddenly how hungry she was.

She turned and climbed out of the ravine as dusk's chill fell upon her. Her leg throbbed as she peered back into the dimming forest, hoping to find the boulders that marked the way out. She had at least six miles to walk before hitting the outer edge of the Moon Woods.

As she navigated the pain in her leg, wondering if she would make it out alive (and sensing for the first time what it might feel like to go missing), a strange feeling clouded her vision. At first, lightheadedness accompanied it, and then tingles rushed down her neck.

Except the tingles came as visuals. *Colors.*

Then Natalie's mind burst open, and everything in front of her went white.

A	T 3:36 P.M. ON THANKSGIVING DAY, in the middle of a very quiet and careful family dinner, the Thorsen family's landline phone rang. Lindsay's father, David, started to rise from his seat, but she was closer to the phone and got there first.

"Thorsen residence," she said.

"Hi, Lindsay. This is Detective Rhymes with the Idle County Sheriff's Department. May I speak with your father, please?"

Lindsay's heart jumped in her chest.

She glanced past GeeMa and GeePa to meet the concerned gaze of Grandma Thorsen, who had arrived yesterday, despite her less-than-glowing feelings about the Thanksgiving holiday. After a fleeting moment of eye contact, Lindsay brought the cordless phone to her father and whispered, "Detective Rhymes." She suddenly realized that all three of her living grandparents, who were visiting Minnesota this year because of the Drew situation, would now understand the macabre anticipation that police calls like this brought.

"Hello?" David said, his face showing the same mix of hope and dread that was crawling in Lindsay's gut. She glanced around the table and saw that everybody, even GeeMa, wore the same apprehensive expression.

*Detective Rhymes wouldn't be calling in the middle of Thanksgiving dinner if it wasn't important*, Lindsay thought.

After a long pause, David said, "Okay, so what do we do from here?" He listened again for another minute, looking almost hopeful, before continuing. "Okay . . . And what about the bloodhounds? . . . Yeah, I'll be sure to ask them if they remember." Another pause, then: "I appreciate the call, Harry." David hung up the phone and set it delicately next to his dinner plate.

"Well?" GeeMa said in her characteristically pushy manner.

"They've identified a man named Lowell Grendel who fits the description Lindsay gave of a man at Spinner's Lake back in August. It was right after Lindsay got home from DC—a picnic with the Johnsons, I guess?"

"The guy with the camera?" Lindsay asked, vaguely remembering the man who had helped Drew pick up the blown-away paper plates the day of the tornadoes.

"He lives on Windsong Road at the far southeast corner of End Haven. Just moved here from California in August, apparently."

*Windsong Road.*

That was the street Alec and Natalie Pent—and Elijah Bryce— lived on. After English class yesterday, as Lindsay walked out the school doors with Molly Butler for the first time ever, Molly had reminded her of this when telling her how Elijah often rode his bike to school.

"Detective Rhymes said that one of the officers canvassing the neighborhood identified and spoke with this guy three days ago," David continued. "They went there again last night to ask him more pointed questions about being at Spinner's Lake on August ninth. Turns out he *was* there. It was his second day in town. He remembered helping Drew pick up the paper plates."

"But who *is* he?" Sandra demanded. "Did he take Drew? Do they actually have any reason to suspect him?"

"No direct evidence, but—"

"Then why the hell did Detective Rhymes interrupt our Thanksgiving dinner?" Sandra cut in.

Anger flowed red into David's face. "Because one of our neighbors, Jean Ramsey, saw this guy's car in our neighborhood on Halloween. He drives a 1994 Jeep Wrangler that's painted in an army camouflage pattern, and it's the only one of its kind in Idle County. It was a unique paint job he did after a short stint in the military. I guess he never registered it in Minnesota after his move."

"So he *was* here?" GeePa said. "Isn't that pretty conclusive? I mean that he's a suspect?"

David gritted his teeth. "Person of interest, yes, but no more than anyone else who was in the neighborhood that day. Apparently he confirmed being in our neighborhood and even in the woods behind our house, because he had a job photographing the interior and exterior of the Laverns' house over on Provell Street. They just put it on the market."

Lindsay's thoughts were running in circles. The Laverns lived behind them and to the right, through a grove of cedar trees. Her family's yard (and the backyard sandbox where Drew had been playing) would have been easily accessible from the Laverns' backyard; there was even a path through the trees.

"I guess they have no other reason to suspect him and no cause to get a search warrant for his property," David continued. "Not unless there's some kind of substantiated evidence linking him to Drew. He claimed that he understood the concern but knew nothing about Drew's disappearance."

"That's bullshit," Sandra said.

"Maybe so, but they have no legal right to force him to provide a scent sample for the search dogs. Though, by now, any trace of his scent left here would probably be long gone."

Sandra threw her napkin onto the table, knocking over her glass of wine with the swipe of her arm. "What do you mean no legal right?"

Only Grandma Thorsen seemed to notice the spilled glass. She stood up slowly and walked to the kitchen for a rag while her son continued his explanation.

"Grendel said he 'didn't feel comfortable' giving them any scent matches for the dogs without a court order. Since it was windy that day, his scent could easily have blown through the trees and into our yard, and he claimed that his voluntary cooperation could 'compromise his innocence.'"

"Compromise his innocence? What kind of bullshit is that?" GeePa growled.

"Detective Rhymes said Lowell has a point, because he *was* basically in our yard that day. It also might make it hard to get a judge to issue a search warrant. They're going to try, but he says the judge here errs on the side of caution in favor of potential suspects."

"Damn it!" Sandra exclaimed, ignoring Grandma Thorsen's reach over her shoulder to wipe up the spilled wine. "What about his car? Can't they use the dogs to see if Drew was in there?"

"He didn't agree to that up front either, which Detective Rhymes will try to use as an argument for the warrant," David replied, shaking his head.

"Did they talk to the Laverns yet?"

"The police? No, not since the day after Drew disappeared. They've been at their new house in Florida since before it all happened anyway. I assume they've cross-checked with the Laverns' realtor about the time frame this Grendel guy was there that day. Grendel said he was gone from the house by four o'clock."

Nobody spoke for a long time. The only sign of life in the house was Grandma Thorsen, who was gently rinsing and wringing out the wine towel in the kitchen sink.

GeePa finally coughed, which caused his ex-wife to perk up.

"So, what about the worst-case scenario?" GeeMa asked, folding her hands so her gaudy bracelets fell toward her elbows. "I mean, I don't want to be a pessimist, but they already told you it's unlikely Drew's still alive, right? If this Lowell Grendel guy *did* take him but they can't find any evidence, do we just go on wondering forever and fall into a pit of despair?"

Sandra glared at her mother.

"What?" GeeMa said. "I'm just trying to inject some *realism* here."

Lindsay looked down at her plate, unable to wipe the image of Drew's ghost from her mind. When she glanced up again, the whites of her father's eyes caught her gaze as if he were reading her thoughts and urging her to stay silent.

"Maybe you just shouldn't say things like that, *Mother*," Sandra hissed.

"Well, somebody has to say it," GeeMa replied. "It's been a month now. We need to start thinking about moving forward."

Grandma Thorsen, who always knew how to speak her mind without cutting into people's feelings, raised her posture. "This might not resolve quickly, Sharon. I see no harm in holding out hope that the police will do their job well and give us some closure."

GeeMa regarded the other grandmother as if she were a stain on an otherwise pleasant gathering. "I'm just trying to be a voice of reason here, *Betty*. It's no use walking around not preparing ourselves for the very worst."

"But I don't *want* to prepare myself for the worst!" Sandra shrieked. "I *want* this Lowell Grendel investigated to the fullest extent of the law, whatever that's going to mean, and—"

"Honey, they can't just trample on his rights—" David started.

"You think I care about his *rights*? If he took my son, he can hang from a noose for all I care!"

Lindsay watched her father's blood pressure rise straight to his face. "Yes—*if*. That's the big word there. If there's no other reason to suspect him, there's no way for the police to make a case."

"I know that!" Sandra bellowed. "I just want some goddamned answers!" She was now shaking with anger as tears ran down her face.

Lindsay's gut reeled. For the first time in what seemed like forever, she was agreeing with her mother.

David now shifted to slow, heavy breaths. "They already had trouble with the bloodhounds because of the wind that day, and it'd be a long shot if any scent lasted four weeks. Drew's scent did track off into that yard, yes, but he could have run back there himself. And since Lowell Grendel *was* in the Laverns' backyard taking pictures, they'd still need more to implicate him."

"If I may," Grandma Thorsen cut in, "considering what Sharon said earlier despite all of us wanting to hope for the best—which, again, I'm not discouraging—we also can't dismiss the other things going on. Namely, what our Lindsay here saw after her gym class and in Drew's bedroom."

Nobody at the table spoke. Lindsay felt her face go beet red, and it took nearly ten seconds for her to realize that Grandma Thorsen was actually defending her.

Sandra glowered at her mother-in-law. "And just how exactly do you think Lindsay's bullshit ghost stories will help the situation?"

Lindsay stared out the window behind GeePa's head. Leaving the table now would cause an even bigger commotion.

"If you'll recall what happened in my garden the week my husband, Nikan, died," Grandma Thorsen said, "maybe you'll consider Lindsay's side in all this instead of blaming her for making it more complicated."

Sandra continued to glare. David looked down at his plate. Grandma Thorsen looked at Lindsay.

"Honey, I don't think I've ever told you this, but before your grandpa Nikan died, he loved white roses. As reductive as it sounds, I think they were one of the few ways he allowed himself to connect back to nature after a life focused on capitalist values. Either way, I had always insisted on having pink roses lining the front of our house in Glencoe. Always pink. Sometimes I even yelled at him about it. They had gone dormant for the season about four weeks before Nikan died—that was mid-November. When I came back after the funeral, though—accompanied by all the guests, mind you—I looked at that garden, cursing myself for always refusing to let Nikan plant his white roses. And do you know what I saw?"

Lindsay shook her head. She had been just four years old when her grandpa Thorsen died, and she barely remembered the funeral. She did, however, recall the man's coffin being carried out a west-facing door— a slightly adjusted version of a Potawatomi tradition for the dead that Grandma Thorsen had insisted upon.

"White roses were budding on my dormant pink plants," the woman now continued. "*White* roses. On every bush. And sure, the roots were probably grafted, which could explain the color change, but for all of them to bloom in one day from the dormant state they were in that morning? Impossible. And do you know what? Since that moment, I haven't for a second doubted that Nikan is alive and well somewhere, even if it's just his spirit—whatever that actually means."

Now Lindsay glanced at her father. He was still looking down at his plate, but a slight smile now warmed his face.

"If Drew is trying to do something similar with his big sister, then it's not all hopeless," Grandma Thorsen finished.

Weeping, she pushed her chair out and stood up slowly, hands balanced politely on her thighs. As she walked toward the bathroom, she held her head high, unashamed. Lindsay was bursting with pride in her grandmother, one of the last people she thought would have given her story about Drew's ghost a second thought.

GeeMa and GeePa glanced between Sandra and David with raised eyebrows, as if hoping for some acknowledgment that Grandma Thorsen had indeed gone crazy by supporting Lindsay. When Lindsay followed their gazes and saw her mother's and father's vacant expressions, however, she knew the truth without a doubt: that facing this challenge of belief head-on, without fear or pretense, was the only path toward real answers.

"YOU'RE TALKING ABOUT Taconite Rose," David Thorsen said to Natalie Pent as they sat on the cliff behind Saint Andrew's Grotto. The young woman had just finished describing her excursion into the Moon Woods with the so-called woman in rags, and her description of the ghost matched almost perfectly the one Lindsay had hesitantly shared with him and Sandra in 2006, four days after her altercation with Lowell Grendel in Arrowhead Hills.

"I did see that name online," Natalie admitted. "Rose Margaret Leyton. She died in the same taconite mine Lowell Grendel took Lindsay to, right? I read that she was trying to find her missing son or something."

David stared at Natalie, stumped. Her near-fatal hike into the Moon Woods had occurred just a few weeks after the candlelight vigil in Heart Park, where she—in her own words—had confronted Victor Zobel's assistant, Raphael Dumont, about an argument he'd had with Jillian Pope in 2007.

"Honestly, from the few things I could find online, it seems like the people who see Taconite Rose all fit into two categories," Natalie continued. "Like, people who've had loved ones disappear, or people who've been accused of killing or kidnapping or something along those lines. That said, I'm basing that off random ghost websites that are probably run by nutbars with too much time on their hands."

David shrugged. "Can't rule it out, I guess. And I'm surprised the police never followed up with you about that Thai candy wrapper from the ravine."

"All they said to me was, 'Thanks, we'll look into it.' Fucking useless. But my gut tells me it's all related—the gas explosion at Alan Sparks's house, the Idle County Seven stuff, Victor Zobel. Otherwise, there are just too many coincidences."

David looked at Natalie, wondering if she had a bigger punch line. When it didn't come, he said, "Are you actually accusing Victor Zobel of something here?"

Natalie sighed. "I'd be ripped to shreds if I said anything publicly about it. People love him."

"But you *did* see Raphael Dumont with Jillian Pope the day before the gas explosion?"

"Yep. She was fucking *screaming* at him in French. Totally irate."

"I remember walking with Raphael during the Moon Woods searches. He seemed proud of that snake tattoo on his neck."

"Yeah. And I actually found him on that new Instagram app," Natalie said. "I screenshotted a few of his pictures just in case it ever matters."

David pulled one of his legs up from the cliff edge, rested his foot on the ground, and leaned onto his raised knee. "Okay, just so I can wrap my head around this: If you had to form a position on your theories, what would it be? I think we both can agree that there's something weird about Idle County—and about that apparent ghost you say you saw—but how would you make an actual case against Victor Zobel?"

"I don't know," Natalie replied. "I just think he intersects with too much of it."

"And you think the whole ghost thing somehow relates?"

Tears returned to Natalie's eye. She shook her head. "All I know is that I saw Lindsay standing over my bed the night Lowell Grendel took her to that mine. Ever since then, I've felt like I was going crazy."

"But I also saw her that night."

"Yeah. Which could mean the other stuff I've seen *isn't* just in my head."

"Your woman in rags, you mean."

Natalie nodded.

"I guess it's possible," David said.

"Yes. Crazy but possible. Did Lindsay ever say anything about Taconite Rose?"

David nodded. "Only twice that I know of, other than when the name Rose randomly came up during the Drew investigation. She brought it up once to the police after the incident in that mine, saying Lowell Grendel thought he was seeing a ghost named Taconite Rose, and once to me and Sandra a couple days later. She didn't say anything else about what she and Lowell might have discussed when they were together. Honestly, she kind of became a lockbox with us after it happened, all the way up until 2010. I'm actually not surprised, given how blatantly Sandra didn't believe her about the ghost stuff."

"What about an old diary? Did Lindsay ever say anything about that?"

*An old diary.*

Heat rushed through David's body as he recalled Molly Butler's peculiar interaction with Max Pope at Benedict Wise University's ghost symposium in 2006. "What do you mean? What diary?"

"It's something my brother, Alec, and his girlfriend, Sarah, told the police about two years ago. Basically, that they walked by Clayton Graf,

Jillian Pope, and Pauline Gilbert at the Bean & Leaf a few weeks before they disappeared. I guess they were all looking at some big leather journal or something. But that's all Alec and Sarah remembered."

Something crept down David's neck—a sense almost like déjà vu, but with dark corners he couldn't see. "Did you ever hear anything about the journals of Benedict Wise?" he asked Natalie, thinking back on Max Pope's mention of them in his opening lecture at the ghost symposium. "He was an old friar who used to run Saint Andrew's Church."

"I've only heard of the university named after him," Natalie said.

With a deep breath, David told her about the email he'd sent to the Idle County Seven parents a few hours ago regarding Molly and Max.

Now Natalie's eyes were blazing. "Sarah actually asked Victor Zobel about the journal at that candlelight vigil. He, like, froze in his tracks, then just glossed over it and said he'd follow up with the police. But we never heard anything."

"I'm surprised they didn't mention that when I called with the Molly-Max story today," David said.

"I heard they're not supposed to release details of open investigations. I saw that on TV."

"Yeah, well, I've been tenacious."

Natalie laughed sadly. "Alec yelled at me two years ago for trying to play detective. The day of that Moon Woods hike, actually."

As the magnetic energy in the young woman's eyes dimmed, David looked back out at the matchbox neighborhoods scattered in the distance. "I guess I never quite considered how all this stuff affected you and Alec. Losing your old friends, I mean."

"It affected me a lot," Natalie said, shuddering in a way that made David wonder what feeling she was deflecting. Her gaze wandered for a moment, then refocused back on reality with a sullen countenance. "You know Victor Zobel's building some huge house in the Moon Woods now, right?"

A bat flying in the dusk suddenly caught David's eye. His heart beat in time to the flap of the tiny creature's wings.

"What do you mean?"

"Alec told me that Tessa Silverman met one of the construction workers at a bar in Blue Hill the other week. He was wasted and apparently told her he's on some crew Victor Zobel flew in from out of town. They're all supposedly staying at that new Hampton Inn by Max Pope's old nursing home." Natalie's eyebrows jumped up and down in quick, exasperated arcs. "I tried driving into the Moon Woods on this new road they built on the south side, but it was all gated off. There's no way to get to the construction site. But you *can* see it from the top of Blue Hill."

David stared at Natalie, struck by her intelligence, determination, and yes, even beauty. He didn't even have to say the question on the tip of his lips, because, the next second, she was already reading his mind when she asked, "Should I drive or should you?"

2039

NOTHER DREAM OF FIRE.

Clovia Bell woke up dripping with sweat, overcome by a sense of anxiety so intense that, for a second, she thought she was in true danger. Over the past few weeks, the dreams had gone from nebulous to specific, warping first into nightmares of being trapped in *WorldLine*'s bombed-out office, and then tonight into one where she'd been locked in a third-floor bedroom, choking as smoke poured through a crack beneath the door. In the dream, Jonathan Flite had been next to her, screaming for her to *jump out the window, jump out the window, jump out the window*. But then—

Relief. Real life. Night's darkness and the sound of her bedroom's low-buzzing air conditioner wandered back into her perception. She was in her small New York apartment, safe in her bedroom for the time being. Her roommates—Jasmine, Christina, and Tova—were nearby.

Yesterday had been May 30, 2039—Jonathan Flite's nineteenth

birthday. Clovia had been forced to send well-wishes via his only friend, Jimmy Barber, who had now retaken the reins as full-time *WorldLine* liaison since Clovia's grievously mishandled conversation with Jonathan the night of her dad's funeral.

At least she wasn't burning alive, though. Thank heavens for that.

The clock on her ActoPhone read 3:42 a.m.

It was Tuesday. She had to be awake in two hours to start preparing for a production meeting in *WorldLine*'s new temporary office. Carrying on with the Jonathan Flite story almost seemed like sacrilege now that seven staff members were dead because of it, but such was the news business. Everyone participating in the upcoming Boulder and Idle County shoots would be at today's meeting, including the physicist Rebecca Sparks, who planned to help the field producers and editors understand her landmark Theory of Everything and its correlating mathematical explanation of the supposed "anomaly" underneath Idle County's ill-famed Moon Woods. Now that Alice Winterblume had pivoted to bring Idle County's peculiarities front and center, Clovia had to make sure every detail integrated properly with the eight-episode arc's new structure. As far as she knew, Alice was also planning to tell everyone today that Raphael Dumont would no longer be part of the story. The FBI angle, however, would stay between Clovia and Alice.

Everyone was set to meet at 9:00 a.m. on the dot. Clovia still had two more hours to sleep.

Her heartbeat finally slowed, but the fire dream had been intense, more real than previous ones.

What even were dreams?

She fell back into them.


IN THE MEETING LATER THAT MORNING, the *WorldLine* team discussed the ten past-life regressions they would be shooting with Dr. Cora Crowe in Boulder—one with Alice, four with random patients, and five with Jonathan Flite. They discussed the follow-up shoot at Dr. Crowe's home, which would outline her family life, the story of her dead daughter, Flora, and her transition from traditional psychiatry into hypnotic regression therapy. They discussed Jonathan's scheduled meetings with David and Sandra Thorsen, who were flying from San Francisco to Denver with Dr. Crowe's daughter Taisha, who'd become Sandra's assistant after their first meeting in 2034. And no, *WorldLine* would not be publicizing the fact that the Thorsens had introduced Alice Winterblume to Dr. Crowe's work; it could make viewers skeptical of the "incestuous" nuts and bolts behind the production.

Next came discussions about Jonathan's tour of Idle County; his follow-up interviews with those connected to the Idle County Seven; and, finally, Rebecca Sparks's controversial Theory of Everything. Rebecca herself explained how it posited an explanation for one of the most puzzling mysteries in physics: why individuals—souls from higher dimensions, she claimed—were able to perceive their own subjective versions of physical reality.

*Breathe*, Clovia told herself as the meeting's second hour came to a close. *You're not even in the thick of it yet.*

Almost as an afterthought came a brief communication—with little explanation from Alice—about the fact that Raphael Dumont's name would no longer appear in the story. Alice explained to the team that Clovia had already spent the last two weeks restructuring the season to account for the change.

Predictably, the room exploded with questions, none of which Alice could sufficiently answer.


AFTER THE MEETING, Clovia was the last person to exit the boardroom.

As she gathered up loose pens, sticky notes, and notepads from the table, she noticed that Rebecca Sparks was waiting in her wheelchair under the door frame, blocking the way to the rest of the office.

Words appeared on her glass tablet. Clovia had to squint to read them from across the room.

> *It's nice to see you again. Did you and Jonathan Flite*
> *make peace yet?*

For a moment, Clovia didn't even register that Rebecca had just invaded her mind. When the realization hit, however, a hot, tingling sensation rose from Clovia's chest to her face. It was the same feeling she had often experienced during childhood, when her father would violate her privacy by reading her diary and then ask about it during dinner.

No sooner had Clovia assimilated this sudden transgression in her own psyche than Rebecca, with a coy smile, sent new words to her tablet.

> *You and Jonathan are task companions. You made cer-*
> *tain agreements before coming into this life, so don't*
> *assume your intersection with him was a coincidence.*
> *Love is already there. It will show itself in time.*

Clovia's sudden urge to scream must have been visible on her face—or perhaps in her mind—because Rebecca, after watching her for a long silent moment, slowly backed her wheelchair up to allow space for Clovia to exit the room.

Clovia kept her mind blank as she walked to the office kitchen for tea. Upon passing the refrigerator, she almost bumped into Zoe Caldiero, Rebecca's assistant. Their eyes locked ever so briefly, and Clovia wondered: What was it like for Zoe to surrender her mental privacy every day in exchange for a job?

For the rest of the day, Clovia finalized her proposed season restructure for Alice while trying to brush Rebecca Sparks from her mind. What plagued her was that today's interaction wouldn't be their last. In just under four weeks, she and the physicist would be face-to-face again, this time in the woman's home region of Idle County, with Jonathan Flite at their side.

ON THE EVENING OF JUNE 12, as Clovia was packing her bag for the six-week Boulder and Idle County shoot, her ActoPhone rang. The number was unknown, from New York.

"Answer on speaker," she told her phone. Then: "This is Clovia."

"Clovia? Hi, this is Special Agent Heather Mousseau with the FBI. We spoke shortly after your father's death. How are you doing?"

Clovia's anxiety surge was immediate, as was her lie. "I'm fine. And you?"

"Very well, thanks. Though I'm calling with some new information regarding your father's death that also might pertain to you and your work on *WorldLine*. We learned a few things this morning about a woman named Jennifer Corino—she was dating your father up until two months ago?"

The agent spoke the last phrase like a question, as if she were trying to soften certain facts about Patrick Bell that Clovia hadn't taken the time to know.

"Anyway, I wanted to tell you that the Nyack PD recanvassed your old neighborhood this week and reported that one of Ms. Corino's neighbors saw a man on her doorstep the afternoon before her death, which happened about two weeks before your father's. Her cause of death was initially listed as a heroin overdose—local PD found recently used drug paraphernalia near her bed—but we ordered a second autopsy and toxicology panel after this neighbor's testimony. Turns out there was trace evidence of the same poison we found in your father's system. Aconite."

Clovia breathed, but barely. "And how does this relate to me?"

"Well, without saying more than I can, this man on Jennifer Corino's porch—we initially had reason to suspect he might've been Raphael Dumont, the old friend of Victor Zobel we asked *WorldLine* not to mention. But that changed when we talked to the neighbor. She described this man as tall, muscular, and bald. Nyack PD identified his rental car via street cameras, and it turns out the car was paid for by a credit card linked to a Delaware shell company with just one listed director—a different man named Ronald Scrant. He's currently also an employee of Advanced Defense Machining."

"That's Victor Zobel's company," Clovia said, her breaths suddenly mounting. She had just referenced Advanced Defense Machining, a weapons manufacturer, in her season restructure.

"Victor is still indeed a majority shareholder and has a number of contacts at the company, yes," Agent Mousseau said.

"So, you *do* still think he sent someone after my dad?"

"It aligns with the fear tactics we've seen thus far, with people linked to Jonathan. Your online professional profiles show that you work directly under Alice Winterblume, so it's not out of the realm of possibility that somebody might have targeted you, directly or indirectly."

"'Somebody' meaning Victor Zobel."

"We can't be sure. But it's possible."

Clovia's lungs froze in her chest. For a second, she couldn't get air. *Now you're in the thick of it.*

She barely heard Agent Mousseau tell her that *WorldLine* had already offered to pay for security services from Global Protection Group, Alice Winterblume's preferred third-party service. Did Clovia have any questions, and was she all right?

For the third time that year, she answered with a lie—yes, she was all right—but no, of course she wasn't.

On June 14, the new security team drove Clovia to JFK airport, where one of the bodyguards, Roger, boarded a plane with her to Denver, Colorado. On the flight, while Roger read a book, she worked and worked, plagued the entire time by worries that this trip wasn't going to go the way she expected.

The next morning, in Boulder, Clovia watched Alice Winterblume undergo a past-life regression with Dr. Cora Crowe. After setting up eight unobtrusive cameras, *WorldLine*'s small crew left the room so that the psychiatrist's office would stay as calm and quiet as possible. It took Alice almost thirty minutes to enter hypnosis, but when she finally did regress into an apparent "past life," she saw scattered images of crowded streets, dirty water, and vividly colored garments—India, she guessed.

While the regression raised questions, it was completely unremarkable.

Afterward, however, as Alice sat with Rebecca Sparks on camera and asked if she had any insight about the session, Rebecca claimed Alice's spirit guides were saying that this life had taught Alice a type of humility that could only come with extreme poverty. Alice openly admitted to doubting the regression's legitimacy, but as she spoke, her face grew stiff and guarded, the way it always did when she was deconstructing a challenge.

The shoot grew even more questionable when Jonathan Flite finally appeared in Dr. Crowe's office the following Tuesday. Clovia's exchanges with him remained strictly professional the entire time—zero flirtations, zero personal talk, and zero verbal hints of their underlying emotional connection.

But she didn't miss Jonathan's many stolen, fleeting glances.

THE YOUNG MAN'S FIVE PAST-LIFE regression sessions with Dr. Crowe revealed nothing definitive about any prior connections to Idle County, but they did burrow carefully under Clovia's skin.

The first life he described was that of a Norse woman during the Viking Age.

The second was of a male child in an ancient yet seemingly technologically advanced cave-dwelling civilization in what he claimed was now modern-day Spain. "*Their caves haven't been discovered by archeologists yet,*" Jonathan said in his highly suggestible state.

The third and fourth alleged lives were lived concurrently as a male shopkeeper in London in the 1600s and a homeless female child who stole food from him every day. When the girl was twelve, the man caught her, killed her, and threw her into the Thames. Jonathan's explanation, caught on camera, had been: "Those lives were meant to teach me the interplay of power, but I didn't learn it very well."

His last regression was mostly nebulous, but it did bring the first possible connection to his current life. He described an experience in which, as a seven-year-old boy, he saw his dead parents standing behind his shoulder in the mirror, crying.

"And your parents—how did they die?" Dr. Crowe asked during the regression.

Jonathan's answer seemed definitive. "They shot themselves."

"Can you tell me why?"

"No. That part is blocked."

"Where is this mirror? Where are you?"

"My uncle's house. I live with him."

"Is this uncle anyone in your life now, as Jonathan?"

Jonathan's face relaxed for the first time since starting the regression. "Oh. Wow. Yeah. It's my biological dad, Dominic Bock. Except he didn't want me around in that life. He wasn't ready to follow through on his agreement with me."

"What agreement?"

"I . . . I don't know. My guides . . . they say it isn't useful for me to know that right now."

When Dr. Crowe attempted to guide Jonathan to other parts of that life, Jonathan only shook his head. "They say it's blocked because it'll hinder what I have to learn in my life as Jonathan. They won't let me see anything."

Next came a question Alice Winterblume had instructed Dr. Crowe to ask surreptitiously, if a good opportunity were to present itself. "Is there any relation here to the crayon drawings you made as a child?" she said. "Particularly the eighth figure you included in the picture you said was of the Idle County Seven dying in the Moon Woods?"

Jonathan started to shake his head, then stopped. "Just that . . . that figure was me. But I already knew that. I was always putting myself into those drawings, because they were my memories."

Watching the camera monitor in Dr. Crowe's office foyer, Clovia and Alice flashed each other curious glances. This was something new.

Alice, holding her ActoPhone, quickly typed a message to Dr. Crowe. A moment later, the woman asked Jonathan, "Is there any possibility that the figure was also meant to be the neurologist Max Pope?"

Jonathan paused, as if searching his own mind. He scrunched his closed eyes, then swallowed. "That was never my intention."

Alice stepped back from the camera monitor and crossed her arms. Clovia could tell this wasn't the answer she had wanted.

Jonathan's guidance from the psychiatrist into his so-called interlife—the supposedly "timeless" period between death in one life and rebirth in another—was a quiet affair. Jonathan lost himself in it for almost thirty minutes without a word. The cameras might as well have been picking up static, except for a few moments of intense expressions contorting Jonathan's face. If he had experienced anything of note during this portion of the regression, he had thus far kept it to himself.

Yet one detail stuck out to Clovia long after the day wrapped: that in every life Dr. Crowe helped him explore, he always visited the same place after his death: a vast grassy field with a lone tree at its center.

On Friday, June 24, after overseeing Alice Winterblume's first interview with David and Sandra Thorsen, the aging parents of the long-missing Lindsay Thorsen, Clovia watched as the security team and *WorldLine*'s camera crew accompanied Jonathan into the large hotel suite where they were shooting.

David Thorsen, after asking Jonathan for details regarding the Idle County Seven's final venture into the Moon Woods, asked ten generic questions with answers Jonathan couldn't possibly know, all about his daughter Lindsay. Jonathan answered each one correctly.

Sandra Thorsen quizzed the young man in a similar way before asking him why he thought he'd been given the gift of her daughter's memories, along with those of her friends.

"I honestly don't think I'm supposed to know," Jonathan replied.

Taisha Crowe, Sandra's personal assistant, watched it all silently—if not quite skeptically—from the corner of the room.

Finally, it was Saturday, June 25—the last day of the Boulder shoot. While standing midway up Dr. Crowe's home stairwell, looking for any remaining pictures around the house that would make for good B-roll cutaways, Clovia's gaze fell upon a small framed photo she hadn't noticed last week. It was of a newborn baby lost in a maze of tubes, tape, and wires, frozen in time.

*Flora, the daughter with the heart defect,* Clovia realized.

The photo hung amid happier photos of Taisha, Dr. Crowe's younger, living daughter, whose growth to adulthood was documented all over the wall. The loss of Flora made evident in the display left Clovia's chest tight around her heart. From what she had gathered over the week, Taisha had been living under Flora's shadow her entire life. She had relocated to sunny California in 2034, after meeting Sandra Thorsen and expressing a desire to move west. Sandra, still on a high from her first past-life regression with Taisha's mother, had offered a helping hand. If Clovia had learned anything about Cora and Taisha Crowe this past week, it was that no matter how much love there was floating between them, both women were bound by personal obligations to spread their own wings.

Footsteps creaked on the second floor above Clovia's head, just down the hallway.

"Clovia Bell, good morning!" came Dr. Crowe's friendly yet authoritative voice. "Doing one last snoop around my house before you head out?"

"For B-roll," Clovia said, trying to deflate her admiration for the psychiatrist with a dollop of dry professionalism—purely an act of self-consciousness she was sure the psychiatrist could see right through.

"I see you found this wall's most *controversial* photo," Dr. Crowe said as she approached Clovia, her gaze darting toward the photo of the baby lost in the tubes, tape, and wires. Her blue eyes, usually radiating a peculiar brand of intensity, grew distant. "People sometimes ask how on earth I could have allowed myself to frame this one," she said. "We took it about two minutes after Flora died, before the doctor unhooked all the IV tubes and tape. We did get to hold her normally, without all the mess, but for some reason, I chose to remember her like this."

Clovia glanced at the photo again. "I think it makes sense, given what you said in your interview the other day about her death giving you a new perspective. The tubes were part of how she lived."

"You have a nice way of putting things," Dr. Crowe replied, flashing Clovia a validating smile.

"Honestly, I'm not sure how you did what you did. Like, losing your child and then jumping into this unknown realm of therapy. When you were saying in that first interview how you got all that guff from colleagues over it—"

"How I *still* get guff."

"Yeah. I couldn't help feeling like all of us taking Jonathan Flite's side on this story are in a similar boat—opening ourselves up to some potentially heavy criticism by embracing all these 'past-life' ideas so publicly."

"I'm glad you're realizing it now," Dr. Crowe said. "From a 'typical' professional standpoint, I lost a lot of credibility after writing my books. Most of my former colleagues no longer take me seriously. The funny thing, though, is that all the ones I've actually spoken with since then haven't read a word I've written—even just to form an educated opinion. I guess it's not surprising, considering a lot of people mistake science for being all there is, rather than being the study of *what* is." The psychiatrist sighed. "I remember waking up in the middle of the night once, about a month after Flora died. All I could think about was why the Big Bang happened, and then what caused it, and then what caused *that*. I kind of freaked out, because I realized how much I didn't know about what the universe actually was. At the same time, I *needed* to know. It was like I was somehow glimpsing infinity, and my mind couldn't handle it."

Clovia grinned. "Maybe you should work that concept into this last interview today."

"Not a bad idea. Though I think part of me will always be skeptical of what I do, no matter how much success my patients have with it."

"Lindsay Thorsen's mom, Sandra, said you were skeptical about Jonathan Flite back when she first met you. Are you still?"

Dr. Crowe took a deep breath, then shook her head. "Honestly, he's been a fascinating study. I was surprised how easily he went into hypnosis. And I do think whatever he experienced was real—as in, he wasn't faking. But there were so many blocks with him—particularly on that last regression yesterday, with the boy seeing his dead parents in the mirror. The blocks weren't unusual, per se, but it won't necessarily help his case."

Defensiveness suddenly rushed into Clovia's chest, and it took her a second to realize it was a reaction to Dr. Crowe's apparent hesitation over Jonathan. "So, it's not weird to get blocked the way he did?" she asked, hoping she still looked neutral. "It seemed like he was doing fine with the first four regressions. Or am I wrong?"

"Oh, he was doing great. But those were supposedly from lives farther back. That last one with the parents in the mirror, though—I wish he could have gone into that further. Mirrors are fairly new in context of history, which means *that* life, if it was real, would have been somewhat recent. Also, Jonathan hasn't met Dominic Bock yet, right? His biological dad?"

"Nope. That's happening after the Idle County shoot, once he's back in Rhode Island."

"Is Dominic going to be part of the show?"

"No. His wife wants to keep their connection to Jonathan private if at all possible. Last I heard from Jonathan's assistant, Jimmy, she has no interest in meeting him."

"How unfortunate." Dr. Crowe's gaze went distant a second time before she refocused on Clovia. "Well, if I could have guided Jonathan into that interlife stage without him shutting down, we could have potentially learned more about his connection to Mr. Bock. *That* could have been interesting."

"Have you ever found a way around blocks like that?" Clovia asked, recalling one of the fleeting glances Jonathan had given her after that regression, when it seemed he was aching to tell her something he'd held back from the cameras.

Dr. Crowe shook her head. "Unfortunately, no. I've had hundreds of patients run into similar issues—memories 'their guides say' aren't productive to remember. I think the idea is that being told why a memory would be applicable to an ongoing life lesson would preclude the person from actually learning the lesson."

"Ha. I wonder what lessons I'm supposed to be learning," Clovia replied.

Dr. Crowe touched the photo of her daughter Flora, almost aimlessly, then gestured for Clovia to follow her toward the kitchen. "Considering that bomb back in April, I'm guessing you're dealing with a lot right now. Anything in particular bugging you?"

As they walked, Clovia fought to organize her thoughts. There were so many things.

"Just life, I guess. Questions."

"You've got passion in your eyes, you know," Dr. Crowe continued as they stepped into the kitchen, where a craft services table had been set up. "I could see this week how much you care about your work. Alice is lucky to have you on her team."

Blushing, Clovia grabbed a clump of grapes and began eating them with fervor.

"Tell you what," the psychiatrist said, stepping toward the bagels and cream cheese. "Why don't you come here after all this *WorldLine* hoopla is done? Fly out to visit. You can stay in my guest room, and we can do a regression or two. See if we can uncover anything helpful."

Clovia stared at Dr. Crowe for a moment, as if recognizing the new, welcoming path the woman's words were opening up to her. It sounded like an interesting offer at the very least, except for one problem. "Honestly, I don't think I could afford it," she said. "I barely make enough to survive in New York as it is."

"Oh heavens, I wouldn't be inviting you if I planned to charge you," Dr. Crowe said with a playful jump of her eyebrows. "And yes, I'm being serious. Save my number and get in touch once you're able to. Promise?"

Clovia was almost too surprised to smile. "Sure. Yes. I promise."

Dr. Crowe gave her an affirming nod, followed by a subtle wave. She left Clovia standing at the craft services table, basking in an indistinct but significant glow as the *WorldLine* crew bustled around the house, preparing for their last shooting day in Boulder.

<br>


AN EXCERPT FROM THE AUDIO TRANSCRIPT of Clovia Eileen Bell's first past-life regression with Dr. Cora Noreen Crowe on October 27, 2040; recovered by the New York Police Department on November 11, 2041:

*Dr. Cora Crowe: Now look down at your feet. What are you wearing?*

*Clovia Bell: Girl shoes. Flats.*

*Dr. Cora Crowe: And how old are you?*

*Clovia Bell: I'm not sure. Maybe six or seven.*

*Dr. Cora Crowe: Okay. Now look up. Tell me what you see.*

*Clovia Bell: I'm in a church.*

*Dr. Cora Crowe: Is there anything else? Or anyone?*

*[Ambiguous mutters from Clovia Bell.]*

*Dr. Cora Crowe: Could you repeat that, Clovia? It wasn't clear.*

*Clovia Bell: I said there's an altar boy. He's staring at me.*

*Dr. Cora Crowe: Can you describe him for me?*

*Clovia Bell: He's standing next to another altar boy. The priest on the stage, near the altar—he's older. With a white beard.*

*Dr. Cora Crowe: And the boy?*

*Clovia Bell: Black hair and dark eyes.*

*Dr. Cora Crowe: What else do you see?*

*Clovia Bell: Not much. I'm just sitting politely with my family. We go to church every Sunday.*

*Dr. Cora Crowe: Have you seen this altar boy before?*

*Clovia Bell: No. He's new. Now he's walking past me on his way out of the church, looking my way. He's smiling. Almost.*

**Dr. Cora Crowe:** *Is there anything else you see in this scene? Any feelings?*

*[Silence for six seconds.]*

**Clovia Bell:** *No. It's basic. Just a church on a regular Sunday.*

**Dr. Cora Crowe:** *Can you see any reason why this memory is surfacing first?*

*[Silence for fourteen seconds.]*

**Clovia Bell:** *The details are blocked. But gosh—the boy's eyes. They're burned into me. It's the first time in this life that I've ever felt attracted to another person.*

**Dr. Cora Crowe:** *Sexual attraction?*

**Clovia Bell:** *Yes and no. I'm too young to know what that is. It's just . . . attraction. Like knowing a person the minute you see them. And this boy—he immediately scared me, but he also made me feel excited.*

**Dr. Cora Crowe:** *Excited how?*

**Clovia Bell:** *Like I know we'll be friends someday.*

**Dr. Cora Crowe:** *Can you tell me what year this was?*

**Clovia Bell:** *I . . . I don't know. It's old-fashioned times.*

*No computers or phones or things like that. But the church had windows, and people were dressed nicely enough. I can't tell what year.*

*[Silence for six seconds.]*

**Dr. Cora Crowe:** *Any other details you can recall?*

**Clovia Bell:** *Yeah. The church window—the big stained glass one in the back. I always love staring at it on my way out of church, because it doesn't really seem all that Christian. You know, the way you'd expect in a church.*

**Dr. Cora Crowe:** *What does it look like?*

**Clovia Bell:** *I can't see the details. I think it shows a garden with some rocks. And people, maybe? All I know is that I always thought it was better than the window at the front of the church. It's beautiful. It always makes me feel calm. Just . . . very calm.*

**Dr. Cora Crowe:** *Is there anything else here that matters?*

**Clovia Bell:** *No, I . . . no. Nothing more.*

**Dr. Cora Crowe:** *You're sure?*

**Clovia Bell:** *Well, maybe there's one thing.*

**Dr. Cora Crowe:** *Tell me.*

***Clovia Bell:*** *It's just this feeling I have, but I'm too young to make sense of it. But it somehow relates to being okay with the unexpected. That sometimes you make connections with other people, but you can't always control the outcome.*

D AVID THORSEN PEERED OUT the passenger's window of Natalie Pent's pink Volkswagen Beetle as they sped around Old Mill Road, on the north side of the Moon Woods. The sunset had finally diminished, giving way to night.

As the Outer Ring's deadened grass zipped past David's eyes, glowing pale blue under the moon, he recalled his last visit to this side of Idle County. He had been walking across the expanse during the first Moon Woods search for Lindsay and her friends. Even in July, the grass had been on the yellower side of green, as if it were struggling to survive.

Now, as they passed the turnoff for Stone Ridge, the small and shabby town that lay north of the Moon Woods, Natalie pointed out the window. "God. That sign for Stone Ridge. It was chipped and faded when I was seven, and nobody's ever changed it. How come people don't care about making things better around here?"

"And to think I came here for a damned job," David said. Looking out the window and considering all he had lost here—and all those related, ambiguous questions with no good answers—David saw nothing of worth.

*So what does Victor Zobel see in this place?* he wondered.

FIFTEEN MINUTES LATER, they rolled into the town of Blue Hill. Smaller than End Haven but exuding what some people might call a more "resortlike" charm, it sat at the western base of a seven-hundred-foot bluff—the highest point in Idle County. The bank was covered in blue spruce trees that shone cool and frosty even in the daytime. Under tonight's moon, their needles glowed with an ethereal quality worthy of the town's name.

Blue Hill's main thoroughfare, Hopewell Avenue, was surprisingly active tonight. In the two years since David had been here, a number of modern restaurants and breweries had popped up. Tonight was warm, and their patios were filled with patrons enjoying life's frivolities.

The town's lights fell away quickly when they reached the end of Hopewell Avenue. Natalie veered right, onto a road marked Sapphire Lane, and within moments, the forest lining the town enveloped the road. Only Natalie's headlights gave them a sense of place as the road circumvented the bluff's main slope, winding upward in a gradual incline.

When the trees finally broke, showing the night sky once again, they were in the empty parking lot of a daytime picnic area. Natalie parked and let her car idle. Dust from the ground floated before the headlights, temporarily blocking their view of the town below—and whatever might be visible of the construction project in the Moon Woods beyond.

"From what that worker told Tessa, it's a huge project," Natalie said. "Apparently they have a twenty-four-hour crew."

"Seems odd if Victor's just building a house," David said.

Natalie pushed her door open and stepped out of the car. David followed, wobbling in his thin-soled dress shoes as he stood up on the parking lot's gravel. When he closed his door, the car's lights went dark, and they had a clear view of the Moon Woods.

Tonight, they weren't just a vast stretch of black, because a swath of bluish construction lights was shining up from their center. When David and Natalie stopped next to the picnic table set along the bluff's edge, the distant sound of work trucks reached their ears. David rested his fingers on the old table's warped wood and listened.

So, it was true. Victor Zobel, despite his fame, had somehow become interested enough in Idle County to build here. Yet judging by the number of floodlight beams at the forest's center, it appeared he was erecting something the size of a large resort.

David shook his head. "He can afford to build anywhere. Why here?"

"I don't for one second buy that statement he made to the *Wind Prairie Tribune* after he bought the land," Natalie replied.

"You mean the one where he said the Moon Woods reminded him of the stepdaughter he'd lost?"

"Yeah. Way too sentimental."

As Natalie stared out at the distant lights, David wondered whether his wife, Sandra, knew anything about Victor Zobel's secret construction project. Had she even paid attention when Victor bought the land early last year? They had spoken so little about the Idle County Seven case since facts began to dwindle and the town began to move on. Gazing out at the Moon Woods now, David imagined his two children's last moments: what their eyes might have seen as the light left them, how hard their hearts must have been beating.

"What do we do?" he whispered to Natalie, unsure what exactly the question implied.

In the darkness, she took a step closer to him. At first, it seemed as though it was merely a gesture to show her support. Then she grabbed his hand. Despite the cooling night, her palm was warm.

David's heart began racing in a way he could only describe as senseless. It was different than his humiliation at being discovered on the ledge behind Saint Andrew's Grotto, different than the adrenaline that had pulsed between them as they speculated about Max Pope, Victor Zobel, and Rebecca Sparks. He squeezed Natalie's hand just enough to tell her that he was there and that he appreciated her gesture.

And then Natalie leaned into him. When he slowly circled toward her and opened his arms, it wasn't a choice. It was some level of instinct, perhaps underscored by desperation.

The contact came with a sense of relief. David made no attempt to sexualize it, but their close proximity by default reminded him of that long-lost surging feeling of life and vitality he'd neglected throughout his adulthood. It burrowed right to the part of him that still felt like a teenager discovering himself, at least for these few, revitalizing moments.

Except Natalie was crying.

So David simply held her. She adjusted her head against his shoulder, and her breath warmed his left ear as she quietly wiped away a tear. "I was planning on jumping tonight, too," she whispered.

David nodded. "You can talk to me. As long as this is okay and you feel safe, you can always talk to me. I'm here."

Natalie remained in his embrace and nodded.

It was almost a full minute before she asked, "Do *you* feel safe?"

A light but crisp breeze bound them as David considered her question. His heart pounded, and heat radiated from his body. "I think you saved me tonight, too."

"I'm glad."

Natalie pressed her body closer. Her warmth had become intoxicating, and David finally allowed himself to breathe in the flowery scent of her hair. His inhale was slow and deep. Even so, through galvanizing visions he was now allowing himself to embrace, he couldn't shake the image of Natalie out on that hockey player's boat, surrounded by water, trapped in a cage with a predator. The violence sparked a protective urge in him. Whether it was fatherly or simply human, he didn't know. But as his sexual arousal mounted, so did his confusion over what was happening and whether the young woman was truly wanting—and allowing—it to happen.

"I won't do anything you don't want me to do," he whispered. "You deserve better than that. And I'm married."

Wiping more tears on his shoulder, Natalie said, "I'm not looking to hurt Mrs. Thorsen."

"Well, then, you should know she's already made her call about me. Let's just say our UPS driver was able to give her more intimacy than I could, even before Lindsay disappeared."

Natalie shrugged in his arms, then nestled further into his chest. "I used to try to hang out at your house when you'd do workouts in your garage, back when I was first friends with Lindsay. I remember her looking at me all confused once, like she somehow knew I was into you. But girls that age weren't supposed to be attracted to men your age."

David breathed. Again: visions in his head. Both light and dark.

"Considering what happened to you in Minneapolis, I just . . . if we did anything, I'd feel like I was taking advantage of your vulnerability somehow," he said.

"Wouldn't I also be taking advantage of yours?"

David remained silent.

Natalie's leg came forward and brushed his inner thigh. "I'm not going to live my life being some victim or letting people paste that label onto me. I think the fact I ran into you tonight proves . . ."

Natalie sighed, letting her half statement hang.

"Proves . . . ?" David pressed.

"Proves that some things are just supposed to happen."

Instead of letting go, David remained in the embrace, allowing Natalie to take control of the moment, and the next, and the next. Finally, she turned her face toward his, and he leaned in to kiss her. When she returned it, he came alive.

Beyond them, Victor Zobel's construction project in the Moon Woods rumbled. Above them, the forest's namesake watched over all.

WHAT CLOVIA BELL DIDN'T EXPECT upon her arrival in Idle County was the quiet comfort the place inspired in her. After the two-hour economy-class flight from Denver to Minneapolis, she made the drive to southern Minnesota alone, in her own rental car, a mile ahead of her bodyguard, Roger.

It was Sunday, June 26, 2039.

Using ActoMaps navigation, she drove in a southwestern zigzag from the Twin Cities' metro area, through the shallow hills of suburbia, and then across a vast expanse of trees and rolling cornfields.

When Clovia reached Highway 12, approaching the bluffs of Idle County from the north, the stresses of life began melting away. Not even the weight of her father's apparent poisoning—to say nothing of the role her connection to Jonathan Flite might have played in it—dampened her sense of peace. The very air here moved at a more leisurely pace than she was accustomed to, and she made no effort to argue away the relaxation it inspired.

Of course, Idle County was no longer a place where people could just disappear. Since Jonathan Flite's story had begun making headlines again last summer, particularly after Weston Carrow's suicide bomb at Winifred Flite's press conference, the region had attracted its increasingly fair share of reporters, gawkers, and people protesting Victor Zobel's local presence—not yet enough to cause significant social unrest, but enough to ensure that the world wouldn't forget about Jonathan Flite and the long-lost Idle County Seven anytime soon.

And word had spread that Jonathan was coming to town. All hints as to the information leak's source pointed to Shelly Bryce, adoptive mother of Elijah Bryce. She claimed her friends at Common Ties Senior Community had guessed what was happening by repeatedly (and maliciously) asking pointed questions about why she'd been seen walking around with Jaret, *WorldLine*'s Idle County location manager.

*"I tell you—questions, gossip, and speculation are rules for the modern elderly,"* she had told *WorldLine*'s team four days ago.

As Clovia drove into Idle County for the first time, it really did feel comforting, almost like coming home. But was it simply because she'd studied maps and lived vicariously through Jonathan's memories for the last ten months? She could barely admit to herself just how much she hoped her shared time with him here might offer a spare personal moment in which she could apologize for pushing him away the night of her father's funeral. If she couldn't reach Jonathan here, they might never get another chance to follow through on whatever connection they had. Jonathan was famous, and famous people always found ways to become inaccessible.

When Highway 12 came to a perpendicular intersection with Hunter Avenue in End Haven, Idle County's most affluent town, Clovia turned left. She arrived at the Fairfield Inn nine minutes later, thankful she had an entire afternoon to herself before tomorrow's shoot. She crashed into bed, fell asleep, and yet again dreamed she was trying to escape from a burning, third-floor bedroom.

MONDAY, JUNE 27, marked Jonathan Flite's first-ever visit to Idle County, and the beginning of *WorldLine*'s production there with him. For the first two days, he and Alice would be miked with lavalieres as a four-person camera crew drove them into town and followed them from place to place. Considering Alice's and Jonathan's levels of fame, it was anyone's guess how long the calm would last. At least they had Alice's regular security detail on them, along with three deputies from the Idle County Sheriff's Department. Sounder, Jonathan's bodyguard, was also with them.

It was nearing 9:00 a.m. when Clovia found herself on Lemon Avenue in End Haven, driving toward the spot where the Idle County Seven's famous old library used to stand. She was scheduled to meet Jonathan and Alice here in just fifteen minutes.

As she approached the site from the west, a two-story house on the left side of Lemon Avenue caught her eye. It had a new tan paint job, but its gardens were depressingly unkempt.

For a single, monumental second, the place looked familiar.

Then, whether because the moment was meaningless or because Clovia was pushing away a sudden urge to cry, the feeling disappeared.

SHE PARKED ABOUT SIXTY FEET from Lemon Avenue's intersection with Main Street in End Haven, just to the right of the old library site. Through her ActoLenses and linked earpiece, she monitored Jonathan, Sounder, and Alice's idle chitchat on their drive south on Highway 12.

Her ears pricked up when Jonathan said, "Oh God, I recognize this." On the video, his eyes had gone wide.

Alice waited for him to continue.

"Change of plan, if it's okay," he said. "Once you get to the Hunter Avenue intersection, can you turn right instead of left? I want to go somewhere else first."

"Of course," Alice said, failing to hide both her excitement and her trepidation. "Where exactly are we going?"

Still staring out the car window, Jonathan said, "Did Kara Butler ever give you a copy of Molly Butler's ghost hunting journal?"

Alice's face lit up. *WorldLine* did indeed have a copy of the journal Molly Butler kept of her 2004 ghost hunt with Jacob Jenkins, her next-door neighbor. Thirty years after its writing, Jonathan claimed the girl had purposefully omitted important details about the summer ghost hunt, particularly regarding her unexpected relationship with the neurologist Max Pope. Despite questions about their association being raised by David Thorsen in 2012, authorities had previously believed Molly and Max first met at Benedict Wise University's First Annual Ghost Symposium in 2006. According to Jonathan, however, the man had joined Molly much earlier, on her final ghost hunt with Jacob. He had also allegedly accosted her on the death day of Mrs. Grime, the librarian, in the old woman's basement.

"I read the journal," Alice said. "Are you wanting to go see the 'place with no name' that Molly and Jacob Jenkins visited?"

Instead of looking excited, Jonathan's face was pale. "Yeah, if it's still there. Assuming it's the same as it used to be, there should be a boulder midway up the hill, in the trees. It'll mark our hike up. Then there'll be old gravestones in a field at the top."

With a smile, Alice said, "Then I guess I'm changing my shoes."

Instead of turning left at the intersection of Highway 12 and Hunter Avenue, the armored Chevy Electrogue turned right. Alice and Jonathan, quietly joined by Clovia via the camera crew's live ActoVid feed, were silent as the car approached a perpendicular stretch of hills on the horizon.

When Hunter Avenue reached a **T** with an old dirt road, Jonathan whispered, "Jesus. I can't believe it's all still here."

He stood alone at the center of the place with no name, which was nothing more than a circular clearing just past the top of the bluff. The center of the small field was elevated just enough to be a dome, and Clovia watched through her ActoLenses as Alice stood back with Sounder and the camera crew to let Jonathan explore the spot quietly. The young man's microphone was still on, however, and as he stood in the strawlike grass, which seemed only half-alive, Clovia heard him say, "It's smaller than it was in my head. For Molly, this field seemed so huge."

One of the camera operators, using a stabilized telephoto lens, caught Jonathan lightly running his foot over something poking out of the dirt.

"Here's one of the old headstones," Jonathan said. "I think these were early settlers of Idle County. This was a cemetery."

Alice directed the camera crew forward, and she finally approached Jonathan at the center of the field. After a few moments of somber silence, she said, "How are you feeling right now, Jonathan?"

"Like I'm in a dream," he replied.

Clovia waited in her rental car on Lemon Avenue, about a hundred feet from the corner of Main Street. She was parked on the road's right side, which was lined by thick maple trees planted every hundred feet or so. Their tall branches domed over the pavement like cathedral arches painted bright green by summer leaves. With a pang of something resembling uncertainty, Clovia realized that they, too, plucked her sense of memory, similar to the tan house she had passed on her way here.

*It's because of Jonathan Flite*, she thought. *You've gotten too close to his story.*

But had she really?

"Clovia, we're approaching," Alice said through the ActoVid feed.

Connected to the woman's tiny earpiece via audio, Clovia replied, "I have your coffee. They actually have a Starbucks here."

"I'll say it again: you know me too well."

Through one of the camera feeds in her ActoLenses' monitor, Clovia saw Jonathan perk up. "Clovia's there?"

Alice glanced at him, and her ActoLenses recorded his surprised expression. "Yes, she's already on site."

Jonathan took a breath as if to speak, then simply smiled, nodded, and turned to look back out the window.

*Maybe because the cameras are on him*, Clovia thought.

Perhaps he'd open up once Jimmy Barber, his personal assistant, arrived. Jimmy was currently driving down from Minneapolis in a rental Porsche Air, an hour behind Jonathan and Alice. He was going straight to the Fairfield Inn, however, as he was contractually obligated to stay off camera during all shooting hours. Oddly, Clovia had seen him whispering with Alice in Boulder about talk shows, agents, and contracts, seemingly planning some big life change but keeping it secret. From Jonathan? From the production team? Clovia had no idea.

Knowing she could distract her mind for only so long, she continued to wait.

WHEN JONATHAN, ALICE, AND THE CAMERA CREW arrived at the corner of Lemon Avenue and Main Street, the site of Elizabeth Grime's famous old library, a moment of electric silence preceded everyone's exit from their cars. Clovia sat in her driver's seat, trying to slow her racing heart.

All she wanted was to apologize to Jonathan for their last conversation, to let him know she respected and cared about him.

*But of course all I can do is be a cog in the production wheel,* Clovia thought as Alice's Chevy Electrogue pulled in front of her rental car, about twenty feet closer to the intersection of Lemon Avenue and Main Street. On the left corner lot stood a house that was much newer than the other ones on the street. A single oak tree towered behind it, at a spot where its branches hung safely away from the house's roof.

The camera crew exited the armored Chevy Electrogue first. Jonathan followed just slowly enough to give them time to set up their shots while Alice opened the opposite car door and stepped out, onto the street's right sidewalk. She stood back to let the camera crew follow Jonathan toward the corner lot.

"Damn. I've seen this house on ActoMaps," he said. "I remember being so bummed when I found out they built it."

He walked closer. Clovia quietly stepped out of her car. When she looked at the modern street-corner home, a sudden and sweeping sense of dejection overtook her. Having read Molly Butler's ghost hunting journal and heard about Jonathan's fond nostalgia for the great library that once stood here, the sense of loss was palpable. Jonathan had described protests organized by End Haven's residents in October 2008 to keep the library standing. During one of them, Molly Butler had suffered the first visible symptoms of her brain tumor.

*After she became obsessed with death,* Clovia thought.

Now Jonathan approached the newer house's front sidewalk, which curved toward a bright red front door. Thus far, nobody from inside had noticed the camera crew approaching, let alone Alice Winterblume and Rhode Island's famous nurse killer.

"There used to be a bike rack there," Jonathan said, pointing toward a spot about fifteen feet into the yard. "Molly used to feel like a grown-up whenever she'd fit her tire into the slot to keep it standing up. Not sure why."

As Clovia stood back, behind the camera crew, Alice followed Jonathan toward the yard.

"What else do you remember here?" she asked in her most somber reporter voice.

Clovia, through her ActoLenses' feed, could see one of the camera operator's profile shot of Jonathan. He was still facing away from everyone, standing with a relaxed posture while staring at the lot.

"A lot of stuff happened here. Not just Molly's ghost hunt. Elijah Bryce got attacked on the street here by Damon Jacoby, just a few months before he and Molly set up their weekly 'ghost' meetings. Then they met Lindsay Thorsen and got to be friends with her here."

Jonathan paused.

"Anything else?" Alice asked.

Through a dazed smile, his hesitation melted just enough to dispel the sense that he was being purposefully cryptic. "Did I ever mention that Pauline Gilbert and her choir teacher broke into this place?"

Clovia's ears perked up. No, he had not yet mentioned this.

Alice also quivered with curiosity. "I don't think I ever heard that story."

"They were trying to find the key to Mrs. Grime's old safe. Her friend Theodore Tarnish inherited the safe after she died, but he never had the key."

"Why the safe? What was in it?"

"An old journal."

Alice immediately looked at Clovia.

Just last week in Boulder, David Thorsen had discussed unanswered questions he had about the lost journal of Benedict Wise, an old friar who lived in Idle County during the late 1800s and early 1900s. Natalie and Alec Pent had also mentioned the same journal in their preliminary interviews. *WorldLine* had of course kept all this secret from Jonathan, and thus far, he wasn't even aware of who actually was scheduled to be interviewed here over the next three weeks.

"Care to elaborate on this journal?" Alice asked him.

Birds tweeted above them as Jonathan stared at the corner lot. He took a deep breath and held it for a moment. "Mrs. Grime kept it in the library until she died," he finally said. "It was written by Benedict Wise, the old friar who ran the church she went to as a kid."

"And Pauline Gilbert and her teacher broke in to find the safe key?"

When Jonathan nodded, he looked as if he were about to cry. "Yeah. And then they got in a car accident on the way home. A lot happened that year."

"And why was Pauline wanting to read this journal?"

Jonathan bristled, as if frustrated by Alice's prying. "It had information in it that she and the others thought might help Molly."

"About the thing in the Moon Woods, you mean?"

Jonathan simply stood at the corner lot for a moment, perhaps trying to formulate an answer, perhaps waiting to see a glimpse of the past. Instead of answering Alice, he glanced left. "Can I walk down the street this way?"

"You can go wherever you want," Alice said.

"Okay. Follow me, then."

The young man began walking west along Lemon Avenue.

With a few dithery glances, the crew followed. Clovia shadowed them as well, catching up with Jonathan's bodyguard, Sounder. "Hey. Glad you guys made it down okay," she whispered.

"Haven't quite been sure what to expect," Sounder whispered back, quietly shaking her hand. "I do know Jonathan was hoping you'd be here today, though."

"He barely said a word to me in Boulder."

"Yeah, but there's something about *here*. Not sure why. Either way, he talks about you a lot."

When Sounder winked, all Clovia could do was stare at him with a warm blush and smile.

But her relief could wait. This wasn't the day or time.

Only one neighbor, a middle-aged pajama-clad woman who was outside watering a slightly wilted garden, noticed them. Creases tilted her eyebrows when she recognized Alice and Jonathan, and she stood staring as they passed. After about five minutes, they arrived at the house Jonathan wanted to see.

It was the tan house that had caught Clovia's attention on her way to the corner of Lemon Avenue and Main Street. As Jonathan approached it, Clovia studied the house more closely. For whatever reason, a sudden image of blue siding and yellow roses flooded her mind, though there wasn't a single hint of either on site.

Her heart started beating faster. It was something deep, a dissonant rush of confusion.

Looking at the house—*this* house—felt familiar. Like home. Like a heralding of her reality crashing down.

Jonathan, seemingly with innocence, turned around to look at the crew.

*Oh God. Please not now.*

Then he looked right at her.

Clovia's anxiety became shortened breaths, then tears. For the first time in her life, she knew without a doubt that the universe was bigger, grander, and more mysterious than she had ever wanted to consider.

*Because I've been here before.*

She and Jonathan stared at each other as the emotions tethering them became visible.

Suddenly, one of the cameras was on her.

Alice looked between them. Staring. Making invisible connections.

Clovia, eyes wide and brimming with unfathomable tears, suddenly shook her head, held a hand up to signal her unexpected need for a breather, and turned away. Walking across the street and back toward her car, she felt the tan house bearing down on her, demanding both her attention and her respect.

Because thinking back to Jonathan's story about Molly Butler's final confrontation with Max Pope in 2004, Clovia now knew whom the house had once belonged to:

Mrs. Grime, the old librarian.

**2005**

"YOU ACTUALLY SHOWED UP!" Molly Butler called from the table under the Lemon Avenue Library's glowing stained glass window. It was the Saturday after Thanksgiving, and from second floor's main aisle, the late autumn's early afternoon light made Molly and Elijah Bryce look almost transparent.

"Hey, sorry I'm late," Lindsay said. "Had to say goodbye to my grandparents. They're going back to Palm Springs."

"Mmm, I'd love to live in California someday," Molly said as the library's clanking radiators drove home the reality of today's cold weather. The dark-haired girl then gestured to the boy Lindsay already knew by reputation. "Lindsay Thorsen, meet Elijah Bryce. Elijah, meet Lindsay. And yes, I told him that I told *you* about me seeing your brother."

Elijah smiled shyly and shook Lindsay's hand. "Here, have my chair," he said, standing up suddenly, seeming to remember courtesy. "I'll grab one of these ones against the wall . . ." Elijah was immediately strange to

Lindsay, solely because he was unlike any other thirteen-year-old boy she knew. The first thing she wondered when noticing his under-exercised body was what he'd look like in gym shorts and kickboxing gloves.

Lindsay accepted his chair once he had unfolded the third one. "Thanks. We were in different classes in fifth and sixth grade, I guess. I've still heard about you, though." As soon as she said the words, Lindsay inwardly kicked herself. All she'd really heard about him was that he was the "big homo" who'd killed Damon Jacoby.

To her relief, he seemed to read her mind. "Ha ha ha. I'm sure you've just heard a lot of crap from Alec and Natalie Pent, huh?" He blushed but didn't smile.

Lindsay could only shrug. "Alec never said anything mean about you. But Natalie . . . Let's just say we're not really friends anymore."

Elijah shrugged. "You don't say."

Fighting an embarrassed flush creeping into her face, Lindsay looked Elijah in the eyes. "Look—I know what people have said. That you're gay or whatever. I don't care about that. I've also started to realize lately just how many jerks live in this town."

"They're calling me a murderer now," Elijah replied, looking at his hands.

"*Us*," Molly corrected. "I got that label just by hanging out with you and being there the day of the tornadoes." She turned to Lindsay. "We met randomly last summer. Outside here, actually, by the bike rack. After Damon died, it automatically made me a 'murderer,' too."

Lindsay nodded but said nothing. Elijah had been interviewed on the news back in August by multiple reporters, including Alice Winterblume, the pretty one from Wind Prairie, and the story he told had been consistent, cut and dry. He had uncovered a jawbone buried in the Moon Woods earlier that summer, and police had identified it as belonging to a long-lost man named Joshua Grime—who, Lindsay suddenly realized, had started this very library with his wife before disappearing in 1947. After Elijah and Molly had tracked down the rest of his skeleton to a spot at Spinner's Lake, they rode their bikes out there, only to be accosted by Damon Jacoby.

*And I thought my life was difficult*, Lindsay thought.

Elijah pressed his pale hands flat against the table. "He was more depressed than I was, I think. Before he leaned backward off that rock, he told us to tell everyone he said goodbye. In case you knew him, I mean. I know Alec Pent did."

After saying Alec's name, Elijah grimaced.

"I only met Damon a few times," Lindsay said. "He did seem kind of sad."

The silence that followed was blunt but not exactly uncomfortable. Something underneath it tugged at Lindsay, though—the pained, perhaps even defensive expression on Elijah's face when he had mentioned Alec Pent's name.

"Alec wasn't the one who spread the gay rumors around school," she continued carefully. "That was Natalie. I was there the day she told everybody at lunch. Alec had only mentioned the tent thing at their dinner table, because he was confused. That was a while after it happened, though. You stopped hanging out with them, and nobody knew why, so Alec finally told his family what happened in the Moon Woods. That's what I got from Natalie's gossip, anyway. I could be wrong."

"See? I told you!" Molly said, hitting Elijah on the arm. "Elijah's spent the last year and a half thinking Alec Pent hates him."

Elijah blushed again, but when he decided to take their conversation toward the even bigger elephant in the room, she could tell he was a hundred times more comfortable. "I'm sorry about your brother," he said.

Lindsay's first urge was to change the topic yet again—but wasn't Drew the reason she had come here in the first place? She forced herself to find words. "Molly said she saw his ghost in the cafeteria at school that one day."

"Yeah," Elijah replied in a matter-of-fact tone.

Lindsay's gut twisted into a nauseating knot. Today was adding yet another layer of finality to the idea of Drew being dead. Fighting tears, she told Molly and Elijah about her ghost sighting of him at Fairfax Community Center, then about her internet search for information about other ghosts in Idle County.

"I think it's practically *normal* around here," Molly said. "Did you happen to notice Jacob Jenkins in class the other day, when your friend Natalie was talking to him and making fun of my collage?"

Lindsay swallowed. "Like I said, she's not really my friend."

"She's not a lot of people's friend," Elijah added.

"Anyway, Jacob has been my next-door neighbor since forever, and, like, a year and a half ago, right after my mom died, he decided he wanted to hunt for ghosts. I think because his dad saw one on Old Mill Road once. You know the story about that soldier people see wandering around there sometimes?"

"I read some article that mentioned him," Lindsay said, remembering the *Renegade* piece about Idle County she'd seen the night of her Googling. "Wasn't he killed by that crazy priest in the forties?"

"Yeah, apparently. Jacob and I went hunting for the soldier's ghost—along with a bunch of other ones—but we didn't see much. We only had three experiences that got weird. And then there was . . ." Molly paused and looked toward the ceiling, as if searching for words. She glanced quickly at Elijah, then shrugged. "Well, there have been a few actual ghosts since then, I think. It always takes me a while to believe it after it happens."

Elijah shrugged as well. "Same here. Some of the time, I still think it's all in my head, even though I know it isn't."

"That's *exactly* how I've been feeling," Lindsay said. "It always feels like a dream, and then I start thinking it didn't happen. Then I feel crazy."

Both Molly and Elijah chuckled, each staring at separate spots on the wooden table as if their thoughts were straying from their smiles. Elijah was the first to look up. "So, you're actually *not* here to make fun of us?"

"Come *on*, Elijah. I already told you she's super nice!" Molly hissed.

Fighting a scowl, Elijah turned toward Lindsay but didn't meet her gaze. "Sorry. I guess I haven't had the best experience with your group of friends."

"Well, I've never made fun of you—swear to God," Lindsay said. "I'm honestly here because I read your blog, and I don't know who else to talk to. I'm not friends with Natalie Pent and her little minions anymore, but if you don't want me here, I can go."

"No, no," Elijah said, his tone finally warming again. "You have to stay. I mean, I've seen ghosts. *We've* see ghosts. I think it makes sense for you to be here."

Lindsay smiled. "So, what do we do now? Do we just sit around and talk about dead people?"

Molly and Elijah looked at each other and shrugged.

"Honestly, we usually just talk about books or school or movies," Elijah said.

Lindsay, rarely one to sit through a whole movie, craned her neck and looked around at the bookshelves that stretched upward toward the slatted ceiling. Next she took in the multicolored stained glass window in front of her. It was immediately odd; instead of depicting something churchy, which she had assumed it did at first glance, it showed the backs of two children in a flowery field, looking on toward the backs of two adults, who in turn were looking at an angel-like figure rising into the sky. The figure was holding what looked like a baby. It didn't seem religious in nature, which made Lindsay wonder what meaning it'd had to its creator.

She cleared her throat. "So, you've both seen ghosts other than my little brother?"

"Yeah," Molly said. "Elijah's actually been seeing—"

Elijah, blushing for a third time, held up a hand at Molly. "I told you, I'm not sure about her."

"Not sure about who?" Lindsay asked.

Elijah and Molly exchanged glances, then looked back at Lindsay.

"The lady in the ratty old skirt," Elijah said. "Just some woman I've seen. I wasn't even sure she was a ghost at first. But I always see her in the same spot, and she always has her back to me."

"But then he saw her once when he was with *me*, and I didn't see her," Molly said. "I only got that weird feeling in my head, like reality was getting fuzzy."

Lindsay sighed and looked at Molly. "But you've seen Drew. I just wonder: Do you think anyone else is seeing him, too?" She turned to Elijah. "And why the heck is it just you seeing some lady in a skirt?"

Elijah's expression scrunched as if he were trying to fit the right words together. "I mean, maybe it's a dress. But I think it's 'all in the eye of the beholder' or whatever." He glanced at Molly. "And what about how I saw Damon's ghost last summer *before* he died? We still have no idea what that was about."

"Wait—*what*?" Lindsay frowned as Elijah's words hit her mind like nonsense.

Again, the boy's face turned beet red, but then he took a deep breath. "The first time I saw Damon Jacoby's ghost, it was during my paper route in the early morning. It was still a few weeks before he died. But he disappeared right in front of my eyes, so I know it was a ghost—or something *like* a ghost. Maybe some mental projection of the future. I have no idea."

"So, you're saying my brother might still be alive?" Lindsay said.

Molly gestured toward one of the bookshelves behind Lindsay, to the left. "I've looked in almost all the ghost books here, and I haven't seen anything about that. It's just a lot of conjecture about consciousness and chakras and quantum physics. I don't think any of it is actually scientific." She plunked her elbows onto the table and rested her chin in her hands. "Maybe time is different once you're dead or something, and ghosts can go back and forth."

"But didn't you say Jacob Jenkins saw ghosts, too?" Lindsay asked.

Molly squinted while pondering the question. "He never actually saw one, but he did hear and feel them—I know that for sure. Sometimes the air gets freezing cold when a ghost is around."

"That's how it feels whenever Drew is standing next to my bed," Lindsay said. She would have shivered if the ghost in question weren't her little brother. Yet Molly and Elijah's discussion of seeing Damon Jacoby's ghost before he actually died was somehow comforting. Maybe Drew *was* still alive.

"Do the police know who took him? Any leads yet?" Molly asked.

"Maybe," Lindsay said. She launched into the story of Detective Rhymes's call about Lowell Grendel during Thanksgiving dinner, including the fact that the man had helped Drew pick up the paper plates at Spinner's Lake on August 9, the day of the tornadoes.

Molly and Elijah, both staring straight into her eyes, listened to every word.

"Apparently, the police can't get a search warrant for this guy's property, because he *was* right by our yard that day, taking photos of a house. Even if the search dogs did pick up his scent, it wouldn't be enough due cause or whatever."

"Weird that we were all out at Spinner's Lake the day of the tornadoes," Molly said. "We brought a picnic out there and ate it in that same park about an hour before the storms rolled in. That's when we got stuck on Spinner's Island because of Damon Jacoby."

Lindsay sighed and leaned over the small wooden table, into her arms. "Do you remember seeing any guy with white streaks in his hair and a camera? Because we were there right around then, too. Probably about to leave."

Molly shook her head, but Elijah furrowed his eyebrows, looking down toward the table. "You said he had white streaks in his hair? Like, oddly prominent?"

"That's what I remember," Lindsay replied. "He moved here late last summer."

Then she remembered where Elijah lived, and her eyes widened.

"Not to freak you out, but he actually lives by you," she said. "You're on Windsong Road, down the street from Natalie and Alec, right?"

For a second Elijah stared at Lindsay, processing her question. Then he turned to Molly with a sudden jerk of his head. "Dude, the house at the end of my street—the new guy who moved in at the beginning of August. I *did* see him at the lake that day. Totally just a glance, but I remember. When we were eating our sandwiches."

Lindsay sat up straighter. "You've seen him?"

"Yeah. He lives to the left of me, at the far end of the street. And weird—I saw his U-Haul when he moved in last summer. I remember there was a tornado watch that day. But man, my mom would freak if she knew this guy was a suspect."

"'Person of interest,'" Lindsay corrected.

The three of them sat there, listening to the library's clanking radiator. There were more people in the library today than last time, so the sounds of footsteps, stray children making breaks from their parents, and the computer's checkout beeping filtered through the air.

After a few more moments of pensive thought, Lindsay asked, "Have you seen anything else weird?"

"Besides that lady?" Elijah asked. "No. I've only seen her a few times."

He sighed, then suddenly raised his eyebrows, as if remembering some forgotten detail.

"The lady," he said. "I first saw her hanging out on my street. I thought she was just someone dressed in old-fashioned clothes, but then I kept seeing her in the same place, like, three times. She was always walking toward this Lowell Grendel guy's house. Always with her back to me."

Lindsay's pulse quickened. "Who do you think she is? Or was?"

"No idea," Elijah replied. "She was the first random ghost I saw. Like I said, I saw Damon's ghost before he actually died. I have no idea why. I think once you've seen one ghost or whatever, it opens up your mind or something. More stuff gets through. Or maybe we're all just going nuts."

"I haven't seen any random ghosts yet," Lindsay said.

Molly, who already seemed like the resident expert, was fidgeting with her hands.

Elijah eyed her. "You're doing that thing again," he said. "Just say what you're thinking."

She took a deep breath, then looked right at him. "I think you should keep an eye out. I mean, not just for ghosts but in general. If you live by that guy, you might see something that could make a difference."

"Only if he's actually the guy who took her brother," he said, gesturing toward Lindsay. "We don't even know."

Molly looked at Lindsay. "But it doesn't hurt to be cautious, right?"

"I'm not the one who lives by him, so it's not up to me," Lindsay said. "But just in case . . . could you tell me if you see anything weird?"

Elijah, beaten, settled into his chair, looking uneasy.


Despite Elijah's reservations about keeping an eye on Lowell Grendel, Lindsay's first week of friendship with the Murderers—or *non*-Murderers—passed with more natural ease than she had ever felt in her life. For the first time ever, her true self came out effortlessly. It wasn't the buttoned-up version she displayed around her parents, and it wasn't the half-interested version she always displayed around Natalie Pent and the other girls. Strangely, it was closer to how she felt when watching Alan Sparks kickbox.

"So, tell us about him!" Molly said at lunch on Friday. "Which one is he? I'm too shy to even *look* at eighth-grade boys."

"Plus they all think we killed Damon Jacoby," Elijah cut in, picking at his ham and cheese sandwich.

Lindsay blushed, but she couldn't help the grin that colored her face. "Well, I doubt Alan thinks that. He's *nicely* athletic—like, not a jackass. I think he swims on the End Haven High team already. Kickboxing is just a side thing for him. At least that's what I heard him say one night after practice."

"So, you're the only girl who goes?" Elijah asked. "Do they treat you all weird?"

"Mostly, yeah. Alan is the only one who doesn't."

"I want to see what he looks like," Molly said, more into the conversation than Lindsay would have thought possible. It was different than the girl talk she'd experienced with Natalie Pent's friend group. Molly had never even kissed a boy, so her fascination with Lindsay's crush on Alan Sparks seemed more about curiosity than typical "boy-experience" comparisons.

"I'll point him out in the hall sometime. Or you guys could just come to kickboxing. He's always there."

"Yeah! That would be fun," Molly said.

Elijah sighed and sank into his sandwich. "I think I might skip out on that one."

Molly rolled her eyes. "You're just scared of being around all those hot boys."

"Whatever," Elijah said with his telltale blush. "They'd probably kickbox us to death because of Damon Jacoby."

Lindsay shook her head. "They all follow Alan like sheep, and he gets pissed when they act like assholes. Seriously, you should come. I bet my dad would pay for you both."

"Maybe I could just watch," Elijah said, easing into the idea with complete discomfort.

"You need a membership to use the fitness center," Lindsay added. "And parents' permission if you're under eighteen. You both turned thirteen already, right?"

Elijah nodded. "I mean, it *would* be fun to get into exercising. I just have no idea how."

Molly giggled. "You just want to get all big and buff so you can look like Alec Pent. Not that I blame you. If I were a boy, I'd want to look like him, too."

"She went out with him!" Elijah said, pointing to Lindsay, who immediately blushed again. They had already discussed this topic multiple times, but Molly and Elijah had not yet tired of it. They had teased her at least five times about how coldly she'd dumped Alec before her summer kickboxing camp in Washington, DC.

They finished their lunches and were just about to leave the cafeteria when Molly stopped midmotion. "Speak of the devil," she said, suddenly looking shy and pale.

Lindsay and Elijah turned around. Alec Pent was walking straight toward their secluded corner table.

*Oh God, I knew this would happen sooner or later*, Lindsay thought, guessing Alec was probably more curious about her falling out with his twin sister than actually feeling bad about it. Natalie wasn't much nicer to him than she was to anybody else.

"Hey," Alec said, looking at Lindsay first, then at Elijah, and then fleetingly at Molly.

"What's up?" Lindsay said, glancing at Molly and Elijah to make sure Alec got the hint that they were now her friends. Molly's quiet but humorous personality had suddenly vacuumed into itself, and Elijah was studying his sandwich's plastic wrap.

Alec, however, was nothing less than courteous. "Just saying hey. Heard you switched lunch tables."

"Yeah. Natalie kind of hates me now."

Alec gave her a knowing sigh, then turned to Elijah. "Hey, long time no see, man. How's it going?"

"Pretty good," Elijah replied, barely meeting Alec's gaze.

His old friend nodded nervously. "So, my family and Alan Sparks's family are having a Christmas party on December twenty-third. It's a Friday. We did a version of it last year and thought it'd be fun to do it again this year, but with more people."

He glanced at Lindsay, whose face went an even deeper scarlet at his mention of Alan Sparks's name. She knew they were family friends, and now that he mentioned it, she had heard social murmurs about a joint Christmas party last year, before her short dating stint with Alec.

"I know things are weird with Natalie," Alec continued, "but I still wanted to invite you. You all, I mean."

Alec gestured at Molly and Elijah. Molly gulped.

"You want me to come to a party where Natalie is going to be?" Lindsay let out an incredulous laugh. "You're kidding. Honestly, I think she and the other girls think I'm a bitch, because I don't like how they keep making fun of everyone."

With a slight chuckle, Alec shrugged. "I think you'll be fine. The party's at our house, and my parents will be there." His gaze shifted from Lindsay to Molly. "And hey, I think I've seen you hanging around at Elijah's house down the street. I'm Alec," he said, extending his hand.

Molly extended her own hand and gave him a rubbery shake. "I'm Molly." It came out as a near croak. She coughed and reiterated her name. "Molly Butler. Sorry—had a piece of celery in my throat."

Alec grinned, and Lindsay couldn't help but feel a flutter of joy over the fact that his expression toward Molly looked more than just courteous. "Anyway, I figured you'd all hear about the party, so I wanted to invite you first," he said. "December twenty-third, starting at six thirty. Don't forget." Before Lindsay could tell him no, he waved and walked away.

For a few seconds, nobody spoke. Molly had frozen like ice; Elijah's shy expression had brightened into something that looked like relief; and Lindsay, horrified at the prospect of going to a party where everybody would be whispering behind their backs, was hoping Molly and Elijah wouldn't even entertain the thought.

"I mean, it might be fun to go," Elijah finally said.

Lindsay grabbed her empty lunch bag and stood up from the table, then glanced at him when he didn't negate his own statement. "I hope you're kidding."

"Think about it. It could be funny if we all show up and freak everyone out," Elijah said. He got up and followed Lindsay from the table.

Molly straggled behind, fumbling to fold the lunch bag she had been recycling every day since Lindsay had met her. Elijah had been doing the same thing, which of course made Lindsay feel guilty whenever she threw her bag in the trash.

"I mean, I've known them since forever, so it wouldn't be overly weird to go to their house," Elijah continued. "Other than the fact that everyone who'll be there probably thinks I'm some killer."

His words unwittingly ushered Lindsay's thoughts back to Lowell Grendel.

"We could make a sleepover out of it," Molly said, catching up to them and throwing her garbage away. "I mean, if nobody wants us at the party, we could just go back to Elijah's house and play board games or something." She raised her eyes at Elijah. "That is, if your mom would let you have two girls over."

Elijah shrugged. "I doubt she'd care now that she knows I'm gay."

"I guess it *could* be fun," Lindsay said, suddenly warming to the idea of attending a party with Alan Sparks—and visiting Elijah's street. Because, in her mind, she was already looking toward the end of it, at the newly occupied house on the left. There Lowell Grendel stood, in the window with his white-streaked hair, waiting to become Idle County's next terrible news headline.

*IF YOU WANT TO GET THE STORIES, you need to look like a real jour-nalist,* Lydia Clark thought as she primped herself at the top of Dominic Bock's home sidewalk in Corpus Christi, Texas.

It was 1:03 p.m. on Saturday, June 25. As she looked up at the Bock family's well-manicured Texas-large house on Lake Superior Drive, a vice grip clamped her heart.

Today would be a moment of truth. Would the information about Jonathan Flite's biological father that Lydia had gleaned from Timothée Boucher, her snake-tattooed French lover, hold up? Three of Winifred Flite's ex-friends in Newport, whom Lydia had found via the woman's ActoHub connections, had corroborated the fact that Winifred had indeed dated this Dominic Bock man in her mid-twenties. But had the two lovers really conceived a child?

The doorbell to the Bock household played a digital tune—a slightly off-kilter version of *Yesterday* by the Beatles. While listening to the chimes and emotionally preparing herself for the door to open,

Lydia took in her surroundings: low palm trees in the yard's circular garden; a neatly trimmed hedge lining the sidewalk; and the house's predictable beige siding, which screamed "not quite rich."

Lydia rang the doorbell again. Social media accounts had already given her the names of Dominic Bock's wife and children, but how obvious should she make the extent of her knowledge? Would showing she had done her research prove her validity or make her look like a stalker?

*Only an amateur would worry*, she told herself. *If you want to be a real reporter, you need to get your hands dirty.*

From behind the door came the shuffling sound of footsteps. Then the turn of the knob, and a whoosh as the door opened.

A young girl, perhaps nine years old, stood behind the storm door, looking at Lydia curiously. Lydia recognized her as Dominic Bock's youngest daughter, Jessa. She'd been named on a digital Christmas card posted on Carolyn Bock's semiprivate ActoHub account and in photos from Dawson Elementary School's last "pick-up-the-trash" volunteer day, which Carolyn had organized.

"Hi there," Lydia said in her rehearsed voice. "My name is Lydia Clark. Is your father home?"

Without addressing Lydia directly, the girl turned and yelled, "Mom! Someone's at the door."

*Goddamnit.*

With a skeptical glance, young Jessa stepped back and waited awkwardly.

Lydia heard Carolyn Bock's much-more-frenetic gait before she saw it. The woman was a basic type of White-suburb pretty: brown hair, a light layer of makeup, fit for over forty. Yet there was something heavy in her eyes. Something recognizable. The weight of life, perhaps?

"Hi, can I help you?" Carolyn said.

"I believe so!" Lydia said in far too cheerful a voice. "Is Dominic home?"

The man's wife immediately stiffened. "No, he's at work."

"Oh, interesting—working on a *weekend*." Lydia knew her indirectness now wouldn't help, but the pierce in Carolyn's gaze had already set her on edge. Before she could think better of it, she added, "Dominic works in wave energy at WaveForm Electric, right?"

Now Carolyn ushered Jessa behind her and stood with the posture of a brick wall. "Excuse me, but what's this about?"

"My name is Lydia Clark," Lydia said, her high heels wobbling. "I'm a reporter from *Providence Today* in Rhode Island, here to follow up on the story of Jonathan Flite, the famous nurse killer."

Carolyn's expression hardened even further. She turned to her daughter and said, "Jessa, could you go water the plants out back please?"

Jessa deflated and again glanced curiously at Lydia. When Carolyn gave her a stern look, Jessa blew out a grand sigh and said in a showy voice, "Okay, *fine*." She stomped off as Carolyn opened the storm door and stepped onto the cement front porch.

"What are you here to ask?" Carolyn inquired.

Quaking once again in her cheap heels, Lydia said, "I have a source claiming to have evidence that your husband, Dominic, is the biological father of Jonathan Flite, the nurse killer in Rhode Island. I'm wondering if you'd care to comment on this."

Carolyn's eyes narrowed. A light breeze fluttered her brown hair as she studied Lydia's face. "I've never heard of your news outlet. What again did you say it was called?"

"*Providence Today*. It's an independent news blog," Lydia explained, still too cheerfully.

"And who told you my husband has anything to do with this story?"

"Unfortunately, I can't reveal my sources. This is obviously a sensitive topic."

"I have nothing to say to you," Carolyn said, turning back toward the house.

Just as she opened the storm door to go back inside, Lydia called after her, "Does Dominic have a work or cell number I could reach him at? I'd really like for this story to break with the full truth. I flew all the way down here to confirm it."

Carolyn froze in her tracks. She waited five seconds before turning to face Lydia again. "First off, no. My husband isn't talking to you. Second, it sounds like you're threatening me. And third, we're doing everything possible here to protect our daughters from the media circus following that nurse killer around. I'd appreciate it if you please leave my family alone—and out of your story."

*There. Bingo.*

"So, you're confirming there *is* a story?" Lydia asked.

"No, I—" Carolyn lost her words midscowl before regaining her composure. "I didn't say anything like that."

"But you do know who Jonathan Flite is? And what he's claiming?"

"All that past-life nonsense about those missing kids? Everyone knows about it. But this is Texas, Miss Clark. Some of us are still Christian down here."

"And what do you think about Winifred Flite telling everyone that Jonathan's father was a sperm donor? Did you know Dominic was the boy's father?"

Carolyn Bock's falsely polite expression dipped five shades darker, and her incredulous smile vanished. "Do you truly have no shame, Miss Clark?"

"I'm just doing my job, Mrs. Bock," Lydia replied over her own stuttering heartbeat.

"Oh. Really. Your job? Who employs you?"

"I told you before, I run my own—"

"Ah, that's right. 'Run your own news outlet,' meaning you have a *choice* here. Well, let me tell you about *choice*." Carolyn's anger was now red, livid, real. "That boy out in Rhode Island is attracting *terrorists.*

Death and violence follow him wherever he goes, and—hell, they're even saying he's linked to that nuclear bomb in Switzerland, which has us all scrambling to build bomb shelters we can't afford. Like I said, Dominic and I have *children* to protect." Fear flickered on the woman's face. "If you would knowingly publish a story made of 'facts' you can't confirm and put my daughters in danger, it would be unforgivable. Now I'm asking you, woman to woman: Do you really have the gall?"

Lydia stood paralyzed atop her wobbling ankles. For a second, she could only stare at Carolyn Bock with her mouth hung open. No dignified words could animate it.

"That's what I fucking thought," Carolyn said. "Have a good day, Miss Clark."

The woman disappeared back into her house—into her perfect little life—leaving Lydia standing on the cement porch with the posture of a prime fool.

When she finally found the gumption to walk back to her rental car, knowing she had just wasted Timothée Boucher's money to fly all the way to Texas for nothing, a new seed of anger—watered by self-doubt and self-loathing—sprouted its first gnarled roots in her.

*And this is why you haven't been able to achieve your dreams*, a nasty voice in her mind whispered. *Because you don't have the guts.*

So what if Carolyn Bock was right? Lydia still hated her for it.

And hate—just like love, she knew—could easily grow wings.

A T 7:15 A.M. ON SATURDAY, DECEMBER 3, Lindsay Thorsen was still sleeping in bed when the cell phone on her night stand buzzed uncontrollably. In a state of groggy confusion—made all the more unsettling by the fact that Drew had been giggling at the foot of her bed during the night—she grabbed the phone and saw Elijah Bryce's name on the caller ID.

"Hey," she growled, sounding more like a cranky lioness than a friend.

"Um, hey, it's Elijah calling," came the boy's voice through the phone.

"Yeah. What's up?"

"I know it's early, but I was doing my paper route this morning and actually did see something. I didn't want to call the police without talking to you first."

It took only a second for clarity to hit Lindsay.

*Police.*

*Drew?*

"Is it Lowell Grendel?" she asked.

"Maybe," came Elijah's reply.

Lindsay's heart jumped into hyperdrive, and a hot wave of tingles washed over her body. "Tell me everything."

"I was delivering his newspaper this morning. It was little bit earlier than usual—four thirty or so—so I doubt he was expecting me to be there. There was a small window on the door to his garage, and when I was walking by, I saw the light on and heard a kind of muffled loud sound, which I think was a vacuum cleaner. I saw him using it in his Jeep, like he was cleaning or something. He didn't see me, though. At least I don't think."

Lindsay jumped out of bed. Wearing her sports bra and night shorts, she bolted from her bedroom and ran downstairs to the den off the kitchen. Her father, in his usual morning work spot, looked up. His tired eyes grew alert as Lindsay spoke again into her cell phone. "Here, talk to my dad." She shoved the device into David's hands. "It's my new friend Elijah."

She paced back and forth as Elijah relayed his story. David Thorsen listened with his lips poised and eyes narrowed, then asked a number of questions once Elijah finished speaking. The phone call lasted five minutes.

"You asked Elijah to keep an eye out?" David said after ending the call. When Lindsay nodded, he walked to the kitchen without responding, looking both vexed and hopeful, then reached for his own cell phone to call Detective Rhymes.


Luck.

A break.

What Lindsay, David, and Sandra Thorsen found out from

Detective Rhymes later that morning was that Lowell Grendel's pre-dawn vacuuming might actually be enough for Idle County's municipal judge to issue a search warrant—because the effort hadn't been a simple coincidence. Something else had happened just last night, so late that Detective Rhymes had planned to wait until morning to phone the Thorsens.

David put the man on speaker phone so Lindsay and Sandra could hear his explanation:

At 10:46 p.m. yesterday, the Idle County Sheriff's Department had received a call from Wanda Jorgensen, a neighbor the Thorsens hadn't yet spoken with since moving to Dollywyn Drive. Lindsay had seen Wanda many times, even avoided a friendly wave from her here and there (living in Chicago had taught her Stranger Danger, after all). As it turned out, Wanda was recently divorced and had gone on three un-remarkable dates with Detective Rhymes last June. They were still on speaking terms, and thus had come Wanda's story.

Wanda did not live alone. She lived with her mother, Eleanor, a senile white-haired woman who liked two things in life: sitting on her front porch to watch the neighborhood when the weather allowed it, and sitting in front of her new high-definition television when it did not. On Halloween, despite the wind, Eleanor had been sitting on their front porch, breathing in the trickling end of the year's autumn air and waiting to see children in costumes.

"Old Eleanor woke up screaming at nine thirty last night, 'absolutely howling,' as Wanda put it," Rhymes explained. "Can't tell her daughter from a chocolate cupcake, but that's beside the point. She was screaming the name Rose over and over, saying that Rose had been there the day 'that boy across the street' disappeared. Now, I've never met anyone in this town named Rose, but what the old lady said next is the clincher: she said that this Rose woman pointed out 'the man with the black-and-white hair who drives the army jeep.' Wanda said she can tell when her mother is having lucid moments, and apparently this was one of them. She's sure Eleanor saw Lowell that day, sitting on their side of the street, watching your house."

"Jesus, God," Sandra said.

Yet Lindsay saw hope in her parents' eyes. Whoever this Rose woman was, she had told old Eleanor Jorgensen that a man with white-and-black hair had taken Drew.

Only one man Lindsay knew of matched that description.

*Lowell Grendel.*

After Wanda Jorgensen had called in with the tip, Detective Rhymes had crawled out of bed to visit Grendel's house with Deputy Eli Thropp. Again, Grendel had denied any wrongdoing and turned the police away. "We insinuated we'd likely be back soon with a search warrant," Rhymes said. "He looked like he might be panicking. Now, thanks to Wanda's mother and Elijah Bryce, we might actually *get* the warrant. My hunch is that whatever he was doing early this morning, he wouldn't have been doing it if we hadn't visited him six hours before."

Deputy Eli Thropp, as Detective Rhymes explained, knew Elijah Bryce through multiple incidents of Damon Jacoby's bullying last summer. They had both visited Elijah's house this morning, just minutes after David had called to relay the boy's story.

"I'll call you the second we have anything more. This is substantial," Rhymes promised them.

Now it was a waiting game.

WHO IS THIS ROSE? Lindsay wondered all the way to the library, where she, Molly, and Elijah were still planning to meet. Something about the name tickled the back of her mind, like a tiny hook at the end of a random life thread. If it were just the rambling of some mentally declining old lady, why did it sound so familiar? Yet Lindsay didn't know of any ghosts named Rose. Did she?

At the library, it was Elijah who offered a bit of progress.

"If it *is* a ghost—which is a big 'if'—what if it's the lady I've been seeing? The one who always has her back turned to me?"

Lindsay could barely muster a shrug. "Could be," she said. "I don't really know how the whole ghost thing works."

"Neither do we," Molly said with a glum look.

"I still don't see that many," Elijah added, looking at Lindsay. "I'm not sure how it'll be for you. I mean, you've only seen your brother, right?"

"As far as I know, yeah."

It seemed pointless to mull over the situation further. Yet that's all they did for the rest of the afternoon.


By the time Saturday came to a close, there were still more questions than answers. Detective Rhymes called at 8:04 p.m, as Sandra was shakily mixing her third after-dinner cocktail. David, who had been on severe edge all day, frowned as Lindsay handed him the phone. Instead of bringing it to his ear, he walked again toward the den's desk, pressed the Speaker button, and set the handset in its holder.

"This is David. We're all on speaker again."

A compulsory throat clear sounded through the phone, and Detective Rhymes continued. "Hello, David. Sandra. Hi again, Lindsay." Instead of waiting for their pleasantries, he immediately shared his news: the police had been granted a warrant to search Lowell Grendel's property. Coupled with a forensics team from Wind Prairie, they had examined his house, garage, and car from top to bottom.

"While we did find certain drug paraphernalia on the premises— meaning syringes and empty drug vials—there was no immediate physical evidence to suggest Drew had ever been there," the man explained. "But the forensics team is still in the process of analyzing fibers from Grendel's Jeep, garage, house, trash cans, and vacuum. We'll be able to identify any hair, red material from Drew's Halloween costume, or bodily fluid, if it's there."

At this, Lindsay, David, and Sandra could only stare at the phone speaker.

"And—I honestly should be keeping this under wraps, but I know you're going through hell over there," Detective Rhymes continued. "Just keep this next bit to yourself, please. No word to any reporters—a few of them did get wind of all this, and I'm guessing his face will be splattered all over the ten o'clock news tonight." The detective cleared his throat again. "Anyway, we did find a few things that gave us pause. The Jeep was freshly cleaned from top to bottom, just like the Bryce boy said. The floor carpet was still wet from the shampoo. And Grendel's computer is a story unto itself, because whatever files he may or may not have deleted, he forgot to clear his internet history after our visit last night. We saw that he had visited a number of sites relating to forensic investigation processes, including vehicle investigation and how forensics teams can find evidence of foul play by vacuuming and analyzing miscellaneous fibers. We'll soon be running a more thorough recovery of all data on his hard drive—deleted files and the like. But the point is, Grendel visited those websites last night, *after* we came to his house. He was definitely scared."

Lindsay looked at her father. His face was shaking. "And did he have any explanation?"

"He tried to make light of it. Said he had taken his new yellow lab pup on a ride and that the dog defecated in the back of the car, stepped in it, and dragged it all over the seat. We confirmed that he did indeed adopt the dog on a trial basis on November fifth. Named it Trevor, then sent it back a few days ago. The forensics team will be testing the carpet for fecal matter to see if what they find corroborates Grendel's story. Either way, Grendel says he has trouble sleeping at night in general, so he decided to do the cleaning in the early a.m. instead of waiting for daylight."

"What about those damned websites?" Sandra slurred. "What did he have to say about that?"

"He says he's writing a book, and he was doing research," Detective Rhymes replied. "Thing is, we didn't immediately find any documents on his computer that resembled book manuscripts. Not to mention that he just happened to go do his 'research' when he realized a search warrant was about to be issued."

"That bastard," David said. "That goddamned *bastard*."

Sandra, almost invisibly, flashed a sour glance at her husband. *What happened to "not trampling on his rights"?* Lindsay imagined her asking with snark.

"Now, are you ready for the weird part?" Detective Rhymes asked.

The ice in Sandra's drink clanked against the glass in a way that sounded heightened, almost surreal.

"This guy is a photographer—Lindsay told us that when we first interviewed her. He was taking pictures out at Spinner's Lake, the day of the tornadoes. Anyway, since he hasn't quite made the leap to digital photography yet, he's transformed one of his basement rooms into a large darkroom. We found hundreds of pictures down there. Some were hanging up to dry, and a lot of them were just reprints of the same ones over and over again. You'd be creeped out if you saw them."

"They weren't of little kids, were they?" Sandra asked, almost spitting out the words.

"Well, that's just the thing. They're not of Drew directly. Actually, we're not quite sure *what* they're of. Some of these photos did have people in them, but not like you'd think. A lot of them looked more like balls of light, all shapes and sizes, and had hazy outlines around them."

David Thorsen's gaze locked on Lindsay's.

*Ghosts*, she could almost hear him thinking.

Her palms began to sweat.

"Looked like something you'd see in one of those haunted-house movies," Detective Rhymes continued. "Creepy stuff. Never seen anything like it, you know? I recognized some of the places in the photos, but a lot of them were focused on whatever these things were, and the background was blurred out."

Detective Rhymes took a deep breath and then paused, seemingly searching for his next words.

"There was this one, though," he finally continued. "Scared the living hell out of me. It was the clearest of them all. A woman in an old-fashioned dress, looking straight into the camera. A ball of light was blocking out most of her face, but you could just see the shadows that would be her eyes. They looked white, like the opposite of a skull. I couldn't quite see how old she was or what she looked like, but Jesus, it was weird. Creepiest thing I ever saw. Taken right outside his house, by the look of it, because I could see Elijah Bryce's house blurred in the background."

Silence filled the room as Lindsay contemplated Detective Rhymes's words.

First, it had been Molly Butler who'd seen ghosts.

Then Elijah Bryce.

Then Lowell Grendel.

Now Lindsay herself.

Who else in Idle County shared this affliction?

David, again locking his gaze on Lindsay, leaned closer to the phone. "You said Drew wasn't in the pictures directly. What did you mean by that?"

For a moment, all they could hear were Detective Rhymes's heavy breaths. When he finally spoke, hesitation colored his tone. "Well, know this up front: I've never believed in ghosts, life after death, or anything like that. Mom got killed by a burglar when I was a kid, and Dad turned to drinking and beat the hell out of me in the years after. I had to see how meaningless life can seem. Nothing in my life made me believe that it goes on, into some other type of hell. But . . ." He paused to collect himself. "Some of these photos did show children. Or the outlines of children. Most of 'em were those bright lights, but you could make out shapes of people behind them. But the faces were impossible to see. No better way to explain it. So, yes, some looked like kids, but no, I couldn't tell if any were Drew."

Nobody spoke.

Lindsay's heart turned in circles. Then new visions came to her:

Alec and Natalie Pent's Christmas party.

A possible slip away, to Lowell Grendel's house.

A secret search for incontrovertible evidence.

*Maybe he has a photo of Drew as a ghost. Maybe I'd recognize it if I could just break into his—*

"That's what I meant by 'not directly,'" Detective Rhymes finished.

In response, Lindsay and her parents could only sit there, in stunned silence.

To be still. Aware. Mindful.

Did life have any other purpose? Did it have a plan? Revis Zobel didn't know. But as he stood alone on the edge of his yacht's diving board, looking into the blue sparkles of the Tyrrhenian Sea, he thought: *Yes. Maybe.*

It was July 1, 2039—the hottest first day of July on Italian record. He had just, for the hundredth time today, forced the panic in his heart to abate. Imagining the reaction his father, Victor, would have to Alice Winterblume's upcoming *WorldLine* season on Jonathan Flite and Idle County—not to mention Revis's involvement in it—had recently become a daily source of concern. Revis would be answering numerous speculative questions from Alice, formulated in conjunction with the FBI, about his father's possible crimes, including the yet-to-be-proven orchestration of the nuclear terrorist attack in Geneva, Switzerland, two years ago.

*And then I'll be excommunicated from the family forever*, Revis thought.

In a forced swath of calm, he dove into the water.

While floating, he considered his demands for *WorldLine*—because yes, they had asked him what he wished for in return for his participation. Alice Winterblume was a back scratcher, a tit-for-tat personality. Even though her Jonathan Flite project had rendered *WorldLine*'s New York office burning rubble, she still wanted to offer Revis something valuable in return for his interview. She was also smart enough to know that money held no sway over him.

Until recently, he'd had everything in life he ever wanted, except perhaps for love—and answers. If crazy Jonathan Flite could offer him anything—whether it be the truth about what had really happened to his half sister, Jillian, or whether Jillian had witnessed any hints that their dead mother, Cassandra, had been poisoned (as the physicist Dorothy Garland, whose real name he now knew was Rebecca Sparks, had hinted at in her last letter)—then this charade with *WorldLine* and the FBI would be worth it.

A meeting with Jonathan Flite. That was what Revis wanted.

And hell, *WorldLine*'s cameras could even record it. If it simply turned into a shitfest on Revis's own father, that was fine; it would be a shitfest well placed and well earned by famous Mr. Victor. But if it were to go further—if Jonathan were to shed some clear, vibrant light on hidden family secrets nobody even knew to ask about—that would be swell as a fucking bell.

As Revis climbed back up his yacht's ladder, toward the ActoPhone lying on a nearby table, a message alert fluttered across his ActoLenses' display. It swiped in just as he reached the deck, overlapping his view of the Amalfi Coast's high ridges in the distance.

The message was from another ActoUser with the screen name "SnakeOil," in English.

*SnakeOil.*

"Open the message," Revis said, immediately suspecting who it might be.

Floating back into his perception (yet partially hidden by the ActoLens display) was the gaggle of scantily clad Italian women drinking on his boat deck. Some were already naked—laughing and teasing and posing as he passed. They were just toys, and they liked it that way. They knew nothing of his real life. Nothing of the concerns plaguing him. Nothing about his true intentions for the future.

As he shut them out, he grabbed his ActoPhone and thought of Natalie Pent, his sister's personal trainer. She was the one woman in recent memory who had seen through Revis's facades. He had been thinking of her every day since.

He walked to his bedroom, then scanned the message from "SnakeOil." It took only one line for him to be 100 percent sure it had been written by Raphael Dumont, his father's old friend, in response to an email Revis had sent him after receiving Rebecca Sparks's letter at the Salerno house.

*Revis, my boy,*

*Poisons? Strange and unexpected that you would ask me of that topic. Where did you get the idea that I would be a valuable source?*

*Now that your father and I are forever at odds, I find it safe to say that he has indeed asked me (and others) to do many dark and terrible things. And yes, in his worst moments, he also considered your mother—and her questions about quantum theory and the nature of the universe—a "threat" to his "image." I did procure for him on numerous occasions multiple types of poisons, though I was never sure what he did with them.*

*He is the monster. But so am I now. All I know of poisons, I've learned from him. And I wasn't his only student.*

*Please also know that I rarely check the email address you sent your last message to. I would think world governments are surely monitoring that account. I'm able to access it from time to time, however. I'm sorry this response comes late.*

*I'm on a mission now, until the end. I hope you understand once it's complete.*

*Affectueusement,*
*Ton « oncle »*

*Your "Uncle."*

"Uncle Raph," he and Victoria had always called him. "Uncle Raph" with his creepy snake tattoo and greasy-ass ponytail. Except now it was clear he cared. Enough to help, at least.

There came a rap on his bedroom door. Knuckles.

Revis knew their unique cadence. It was Lucia—the most domineering of his yacht guests, probably looking for fun. But she was nothing. He wasn't in the mood for her artificial type of love today.

"Not now," he politely called out.

After quickly forwarding Raphael's message to Special Agent Heather Mousseau in New York—which was technically unnecessary, seeing as the US government was surely monitoring his Acto account—he copy and pasted it into a text message to Natalie Pent. Because why not reach out again? Why not show her that he had listened to her valid concerns about Raphael Dumont that night in Minneapolis?

Under the pasted message, he added:

*↑↑ From your little friend Raphael Dumont.*

Refusing to hope for a response but hoping anyway, Revis locked his phone carefully inside his safe and walked back out onto the boat deck with a pasted-on a smile.

"NO FORENSIC EVIDENCE." That was the word from Detective Rhymes. Despite having charged Lowell Grendel with a petty misdemeanor for possessing a bag of empty drug vials and syringes, the police hadn't been able to arrest him. As a result, the news reporters who had flocked to his doorstep ten days ago were losing interest. Lowell was, by all accounts, a free man.

On Tuesday, December 13, Lindsay's eyes were heavy all day. When the bell rang to let her and Molly out of English class, they were still gathering their books when Ms. Olson motioned with her head for them to stay behind a second. When the last remaining students filtered out of the room, they both took seats on top of their desks. Ms. Olson approached them, holding out what looked like a newsletter.

"I've got something for you both," Ms. Olson said. "Well, I thought of Molly first when I saw it, because of her collage, but seeing as you two are all chummy lately, I thought it might be interesting for both of you. Maybe even that friend Elijah of yours."

"What is it?" Molly asked, taking the newsletter from Ms. Olson's hand.

Lindsay leaned in for a closer look. Their teacher had folded the newsletter back to one of the pages near the end. Across its lower half was an ad.

*Benedict Wise University's*
### FIRST ANNUAL GHOST SYMPOSIUM
*February 3 – February 5*
*Cougher Hall*

*~ Please join us for a weekend of academic mystery, inspired by the late Elizabeth Anne Grime, one of our most cherished benefactors. Come as we host a wide range of guest speakers and organizations dedicated to studying the greatest mysteries life has to offer.~*

*Space is limited, so please call our campus life office at 237-875-0999 to book your spot. Tickets are $75 for the entire weekend and include assured lecture seating, catered lunch and dinner each day, and parking.*

Ms. Olson let them skim the ad before she spoke. "My partner gets this newsletter—it's her alma mater. I read it sometimes when I'm trying to talk myself out of a PhD."

Lindsay's first reaction was to blush. Molly, however, held the pamphlet with the same type of reverence priests on television used when holding Communion wafers.

Ms. Olson watched them both carefully. "I could probably be fired for giving you something like this, because of what it implies about spiritual beliefs and such, but I decided to risk it. No problem if you don't want to go. You both seem less than excited."

Out of habit, Lindsay pasted on her best business-casual face. "I think it looks interesting, actually."

"Me too," Molly added. "But it's just . . ." She paused, staring at the paper.

"Just what?" Ms. Olson asked.

Molly's expression grew somber. "I knew the benefactor they're talking about. Mrs. Grime. We got to be good friends before she died."

"You mean the old lady with sparkly eyes from the Lemon Avenue Library?" Ms. Olson asked, looking completely unsurprised at Molly's proclamation. Most kids who grew up in End Haven had known Mrs. Grime.

Molly nodded, then looked at Lindsay. "Tickets are expensive, but it'd be great to go to this. Especially if these people knew Mrs. Grime."

"Why? Did Mrs. Grime believe in ghosts, too?" Ms. Olson asked in a lighthearted tone, as if suddenly unsure whether to be serious.

"She did, actually," Molly replied. "I never got the details on what happened, but I think it was back around the time her husband was killed by that serial-killer priest guy."

*Joshua Grime.*

His was the skeleton Molly and Elijah had found back in August, buried in the cave on Spinner's Island.

Ms. Olson's curiosity perked up even more at Molly's mention of the man, but she tried to cover it with a shrug. "Well, cool. I'm glad you're interested. The ad doesn't say anything about age requirements, so I'm assuming anybody can go. You'd need a parent to go with you, obviously. If you run into any trouble buying tickets, I can have my partner, Judy, get them for you—she's connected."

A few moments later, in the hallway, Molly asked, "Can you believe how cool this would be?"

For once, Lindsay's enthusiasm was almost a match for Molly's. "Yeah. I feel like it's a sign or something. We should definitely get tickets."

Then, remembering the look on her father's face when Detective Rhymes had discussed the mysterious photos hanging in Lowell Grendel's basement, she added, "My dad might also be interested. I'll see if he can drive us and pay for a hotel."

Molly beamed.


It was Elijah who pointed out the obvious on their way out of school. "You do know this is going to make it pretty clear to our parents that we're crazy, right?" Yet the determination in his eyes made it clear he was just as excited about attending the symposium as they were. "Just wanted to bring it up so we all know what we're getting into. If we ask to go to this thing, it'll be obvious that we believe in ghosts. Just saying."


Later, however, over a lukewarm dinner of Tickle Me Thai takeout—Sandra Thorsen was already in bed for the night—David Thorsen listened to Lindsay's proposal to attend the ghost symposium. Just as she predicted, he offered to pay for everybody, including their hotel stay for a night in Wind Prairie.

"Sounds like you're really liking your new friends," he said after Lindsay thanked him.

She blushed, then added, "Yeah. And don't worry. Elijah is gay, so it won't be weird staying overnight with him."

With only a slight furrow of his eyebrows, David chuckled and nodded.


On Monday, the nineteenth of December—just four days before the Pent-Sparks Christmas party—Lindsay walked onto the kickboxing floor flanked by her two new friends. Her extremely late birthday presents to Molly and Elijah (also paid for by David Thorsen) had been two yearlong passes to the Fairfax Community Center's gym. It had been obvious from the get-go that neither Molly's father nor Elijah's mother had as much money to spare as her own parents did, and she wanted them to join her for kickboxing without pressuring them to pay. After David had agreed to front the money, Lindsay had called both Molly's father and Elijah's mother to get sign-off. Each did so with measurable enthusiasm; Shelly Bryce had seemed particularly keen on the idea of her son spending his time exercising instead of digging up skeletons.

"Are you sure I have to do this?" Elijah asked as they entered the community center.

"Come on, Elijah! It was a birthday present," Molly replied, even though she now sounded more nervous than before about the prospect of exercising in front of other people.

Coach Martinez beamed when he saw them, but Lindsay had to ignore the stares Elijah got as the other boys donned their boxing gloves and took spots at the hanging punching bags.

Alan Sparks was the last one out of the men's locker room. He caught Lindsay's eye and smiled as he took a punching bag two spots down from hers. His smile faded, however, when he saw Molly and Elijah. Lindsay couldn't tell whether his expression was one of simple surprise or one laced with contempt over the Murderers' presence.

*If it's the latter, you just lost all your points,* Lindsay thought.

"Hey, Sparks!" Robbie Wheeler said, knocking Alan on the shoulder and leaning close to whisper something in the black-haired boy's ear. As he pointed toward Molly and Elijah, a few other boys chuckled and shook their heads. From three spots down, near Alan, Lindsay heard somebody whisper, "What's the faggot doing here?"

Coach Martinez, who was on the other end of the room examining Dan Nelson's injured wrist, seemed completely oblivious to the slur. More whispers of *"I don't know"* and *"I think he came with Thorsen"* followed. Lindsay turned to check on Molly and Elijah. Like Coach Martinez, they both appeared oblivious to the comments; they were laughing about something to themselves.

That Alan Sparks stood in the bullying circle boiled Lindsay's blood even more than the name-calling. Clearly, he was no different than the other boys. Wouldn't he be defending Elijah otherwise?

*Yeah, and you should be, too,* one of Lindsay's less judgy inner voices piped up.

Just as she mustered the courage to unleash hell, however, Coach Martinez starting calling the shots for their warm-up. Ten right hooks. Ten jabs. Ten left hooks. Leg kick. Push kick. Cross, uppercut, and roundhouse, all times twenty. Go, go, go!

With each punch and kick, Alan's face grew clearer and clearer in Lindsay's punching bag. She thought of him next to the Pent family Christmas tree this coming weekend. In her imagination, she pushed him right the hell into it.

Two jabs followed by a left hook. *Maybe it isn't worth making a scene if Elijah didn't hear the bullying.*

Leg kick. *That's not the point.*

Push kick. *Yeah, then what is the point?*

Uppercut and a whopping roundhouse. *The point is to make this world a less crappy place!*

Midway through, Coach Martinez had them switch to the mat in the main atrium—an unexpected move for a Monday. "Sparring practice! Get a partner, everyone. I'm going to teach our newcomers a thing or two on the punching bags. You all: practice for the tournament!"

Lindsay watched Jeff Miles punch Alan on the shoulder to claim him as a fighting opponent. The other boys paired up until only one was left: Robbie Wheeler, the jerk who had pointed at Elijah.

"Hey, Thorsen, I guess we're fighting tonight."

With a deep glare, Lindsay put her helmet on and threw in her mouth guard. "I guess we are."

"And why'd you bring *those* two here?" Robbie gestured at Molly and Elijah, who had finally both slipped on some spare boxing gloves.

Lindsay adopted her fighting stance. "Why do you care?"

Robbie snickered. "I just didn't know you were dating queers now. Alan Sparks thought he had a chance with you."

Lindsay attacked. Her fury caught Robbie off guard, and his smirk became wide-eyed concern as she sent a right hook into his leering jaw. She hit him with a solid leg kick before he finally stepped back and adopted his fighting stance.

"Good one, Thorsen." He was already breathing fast, on an unexpected defensive.

*You're just one boy I'll smack down on my way to Alan Goddamned Sparks*, she thought at him, diving below one of Robbie's hooks. They had circled the mat, so Lindsay now faced the smaller punching-bag atrium. She had just enough time to glimpse Elijah in a surprisingly solid fighting pose before twisting away from Robbie's leg kick.

Two minutes into their fight but not quite breathless, she said, "You're an asshole for making fun of Elijah."

Robbie fell into the circular dance Lindsay was making around him. "Oh, is that his name? I forgot. All I know is that I saw him on the news last summer after he killed my friend."

Lindsay faked a right hook before landing a left jab on Robbie's helmet. "They didn't kill Damon Jacoby!"

"Yeah, right. I'll believe that when I see the evidence." Robbie's breaths were heavy. "Don't you realize what being friends with them is doing to your reputation? Alan knew about it from school, but he was surprised you actually brought them here."

"What the hell does he care?" Lindsay rejoined. She ducked away from Robbie's roundhouse but fell right into his hook. It came with the boy's full force.

*Yes. Finally. He's actually fighting me.*

Lindsay ramped up her efforts.

"Are you totally blind?" Robbie asked between pants. "Alan is totally into you, and you're not doing anything about it. I'm betting he's freaked out now, though, because you're friends with the people who killed Damon. He and Damon played baseball together in sixth grade!"

Lindsay channeled all her feelings into another fake out that Robbie fell for. She landed a double punch: a hook, then a jab. "Does he know that Damon tried to kill Elijah?"

"Damon was from a messed-up family," Robbie said. "Doesn't mean they had to go push him off a rock and crack his skull open. I'm just saying it'll probably be tough for Alan to ask you out if he knows you're hanging out with that killer fag and his hag!"

That did it. Lindsay lunged at Robbie, ducking under his hook and landing a kick on his leg. He winced, then snickered. It was the hardest Lindsay had ever worked to overcome an opponent, and for the first time, Robbie was really trying.

And his height left him at a disadvantage. Where he bested Lindsay in strength, she bested him in adroitness. She was smaller and faster. It was all about landing the kicks and the punches, and she was doing a better job.

They had both worked themselves into a dripping sweat by the time Coach Martinez finally remembered to blow his whistle. "Time! Got carried away helping our newbies learn some of the moves!" he said. "Switch it up!"

For the next forty minutes, Lindsay worked her way through

kickboxing partners, getting closer and closer to Alan Sparks. Each time she tried to claim him as a partner, however, he had already chosen another.

"Eight o'clock!" Coach Martinez yelled. "Your rides are waiting!"

Jeff Miles backed off from Lindsay, panting as he bent over and held his knees.

"Good fight, Thorsen," he said. "But you might not want to bring those two back here." He got up and walked toward the spot where his friends were congregating.

Alan's piercing black hair caught Lindsay's eye as two of the boys in the circle departed for the locker room. Without thinking, she veered toward him, keeping her strides long and fast and her footsteps heavy. Alan turned and, with a smile on his face, said, "Hey, good job. Looks like you creamed Robbie, Steve, and—"

"You're a total jerk," Lindsay hissed. "Robbie said you didn't like that I was hanging out with Elijah Bryce and Molly Butler." She pointed a finger at her two new friends, who were still talking to Coach Martinez across the atrium. "You guys make fun of Elijah for being gay and Molly for being his friend, and then you keep spreading the stupid-ass rumor that they killed Damon Jacoby."

Alan took a step back. "Wait, I—"

"Don't you realize that Damon did the same thing? And that it got so out of control that he tried to kill both of them?"

"I said I—"

"Elijah and Molly almost *died* out on Spinner's Island because of that bullying shit. Have you even had to think about how awful death actually is?"

*Now it's about Drew*, Lindsay thought, inwardly shrinking. *And they all know it.*

"I just thought—" Her voice faltered. "I just thought you were better than that."

Lindsay turned around and stormed back across the mat, away from the boys. If she hadn't been the girl with the missing brother, they would have surely laughed off her little explosion. But she *was* the girl with the missing brother, and they all remained utterly silent as she left them in her dust.

2039

Lydia Clark, rolling with drunkenness from her third glass of chardonnay, hovered over the Publish button on her *Providence Today* blog. It was 8:32 p.m. on July 8, 2039, and she had been sitting on the Dominic Bock story for almost two weeks. If he really was Jonathan Flite's father, which his wife, Carolyn, had all but confirmed in Corpus Christi two Saturdays ago, someone was going to find out sooner or later. Someone was going to publish it. Someone was going to get all the credit.

*Real reporters tell the truth even if it makes people's lives harder,* Lydia told herself as she stared at her computer.

And hell, look at Alice Fucking Winterblume. She was still plowing ahead with her "secret" Jonathan Flite documentary for *WorldLine,* even after one of her employees had protested the project by detonating a goddamned suicide bomb.

Lydia took the last sip left in her glass, poured the rest of the bottle, and checked her ActoPhone again.

Still no response from Timothée Boucher. Either he had found some other woman to dangle a carrot in front of and was no longer interested in her reporting career, or something had happened. He hadn't returned her calls in over a week.

*Fuck it.*

Through a drunken haze, Lydia clicked Publish.

There.

Her story was live.

So what if she felt guiltier than ever for dragging Carolyn Bock and her poor little family into the unforgiving media spotlight? The world would now know that Jonathan Flite had a biological father named Dominic Bock. That Mr. Bock had been kept in the dark about his relation. That Jonathan's mother, the vicious bitch Winifred, had told everyone that Jonathan's father was a sperm donor. It had all been there, in the hacked text message threads between Jonathan and Jimmy Barber, so why shouldn't the world know?

Lydia shared the post to her ActoProfile. Then she submitted an anonymous story tip about it to the *New York Times*. And the *Wall Street Journal*. And *USA Today*. Then came the *Los Angeles Times*, CNN, the *Washington Post*, and the *Daily Gossip*. The list went on and on until she was halfway done with her second bottle of wine, feeling blue in the face.

After targeting every American publication she could think of, she sent a text message to Timothée Boucher, her smarmy French lover who clearly thought she was nothing more than a saggy old gold digger.

> *There. It's done. The world knows who Jonathan Flite's father is. Now, where the hell are you? I want you. Please.*
> *I really want you.*

Lydia waited for a response. Or an indicator that Timothée was typing.

But no. Nothing came. Not even a hint that life would, for once, go her way.

She fell asleep drunk and crying.

THAT SAME NIGHT, two hours later and halfway across the country, Clovia Bell stood outside room 406 at the Fairfield Inn in End Haven, Minnesota. It was Jonathan Flite's room, a top-floor suite—and she was about to knock on the door, despite her throbbing heart.

They were going on day twelve of their Idle County shoot, and due to how emotionally draining it had become, Jonathan disappeared into his room every night. He had now met personally with multiple family members, friends, and acquaintances of the Idle County Seven, including Shelly Bryce, Eloise Creed, Lynn Peabody, Claire Gilbert, Emily Tarnish, and Natalie Pent. Alice Winterblume had interviewed each person both before and after their recorded visits with Jonathan, and thus far, Jonathan had convinced every single one of them that his memories were legitimate.

Shelly Bryce had quietly shed tears when Jonathan recalled a life-altering argument she'd had with her son, Elijah, in the summer of 2005.

Eloise Creed's face went pale when Jonathan asked her if she still had the psychic gifts her brother Gabriel had witnessed the night of the gas explosion at the Sparks house.

Lynn Peabody, who had been the interim librarian at the Lemon Avenue Library from 2004 to 2008, almost turned a shade of gray when Jonathan recalled her first meeting with Lindsay Thorsen, which occurred just days after Lindsay's brother, Drew, had been murdered. Lindsay had been crying in the library's legal section, watching Elijah Bryce and Molly Butler through the book stacks.

Claire Gilbert, now a resident of Montana and by far the most skeptical of the Idle County Seven parents, had frozen midstep on Windsong Road's sidewalk when Jonathan described the true nature of the secret pregnancy her daughter, Pauline, had in tenth grade. The biological father hadn't been Jacob Jenkins, Jonathan claimed, but rather Pauline's high school choir teacher, Mr. Boltan.

Natalie Pent's stoic demeanor had turned brittle the moment Jonathan recounted a bathroom conversation she'd overheard between Lindsay Thorsen and Jillian Pope the day after the 2007 gas explosion at the Sparks house. The entire *WorldLine* crew was silent as Jonathan confirmed that Jillian had indeed suspected Victor Zobel of causing the gas leak and that she had been too afraid of him to go to the police. When Jonathan also added almost nonchalantly that Lindsay had noticed Raphael Dumont following her the afternoon before her disappearance in 2010, Natalie—still unaware that *WorldLine* wouldn't be naming Raphael in the documentary—burst into tears, removed her microphone, and walked off camera.

And then came Jonathan's meeting with sixty-six-year-old Emily Tarnish, who grew white as a ghost when Jonathan explained how her dying father, Theodore Tarnish, had given Clayton Graf and Elijah Bryce the final, missing journal of Benedict Wise in 2010. It had been sitting in his bedroom closet, in an old safe that had once belonged to his best friend, the late librarian Mrs. Grime.

*Whose old house I couldn't even look at, because I'm losing my mind,* Clovia thought now as she stood outside Jonathan's hotel room door.

Yet being here in Idle County had awoken something in her that she couldn't describe. Even the cameras had recorded it—the intangible energy passing between her and Jonathan that first morning, in front of the tan house on Lemon Avenue. He had confirmed later that it had indeed belonged to Elizabeth Anne Grime, the mythical librarian who died on September 3, 2004. Her ghost was, according to Jonathan, the first one Molly Butler ever saw.

If Clovia tried hard enough, she could almost remember the moment: eleven-year-old Molly walking down the old library aisle, her dark eyes widening in shock as she clutched her homemade stained glass window—a gift she had been planning to give to the old woman.

*Or you've just heard Jonathan's story one too many times,* Clovia thought.

She knocked on his door.

After a few disquieting moments of silence, footsteps rustled up to the other side of the peephole.

"Oh, whoa—I'll be right there," were the first words Jonathan had spoken to Clovia in weeks.

Was Sounder in there, visiting from his adjacent suite? Or Jimmy Barber? If so, she might be making a fool of herself within seconds.

When Jonathan opened the door, he was wearing gray sweatpants and a plain blue T-shirt, one that hugged his ropy frame. Attraction rushed through Clovia when she saw the contours of his muscles.

And it was just the two of them, face-to-face. Finally.

*He's a killer. Remember that.*

Except he was gentle. He was kind. He was damaged, perhaps, but intensely caring about those around him. All week, Clovia had watched him interact with people from Idle County, seeing him appear at ease, unworried and validated, for the first time since their initial meeting.

"Can we talk?" she whispered. "No cameras."

Caution sharpened his expression, but he quickly said, "Sure—let me get my flip-flops."

"Flip-flops?"

"Yeah, to walk outside. So you can feel safe, I mean."

Embarrassment flushed Clovia's face as Jonathan nodded cordially and turned to fetch his flip-flops. If he weren't Rhode Island's famous nurse killer, she'd be listening without question to the push in her gut telling her that he was it; he was the one; he was about to become the best friend she would ever have in life, if only she were to forget her own fears.

*To run backward or to leap with faith?*

It was the question of the hour.

"Okay, let's go," Jonathan said. "We might have to sneak out the back of the hotel. I saw a bunch of reporters out front earlier."

Clovia moved away from the door frame to let Jonathan through. He passed her, and as they turned in tandem toward the hotel elevators, his hand brushed the small of her back. The gesture seemed effortless. Caring. Nurturing.

*To leap with faith, then,* she thought.

They made for the elevators.

AFTER FINDING A PAVED BIKE PATH behind the hotel parking lot, they walked. For the first time in her life, Clovia knew what it meant to have a soul mate. Her apology for hurting Jonathan's feelings in April came quickly, as did his forgiveness and understanding. He explained that in the lead-up to their derailed conversation following Patrick Bell's funeral, he'd allowed himself to feel comfortable with Clovia beyond the professional connection they shared—similar to how it used to be with Mason Witzel, his friend who'd been killed at Crescent Rehabilitation Center.

"But then I realized you had concerns about me, and I felt stupid for even calling," he said now under the stars. "Like, how could anyone ever love me?" His voice immediately caught on the word "love," and he chuckled. "By 'love,' I mean 'like,' or—"

"I know what you meant," Clovia said, smiling.

"Probably weird for me to be talking about these types of things," he said. "Other guys my age seem so . . ."

"Silly? Not self-aware?"

"I was going to say 'happy-go-lucky.'"

Now they both chuckled.

"Trust me, being deep is a *good* thing," Clovia said. "I just wish it weren't so complicated."

They walked for a few moments in silence before Jonathan continued. "Something happened to you the other day, at Mrs. Grime's old house."

A mix of uncertainty and shame thickened Clovia's throat. "Yeah. I can't really explain it. But when I looked at that house, I had this crazy feeling of . . . well, not quite déjà vu. But something close to that. I think being here with you, working on this story, is making me feel like . . ."

"Like you once had a past life here?"

Two cars zoomed by them on the road lining the left side of the bike trail. Clovia noticed Jonathan turn his face away from them as if on instinct.

"Or like I was supposed to come here and realize it," she resumed, barely above a whisper. She looked over her shoulder, afraid one of the reporters or oglers might have followed them from the hotel. But the flock was still a block away, on the sidewalk in front of the building. Even so, Clovia's next words remained tangled in her throat.

*I think I might have been Elizabeth Grime.*

She settled for: "I feel like once you start wondering about all this stuff—the nature of life and death or whatever—it's easy to start imagining things that might not be real."

"Like reincarnation."

"Yeah. I mean, where's that line between fact and belief, even in the face of possible proof?"

Jonathan took a step closer to her, then chuckled sadly. "Welcome to my happy life. I basically spent my entire childhood reading about all the reincarnation studies out there—like, psychiatrists and therapists who spent their careers studying kids with memories of 'other mommies and daddies' and 'other houses' and 'days they died.' I'm not the first kid to make crayon drawings of that sort of thing. I'm guessing *WorldLine* is aware that it's not exactly a new topic?"

"Alice is definitely aware," Clovia said. "So are a few others in the office who've really gotten into the idea."

"Ha. And are *you* into the idea?"

Self-consciousness rushed like heat into Clovia's chest. "No. I mean, not until recently. But this year . . . this shoot . . . let's just say it's opened my mind a bit. It's also been so crazy with all the deaths. I feel like—"

*Don't say it. Don't blame him for the bombing. Or Dad getting poisoned. Or other people's horrible choices.*

"—like I'm a hamster on a wheel, just trying to process it all," she finished.

"It's been a lot," Jonathan replied, seeming to pick up on what she didn't want to say. "And I'm so sorry. It really is all my fault."

"It isn't, though," Clovia said. "It's just circumstance. We're all choosing to work on this project. I'm choosing to know you."

Jonathan scrunched his shoulders in an uncomfortable shrug. "I guess I'm still not used to talking so openly about all this. Like, I never told anyone that I was always imagining myself in those memories when I made those crayon drawings. I'm kind of surprised I said that on camera, actually. I guess because—"

He stopped as if he'd crossed some invisible line he wasn't yet ready to invite anyone else over.

"I just mean . . . being born with all that in my head did a number on me. When all the other kids were playing with blocks and trucks and dolls, I was wondering why I knew French." Jonathan glanced nervously at Clovia. "Either way, I think my having a photographic memory kept the memories there until I was old enough to process them. Like I was born with exactly the type of brain I needed or something."

"But why seven sets of memories?" she continued. "A lot of people are hung up on that, I think."

Jonathan took a deep breath and walked in silence for a moment. "There were some things in Boulder."

"What do you mean 'things'?"

"Like, relating to what Dr. Crowe's patients have said about reincarnating in soul groups—how we apparently come back together in life after life, playing different roles."

Clovia liked the idea, but admitting it in actual words still felt like walking along the brittle edge of sanity.

Jonathan didn't seem to notice her mounting breaths. "I was listening to the recording again, and remember how Dr. Crowe kept bringing me through my deaths in those lives, to that intermediate stage between dying and choosing the next life? The image I kept getting in my head— that tree in the middle of the field—I didn't really say it on camera, but it was like I was one of the branches, and each branch was a different person. But I was also the tree. It sounds so stupid when I say it out loud."

"Maybe it was symbolic," Clovia suggested. "Like, what if your soul group is the clump of branches or something?"

"And the tree?"

"I'm not an arborist. I couldn't say."

Jonathan let out a guttural laugh—bigger than any Clovia had ever heard from him. "Well, damn. But yeah—I guess it maybe felt like a hint about what all this actually is. Life, I mean."

"All I can say is that I've felt almost crazy since getting here," Clovia said. "Like, not necessarily in the way you've said that Damon Jacoby kid felt. But, like, I'm starting to see why people don't want to ask big questions like this."

"It can be lonely," Jonathan replied. "Overwhelmingly so."

Clovia shook her head as they followed the bike path in a curve toward End Haven's mall. "All these New Naturalists just walk around, taking their existence for granted, and then conversely try to explain it away as being some fleeting cosmic accident. But *something* sparked the universe. It's baffling to me that people don't question that more often. Even scientists don't have a clue what the underlying nature of it all actually is."

Jonathan chuckled. "Everything is made of particles, but what are the particles?"

Clovia looked at him with a beaming smile—partly a laugh, partly understanding, partly relief that she had met him and that they were here, together. The night felt potentially endless.

The bike path stopped at an intersection across from the mall, which was shuttered for the night but still lit up in that great American way. *For all of you driving by in the dark, look at our store fronts! Come buy our stuff tomorrow!*

Without waiting for the stoplight to change, Clovia led Jonathan across the empty road, toward the mall's parking lot. They walked over its faded parking lines, toward the bright lights of an Amazon store.

Outside its locked doors was a bench. Clovia sat. So did Jonathan.

"Were there any other reasons you killed Ellen Graber?" she asked. "More than what you've said on camera, I mean?"

Jonathan's expression became grave—almost green. Suddenly, Clovia knew she needed a full answer.

"I mean, I know you've said you wanted someone else to know you weren't crazy for believing in life after death," she said, "but there had to have been more going on in your head."

From the bench, Jonathan stared across the parking lot and street, toward the Fairfield Inn. "I guess there's one thing I didn't say on camera—I'm probably too embarrassed still. But the morning before it happened, I went down to the kitchen and heard my mom telling her friend Delilah that she wished I'd never been born."

Tears now formed his eyes.

"That's when I kind of snapped. I broke my mom's favorite vase and ran upstairs to cut my wrists with the glass. To me, the only thing that made me worth anything was my weird brain—my memories that no one believed in. Then Ellen Graber . . . she was just so nice to me in that hospital. I was dying to share everything in my head with anyone who might listen, so I just . . ."

Clovia gripped the edge of the bench. "Are you saying you *were* actually trying to kill her?"

"Not directly." Jonathan subtly inched toward the bench's far side. "But I guess I already felt like I was in prison. When I realized what I was doing, I just held on and didn't stop. It was like a nightmare. Still is, actually. Craig Graber has no wife. His kids have no mom. I should probably be in jail forever, even though I'd never do anything like that today. Maybe it serves me right that I got famous. It's basically another type of prison, isn't it?"

Feeling her apprehension soften once again, Clovia asked, "Would you tell your younger self anything now, if you could go back?"

Jonathan shrugged. "Maybe just to keep telling the truth. But to find a better way."

When he looked into Clovia's eyes, her heart grew wings.

"I'm glad you're telling the truth now," she whispered. And then she kissed him, right there on that bench.


IT WAS JONATHAN'S FIRST KISS, outside of his own mind. He admitted it to her as they walked back to the Fairfield Inn, though he was quick to say he still had "memories" of kissing and sex from the lives of the Idle County Seven. Clovia also shared that her own love life had been limited to one disappointing boyfriend during her freshman year at New York University.

When they walked back along the dark bike path to the rear side of the hotel, a black Chevy Electrogue sat with blinking lights near *WorldLine*'s grip truck. One man sat behind the wheel, and another was holding the car door open, letting a woman out.

It was Alice, back from her board meeting in New York.

*Christ, I forgot she was due back tonight*, Clovia thought. Tomorrow's call time was 7:00 a.m. for everyone. They'd be meeting with Rebecca Sparks at the site of her old home, where her entire family had perished in 2007, following the gas explosion that certain people—Jonathan and Natalie Pent included—now believed Victor Zobel had orchestrated.

Alice was already watching them approach when she stepped out of the Chevy Electrogue. Noticing the concern creasing her face, Clovia blushed, thinking the woman might be angry that her subordinate was spending time alone with their star subject. When Alice spoke, however, it was with her typical courtesy.

"Miss Bell. Mr. Flite. Good evening."

No mention of their being out late together. Or of Jonathan looking flushed from his first kiss.

"Good flight?" Clovia asked, her wits mostly collected.

Alice cocked her head. "Did you get my text?"

Clovia shook her head, then dug into her pocket. Her phone wasn't there.

"Damnit, I left my phone in the hotel room," she said.

"Well, it's probably a good thing we're almost done shooting here," Alice replied. "I'm afraid it's going to be a zoo tomorrow at the Sparks house location."

"Why? What happened?"

Alice now looked at Jonathan. "Jonny, my boy, you might have yet another problem. I know you were planning on meeting your biological father after our shoot and that there were issues with his wife wanting to keep their family out of the spotlight. But that Lydia Clark woman from Providence just leaked his identity to the press. CNN ran with it, and now the name Dominic Bock is all over the news."

Jonathan simply stood there, in the parking lot, watching Alice's grim face. Clovia took a step closer to him.

"And there's nothing anyone can do?" he said. "No way to make sure his family has privacy?"

Alice shook her head. "I'm afraid they're now riding the wave. And since we're obligated to deliver this documentary to CBS next May, I'm guessing it'll only get worse the closer we get. I'm so sorry, honey."

The harsh parking lot lights threw Jonathan's face into shadowy relief as he turned to Clovia with a despondent shake of his head. And right then, she saw it in his eyes: a resolve to disappear.

# PART 4

# SPARKS

"Y ou do realize I'm *famous*, right?" were Jimmy Barber's first words to Julietta Flite at New Dawn Recovery Center, after her immediate declaration upon entering that only blood relatives should be present for Jonathan's first meeting with his biological father, Dominic Bock.

Jimmy's words, spoken through the most unfazed, overconfident scoff Winifred Flite had ever seen, made Julietta pucker her lips and blaze with anger.

"Do you honestly think I care that you're famous?" she spat back at the young man. "This is a family affair, and pardon me, but you're *not* family."

Jimmy chortled. "Some of us *choose* our family these days. And please don't pretend that orchestrating this meeting with a man you've never met means you've been a supportive grandmother to Jonathan all these years."

Jimmy took a drag from his shiny white cannabis vaporizer before handing it to Winifred. Winifred chuckled at her mother's boiling red face, then also took a drag. It took only seconds for the wave of euphoria to hit. She could almost feel her damaged cognitive function, crippled legs, and slurred speech doing a monkey dance.

*Because you're going to need a bit of fun today*, the monkeys whispered.

It was Friday, July 29, 2039. Dominic Bock, the boyfriend she'd lied to and discarded like trash nineteen years ago, would be arriving within the hour—hopefully without a herd of news vans and cameras trailing behind him. Now that Lydia Clark had leaked his identity to the press, however, any hope for privacy seemed futile.

Two days ago, Winifred had been ready for Dominic's visit, even excited to finalize the amends she had recently made with him over ActoVid. Yet anxiety had taken hold of her today—the first hint of her old self that she'd experienced in a long while. All she could envision was Dominic showing up, holding a grudge, and validating every guilty feeling she ever had about leaving him so coldly in her dust. Part of her wished Dr. Lumen were here to buffer the encounter, but no, he hadn't visited the East Coast in over six weeks. Was it because she was now an invalid? Winifred didn't know, and perhaps it'd be worse to seek an answer.

Jonathan sat in a chair next to her bed, fidgeting with his hands as he stared out the window. She held the vaporizer out to him, but he shook his head. "No thanks. I'd rather keep my faculties for this."

Winifred glanced at Jimmy again and shrugged. Jimmy took the device, shut it off, and put it in the leather satchel he had strapped to his torso.

"Now it smells like *drugs* in here," Julietta said.

"Pleeeease," Winifred replied. "I found cocainnne in your sock drawer at least ten times when I waaaas a kid."

"You can have a drag if you want, Julietta," Jimmy said, dripping with sarcastic charm. "It might calm your nerves."

"You rrrreally shouldn't have come, Mom," Winifred added.

Julietta glared at Winifred. "Excuse me? I resent that."

"Resent away," Winifred replied.

"Sorry, but your father's business is in a PR nightmare because of all this." She glanced sourly at Jonathan. "Considering how things just seem to get worse and worse around here, *someone* had to come and oversee it all."

"While Dad's philaaandering around in Greece, you mean?" Winifred said.

Julietta crossed her arms in a huff. "There's no need to be *crude*, Winifred."

As if that settled it, she turned toward the window and began pacing.

No one talked for five minutes. Jimmy, glued to whatever images his ActoLenses were projecting into his eyes, seemed perfectly content staring into space. One would never suspect he had helped the FBI apprehend Nicolas Rim, Jonathan's would-be assassin from Crescent Rehabilitation Center, last August.

Anxiety flickered again in Winifred's heart. Would all this simply bring more Weston Carrow types out of the woodwork? Would there ever be an escape from the violent clash of ideologies Jonathan seemed to be shoving on the world?

But a comforting voice hit Winifred's senses—a wise one she now almost recognized.

*Sit back. Remember what happened* after *the press conference explosion. Your little jaunt into kingdom come changed you for a reason.*

There it was: that calm, out-of-body relaxation.

*Or maybe it's just the monkeys,* she thought amid her buzzy cannabis high, trying to ignore the slight torture that now accompanied the illusion of reality around her.


"Knock-knock," came a male voice from just outside her open room door, in tandem with a rap of knuckles on wood. Winifred must have lost track of time in her relaxation and dozed off, because when she jumped back to attention, the moment had come. The man's voice was familiar. She ached hearing it.

Everyone in the room had already looked up by the time Winifred's gaze found Dominic and sent an old yet familiar rush of attraction through her body. He was holding a bouquet of roses—coral-colored, her favorite. Fit as ever, he still resembled a gentle golden retriever, just as he had when she "visited" him during her near-death experience last August.

Winifred glanced at Jimmy, who was already staring at Dominic with fixation. It appeared to be a mix of admiration, intimidation, and—as was typical for Jimmy when eyeing muscular men—lust.

Next to Jimmy, Jonathan stood up and instinctively wiped his hands on his jeans. If there was one thing Jonathan had in common with his father other than his eyes and nose, it was his tendency to get anxious—complete with sweaty palms—while overthinking every little thing.

Dominic's gaze flitted from Julietta to Jimmy, then to Winifred. When it finally found Jonathan, who was standing there, patiently waiting, the man's nervous expression softened into his best smile—the one that could melt ice.

"Hi," he said. "I'm Dominic."

Jonathan stood with his mouth open. His lips shaped around possible words.

*"My terrible mother told me I was a test-tube baby,"* Winifred's mind filled in for him.

The weight of her lie, now rectified, lifted as the two men shook hands. On the sidelines, Jimmy watched with an oddly steady gaze. It took Winifred a second to realize he was likely recording the encounter via his ActoLenses.

"I'm not sure what to say," Jonathan said.

Dominic chuckled through a heavy throat. "I think we say 'holy shit.'" He took Jonathan into a hug and whispered something in his ear. Winifred couldn't hear most of the words, but she did hear the last ones: "*I should have said something.*" When Dominic pulled back from the hug, his cheeks shined with tears.

Finally, he turned to Winifred, who couldn't even stand up for a greeting. She knew she looked worse than ever—pale, out of shape, every wrinkle of her forty-seven years showing beneath her minimal morning attempt at painting on makeup.

"Hey, Win," Dominic said. He'd given her the nickname on their fourth date, after they had first slept together and he, in his words, "had won."

When she answered, it came out garbled. "Thaaanks for commming."

"Thanks for finally letting me."

Winifred glanced at her mother, then back at Dominic, before rolling her eyes.

Dominic turned to Julietta. "And we never actually met," he said. "I dated your daughter for almost two years."

"So I've heard," Julietta said with an icy chill.

As the Flites glanced awkwardly at each other, Jimmy Barber jumped to his feet and held out a hand to Dominic. "Mr. Bock, my name is Jimmy Barber. I'm Jonathan's personal assistant. It's a *glory* to meet you." He inhaled as Dominic stepped forward to exchange handshakes.

With a taken-aback blush, Dominic said, "Great to meet you, too, Jimmy. I'm a bit late to the party, I'm afraid."

"But a *most* welcome addition."

Looking flustered as Jimmy gave his hand a final pump, Dominic smiled and looked between Jonathan and Winifred. "I guess I—" he started, but Jonathan cut in.

"Maybe we could go out to the beach for a walk?"

The young man's gaze flitted between Jimmy and Julietta, as if to send his father a silent plea for privacy.

"I'd love to," Dominic replied. "But first, I have something for your mom."

He walked across the room and handed Winifred the bouquet of coral-colored roses. Their fingers touched as he handed them off, and she instantly felt the years dissolve between them. It was an apology. It was forgiveness. It was a clean slate.

"I'm so sorry," she whispered as Dominic hugged her.

"I know. But let's bury it."

"Life," was all she could say in response.

For a moment, she wondered if Dominic was going to kiss her forehead, the way he used to after their lovemaking sessions. Instead, he ran a hand over her hair, which she had left long for their meeting.

"I'm going to go meet my son," he said.

They left the room.

Julietta, watching Dominic and Jonathan walk down the hall, whipped out her ActoPhone and furiously placed a call, likely to Winifred's yacht-bound father, Stanley. Jimmy started examining himself in the room's mirror. Winifred simply sat back in her bed, tickled by an undivinable sense that life's wheel was yet again steering her ship toward uncharted waters.

T HE NUMBER OF STARES Lindsay, Elijah, and Molly got when they walked into the Pent-Sparks Christmas party made their entrance nothing short of spectacular.

"Oh—my—effing—God," Natalie said as she stood against the high railing ledge lining the raised living room of her family's split-level house. Lindsay looked up at her and waved. Natalie scowled and stormed off toward the kitchen.

The attendance verged on a crowd, and nearly everyone was holding a red plastic cup, presumably filled with punch. A frightful choral rendition of "Frosty the Snowman" blared from the living room, where multicolored lights glowed on a Christmas tree at least eight feet tall.

"Well, we're here," Molly said in a low, exhilarated voice. Right then, Roberta Pent, Alec and Natalie's mother, walked out of the kitchen with a large tray of Christmas cookies. Upon noticing everyone staring at the foyer, she turned (almost severing Candace Dickson's head with the tray) to see who was generating all the fuss.

If she was aware of the recent fallout between Lindsay and Natalie, she made no indication of it. "Lindsay! Well, hello, hello! And is that—wait, Elijah Bryce?" Roberta's face adopted a more serious look of surprise as she craned her neck to see behind Lindsay. Roberta handed the tray to her scowling daughter (who had just reappeared from the kitchen), rushed down the stairs to the entryway, and wrapped Lindsay into the warmest hug she'd had in years. Lindsay broke the hug first, but not before Roberta could whisper, "You're looking good, Linds. Keep your chin up."

Then she turned to Elijah. "And you, Elijah! I'm so glad to see you. *So* glad." She hugged him with even more intensity than she had hugged Lindsay.

Lindsay took her jacket off and handed it to Tim Pent, Alec and Natalie's father, who had appeared from the basement, where he was presumably stashing each new batch of coats.

"How's it going, Sport?" he said, attempting to ruffle Lindsay's pulled-back hair. Then in quieter voice: "Saw your dad the other day. He's looking good. Looks like things are getting back to normal, at least a little bit. And you let him know we're keeping our eyes out on that new neighbor down the street, will you?"

Elijah and Molly, glancing awkwardly at Lindsay, piled their jackets into Tim's arms. He turned and carted them downstairs as Elijah introduced Molly to Roberta.

Lindsay, meanwhile, took another look at the party. Pauline Gilbert was standing with Sophie Higgins near the stairway, appearing slightly out of place. She waved at Lindsay with a warm smile, and Sophie did the same.

"Alec, come and show your friends the food and punch!" Roberta hollered toward the living room. She turned back to Lindsay, Elijah, and Molly. "Natalie insisted on serving only healthy food, so I hope you don't mind vegan everything. Some of it's actually good. Especially the chicken sausages Maureen Sparks brought over." Roberta winked and ushered them up to the house's top level.

Before they could ascend, however, Alec emerged from a circle of popular eighth graders and hopped down the steps. He smiled at Lindsay when she greeted him, then turned to Elijah and Molly. "Glad you guys could make it. Didn't think I was going to see you."

Elijah blushed. "Yeah, haven't been here in a while."

Despite his apparent timidity, something had come alive in him. Lindsay guessed it was either a vague shadow of the way he used to be with Alec, or an uncontrollable reaction to Alec's arms, which had doubled in size since summer.

She did her best to suppress a smile as Alec turned to Molly and faltered over his words. "Mandy, right?"

Molly grinned and said, "Molly Butler, actually. Thanks for inviting us." Despite her undeveloped chest and her small stature, the girl had a particular type of grace Lindsay was envious of. While she didn't need makeup to be beautiful, it was, tonight, the finishing touch.

"Oh God, sorry," Alec said. "I knew your name started with an *M*! Here—come on upstairs. I'll show you around." Lindsay and Elijah stood aside as Alec ushered Molly away, seeming to forget about them altogether.

"Well, looks like he might finally be over you," Elijah said. With a laugh, he led Lindsay upstairs, to the house's main level. They snagged more gazes as they emerged into the darkened living room, but after a few seconds, most people turned back to their conversations. Natalie had once again disappeared into the kitchen, and Tessa, Candace, Karly, and Sarah were the only ones to give Lindsay and Elijah truly demeaning looks. They were wearing miniskirts and standing in a circle of boys—one of whom was Jacob Jenkins, Molly's next-door neighbor.

In the back corner of the living room, next to the Christmas tree, a middle-aged woman with a heart-shaped face and thick jet-black hair was feeding a seated teenage girl with an equally heart-shaped face. The girl had blond hair and glasses, however, and her hands were resting at her sides. It took Lindsay a moment to realize she was sitting in an electric wheelchair.

The second it became apparent, the girl looked up, straight into Lindsay's eyes.

Lindsay glanced back at Elijah quickly, then breathed a sigh of relief when Pauline and Sophie reappeared in the living room with plates of food.

"Hey, long time no see, both of you," Pauline said as she approached. "I'm kind of shocked we're all here, to be honest. But I couldn't say no to Alec."

Lindsay smiled. "We didn't get the invite from Natalie either."

Pauline, who was wearing her black hair in a halo braid, opened her mouth to respond to Lindsay, then instead cocked her head toward Elijah. He was standing halfway out of their small circle, probably blushing under the dim Christmas lights. But Pauline grabbed his arm. "And you. You stopped calling me back."

"Yeah, well . . ." Elijah squirmed a bit, then cracked a smile. "You know how it all went down after we went camping that summer . . ."

Pauline bit her lip and nodded. "I guess. I stopped by one night after the Spinner's Island thing to see how you were, but you were out visiting your birth mom or something?"

"Yeah, Cynthia Foster. She lives over on Cage Street, a few blocks off Hunter Avenue."

"God, so weird. Remember how we used to sit out back in my playhouse and make up stories about who your birth parents were?"

As Elijah began updating Pauline on his life, Sophie escorted Lindsay to the food. When they entered the kitchen, Molly was already helping Roberta Pent spear the glazed chicken sausages onto toothpicks and set them on a tray. Alec was leaning over the table next to them, looking befuddled at Molly's sudden affinity for his mother but completely comfortable with it. Lindsay caught his eye and pointed at Molly with raised eyebrows. He only shrugged and turned away with a wide grin.

When Lindsay had a full glass of punch, she turned around and almost spilled it on Natalie, who was waiting in line behind her, holding two empty cups. She was staring at Lindsay with an expectant narrow-eyed smile. "Do you mind moving your fat ass? Some of us are thirsty." Her words were quiet enough under the Christmas music for her mother and brother not to hear.

Lindsay stepped out of the way without a word, and Natalie rushed in to fill the two glasses. *Just stop caring*, Lindsay told herself while following Sophie back to the living room. *It's not your fault Natalie's acting like a—*

But Lindsay's feet suddenly became dead weights. Alan Sparks was now standing in Jacob Jenkins's circle of boys with his hands in his pockets, quietly watching Tessa Silverman mime something she clearly thought was hilarious. Lindsay spun toward Elijah and Pauline, who were still talking quietly in the corner, looking as if they didn't want to be interrupted. Just past them, however, was the hallway leading toward Natalie's bedroom and the upstairs bathroom.

"Be right back," Lindsay told Sophie before rushing toward the hallway. As she approached it, she turned her face away from Alan, which meant she was facing the Christmas tree—and the blond girl in the wheelchair.

Looking closer, Lindsay saw that she had an electronic screen and typing keyboard attached to her setup. As Lindsay passed, the girl stared after her with a mysterious smile.

And then came the bathroom. *Relief.*

Lindsay closed the door, clicked on the light, and set her punch on the vanity. In the mirror, she looked desperately alone.

*I shouldn't be the one hiding,* she thought. *Alan should be, considering what his friends said about Elijah.*

Even so, Lindsay stayed in the bathroom for ten minutes. Twice there were loud knocks on the door, followed by giggles after she said, "Just a minute!"

She'd never escape the party without seeing Alan face-to-face, so she started rehearsing what she'd say once it happened. After getting a grip, she checked the mirror again to make sure her face wasn't flushed.

*Okay.*

*You're good.*

*Stop acting like Natalie Pent.*

But just as Lindsay opened the door and crossed back into the hallway, a deep and perfect voice dug straight into her heart.

"Hey, Thorsen."

It was Alan Sparks.

Cornered in the hallway with nowhere to run, Lindsay donned her fighting mindset, then looked up. Alan was leaning on the hallway wall, just past the girl in the wheelchair. He wasn't smiling, but he wasn't glaring either.

"I was just leaving," Lindsay tried to say, but the words broke into nonsense as they left her mouth. Out of options, she simply stood there, waiting for Alan to address the incident at kickboxing on Monday.

Instead, he used his torso to push his body off the hallway wall. "You didn't message me back this week."

"I blocked you," Lindsay said.

"I know. I had Alec check to see if you were still online."

Before she could help it, Lindsay sniggered. "Um, okay, Creeper."

No sooner had Alan taken a hesitant step toward her than the blond girl in the electric wheelchair whirred toward them from her spot by the Christmas tree. She looked straight into Lindsay's eyes for the third time that night.

Alan gestured down at her. "Lindsay, this is my sister Rebecca. Rebecca, this is Lindsay."

Rebecca's face warmed under a wide smile, and Lindsay's heart calmed. The girl's fingers slowly moved over the keyboard connected to her wheelchair.

As if it were second nature, Alan looked down at the adjacent screen, which Lindsay now surmised had words on it.

"She says it's up to me to make a move here," he said. "And that if you're pissed at what I have to say, you can blame her."

Lindsay thawed, just a bit.

"Can we go for a walk?" Alan asked, gesturing toward the front door. "I just want to explain what *actually* happened the other night."

Rebecca watched carefully from behind him as Lindsay fought the urge to give in easily. But her best efforts melted away when Alan scratched the dark stubble on his chin.

"My jacket's downstairs," she said.


Two minutes later, they were walking down the Pents' front sidewalk as large snowflakes fell into Alan's thick black hair, sticking to it like shimmering moonlit dust. Lindsay shoved her hands deep into her jacket pockets and scrunched her shoulders in the motion of a shiver, even though she wasn't cold. The night was sharp and fresh, perhaps even invigorating. Its wintery non-odor calmed her—it was the smell of ice, of nothing, of a blank slate.

When they reached Windsong Road's main sidewalk, Alan turned right, toward the south end. "I'm sorry for what it looked like the other night," he said after a few slow footsteps. "I wasn't making fun of your friends. Those other guys were, but I wasn't."

"You should have told them to shut up," Lindsay replied.

"Okay, maybe," Alan said. "But from what I hear, you just started hanging out with them a few weeks ago and didn't act much differently before that."

"Who told you that?"

"Tessa Silverman."

A flush of guilt colored Lindsay's cheeks; thankfully, the night was too dark for Alan to see it.

"And whatever Robbie said when you guys were sparring, it's total crap," he continued as the snow crunched under their feet. "He likes to stir the shit."

*He said you were going to ask me out until you learned I was friends with Elijah and Molly*, Lindsay thought but didn't have the gumption to say. Instead, she kept her guard up. "He said you think Elijah and Molly killed Damon Jacoby. It's not true."

"I know that! God, Robbie is just—I never said that. I didn't know Damon very well, and all I said to Robbie two weeks ago was that it seemed like you were dealing with a lot and finding new friends. I was worried you'd quit kickboxing."

"Kickboxing is the only thing I *have* right now," Lindsay said. "Well, other than Molly and Elijah. Compared to Natalie's friend group, they're a breath of fresh air."

Alan exhaled a white cloud. "I'm jealous. I don't have a lot of close friends."

Lindsay shot him an incredulous glance. "Yeah, right. You're always, like, 'Mr. Calm and Cool' at kickboxing. And in the halls at school."

His right eyebrow shot up. "You watch me in the halls at school?"

For a horrified moment, Lindsay couldn't breathe. Then Alan laughed quietly.

"Totally kidding. I watch you, too. I mean, I've noticed you. Whatever."

"Thanks, Creeper," Lindsay said.

A peculiar warmth rose in her chest and tingled through her body.

She basked in it for a timeless, unblemished moment until a slow, creeping realization dawned on her.

They had reached the end of Windsong Road.

Lindsay stopped dead in her tracks and grabbed Alan's hand without thinking.

Across the dead end from them was a small house with chipped siding that might have looked white in the daytime. Tonight, however, it was hiding in the dark, at least a hundred feet away from the closest streetlight, just left of where the road ran into an undeveloped field. There were no lights on inside, at least on the above-ground floors.

"What is it?" Alan asked.

The warmth in Lindsay's chest turned into a sweaty panic.

"That's his house," she whispered. "Lowell Grendel. The guy we think took Drew."

Alan jerked his head toward the shabby structure and clutched Lindsay's hand tighter.

Nausea curled Lindsay's stomach as she remembered Lowell Grendel ruffling Drew's hair after helping him pick up the flying paper plates at Spinner's Lake.

"Wait—have the police done anything?" Alan said.

"They got a warrant but didn't find anything to make a case," Lindsay replied. "The weird thing is that they *did* find pictures in his basement. Not specifically of Drew, but of—"

How could she explain the pictures? She couldn't. Not without looking crazy.

"The people in them were . . . not there," she said. "The cops said they looked like ghosts. And they were on real film negatives—they weren't Photoshopped."

A gust of wind kicked up, and dusty snow spiraled around them.

"He actually caught something like that on camera?" Alan said with an edge of curiosity. "Like, real ghosts?"

Suddenly remembering how Alan had hinted that he believed in such things the first night they ever chatted online, Lindsay told him about the mysterious woman named Rose her elderly neighbor Eleanor Jorgensen had seen and the photos Detective Rhymes had found of the woman in an old-fashioned dress. As the snow fell around them, the story's oddness sank in.

"Weird—especially the thing about the light covering the ghosts' faces in the pictures," Alan finally said. "My sister sees things like that, but I've never heard of anyone actually getting a picture of it."

Lindsay cocked her head as more gears clicked into place. "Wait, which sister? You mentioned something about that when we first IM'ed each other."

"Yeah—Rebecca, the one in the wheelchair. You met her inside." Alan smiled in a strange, gentle way, but his tone remained cautious and careful. "She's sixteen. The reason she can't really walk or talk is because she has this thing called agenesis of the corpus callosum."

"Agenesis of the *what*?"

"The corpus callosum. It's the band of neural fibers in the middle of your brain that connects the left and right sides. Not having one affects everyone differently. She had seizures a lot when she was a baby, but luckily she's perfectly 'there' mentally. She uses that computer thing to communicate, because forming language verbally is hard for her. So is walking."

"And she sees ghosts?"

Alan's lips curved into a troubled half smile. "Yeah—that, and then some." He scratched his head as if it might help organize the thoughts swirling in his brain. "She's also kind of psychic. She can read minds. Like, she always knows what people are thinking when they walk into a room, and she also says she sees spirits and stuff. And that we apparently all have 'spirit guides' that help us achieve our life goals—teachers on the spiritual side of things, basically. She says people's guides—and her own—tell her things. That's how she sometimes predicts stuff that actually ends up happening."

As novel as the concept might have seemed to others, it felt unusually familiar to Lindsay. This itself brought a quiet sense of foreboding.

"What else has she said about ghosts?" she asked.

"I guess that's a long story," Alan said, shifting on his feet. "We actually stopped telling people about Rebecca after I had the baseball team over last spring. Something weird happened with Damon Jacoby."

Lindsay's breath stopped short. Damon's ghost was the first one Elijah ever saw—*before* the older bully died.

"I'd always kind of ignored the stuff Rebecca said about seeing 'spirit guides'—how they would tell her things about possible futures and all that," Alan continued. "But I had the baseball team over for a barbecue at the start of the season last year. It ended up raining, so we were all inside playing Nintendo, and my mom was helping Rebecca eat dinner in the kitchen. When Damon walked in to throw his plate away, Rebecca stopped eating and started staring at him. My mom tried to snap her out of it, and everybody heard her tell Rebecca to get out of Damon's head. It was all super awkward, and Damon felt really weird, I think. I got all mad at Rebecca later that night, but then she told me something kind of crazy. It freaked me out, even before last August."

Alan bit his lip and shook his head. Lindsay stepped closer to him.

"She basically said Damon was going to die soon. That Idle County was making him psychic like her, and he was starting to feel crazy. Then, when he died in August, I could barely keep it together. I guess when I saw you hanging out with Elijah Bryce and Molly Butler, it was a little weird, considering they saw Damon die."

"Rebecca looked right at me the second I noticed she was in a wheelchair," Lindsay said.

"Yeah, that's just kind of how she is. No doctor can explain the mind-reading stuff, obviously, even though they've proven it's real with a bunch of tests. They're all scared to go public with it, despite my parents and Rebecca giving their consent."

"And the predictions?"

"Nobody knows. But the funny thing is that she told me Damon is actually all right. Like, she's seen him hanging around and said that time is messed up for him, because he's still trying to understand why life went so wrong."

Lindsay thought of Elijah seeing Damon's ghost before his death. "That might explain a lot," she said.

"So, you actually believe this stuff, then?" Alan asked.

Lindsay's nerves fluttered at the question, and the fence around her heart—that defensive barrier her mother had so successfully instilled in her—broke down completely. "That night at the community center wasn't the only time I've seen Drew," she whispered.

The truth in her words was enough to stop Alan's breath. He turned, saw the tears in Lindsay's eyes, and wrapped her vulnerable body in his strong, warm arms.

2040

WINIFRED FLITE'S ROOM DOOR at New Dawn Recovery Center was open when Dominic Bock approached it on June 13, 2040—already almost a year since his first introduction to Jonathan and just fourteen days since the premiere of *WorldLine*'s earth-shattering new season. Alongside him was Dr. Thomas Lumen, Winifred's anxious psychiatrist friend, whose everpresent limp was more pronounced today than it had been back in January, the only other time Dominic had met him face-to-face. As if to punctuate it, a shadow of melancholy dimmed the doctor's eyes, seeming to herald troubles yet to come.

It was 4:01 p.m.

Outside, thunder rumbled.

Dominic paused at Winifred's door and glanced out the hallway window. In the air above the Atlantic, a lone double-crested cormorant floated on the approaching storm's wind. How lucky the creature was to be so oblivious to the events that had upturned Dominic's corner of society in the last two weeks—*WorldLine*'s premiere following Jonathan's purposeful disappearance, Natalie Pent's follow-up op-ed about Raphael Dumont in the *New York Times*, and Dumont's targeting of Dominic's daughters at their San Antonio hotel just four days ago.

*"If you don't cancel your flight, I might seriously think about getting a divorce,"* his wife, Carolyn, had told him this morning, just before he dishearteningly called her bluff and left for the airport.

As if to underscore the reason for Dominic's troubled marriage, Jonathan's familiar voice suddenly sounded from inside Winifred's room.

*"It's a cold room, especially at night, when the fire goes out."*

Dominic's heart leapt with excitement—had Jonathan returned from his secret attempt to get off the grid? Had he decided not to take Victor Zobel's bait to visit Star Island?

Then Dominic realized he knew exactly what Jonathan was going to say next.

*"I'm looking in the mirror, dressing for church. My uncle always wants me to look into it when I comb my hair, but I'm always so scared. I know he'll never believe me if I tell him I'm seeing my dead parents behind me, in the mirror's reflection—he kind of dismisses everything I say."*

It was audio from his last past-life regression with Dr. Cora Crowe. Coincidentally, it was nearing the very part where Jonathan claimed his "uncle" in that life had been some past version of Dominic. Carolyn had scoffed when streaming the episode, but Dominic's heart had done somersaults.

Silence. Then:

*"But my parents—they're always staring at me, crying,"* Jonathan's voice continued. *"Their mouths are moving, but I can't hear what they're saying."*

More silence before Dr. Crowe's voice cut in. *"Can you see anything else in this particular moment?"*

*"Darkness. It's black."*

*"Do you mean your guides are blocking it?"*

At the exact moment Dominic peeked into Winifred's room, Jonathan's face, recorded last summer, scrunched up on her television screen. He was lying on Dr. Crowe's couch with closed eyes, and a smile touched his troubled expression. The camera lingered on him for a few seconds before the show cut to his postregression interview with Alice Winterblume. In the television's frame, Jonathan sat across from Alice, looking tired.

*"You didn't answer during that moment,"* Alice said in the interview. *"Can you tell me what you were seeing?"*

Jonathan fidgeted on camera. *"I'm not sure. So much of it was blocked."*

*"And do you think it had anything to do with Idle County? Why your subconscious chose this life to review?"*

Jonathan shrugged. *"I don't quite know. I think I'm supposed to learn something about forgiveness, but I don't know what. Or why."*

Dr. Lumen, glancing at Dominic, nodded toward the room. They stepped inside as the *WorldLine* episode continued playing.

"Knock-knock," Dominic said. A second later, the television wall in the room paused.

Winifred didn't greet them as they walked in. Instead, she was sitting on her bed in what looked like a state of blunt, extended shock. Concentrating through her words, she said, "I started rewaaatching the show yesterday to see what all I missed the first time through. And—God. No wonder Jonathan waaaanted to disappear. Jesus fuuuuckkkinggggg . . . *Christ.*"

Dominic smiled. In some ways, this was the same old Winifred, because, when their eyes met, she smiled back. Despite Weston Carrow's suicide bomb having broken her physically two years ago, something about her spirit had changed—possibly for the better.

"He . . . he sure is . . . *maaaakinggg a splash*, isn't he?"

"You've heard about Victor Zobel's offer for him to visit Star Island, right?" Dominic said.

"Of course. It's why I started rewaaatching."

Dr. Lumen took a seat on the edge of Winifred's bed. "We're hoping you'll tell us where Jonathan is, so we can go talk with him. We're just worried. That's all."

"He and Cloviaaaa wanted to get off the grid before the showww aired. I need to honnnor that."

"And we want to help them do whatever they need to do," Dominic said. "But within reason. If it involves going to visit Victor up on that damned space yacht, someone needs to stop them."

"Youuu think I don't waaant to do the exact same thing?" Winifred said with a snap of her old snark.

"Then help us get to him," Dominic pleaded. "He shouldn't be deciding this alone."

Winifred sighed, sat back in her bed with crossed arms, and looked out her window just as lightning flashed over the Atlantic. "He asked meee not to tell *anyyybody* where he and Clovia are. Only theirrr security teams and I know."

"And Jimmy Barber?"

"Jimmmmmy got an agent just before the premiere and is dddeveloping a . . . taaalk show," Winifred said.

Dr. Lumen sighed. "What about the FBI?"

"I'm guessing they got whaaattt they wanted out of *WorldLine*. The whole worrrld is blaming Victor Zobel for the Geneva bombing, all because of that meeeeting of physicists. He won't beee able to come back down to Earth from this. Liiiiterally." Winifred gestured toward the TV wall, which still showed the documentary paused on Jonathan's face. It was the fourth episode, if Dominic remembered correctly—the one that introduced Dr. Cora Crowe and all her so-called evidence for reincarnation. Since the premiere, people around the world had begun corroborating the woman's claims, speaking out with stories about their own children saying odd things that seemed to be recollections from other lives. For the first time ever, the media seemed to be listening.

Dominic thought back to *WorldLine*'s most riveting snippets, particularly Jonathan's story about Lindsay Thorsen grabbing Elijah Bryce's flashlight during an out-of-body experience. It would have been quite the long con for a group of thirteen-year-olds, along with the girl's father, to conjure that event up—let alone for Jonathan to somehow be in on the trick thirty-four years later. The only publicly recorded mention of the flashlight incident prior to Jonathan's first interview had come from Rebecca Sparks in 2034, when she predicted that the young man would eventually discuss it with Alice Winterblume—and inadvertently give *WorldLine* the proof it needed to fundamentally shift the social psyche toward curiosity. Jonathan had been just thirteen when that interview took place, not to mention incarcerated, with all external communication monitored. To everyone's knowledge, he hadn't yet interacted with the then-obscure physicist at that point.

Rebecca Sparks herself was now shaking up every talk show, news outlet, and public auditorium with her demonstrable clairvoyance and controversial Theory of Everything, the latter of which purported to explain how Lindsay Thorsen was able to grab the flashlight in 2006. Yes, Rebecca's explanations required a belief in higher consciousness, but, quite conveniently, her psychic abilities were overt proof of that. It seemed she'd been waiting to unveil her wonders publicly at just the right time, to coincide with *WorldLine*'s exposé.

*And people are finally connecting the dots*, Dominic thought.

Dr. Lumen stretched his bad leg horizontally off the edge of the bed, then let it down again. With his ever-present grimace, he looked into Winifred's eyes. "What did the feds say about Victor's invitation to Jonathan?"

"Nothing," Winifred replied. "Theyyy haven't even spoken to

meee since the premiere. I don't know yet if theyyy've reached out to Jonathan."

Dominic took a step closer to her bed. "Look, there's a legit chance Victor Zobel is a national security risk. The fact that he made this offer for Jonathan to visit *after* he knew the entire world was watching him is fishy as hell."

"Then whyyyy do you think Jonathan would be stuuupid enough to go up there?" Winifred asked.

"Well, I've only known him for a year, but it's already obvious that he's spent his whole life looking for answers," Dominic said. "And you saw it on *WorldLine*: Jonathan officially believes in reincarnation and thinks life is all about coming in with a goal and going out having achieved it. If he sees this as being part of some 'big life purpose,' I just think . . ."

Dominic shot Dr. Lumen a pleading glance.

The psychiatrist scooched closer to Winifred on the bed. There was patience and understanding in his eyes, perhaps even love. "Winifred, I think we both know that Jonathan's spent his whole life not having a choice in what he does and that he doesn't really have a means to measure himself against public expectation. All we're hoping for is to talk with him before he does anything too dangerous. Help him if he needs it. That's *all*."

"Then I suggest youuuu both consider that life really *might* be all the things he and this Rebecca Sppaaaarks woman say it is," Winifred said, gesturing toward the television. "Seems like the world is finally wakinggg up to the illusion phyyysiciiists have known about for decades. And don't illusions uuusually have purpose?"

*Jesus. She sounds just like Jonathan*, Dominic thought. Twenty years ago, the woman would have approached this topic like a militant New Naturalist.

Dominic opened his mouth to speak, but his words caught on a feeling that had been growing in his heart since the *WorldLine* premiere—a mixture of his usual everyday attitudes combined with a new amalgam of terror that life wasn't what he thought it was, that it was somehow just a simulated experience of perception in a shapeless, infinite abyss. Religion had always presented these incomprehensible ideas in a neat little box whose contents he'd never truly contemplated, because he'd considered the box proof enough of their validity. Now staring these bigger existential questions in the face, he was unsure what their answers might mean for his life, his marriage, and society. Not knowing felt like trying to scream without a voice.

"Win, please," he said. "Could you just tell us where Jonathan is? Or tell him we want to talk somehow, without the press following us?"

Winifred stared at her son's face on the paused television. For the first time ever, Dominic saw tears glistening in her eyes. "I betraaayyyed him his whooolllee life," she whispered. "I can't just do the same thiiing as before and hope he'll keep forgiving me . . ."

She looked at Dominic. All their unrealized possibilities flashed between them: the continuation of their relationship so long ago, their tandem raising of Jonathan, the different paths other choices might have offered them.

"Letting him go through this alone *would* be doing the exact same thing as before," Dominic said. Tears welled in his own eyes as he considered their twenty-year-old son, who—along with Alice Winterblume—had just unleashed an unprecedented mystery upon the world. Choices and intentions, Dominic knew, might matter now more than ever.

After a deep sigh—and with particularly strained words—Winifred said, "If I tell you whyyy Jonathan and Clovia left and where they went, youuuu can't tell a souulll."

2039

*F*OCUS, *FOCUS FOCUS*, Clovia Bell thought as the familiar swoosh of a message alert sailed into her ears—the hundredth email of the morning. It was only 9:58 a.m. on August 29, 2039, and the three tasks she was juggling in preparation for Jonathan Flite's Friday interview with Revis Zobel had already been interrupted fifty times.

But focusing was impossible when a hundred things had to be done before lunch. She opened the message.

It was from Jamal Harris, their new lead editor.

> *Hey Clovia: Possible issue with Rebecca Sparks story for the Idle County exposé. Running through the interviews relating to the gas explosion at her house in 2007, and it looks like Gabriel Creed's sister Eloise made a statement that contradicts the ones made by Rebecca and Jonathan Flite. Not sure if anyone flagged this yet? Might be easier to discuss in person.*

Clovia closed her eyes. Apart from the fact that Jamal had recently shown signs of having a quiet workplace crush on her, this was the worst possible thing she could be hearing today. A contradiction about the Sparks-house gas explosion, if it were substantial enough, could throw an even bigger wrench into the season's narrative than the loss of Raphael Dumont. Not to mention that Clovia and Jonathan had unofficially started dating, and they were still at that fledgling point where even the tiniest breach of trust could clip the relationship's wings.

*Just breathe. Nobody is dying here. At least not today.*

With an unexpected sullen sense that she was building her future on shaky ground, Clovia stood up from her desk and walked straight to Jamal's desk.

"RIGHT HERE," Jamal said a minute later, pointing to the written interview transcript on his monitor. "See? Eloise even stutters over it a bit. First, she says she had 'psychic episodes' as a kid and that she woke up the night of that gas explosion 'worried about the girl in the wheelchair'—meaning Rebecca Sparks. Then she goes on to say that she saw her brother Gabe 'run across the street and get in a car with'—but then she stops and changes directions. She jumps right into saying, '. . . When Gabe got to the Sparks house . . .' yada yada yada."

"Gabriel Creed took a taxi to End Haven that night, with cash," Clovia said. "That's what he told the Idle County Sheriff's Department, anyway. Jonathan and Rebecca also backed that up."

"Yeah. But doesn't it sound like Eloise was about to say something else? Like, that maybe Gabriel got in a car with someone familiar instead?"

"Who are you suggesting?"

With a flicker of eye contact, Jamal said, "Well, I saw in the notes that Max Pope lived across the street from Gabriel at the time. It was right after his Gateway Project stuff imploded."

Clovia stared at the transcript.

Had *WorldLine* missed something?

"I'll look into it ASAP," she said, calling on every positive emotion she had left to prop up her sinking heart. "Thanks, Jamal."

"No problem," he replied under a subtle blush.

As Clovia walked back to her desk, her morning stress hit a crescendo. If Jonathan and Rebecca had lied to *WorldLine*, it could potentially compromise not just their new season's integrity but also everything the crew had left to shoot. Even worse, if *WorldLine* couldn't trust Jonathan Flite, then neither could she.

And *that*?

That would clip their relationship's wings indefinitely, sending them both tumbling down, down, down.

2039

WHAT REVIS ZOBEL NOTICED first in Jonathan Flite's eyes on September 1, 2039, was recognition. They sat opposite each other inside a Four Seasons suite in New York and had just made eye contact after the famous nurse killer's unusually long study of Revis's hair, cheekbones, and clothing.

Were the cameras capturing that look on Jonathan's face?

Revis hoped so. He fucking hoped so.

"You look like you've seen a ghost," he said to the young man.

On the cameras' sidelines, *WorldLine*'s minimalist crew watched in silence alongside Special Agents Heather Mousseau and Amed Antar, Revis's two FBI contacts. Per their joint endeavor with *WorldLine* to keep today's shoot under wraps, there were only three other people in the room besides Revis, Jonathan, and the two special agents: Alice Winterblume, a hair and makeup artist, and a young creative producer named Clovia Bell.

That was it. It was as bare bones a shoot as Revis could have imagined. But it had to be, according to Alice, because the FBI wanted to keep his involvement silent until the last big marketing blitz before the season's premiere next May. Revis had already given an initial "pre-Jonathan" interview with Alice Winterblume and spilled as many details about his father as he could: the childhood beatings, the death threats, the manipulation of people, the rumored "consciousness tests" performed on humans in Estonia.

And the man's hypocritical "peace-first" public mentality? That was a farce. He had controlling shares in three weapons manufacturing companies—not to mention global connections in the shipping and logistics industry that made his rumored involvement in the 2037 nuclear attack in Geneva more than plausible.

Yes. Yes. Yes. Anything else?

Revis, recalling that off-kilter feeling he'd always felt in Idle County's infamous Moon Woods, now stared at Jonathan Flite, his father's newest nemesis.

"You're the first of my father's enemies I've met in person," Revis started.

"And you're the first Zobel *I've* met in person," the young man replied.

Revis chuckled. "Pray I'm the only." And because he had no energy for further pleasantries, he immediately added, "You say you have the memories of my half sister, Jillian. I hope you don't mind if I ask you to prove it."

"I definitely will if I can," Jonathan replied.

"Okay, then. What was the gift she gave me for Christmas when I was four?"

Jonathan, who didn't seem to enjoy being on camera, adjusted his posture. "I'm not a hundred percent sure how old you were, but are you talking about the Christmas after you stepped on that nail? Like, the year Little Nick's dad built that addition onto your house in Gland?"

Fear trickled down the back of Revis's mind.

*Little Nicolas Rim, whose dad died after digging that elevator shaft at the Moon Woods compound.*

Nicolas had called Revis out of the blue late last year, and they had discussed the incident. But since then? Radio silence.

Yet Jonathan knew about the Rim family. Somehow.

*That doesn't prove anything,* Revis thought. *There are a lot of ways Jonathan could know about them. Maybe the FBI told him about Nick's phone calls.*

"Don't stall on me," Revis continued, more as an intimidation tactic than anything else. "If I was four, it would have been Christmas of 2002. What present did Jillian get me that year?"

Suddenly looking cautious, Jonathan glanced up at the people standing to his left—first Alice, and then the Clovia Bell girl.

He cleared his throat. "Well, I remember Jillian hating that your dad, Victor, forced everyone to dress up on Christmas, even in the morning," Jonathan said. "She gave you two normal gifts that year, in front of the family—paid for by your mom. I think one was a stuffed elephant. The other was a toy tool set. She was hoping it'd help you get over your fears of hammers and nails after the whole construction site thing."

Sweat began beading on Revis's forehead.

"But there was also something else. Jillian loved you a lot—she always felt really sorry for you and wanted to give you something your dad wouldn't see: a set of kid watercolor paints, because you liked to make art whenever he wasn't home. She used money from her allowance to buy them. I remember she gave them to you later that night, in your bedroom. She was nervous Victoria would make fun of you for having them and tell your dad about it, but it never happened. At least not when Jillian was living there."

Tears formed in Revis's eyes. He thought back on those watercolors and the pictures he'd painted with them—mostly of Lake Geneva and its surrounding mountain range. If he weren't mistaken, Victoria still had one framed in her New York apartment.

"I think Jillian was ten or so," Jonathan finished.

And Revis's stomach dropped.

This was it. A turning point. The world had to know about Jonathan Flite. About his memories. About the very fact that consciousness wasn't just limited to the physical brain, wasn't just a random byproduct of universal luck, and wasn't just a cold unreality that scientists, New Naturalists, and his abusive, murderous father could explain away with myopic logic. Jonathan's memories were proof for society that life transcended death, which in itself could give humanity a means to stop its cyclical hating, warring, and—

*STOP.*

*Calm.*

*Breathe.*

Revis had to keep his wits about him. Had to keep it together. He was on camera for the world to see, and despite his contractually ensured control over what Alice Winterblume could and couldn't include in her documentary, he wanted this interview to ring true. The world needed to know that the closed-minded nature of his father's New Naturalism philosophy was scientism, not science, and that the theories and paradigms supporting it were just that—theories and paradigms.

*And if they don't have room for whatever Jonathan Flite is proving here, they'll need to change.*

With that, Revis stood up from his seat, took two long strides, and bent down to grab Jonathan in a hug. Tears fell from his eyes, onto the young man's shoulder.

"Thank you for proving it," Revis whispered.

"I don't know why I have Jillian's memories in my head," Jonathan whispered back as the Clovia Bell girl rustled about, probably using her tablet to control the cameras' zoom lenses.

For the next five minutes, Revis couldn't shake his tears or his awe that the young man in front of him was somehow connected to his dead half sister.

But then he gathered his wits.

In front of him now was ActoLens footage recorded by a young woman named Kara Butler. She had shot it in the driveway roundabout of his father's Moon Woods compound, near that god-awful fountain his sister, Victoria, had always liked. Revis watched the ActoVid's subject—a frail Idle County local named Shelly Bryce—step out of her car. When she stood up, she suddenly looked faint.

Next to Revis, Jonathan was also watching, rapt. Four *WorldLine* cameras were recording their reactions.

"Have you seen this before?" Revis asked Jonathan.

The young man shook his head. "No. First time. I had no idea this even—"

Shelly Bryce suddenly flickered white on the video. Digital noise blurred where her clothes should have been. Then she flickered again before disappearing altogether.

"What in the bloody hell," Revis said.

Next to him, Jonathan was silent. He gestured for Revis to rewind the video. Revis did. They watched it again.

Finally, Jonathan shook his head. "I can't believe they got this on camera."

"You know what's causing it?"

"No, but I'm guessing Rebecca Sparks might. She's the physicist who—"

"I know who she is. She's been taunting my dad with letters for almost two years."

Jonathan looked confused for a moment. "Oh. Okay. Well—I think it's because of that thing under the Moon Woods. Jillian and the others had weird whiteout experiences right before they died."

Revis's mind began reeling once again. Within seconds, it careened out of control.

*BREATHE.*

As Revis continued, his lungs could barely hold air.

"Okay. I just have to ask . . . regarding my mom's death back in 2006 . . . did Jillian know anything I didn't?"

Diving through Revis's mind like spastic seabirds were thoughts of poisons; of the letter Rebecca Sparks had sent to his Italy house; of the recent ActoMessage from Raphael Dumont, his father's slippery ex-friend and assistant, who now claimed to be on some sort of mission against his old boss, to the end.

Some invisible emotion burned behind Jonathan's hazel eyes. Yes, he had the expression of a student taking the biggest test of his life—to see if his very nature might pass society's analysis of what was or wasn't acceptable. But this was something more, perhaps true fear of that test's ramifications.

"There were emails," he said to Revis.

"What do you mean?"

"There was a night in Gland—it was in 2004, I think, a few weeks before Christmas. Your dad started screaming at your mom over an email she was writing to Jillian's dad, Max. Jillian was so scared. She thought your dad was going to do more than just hit your mom." Jonathan's words were slow, careful. "I'm not sure if you ever knew about the hitting?"

"I knew about the goddamned hitting," Revis said, his voice low, almost a whisper.

"You were upstairs, and Jillian was trying to distract you and

Victoria in her bedroom. She put on a movie—*The Lion King*, I think. But then she left you there and went downstairs to see why your dad was screaming, and it was about these emails. Your mom was having debates about physics and consciousness with Max Pope, Jillian's dad, and *your* dad was freaking out over the fact that they were still in touch. Jillian actually went snooping in Max's emails later, after she was living with him in Idle County. She'd heard Max mention stuff about the Moon Woods being weird, and she got curious if he and your mom had discussed it. She also noticed that your mom started getting sick with her heart issues right after that big fight. Your mom died a year and a half later."

"And did Jillian have any theories about my mom's death?" Revis asked.

Jonathan Flite nodded. "Poison of some sort."

*Poison.*

Revis could barely contain himself. He needed a drink. He needed two drinks. He needed to face his sister, and then his father, and then the whole fucking world. Everyone needed to know just how big a monster their New Naturalist darling, Victor Zobel, really was.

"But honestly, it was only because she'd heard one of your dad's friends mention poisons in passing about a year before, in the driveway in Gland," Jonathan continued. "The friend was talking to some other friend, and he said the French equivalent of something like, 'He's going to aconite your ass if you don't be careful.' She didn't know who 'he' was, but she thought later that they might have been talking about Victor. She also had to Google what aconite was afterward."

"And which friend said this?"

Once again, Jonathan glanced uneasily at Alice Winterblume.

"It's okay," Alice suddenly said. "We'll edit around it."

When Jonathan finally said Raphael Dumont's name, Revis's mind immediately fell off a cliff, racing to find wings as dueling mental images dragged him down: first, his father, Victor, ordering Raphael around on the regular all those years ago; and second, Natalie Pent sharing her theories about Raphael back in April.

*Maybe life really is a fucking circle.*

"Why would you edit around Raphael?" Revis asked Alice Winterblume slowly, amid his mental tumble.

One of the FBI agents—Special Agent Antar—cleared his throat but didn't speak. Nobody around him said a word.

"Is there something I don't know?" Revis pressed.

Agent Mousseau, the FBI agent Revis had been working with most closely, nodded to Alice, who then responded in a way that sounded rehearsed.

"Due to extenuating circumstances, we won't be incorporating Raphael Dumont into this new season's story."

"*Excuse* me?" Revis said.

"We're taking care not to compromise an ongoing investigation," Agent Mousseau added, taking a small step forward.

"What ongoing investigation?"

"I'm afraid I can't say."

Revis's chest suddenly constricted, and he immediately wanted nothing more than to debrief with Natalie Pent, who since 2010 had put in too much time and effort finding evidence against Raphael and his father to watch it all go up in smoke.

Yet giving Natalie details of today's interview would break his non-disclosure agreement with *WorldLine*. Nobody outside this hotel room was supposed to know what had been recorded.

*Unless I take a leaf out of her book and talk anyway.*

"If you'll excuse me," Revis said, standing up from his chair and switching off his microphone. As he walked off camera and left the hotel room, he heard the show's small crew—and the accompanying special agents—descend into whispers.

ATALIE PENT'S LUNGS AND BODY were breathing, yet they now felt detached and far away. She was moving toward a ring of light that beckoned with a level of brightness and warmth she'd never before experienced.

Was she still in the Moon Woods?

Was her leg still injured from her tumble into that rocky ravine?

Was she going to be stuck in the forest all night, in her ill-equipped exercise tights and jacket, a victim for the cold?

It didn't matter anymore, because the answer to all her questions was no. She was somewhere altogether new.

It was here. It was now.

*She* was now.

SHE WALKED. Around her, the Moon Woods were bathed in light, growing and shrinking colossally as if they were breathing. Natalie's senses danced around the trees; she tasted the smell of their bark, saw the sounds of their clacking branches, and heard the touch of the wind through the spaces between. She was somehow outside the physical dimension the trees occupied, and while their world—*her* world—existed in the truest sense of the word, she now realized it was a world limited by filters of perception.

Somehow, she was operating outside their bounds. The personality of Natalie Pent, the girl from End Haven, Minnesota—the one with all those unclarified goals and dreams—was a shell. A vehicle. A fragment of energetic essence, ever evolving and ever safe. No matter that she saw ghosts or that her old friends had disappeared—that was all part of a greater purpose. One they all shared.

*"Natalie!"*

She saw the voice instead of hearing it. It sparkled.

*Behind you*, she thought. *It's coming from behind you. From the ravine.*

Natalie turned to greet whoever had just spoken her name. And what she saw was—

—HER LIFE AS A SERIES OF MOMENTS. A decision to enter life, to share a womb with the essence fragment who would later become her twin brother, Alec, at least for this leg of their journey.

Early childhood had been troubling. The world around Alec seemed to settle onto him like a comfortable winter coat, but for Natalie, the world had immediately been cold, heavy, and uncomfortable. She had come into life with fear. With disbelief in herself. With certainty that she would fail at her life's work—the one main goal she had.

*Yet part of the goal was to recognize the illusion of failure, was it not?*

This voice came from somewhere deeper. From the source of whatever part of her did the perceiving.

The life she lived as Natalie Pent became clearer. She could see it from the outside now—all its moments—as if looking into a crystal ball. In her reverie, she walked through this in-between place, one foot in front of the other.

And that was the point, wasn't it?

Walking, not arriving.

*But why?* she thought. *Why is there a journey at all? Isn't existence without goals the same thing as nothing at all?*

She thought about the world. About the limited culture around her, and the cultures she had read about in school or learned about on television. They were all part of the illusion—rules and regulations that sought to capture and categorize the building blocks of an edifice that meant very little here, on this side of perception. The true world—the true *self*—was so much grander. And wherever Natalie was now seemed to be just the beginning of it, her first glimpse of the shapes making the shadows.

SOMETHING WAS FOLLOWING HER. Or someone. A man made of sorrow. Was he weeping?

*"Please help me,"* the man said, though Natalie couldn't bring herself to turn around. *"Please, I didn't mean for it to happen. I didn't want this!"*

The voice was inside Natalie's head yet somehow clearer than the loudest sound she had ever heard. Again, it came from multiple senses—all of which were now blended together.

*Or unified?*

*"Please don't leave me!"* the sorrow man screamed somewhere behind her. *"It was all my fault! It was all my fault, and now they've left me. I'm alone! I'm all alone."*

Whispers passed Natalie's eyes. They were bright. Made of colors she had never seen before. They reached her mind with sharp clarity.

*"You're on your own journey, just as he is,"* the sparkling voice behind her said. *"Leave him be."*

But who was the sorrow man? She had to know.

*"Just a fragment coming to terms with his choices."*

And just as Natalie turned to look at the man—the *ghost*—she felt her mind falling upward, folding in on itself.

*No,* she thought. *I'm not ready.*

Yet it came like the feeling of waking from a dream, of losing her balance and falling—

NATALIE WOKE UP warm in her bed. She was gasping, looking at her ceiling, realizing she was safe at home on Windsong Road.

*The Moon Woods,* she thought. *I was in the Moon Woods. First at the Knoll with Alec, and then by that ravine—*

She felt around her pockets for the blue Tickle Me Thai candy wrapper she'd plucked from the dirt. But she wasn't dressed; she was clad only in her sports bra and underwear, the way she always was at night.

And then Natalie realized there were eyes in the room. Seven pairs. She was being watched.

She bolted upright in her bed and saw them staring at her: the Idle County Seven, four of whom had, at one point or another, been her friends.

Pauline Gilbert.

Lindsay Thorsen.

Elijah Bryce.

Gabriel Creed.

Molly Butler.

Clayton Graf.

And Jillian Pope. Beautiful Jillian Pope, with her flowing red hair—the envy of every girl at End Haven High.

They were all smiling.

*"We're okay,"* Lindsay Thorsen said. *"We're all okay!"*

*"Just promise to get nicer,"* Elijah Bryce said, grinning.

Natalie sat paralyzed as Pauline Gilbert leaned in toward her ear, also smiling. *"You'll always be my first friend. I love you and miss you. But I'm here with you. We're all here."*

All the others simply smiled down at her.

Emotion—an amalgam of grief, joy, and gratitude—surged through Natalie's body. It was with incredible relief that she felt herself falling upward again, as if all her perceptions were tipping upside down. And then—

—SHE WAS BACK IN THE MOON WOODS, stumbling through her bright, overloaded sensory experience with a sense that every event in her life was *now*, that time, always moving forward, was simply an illusion created by the perception of possibility.

Behind her, the sorrow man was still shrieking, *"Please, help me! Please!"*

Then she fell upward again, and—

—A TERRIBLE BEEPING SOUND pinged in Natalie's ears. Stars twinkled above her head. It was freezing cold, and dead grass poked into her back, through her thin athletic jacket.

She was still outside.

Outside, and it was night.

*I'm still in the Moon Woods.*

Except there were stars above her. No trees.

Natalie sat up when she realized the piercing pinging sound was coming from the iPhone in her pocket. It was a chime from the new

Find My iPhone app, which Alec had set up for her in July, just two weeks after the Idle County Seven disappeared.

From somewhere behind her came the sound of an approaching car. She gathered her wits, then turned around and saw headlights through a thin layer of trees—they were less than a hundred feet away. Only then was Natalie able to place herself.

*The Outer Ring. I'm in the Outer Ring of the Moon Woods, and that's a car driving on Old Mill Road.*

The car and lights came to a stop. And then she heard a car door slam, and the voice of her brother, Alec. "Natalie! Where are you? *Natalie!*"

In a daze, Natalie lit up her phone screen and began waving it in a wide arc over her head. When Alec screamed her name again and ran to her, gasping, she fell into his arms and began to weep.

**2005**

IN THE DEAD OF NIGHT following the Pent-Sparks Christmas party, Lindsay Thorsen awoke to a tapping noise at the window. She opened her eyes in the darkness.

These weren't her normal bed covers. This wasn't her bedroom. Or her house.

*Elijah's. You're sleeping over at Elijah's.*

Relief flooded her as images from the night before flashed across her memory: Alec and Natalie's party, Elijah's reunion with Pauline, and Molly helping Roberta Pent in the kitchen. Then had come her walk with Alan Sparks. He had hugged her. Then kissed her.

Smiling, Lindsay turned onto her side and buried herself deeper into the sleeping bag.

The window tapping caught her attention again—a childish rap on the glass of Elijah's living-room window. It was quiet; the fist making it was small.

Lindsay opened her eyes and turned her head. The snow outside must have stopped, because now moonlight shone through the back family room's thin curtains.

A shadow stood behind them, blocking the bluish glow. It was in the shape of a person. A child.

Lindsay blinked hard three times. The figure was still there, standing outside.

Then came giggles through the glass.

*Drew.*

Lindsay peeled her sleeping bag back, looking left at Molly and Elijah, who were both fast asleep. Elijah's mouth hung open, and Molly was lying flat on her back with coffinlike stillness.

Another giggle.

*What are you trying to tell me, Bugger?*

Drew tapped at the window again, then disappeared to Lindsay's left. He was running around the house, toward the front door.

In her bare feet, Lindsay carefully stepped around the coffee table Elijah had moved to make room for the sleeping bags. Trying to remember the layout of his house, she followed Drew toward the main dining room and then the front foyer. Through every set of curtains, she saw his shadow and heard his knocks on the house's siding.

*Shoes. You have to get your shoes on.*

Lindsay found her boots in the dark, then unbolted Elijah's front door.

*He'll be gone when I open it. This is a dream, because I'd never do this in real life.*

Lindsay eased the door open. The only thing separating her from the cold winter night was a flimsy glass storm door. It shook in the wind that had risen after the night's snow clouds blew out.

When she opened the storm door all the way, Drew doubled over in laughter on Elijah's front porch. He was wearing his red Doctor Deadlock costume.

*It's too cold for you to be wearing that, Bugger!* Lindsay thought, her heart shrieking in her chest.

Then Drew turned and ran.

A second later, Lindsay was outside in her boots, chasing him into the freezing night. He did not speak; he only giggled in his unique, beautiful, forever-lost way. He cut left, across Elijah's front yard, messing up the fresh and perfect blanket of snow that glistened in the moonlight. Lindsay followed, feeling the iciness melt through her pajama bottoms.

*It can't be a dream, because you only ever wear pajama bottoms when you're sleeping somewhere other than home. You're at Elijah's house. This is real.*

Another twenty yards passed under Lindsay's feet, and the snow-powdered silence of Windsong Road made her breaths sound heavy, desperate, alone.

She knew where Drew was leading her before they reached it.

Lowell Grendel's small sagging house was now right in front of her—perhaps ten quick steps to the front porch.

But Drew kept running, so Lindsay panted after him. In a dream, the boy would have disappeared as consciousness overtook her, but he was clear as ever now, dragging his feet through six inches of snow.

*They're bare, his feet. Oh my God, they're—*

"Drew!" Lindsay whispered in the darkness. "Bugger! You're going to freeze if you don't—"

He only giggled madly. Lindsay rushed after him, mowing through the trail he was leaving, desperate to catch him, to hold him, to bring him back to her family as proof that he wasn't really gone.

*You're almost there,* she thought. *You'll be able to grab him if you just—*

But no.

It wasn't going to happen.

It took Lindsay two and a half laps around Lowell Grendel's small white house to realize she would never catch Drew.

Yet there would be no more wondering, no more second-guessing. She knew it now: Lowell Grendel had killed her younger brother.

And Lindsay was now alone in the murderer's backyard. The night was eerily quiet, and her legs were freezing. Attached to his house, facing her, was what appeared to be a cellar door—the type she'd seen only in movies. This one, lying diagonal against the back of the house, was surely the gateway to Lowell Grendel's basement photography darkroom.

Lindsay stepped forward. Above her, the moon was bright enough to cast her shadow, which melted into the darkly painted cellar door flaps as she approached them. A small hasp lock, hooked with a padlock, connected the two flaps. Lindsay leaned closer for a better look.

The padlock was twisted open. Unlocked.

*Are you down there, Bugger?*

It was a ridiculous thought. And yet—

Something caught Lindsay's eye. Movement.

A curtain covering one of Lowell Grendel's back windows had shifted open a crack. Where before it had been completely covered, there was now a narrow strip of black, a sliver of view into the house.

*Oh my God, he's watching. Get out of here now, now, NOW—*

The curtain slammed back into place. Whoever was standing behind it—surely Lowell Grendel—had just seen her looking in.

Lindsay ran.

The snow seemed ten times as thick on her way back to Elijah's. Certain the murderer was behind her, she saw and heard nothing but her own footsteps between her panting breaths. Lowell would also be in his pajamas (did killers even sleep?), gaining on her, close enough to grab her.

Ahead of her was Windsong Road's last streetlight, the one in front of Elijah's house.

*Turn. You're here. Get inside!*

Elijah's front door was still open. As Lindsay tumbled through the storm door, she fell to her knees, gasping for air as if she had just broken through the surface of an icy early grave. A light burned to life above her head, and Elijah's whisper cut through the darkness.

"Lindsay? What the—?"

"It was Drew!" she croaked. "I saw him outside the window. I chased him, and we ended up in—"

"*Please* don't tell me you ran to that creep's house!" Elijah said, stepping over her. He closed the main door and bolted it shut.

Molly, wiping her eyes, stumbled into the front foyer. "What's going on?" Her words came out in a yawn.

"He saw me," Lindsay whispered. "I was standing in his backyard, and he saw me! He knows I know it was him."

"But you *don't* know it was him!" Elijah said. "I thought the police said—"

"It doesn't matter what the police said. I *do* know. Drew was knocking on your window—it woke me up. I followed him outside, and he was running in circles around Lowell Grendel's house."

Instead of arguing, Elijah only shook his head—either in exasperation over Lindsay's nighttime choices or in fear of what they might lead to.

It was Molly who suddenly pointed through the front door with an excited yet agitated expression. "Look," she said, stepping toward it, over Lindsay. "Elijah, shut that light off!"

*It's Lowell Grendel,* Lindsay thought. *He's outside, watching us from the front sidewalk.*

She was about to scream for them all to run, to grab a cell phone, to call 911 and hide, but Elijah's words made her stop. "Holy shit. It's actually her."

Molly whispered: "Lindsay, stand up quick. Is that your brother out there, with that woman?"

Lindsay stood up and forced herself to look out Elijah's window. Instead of seeing Lowell Grendel's face looking back in at her, she saw a woman in an old-fashioned dress standing under the streetlight with her back to them. Wrapped around her waist, peering backward like a shy, tethered child, was Drew. He was wearing his red Doctor Deadlock costume, and even at a distance, Lindsay could see it in his eyes: the gentle promise of death, and a whisper that he was okay on that other, harmless side of reality.

"I MUST CONFESS, I was hesitant to take you on," Dr. Cora Crowe said to Sandra Thorsen and her husband, David, once they were finally seated in the woman's Boulder office—Dr. Crowe behind her desk, and Sandra and David in two chairs facing it. The psychiatrist's dark complexion and lustrous blue eyes underscored an air of somberness, confidence, and overall satisfaction with life that for some reason summoned all of Sandra's defenses.

"Why hesitant?" Sandra asked.

"Because of your connection to this Jonathan Flite boy out in Rhode Island. His situation seems questionable, to say the least. I'm nervous it's going to make what I do even more controversial."

"I'd have thought our connection to his story would make you curious," David said. As always, he was being careful to keep his tone light, friendly, and unthreatening.

Dr. Crowe offered a lukewarm smile. "To be frank, I'm a skeptical person. With what I do, it has to be a rule. Also, anyone who claims to have past-life memories of someone prominent—let alone seven kids who all disappeared at the same time—needs to be fully vetted. Most people who do these past-life regressions come out with stories of other lives that were inconsequential in context of fame, celebrity, and earth-shattering heroics. Lives are typically basic, for lack of a better word. Since your daughter and her friends were famous enough to be researched, it's all a bit convenient."

"But *could* this kid be the real deal?" David asked.

Dr. Crowe shrugged. "Honestly, some patients have remembered living multiple concurrent lives. It's not out of the question, as far as my experience goes. Maybe if that physicist you mentioned ends up being legit, and if Alice Winterblume *does* make that documentary, I'd have more to go on. But people can be dishonest. Unfortunately, I always have to consider that."

At Dr. Crowe's words, the unutterable truth Sandra had sensed earlier, outside the office door—that it hadn't been grief plaguing her after Lindsay and Drew disappeared, but rather something disgraceful—crept back into her mind.

"I think it might have been a mistake for me to come here," she said suddenly, turning to David. "I'd like to go."

"Sandy, wait. We just got here—"

"I know, but I don't think I can do this. It doesn't feel right."

"If I may?" Dr. Crowe cut in, again with that self-assured, patient air Sandra could only envy. "You don't have to believe in past-life regressions for this to be an enlightening experience. Hell, I still doubt the nature of my work every day. But it doesn't change the fact of what I've seen in my patients—quite often full reversals of the psychological problems they came in to treat. More often than not, it happens with the ones who don't expect anything to happen at all."

"I almost trained in clinical hypnosis a few times when I was getting my psych degrees, but I never actually followed through," Sandra said, inching back toward warmth. "I was always nervous it'd make me look crazy."

"We still have a long way to go in understanding what hypnosis actually is," Dr. Crowe conceded. "Suffice it to say that the clinical definition is that it's simply an altered state of consciousness. It makes you more susceptible to suggestion and direction by inducing a decreased amount of activity in the brain's dorsal anterior cingulate—that's part of the salience network that tells us which physical stimuli to pay attention to. More or less, it changes the brain's processes and seemingly disconnects our actions from our awareness of them."

"So, it could all be nonsense," Sandra said.

"You're going to get a lot of opinions, that's for sure," Dr. Crowe said. She leaned forward in her chair slightly. "Honestly, the only reason I was open to treating people with hypnosis earlier in my career was because I experienced an early childhood regression myself during med school, which brought up memories from all the way back to when I was three months old—mostly of incidents in my parents' marriage that I was witness to and that they thought I'd never remember. I asked my mom afterward if the memories were legit, and she almost jumped out of her skin before confirming that yes, they were."

"Why don't more therapists use hypnosis, then?" David asked.

Dr. Crowe shrugged a second time. "Because it's never a sure bet. It's not black-and-white, and a lot of therapists don't consider it scientific due to its subjectivity. People can also fabricate memories, even if their therapists do a good job guiding them. I like to tell people that doing a past-life regression is more about being open to vulnerability— and to whatever answers come to you."

Sandra's pulse slowed, and there it was: calm, somewhere behind her fear. "I'm not sure I'm an open person," she said.

"Are you at least open to the possibilities of what might come from trying something new?"

With slowing breaths, Sandra replied, "I just want to know why I lost both my children."

For the first time since their arrival, Dr. Crowe's posture shifted toward relaxation, and she nodded. "Well, then, let's get started."

I N THE MORNING FOLLOWING THE APPARITION of Drew and the woman in rags, Lindsay Thorsen couldn't remember falling back asleep. Yet five hours later, she, Elijah Bryce, and Molly Butler woke up within minutes of one another to the sounds of Elijah's mother, Shelly, grinding coffee.

Lindsay was once again struck by the sights, smells, and sounds of a different house. She used her elbow to hoist herself up, then noticed that Molly was already sitting vertically, staring out the window. Just as she turned her head in a slow, groggy manner and locked eyes with Lindsay, Elijah bolted upright, as if suddenly remembering the previous night.

"Are we going to tell the police?" Molly whispered, answering all of Lindsay's questions in a single moment.

Elijah held up a hand to shush her, gesturing toward the kitchen, where his mother was. "We'll talk about it later."

"Good morning!" came Shelly Bryce's voice from the kitchen, with a forced-sounding sing-songiness. She was a small and squat blonde who moved with heavy footsteps and a flushed smile. Unlike Lindsay's own mother, Shelly seemed genuine on all the levels that mattered, clearly hard working at her nursing job and serious about keeping her family of two afloat.

Today, she walked with a slight bounce in her step. She had done Elijah's paper route for him earlier due to the sleepover, and the fresh snow seemed to have invigorated her.

"Is anyone interested in coffee other than Elijah?" she asked, leaning through the kitchen door and peering into the family room.

Molly shook her head and scrunched her face. "Tea person here. Thanks, though."

"I'll take it black," Lindsay replied. She had never tried coffee before, mostly because her parents drank it religiously and always got headaches whenever they didn't. But today seemed like a good day to start.

Elijah switched on the television. Children's cartoons blared on almost every channel, and only when they glimpsed footage of lions roaming the African savannas did Elijah put the remote down. It was ideal for Lindsay, somehow, sitting with her friends and not having to talk. They all knew what had happened last night and what it could mean: Lowell Grendel, if he really had been peeking through that slit in his curtains, now knew Lindsay was watching him.

She had to tell her parents and the police, even though it would mean admitting to trespassing in the man's yard during a moment of nighttime confusion. While that part might be believable enough, the vision of Drew with the woman in the dress would not be. That part had to remain a secret.

As if to punctuate the strange juxtaposition of frightening speculation and real, everyday life, Shelly announced breakfast just as the credits rolled on the lion program. Lindsay, Elijah, and Molly stretched in unison before standing up—which inspired sleepy but comforting chuckles—and headed for the kitchen.

Shelly scooped hefty piles of cheesy scrambled eggs onto their plates and set a platter of out-of-the-box waffles in front of them. The maple syrup was the fake kind—Mrs. Butterworth's—but Lindsay politely accepted it, trying not to think about how her own mother would probably call Elijah and Shelly "cheap." Yet it all tasted good, even the coffee. Just as Lindsay was about to reach for a second helping of waffles, however, the doorbell rang.

"I'll get it," Shelly said with a quiet sigh. She wiped her sudsy dishwashing hands on a towel and plodded toward the front door. Elijah shrugged and turned back to his breakfast, but Molly eyed Lindsay, clearly thinking something but not voicing it.

When Shelly spoke a few moments later, she sounded exaggeratedly friendly, but in a shaky way that indicated she was feeling anything but. "Kids, could you come here for a minute?"

Lost in his waffles, Elijah yelled, "Just a second!" He took a sip of coffee, then stood up. When Molly followed him with a pale face, Lindsay realized what she was thinking: that the person at the door might be Lowell Grendel.

*Oh God. Please no.*

But yes. It was him, the man who had killed her brother. He was standing on Elijah's front porch.

Shelly held the screen door open with her left hand, at least having retained the smarts not to invite the man inside. But her face was pale and shaking.

Lindsay stopped under the archway to the front living room, carefully barricaded behind Elijah and Molly. It took only a second for Lowell Grendel to look at the three teenagers. His gaze rested on Lindsay for only a brief moment, but during it, she saw a fleeting glimmer of annoyance and then something else. Was it recognition?

"What does he want?" Elijah asked in a solid, serious, and altogether dangerous-sounding tone. Everyone had heard the story of how he had carried his dead enemy's body away from Spinner's Island, but this was the first time Lindsay had ever seen his boldness in person.

Shelly spoke in a trembling voice. "That's no way to talk to a neighbor, Elijah." Despite the words, a slightly judgmental tone—aimed at Lowell Grendel—had escaped her voice.

"I'm not here to cause any trouble," Lowell called through the door, addressing Lindsay, Elijah, and Molly specifically. The wavy strips of white in his otherwise dark hair shimmered in the morning light, making his face look impossibly young. "I know people've been afraid of me lately, though—especially since the police showed up and brought that flutter of news reporters. But it's all been a huge misunderstanding."

He shivered in the cold morning air before frowning.

"That said, I can't just sit here and take harassment from people who refuse to believe I'm innocent. I know I'm new to the neighborhood, but that doesn't give anybody the right to spread lies about me or vandalize my property."

"He says someone was in his yard last night," Shelly added, crossing her arms over her chest in a futile self-hug.

Lindsay could neither think nor speak. She simply stared at Lowell Grendel, allowing the reality of him to creep into her life. He was not just a vaguely recollected face now; he was right there, talking to her.

Elijah's stance grew taller. "How come you think one of us was in your yard? Have you been watching us?"

"He says there are a bunch of footprints circling his house," Shelly said.

"Could have been the paperboy," Elijah replied with a smirk.

Lowell sighed in a way that turned Lindsay's legs to jelly. The grimace distorting his face looked fake, like that of a bad actor, as he shook his head. "Either way, my first bit of snow on Windsong Road is ruined," he said. "The yard is full of your footsteps."

With a sudden shift of his eyes, he looked straight at Lindsay.

She wanted to scream, but nothing came out.

"I'm just trying to be civil here," he continued. "I know it was you kids, because the tracks lead right back to your front yard. I'm not trying to be that catty neighbor, but I'd like some respect." Again came his actor's grimace. "Okay? Sound good? No more chasing games through my yard?"

Something behind the man's expression faltered—was it panic?—as Lindsay's breath caught in her throat.

*How did he know I was chasing someone?*

Lowell Grendel swallowed. "I'll be seeing you all around, then." He looked at Elijah, again with that awkward expression. "And you. Great job getting my newspaper to me on time. I'm up early, and it's spot-on everyday. I'll be leaving you a nice Christmas tip."

He attempted to smile, then turned and hopped down the porch steps.

When Shelly closed the door and turned to see Elijah and Molly still standing in a protective manner in front of Lindsay, she lowered her polite posture and shook her head. "What was that about? He said you guys were laughing and running in circles around his house and mocking him! Elijah, you wouldn't, would you?"

"Not in a million years. And I'm never delivering his newspaper again." Elijah lumbered to the living room window and looked out, after Lowell Grendel. "He's lying, and he knows we know it. You could see it in his face!"

"I don't know *what* I saw in his face," Shelly said, now fighting tears. "I should never have called you all in here, but he seemed so polite when he knocked on the door. I wanted to give him the benefit of the doubt, you know? And you, Lindsay—I'm so sorry. Has he seen your face on the news since . . . you know?"

"He recognized her," Elijah said, and Molly nodded in agreement.

Self-consciousness rode a wave through Lindsay, because in that last flicker of eye contact from Lowell Grendel, she had become a target. Now there was nothing she could do except nod at Shelly. "Yeah, he knew who I was."

Shelly rushed forward and put her hands on Lindsay's shoulders. "I'll drive you home right now. Get your stuff together. We're not going to let this ruin your Christmas, okay? Don't you worry. I'm keeping my eyes peeled on that man. I don't know what it was, but something about him just seemed off. I *do* also need to tell your parents what happened, okay?"

Lindsay nodded.

"Oh. And there was one other thing that sounded weird." Shelly took a step back. "Just before I called you guys in here, he said something really odd. He said, 'Gosh, you know, kids will be kids. Their souls are the brightest ones out there.' Any of you know why he'd say something like that?"

As Elijah and Molly shook their heads, Lindsay remained stoic, because all she could think about was the man's basement and his unearthly photos of her dead, laughing brother.

O N SEPTEMBER 29, 2039, under mounting guilt over keeping Jonathan Flite's possible lie about the Sparks-house gas explosion secret from Alice Winterblume, Clovia Bell needed solitude—a chance to walk, to think, to be just another person alone on New York City's crowded sidewalks.

For the first time in weeks, she left *WorldLine*'s new office without calling Roger from Global Protection Services, who had escorted her everywhere since the FBI's mandate back in June.

IT WAS RAINING when she finally approached her apartment building. She was fifty feet from its grubby glass door when she looked up and registered something strange: a crowd of people standing outside it.

They had lights. And cameras.

Clovia immediately regretted her decision to travel home without security, because the flock was already upon her.

*"Miss Bell! Is it true you're in a relationship with Jonathan Flite?"*

*"Has it put your position at* WorldLine *at risk?"*

*"Do you think you're in danger from Victor Zobel or other possible extremists now that you're publicly aligning yourself with the Rhode Island nurse killer?"*

*No comment, no comment, no goddamned fucking comment,* Clovia thought, pushing through the crowd to her apartment-building door, wondering who-oh-*who* had given these reporters a reason to stake it out. Had it been Lydia Clark, the blogger who had outed the identity of Jonathan's father? Or perhaps someone here in New York?

Realizing it could have been anyone, Clovia rushed inside. Her heart ballooned with anxiety as she climbed the stairs, knowing her life spiral had just taken another loop downward.

When Clovia reached her third-floor apartment in a doglike pant, her roommate Tova was standing at the window, looking out at the street. She didn't look toward the door as Clovia entered.

"What the hell did you do?" Tova said in a low, accusatory voice. "They were out there when I got off work today, screaming at me about some dinner you had with Jonathan Fucking Flite."

"What do you mean? What dinner?"

"Check your precious news."

Clovia slumped onto the couch and pulled out her ActoPhone. Within seconds, there it was: a photo of her and Jonathan at Mitéra Mediterranean restaurant just last night, before he drove back to Newport in his Lexus SE7.

*Oh Jesus. Please no.*

"Looks like the cat's out of the damned bag," Tova said. "Someone even posted audio of your conversation. They were recording from the next table. And—God. I didn't know you two were actually *dating*."

Tova shook her head, folded her arms, and sat down in the living room chair farthest away from Clovia. "I'd have thought somebody in your position would've been more careful with this sort of thing. I mean, the fucking media is just—"

She glanced up at Clovia, the *WorldLine* employee.

"Sorry. I just . . . I didn't sign up for this. And if you bring that murderer anywhere near this apartment, I'm moving out."

Tova stood up in a huff and tromped off toward the kitchen.

*And she was the one person I thought would understand*, Clovia thought.

Knowing it didn't bode well for the dynamic with her other roommates, she stood back up, found a hat and sunglasses, and left her apartment—even though it meant fending off the reporters once again. Tonight, despite the rain and no security guards, dinner would be out. Anywhere but here.

AFTER HAILING A CAB and traveling to the West Village, Clovia found herself seated in her favorite corner of Takashi Ramen Bar, with her back to the wall and her eyes to the door. Thus far, nobody had recognized her.

She kept her sunglasses on. Sipped her ramen.

She called Jonathan four times, only to get his voice mail.

Finally, she sent a text message, telling him she needed to talk. About the reporters? About her concerns regarding the night of the Sparks-house gas explosion?

No.

Not tonight.

Right now it was all too much. Clovia suddenly and hideously envied Victor Zobel, who got to spend the majority of his time on Star Island, orbiting around Earth's squabbles.

*Just breathe. Get through it. Life has to go on.*

For the first time in weeks, Clovia opened the ebook she was reading—her one form of relaxation. It was *Little Women* by Louisa May Alcott, her seventh time through it.

Outside, the sky dimmed. Clovia remained in her corner, breathing through each page, willing herself to remember how things were before *WorldLine*, before orphanhood, before Jonathan Flite. Everyone wanted the power that came with fame—or at least the association with it—but now she knew the truth. Anonymity was golden.

Yet she also loved Jonathan. Truly. Yes, they were young, and yes, they had only known each other for a year. They had also been reckless by building a relationship outside of *WorldLine's* boundaries. But this was more than just a mutual infatuation, and they both knew it.

*Unless I'm going crazy*, Clovia thought.

As she flicked to the next digital page of her ebook, she noticed a bald, middle-aged man watching her from two tables down. He was built like a bulldozer and might have had the face of a fitness model were it not for a spread of unflattering pockmarks.

Clovia looked up at him, and he immediately looked away. Then his gaze rolled back toward her, over an angular grin.

The restaurant's other patrons were all sitting on the opposite end of the dining room, near the door. As a waitress with a full tray bustled past Clovia, the bulldozer man stood up and started his approach. To deflect what she already knew was happening, Clovia looked out the windows. Beads of rain raced down them, and outside, it was dusk. A darkening, cloudy sky arched over wet pavement that was painted with reflections of streetlights, headlights, and lit-up storefronts.

Clovia squirmed under the discomfort of her pounding heart, and before she could tell the man no, he sat down at her table.

*Say something, say something, say something—*

But the man spoke before she could gather her wits. "You should know that it's not just the reporters watching you, Little Miss Bell."

He had an accent. It immediately reminded her of Raphael Dumont, the man Natalie Pent had captured on video in France in 2012 and the one *WorldLine* now couldn't mention. Except this man sounded Russian—similar to Fredek Bobrov, her Expository Writing professor at the Tisch School of the Arts. And despite the bombing at *WorldLine*, the peripheral death threats since, and the days spent walking New York City on foot with Jonathan, Clovia couldn't move. Her street smarts were nowhere to be found.

The restaurant bustled around her as the bulldozer man's gaze pierced hers, feeding what was sure to become a post-traumatic stress response.

"I'll keep this brief," he said. "I have a message for you to give to Alice Winterblume, and it's this: She needs to stop whatever documentary she's making. This is her last warning. I know you have her ear. I could also kill you right now, so if the fact that you almost died tonight isn't enough to make Alice pull the plug, she's going to regret it one day. Mark my words."

Clovia's entire body shook. Her legs were hot, tingling, jelly.

"You need to be careful who you spend your time with," he continued. "Someone could use you to get to those people. Or to make a point."

*Victor Zobel. He's talking about Victor Zobel.*

"Do you see?" the bulldozer man said. "I trust you're receiving the message loud and clear? Say yes."

Clovia couldn't speak. The man leaned closer.

"I said, '*Say yes.*'"

"Yes," Clovia whispered.

The forced response violated her.

And then the bulldozer man stood up, turned around, and left a fifty-dollar bill on his own table before walking out of the restaurant, into the rainy night.

*The FBI. Call the FBI right now.*

Yet it took Clovia almost a minute to pick up her phone. When she finally made the call to Special Agent Heather Mousseau, she did so with shaking fingers.

2005

NO MORE CHASING GAMES. *No more chasing games. No more chasing games.*

Lowell Grendel swore as the phrase he had used in front of Lindsay Thorsen beat through his brain like a rhythm of stupidity, showing him only dark paths forward. He was sitting in his living room on December 25, 2005, starkly alone and starkly still. It was nearing 2:00 a.m. on a very early Christmas morning.

Next to his left ear, screaming at him in words he couldn't hear, was Taconite Rose, the woman in rags. It was always like this now, at least whenever Lowell's mind wasn't strong enough to block her out. The ghost woman was now like a rabid sentry blocking out the world he wished to study, to enter, to make sense of. Didn't she realize that this was why he was driven to take and kill, take and kill, take and kill?

Drew Thorsen had been a mistake. The biggest mistake. Yes, the boy was innocent, and that in itself dragged across Lowell's conscience like a bludgeoning stick spiked with nails. Yet he had been unable to control himself, to dismiss the urge, to unsee the boy's orbs of light—those bits of proof that the world Lowell himself remained stuck in was a smoke screen for something so much bigger and (hopefully) endlessly forgiving.

And now he had all but given himself up to Lindsay, the boy's sister. He had attempted to act like Elijah Bryce's friendly neighbor, despite the small barrage of reporters who had flocked to his door for a short time following the police's raid. He had tried to show everyone that he was innocent, that he wasn't watching their every move like a hawk, and that he wasn't plotting the only way out he could think of. Now that he had seen the girl, Lindsay, chasing her younger brother, however, Lowell knew that she could see the other side of reality as well. That he wasn't alone.

If only he could bring her to Taconite Rose. To show the screaming dead woman not just that others could see her but also that he did indeed have the power to control himself. He wouldn't have to kill Lindsay, but she could be an offering nonetheless. An oblation to bear his regrets openly to Rose and prove he wasn't a monster.

Yes, taking the girl could incense the ghost further. But how else could he ever find peace?

*Turn yourself in. Tell them what you did with the boy's body.*

Except he couldn't. They were already so close to nabbing him, to finding out the truth, to giving him life in prison. He couldn't walk into such a punishment graciously, with open and guilty arms, even if it *was* the only way Rose would leave him alone.

She came closer to his ear. He could almost feel her cold breath, hear her words, and smell her hate. She was intent on seeing him caught or behind bars or dead. That was what child murderers deserved, wasn't it?

Oh, he should have known. He shouldn't have listened to the man at the bar in Laguna Beach—the drunk one who looked like a movie star, who had been discussing Idle County's peculiarities with the old man who looked like Colonel Sanders from KFC. If they hadn't been sitting in the adjacent booth that night, Lowell would have never known to search out this awful, unlocked place.

He dared a glance to his left.

Taconite Rose was still screaming.

*And she'll keep on doing that until you show her you're not a terrible man,* his last remnants of optimism whispered. *If you take Lindsay to where Rose died—and prove you don't always have to kill—it might get her off your back. Maybe even help her move on.*

But Lindsay would never go with him on her own volition; that was obvious. Which meant Lowell would have to kidnap her. Probably after a choke hold and a ketamine injection. He would have to get more vials and syringes, since he had so stupidly forgotten to hide the ones he'd had in his bathroom vanity at the beginning of the month. And finding the drug would be easy. It always was.

Yet it would create another horrible loop, one that could land him in prison unless he was more careful than ever before.

As Taconite Rose continued to bellow her ghostly screams next to him, he began to see the path forward—and the way he might finally bring the woman, and himself, peace.

O N December 27, two days after a silent Christmas, Lindsay Thorsen was just about to finish a bout of homework on her new laptop—the only holiday gift she had truly wanted—when an AOL Instant Message came in from Alan Sparks.

*hey, want to come over for new years eve? bring molly and elijah? might be cool to hang with like-minded people for a change*

A warm thrill of attraction rushed through Lindsay, and with it came a feeling of life clicking into place. Of course she wanted to go, and she told Alan so.

They chatted for ten minutes. When she said goodnight, signed off, and closed the new laptop, a swarm of butterflies fluttered in her stomach.

They settled, and she wondered: *Is this what it feels like for life to move on?*

On New Year's Eve, Lindsay's father, David, drove her, Molly, and Elijah to Alan's house for the gathering. The house was large and white with a tapered roof—somewhat rundown, save for a modern-looking wheelchair ramp zigzagging down from the large front porch. Midsize pine trees lined the lot on each side, giving the yard a dark, slightly shuttered feeling.

When David accompanied Lindsay, Molly, and Elijah inside to meet Alan and his parents, Lindsay's chest was a hurricane of nerves.

"I guess we have to get used to the idea of Alan having girls over," Maureen Sparks said with a cautious smile as Alan took everyone's coats. She was indeed the woman Lindsay had seen feeding Alan's sister Rebecca at the Christmas party, and while her heart-shaped face exuded politeness, her eyes and forehead were creased with stress lines. Her hair was solid black—the color of cheap hair dye—but it suited her in a no-nonsense way that, strangely, made Sandra Thorsen's expensive dye jobs seem completely unnecessary.

Apart from Rebecca, Alan had three other siblings: a sister named Gladys, who was eight, and twin brothers named Lukas and Bailey, who were six. His father, Nathan, was a dental hygienist at an office near Skydale Mall in End Haven while Maureen stayed at home—mostly, she said, to care for sixteen-year-old Rebecca. Money was tight in Alan's family, but unlike Lindsay's well-to-do one, they seemed generally happy.

When the conversation between the parents inevitably turned to Drew, Maureen handed David a hot toddy before they descended into hushed voices. Rebecca, who had wheeled up to them shyly, watched intently as their quiet conversation progressed.

"So, is it really just us three coming tonight?" Lindsay asked Alan while he led everyone toward a tray of chips, salsa, and guacamole set out on the living room coffee table.

"Yeah. Rebecca was actually the one who told me to invite you over—probably because she knew you were on my mind." He said these words with a smile before gesturing toward Elijah and Molly. "She was also curious to meet those two."

Lindsay blushed. Alan knew she'd told Molly and Elijah about Rebecca's alleged ability to read minds, but he didn't know that she'd also told them about the kiss he'd given her under the snow after their walk toward Lowell Grendel's house during the Christmas party.

Elijah had been the one most preoccupied with Lindsay's relayed story about Rebecca. *"Read minds?"* he had asked, trying to mask his apprehension with incredulity. *"I don't know if I'd want anybody doing that inside my head."*

Apparently, his last encounter with a supposed psychic—his birth mother, Cynthia—had ended with a prediction of his death, which had nearly come true.

Molly, on the other hand, had listened to Lindsay with an open mind from the outset and seemed very interested in Alan's family.

Now all three of them listened as Alan explained how Rebecca had adopted a peculiar guise of shyness that afternoon. "It's weird—she was aware I invited you guys over, but she kind of already knew about you."

"What do you mean?" Molly asked.

"I mean, like, when I mentioned that you were coming, she said she'd been looking forward to meeting you for a long time."

Elijah's acknowledgment of Alan's statement came out as an audible gulp. Molly, however, simply nodded as if it weren't strange at all. "Lindsay told us that she's missing part of her brain or something?" she said.

"Her corpus callosum," Alan replied with a nod. He then recapped what he'd told Lindsay at the Christmas party. Every time they exchanged glances, his eyes glimmered, as though he, too, were still fixated on the kiss they had shared under the snow.

Thankfully, it took only twenty minutes for the conversation to turn to kickboxing, which Elijah had taken a liking to after two private training sessions with Coach Martinez. As Alan dipped two chips at once into the bowl of guacamole and stuffed his face (Lindsay exchanged perturbed glances with Molly), he invited Elijah back to the community center. "I could totally show you more stuff, including how to beat Lindsay."

"Ouch!" Molly said with a laugh. She turned to Lindsay, who narrowed her eyes at the boy who was now seemingly her boyfriend.

"Keep on laughing," Lindsay added, mentally sending Alan to the floor with a right hook from hell. "And don't forget about the tournament. You'll be in for a surprise."

"Bring it on."

Alan had to twist his body away as Lindsay rammed her heel into his unsuspecting shin. They all broke into laughter, and for the next half hour, Lindsay and Alan tried to catch each other off guard with kicks.

Finally, David Thorsen, looking a bit red in the face from his hot toddy, passed through the living room to say goodbye. Maureen and wheelchair-rolling Rebecca were close in tow. Lindsay waved goodbye quickly, then turned back to her friends, who were still in the living room.

For the second time that season, Molly made friends with the mother in charge, and by eleven thirty, she and Maureen were cleaning the counters, stovetop, pans, and dishes together as Alan, Elijah, and Lindsay watched the live New York ball-drop celebration on TV. It was already past midnight on the East Coast, so now it was just a mess of rowdy people, lights, and confetti.

Molly pranced into the room excitedly, wiping her hands on a dish towel. "We're getting glasses ready for the sparkling grape juice at midnight, so you better—oh!"

Confused at Molly's sudden interjection, Lindsay followed her gaze toward the living room's adjacent hallway. Sitting there, watching them with an expressionless face, was Alan's sister Rebecca.

"Are you finally joining the party?" Alan said, jumping off the couch and running to her side. "Guys, this is Rebecca. Rebecca, you know Lindsay from the other party. But this here is Elijah Bryce, and that's Molly Butler."

Rebecca didn't move her wheelchair, which appeared to be controlled by a small knob in front of her right hand. Instead, she turned to the small typing keyboard that sat on a platform to her left. Her hands moved slowly.

"Ha. She says, 'Nice to meet you,'" Alan said, angling her tablet toward Lindsay, Molly, and Elijah. He then turned back to his sister. "PS: I saw you with Lindsay's dad before he left. What'd you talk about?"

Rebecca scrunched her face and shook her head. She moved the wheelchair through the door, which Lindsay now noticed was extra wide. Red barrettes held back the girl's long blond hair, and her sharp, alert eyes intensified her otherwise soft features. With some effort, she held a hand out to her family's three guests. Her shake was firm enough to indicate that she was truly happy to see Lindsay again. Still, what Alan said—*she can read minds*—made Lindsay feel naked.

After shaking Elijah's hand, Rebecca suddenly laughed.

"Were you just thinking about how weird it is that she might be seeing inside your head?" Alan asked. Elijah instantly blushed as Alan chuckled. "She always says people feel weird when they meet her, if they know about her mind reading ahead of time."

Sure enough, Rebecca grinned. Then she bent down to her computerized speaking assistant to type.

*You're all very bright people.*

As she finished typing, she beamed at Molly and Elijah. When she looked at Lindsay, however, something in her expression flickered.

Alan smirked at his sister. "See? They're nice. Why were you being so shy?"

Rebecca slowly pressed her fingers on the keyboard again.

*Because I was afraid of knowing their secrets.*

For some reason, it was Molly who immediately blushed upon reading this. Saying nothing, she simply looked away from Rebecca, who glanced after her with a curious smile.

Alan shrugged. "I guess that means she'll try to respect you," he said, jokingly grinding his knuckles into Rebecca's hair, just enough to mess it up. Looking miffed, Rebecca backed up, then wheeled around them, into the kitchen. "Alan!" came his mother's call from the kitchen a moment later. "One more time of messing up her hair and you won't eat for a week!"

"She's probably serious," Alan said. He grinned and turned back to the television. It was ten minutes to midnight, and the news had turned local now as a live broadcast from Minneapolis's Target Center overtook the screen. "By the way," Alan continued in a quieter voice, "Rebecca already knows that you guys, like, see ghosts and stuff."

Elijah and Molly looked cautiously at each other, then at Lindsay.

"Honestly, that's kind of why I wanted to invite you all over tonight. It's nice to finally know people who like to talk about the bigger stuff—not just school drama."

"Unless you're talking about Lindsay's fights with Natalie Pent," Elijah said with a smirk. Molly and Alan laughed while Lindsay faked a scowl.

"Whatever," Alan said. "It's almost midnight. Let's get the sparkling juice ready."

"Already done, but I'll bring it out!" Molly said, zipping away into the kitchen.

Four minutes later, the clock counted down from ten to zero, and the year was new: a fresh start ahead of them all. The events of the past few months flowed backward through Lindsay's mind and tumbled over last year's edge with abandon. At least for tonight, and it was time to look forward.

Alan took Lindsay's hand. His palms were solid but soft. The gesture was invisible to Molly and Elijah, who were standing in front of them, watching the television and drinking their sparkling juice. Alan turned and looked into Lindsay's eyes.

*Kiss him*, Lindsay's body urged. But they were not alone and not even officially going out. Alan himself didn't hint at making a move. It could wait. *They* could wait.

At ten minutes past midnight, Maureen Sparks rounded up Lindsay, Molly, and Elijah and readied herself to drive them home. It was a cold night—just above zero degrees—and the woman spared no precaution against it, taking nearly five minutes to put on her winter gear.

This gave Alan time to "show Lindsay something" in the kitchen. He pulled her through the door, and once they were around a corner where nobody in the living room could see them, he kissed her fully on the lips. It was Lindsay's third-ever kiss from a boy, and it was by far the best.

"Thanks for coming over," he whispered.

"I had a great time," she whispered back.

Then the sudden mechanical whirring of Rebecca's wheelchair made them jump off each other in a rapid twist. Alan itched his head on impulse, and Lindsay pointed to a random photo on the refrigerator. "This is a funny one," she said idly, just before realizing the photo was a pretty one of Rebecca, younger and smiling in her wheelchair, surrounded by about fifteen other kids.

In the doorway, however, Rebecca's smile was even wider.

Alan glanced at the picture, raised one eyebrow, and smiled. "Yeah, that was during some study in Chicago that she was a part of—for psychic kids, I mean." He turned around. "Um, hello, Rebecca."

She began typing.

*I won't tell Mom.*

"Ha ha, funny," Alan replied.

*Wanted to say bye.*

Rebecca looked at Lindsay as she typed it.

"It was nice meeting you again, Rebecca," Lindsay said. "I hope we weren't too annoying."

Rebecca offered Lindsay a slight shake of the head as the smile on her face faded. Again, her fingers twirled slowly across the keyboard.

*Don't give up with Lowell Grendel. Your brother says he's
the one. And yes, Drew is dead. But not gone.*

Rebecca's face was deathly serious now. She continued typing as furiously as she could—which was still slow.

*Lowell has seen Rose, too.*

*Rose.*

It was the same name Wanda Jorgensen's mother, Eleanor, had been screaming about a few weeks ago.

Lindsay took five steps toward Rebecca and knelt next to her wheelchair. "Who is Rose?" she whispered. "Was she the woman standing under the streetlight with Drew?"

Rebecca closed her eyes and nodded. Her fingers moved again.

*She doesn't show her face to good people, because she's embarrassed that she can't move on. She only chases people who've done bad things.*

Tears formed in Lindsay's eyes. "Do you know where Drew's body is?" she whispered.

The young woman's gaze dropped into her lap just as Alan's mother called from the other room. "Alan? Where are you and Lindsay? It's time to go!"

Alan circled the wheelchair and grabbed the back of it. In a low voice, he said, "Rebecca, if you know something, you need to tell us."

Maureen's booted footsteps stomped across the living room as Rebecca's fingers moved slowly over the letters on her keyboard.

*Go faster*, Lindsay thought. *Come on! Hurry it up!*

Rebecca looked up with a stubborn, wounded expression.

*Damn it. If you're reading my mind, I'm sorry for being rude.*

Bristling, Rebecca started typing again, but almost in a grudging manner.

*Drew isn't saying where his body is. But his guides say that you're going to an event in February that will eventually lead you on the right path. You will find his body in the end.*

"What event?" Lindsay whispered. "Do you mean the ghost symposium? The one at Benedict Wise University?"

Just as Rebecca began to nod, Maureen reached the hallway, causing Lindsay to stand up in reflex.

"Okay, time to head out," the woman said with a tired smile. Then she turned to Rebecca, who was already starting to backspace over her words. "Honey, Dad is sleeping upstairs, but Alan'll be here in case you need anything. I'll be back in half an hour or less."

Alan's face flinched, and he looked at Lindsay. "Guess I won't be going with to drop you guys off. But thanks for coming tonight. I had a great time."

*Go, before my mom asks questions*, a serious look in his eyes told Lindsay. *I'll cover for you here.*

Lindsay nodded and waved to Alan. With a polite "thank you," she grabbed the jacket Maureen was holding out to her and walked to the front hallway off the living room, where Molly and Elijah were joking quietly with each other.

But then they saw the shadow in Lindsay's eyes.


BY THE TIME LINDSAY CLOSED HER EYES IN BED, it was almost 2:00 a.m. Her head was heavy, and her nose was dry and clogged. Through muffled sobs in her dark house, all she could think about was Rose, the mysterious ghost in the old-fashioned dress, who now, for some reason, had taken Drew under her wing.

Most frightening to Lindsay was her new truth: that she was now stuck on this side of death. If life was a big stage play with the curtain still up, as Rebecca Sparks had once told Alan, when-oh-when would the curtain close? And why did she have to play this role in the first place?

That night, for the first time ever, Lindsay wondered whether there were consequences for souls who were plucked out of life too soon.

2039

I T WAS ALL CRASHING DOWN; Clovia Bell could feel it between her panicked breaths.

As the FBI overtook Takashi Ramen Bar on the rainy night of September 29, 2039, she told and retold them about her faulty choice to leave home without the service of Global Protection Group and then about her encounter with the bald bulldozer man, who had threatened her life. After giving her statement, she learned a new fact: that this man had the same description as the one suspected of poisoning both her father, Patrick, and his girlfriend, Jennifer Corino. The night passed before Clovia's eyes, and all the while, she thought: *This is how it ends. My ability to feel joy.*

As she answered the police's questions—one after the other after the other—all she could think about were the balls she had been juggling and how they had finally all dropped. They were now rolling toward a future she could neither predict nor welcome with open arms.

IN THE DAYS THAT FOLLOWED, normalcy fell by the wayside before re-inventing itself. Clovia, now forced to find a safer place to live, holed up in one of CBS's corporate condos with round-the-clock security. The FBI now knew about her relationship with Jonathan Flite—not just that they had become close but also that they were flirting with the idea of becoming lovers. Clovia had thus far waited with Jonathan, because she wanted to be sure—absolutely sure—that diving headfirst into a rela-tionship with him was something she truly wanted.

Her hesitation wasn't just rooted in him or his past; it was also rooted in his fame, the magnifying glass he lived under, and the irrevo-cable track she had already found herself shuffling down with her eyes wide open, even as it led toward uncertainty, terror, and the possibility of more death.

Since it could still get worse, she had to keep waiting.

ON OCTOBER 1, Clovia followed Alice Winterblume into her newly re-modeled office, which was even more polished than the last one but lacking in woodsy charm. Yet perhaps this was purposeful. Alice had spent the last thirty years obsessing over Idle County's Moon Woods; maybe she was now readying herself to move past them.

"But *no*—you absolutely can't pull the show," Clovia said after Alice unveiled her fear that canceling the Idle County season might be the wisest choice for *WorldLine*. "We've worked way too fucking hard to just give up. Not to mention, it's the story of your career. You can't pull it because of me."

"I hate to burst your bubble, but it's not *just* because of you," Alice said, sipping her 3:00 p.m. vodka. "I'm a journalist, so you know I'm not proposing this lightly. But people are *dead*. Our coworkers are *dead*. Your dad and his lady friend are *dead*. I've been stubborn all year about the question of whether I'm responsible, and now I just . . ."

"You have to count me as a journalist, too, though," Clovia said. "It's our *responsibility* to tell this story, even if Victor Zobel sends his whole damned army after us."

"Yes, but do we really want to wake that beast?" Alice asked.

Clovia twirled her own glass of vodka in her hand; she hadn't the heart to tell Alice that she'd rather have tea. "I just think that if he's scared enough to send people after someone like me, then the story *needs* to be told. Not just his part in it but also Jonathan's. I mean, think about it: people wake up, go to work, learn things, and believe in things, day in and day out. But how often do they really stop to question any of it? What would happen if they *did*? It could totally change the way they approach life—for the better, I think."

"Okay, then that brings me to another question," Alice said. "Are you actually ready for what all this—and a relationship with Jonathan Flite—might mean for *your* life?"

Clovia wanted to laugh, but instead, she wiped five big tears from her cheeks. "No. Not in the least."

As the conversation veered toward a debate over whether people could ever truly be compelled to grow, Clovia made her first official break from *WorldLine*—and Alice—by holding back once and for all her suspicion that Jonathan and Rebecca Sparks had lied about Gabriel Creed and Max Pope's role in the 2007 gas explosion that killed Rebecca's family. What the truth was, Clovia couldn't say. But something in her gut—she had no idea what—urged her to remain silent.


On OCTOBER 3, Clovia left three voice mails for Eloise Creed, Gabriel's younger sister. Eloise was the only Creed sibling who had participated in the *WorldLine* interviews back in July—partially because she was the only one who still lived in Idle County. She had moved back from Minneapolis last year to take care of her bedridden and morbidly obese mother, Abigail, whose religious fervor had seemingly crossed the line into undiagnosed delusional disorder.

*Are you hiding from my call?* Clovia wondered at Eloise, on her third voice mail attempt.

ON HER WAY HOME THAT EVENING, Clovia treated herself to a bouquet of yellow roses—just like the ones that used to grow outside the houses of her old neighbor Ernie Ducey and the librarian Mrs. Grime. Because why not sing with the angels for a day or two?

WHEN JONATHAN CALLED at 6:00 p.m. that evening, Clovia didn't answer. They had spoken briefly after her shell-shocking encounter with the bulldozer man, but in the five days since, she had purposefully disappeared into her work. She needed time. Space. Perspective. She let him know it in a text message.

Furthermore, talking to Jonathan now would also mean hiding her suspicion that he'd lied to *WorldLine*. She wasn't allowed to discuss with him any parts of the show he wasn't involved with; it was a boundary she had established shortly after they'd met, and one she was professionally bound to by her staff position.

If Jonathan truly did have a ruse, the time to confront him would come soon—once she was confident *WorldLine*'s new season was absolutely moving forward, come hell or high water.

NIGHTMARES PLAGUED HER in the nights that followed. Not just of the bulldozer man chasing her through a house with no doors but also of her father, Patrick, repeatedly drinking a pink cocktail with the widest of smiles, failing to realize it was spiked with aconite.

*"Here, honey! Take a sip!"* he said on the first night she dreamed of him. On the second night, in a dream that picked up where the first one left off, he said, *"It'll take you right down the rabbit hole!"*

And then came more dreams of fire. Always the fire. Clovia was yet again stuck in a third-floor bedroom, screaming out the window. This time, Jonathan stood two stories below her in the grassy front yard, with his arms wide and ready to catch her. Only now he wasn't Jonathan. He was an old man with a white beard, dressed in some sort of brown religious robe.

On October 8, after a week of communicating with Jonathan only through text messages—and being bombarded with hyperlinks to New York City condos he and his mother were legitimately offering to buy her, for her own safety—Clovia made the mistake of searching her own name online. Immediately, she saw the array of pictures snapped at Mitéra Mediterranean restaurant just over a week ago. Slowly sinking into the humiliation of knowing that her private, vulnerable date with Jonathan was now smeared across device screens worldwide, she pressed Play on the ActoVid snippet of their recorded conversation.

*"Do you think it's even possible to live normally?"* she had asked him.

*"Normal like how?"*

*"I don't know. Maybe just, like . . . waking up and living and doing whatever makes you happy?"*

Jonathan had paused for almost ten seconds before saying, *"I've only experienced 'happy' recently, and it's still shaky. As you know."*

Yes. Still shaky.

Clovia knew what that meant now. After her father's apparent murder, the bombing at *WorldLine*, and her personal life being smeared all over the media, she had now been personally targeted by Victor Zobel, assuming that was whom the bulldozer man worked for. If life had been tremoring before, it was now officially quaking.

CLOVIA COULD STILL WORK—still *wanted* to work, even though it was the source of her strife—but she didn't make enough money to rent an apartment with the security level of CBS's corporate condos. She also couldn't ask *WorldLine* to foot the bill for her living expenses forever, especially if she wanted a creative future independent from the show.

*Which might mean leaving New York City*, she thought. *Going somewhere cheaper and more obscure. But wouldn't that stop me from achieving my goals?*

Media outlets were now sending direct ActoMessages left and right, offering her money for exclusive interviews about her relationship with Jonathan. But no, she could never become one of those people who sacrificed another person's dignity to earn a living. In some ways, she was already exploiting Jonathan by working for *WorldLine*. She couldn't also do it personally.

Could she?

The sour truth—at least the only one she could see right here and now—left her one option: to accept the new housing option he was offering.

ON OCTOBER 17, JONATHAN AND WINIFRED FLITE closed on a two-bedroom high-rise condo in Chelsea.

"It's yours," Jonathan said on the phone that night, after breaking the news. "Rent-free. You wouldn't be in this position if it weren't for me, so please—don't object."

"It just feels too weird," Clovia told him, sensing for the first time in her life what it might feel like not to have to worry about finances. "If I let you do this, it'd be completely—"

"Completely what? Wrong not to have to worry about money for a while?" He laughed. "Seriously, I don't need yours. Save it. Use it for something better."

*Something better.*

Right then, a new project idea hit Clovia's mind like a freight train. And heavens, was it ever a fast one.

OVER THE NEXT SIX WEEKS, the project baked, slowly but surely, in the secret mental corner where her creativity lived. This was her happy place, her true home, her greatest source of joy. With relief, she allowed the process to lift her up while life around her fell.

ON NOVEMBER 21, Clovia called Eloise Creed again from Jonathan's new condo (a special type of prison she would never call her own), and this time, she got an answer. Despite now being trapped literally and figuratively by the Idle County story, Clovia still felt a spark of journalistic vigor when she heard Eloise's voice. Hopefully it meant the new idea baking in her mind might actually fly, once it had wings.

"Clovia, hi," were Eloise's immediate words after she answered her phone. "I'm sorry I haven't been answering."

Clovia hadn't prepared herself for the woman's directness. "Hi, I—no problem," she started. "I'm sorry for all the calls. I've just been trying to follow up with a question about something you said in your interview with Alice Winterblume back in June. It had to do with the night of the gas explosion at the Sparks house in 2007. We're trying to make sure we get all the details correct in the show."

Clovia waited through the ensuing silence. In the background, she heard someone rambling—a woman, loud-mouthed. Surely Eloise's mother, Abigail?

Then from Eloise: "Is this about how my brother Gabe got to Rebecca's house that night?"

*She didn't even need me to tell her*, Clovia thought.

"Yes, actually. It sounded in your interview like you were about to say something different than what we'd heard before. Our editor wanted me to follow up on it, since it could have implications on the story."

Eloise let out a deep breath. "I guess there's no reason now to keep it a secret. But when Rebecca Sparks and I met on-camera in June—talking about the explosion and all that—I got a sense she wanted me to stick with the story they told the police back in 2007."

"Got a sense?"

"As in . . . she talked in my head. Just like she did those few times I met her as a kid."

Tingles ran down the back of Clovia's neck. "You mean your psychic flashes are happening again?"

"Yeah. Ever since I moved back to Idle County to help my mom."

*So, why the hell didn't she tell Alice this?* Clovia wondered.

Eloise was silent for five seconds before she said, "Let me get somewhere more private."

Through the phone, Clovia heard footsteps on a creaky floor, then a door opening. The sound of Abigail Creed's loud-mouthed rambling faded.

"Okay," Eloise finally continued, her back-and-forth pacing sending loud creaks across her mother's dilapidated front porch. "It was just one thing—and honestly, I was five. I might not be remembering it that clearly. But I don't think Gabe took a taxi to Alan and Rebecca's house that night."

"What do you remember?"

"Well, first, I woke up with Rebecca Sparks screaming inside my head for help. We'd only met and talked that way a few times before, when she came with her brother to volunteer at that old nursing home."

Clovia recalled the patchwork of stories from the Idle County Seven parents about Max Pope, his secret neurological tests during the Alzheimer's drug study in Blue Hill, and his eventual fall from grace.

"Anyway, I walked to Gabe's room that night, feeling all special for getting Rebecca's psychic SOS message," Eloise continued. "After I told him, he ran out of the house, toward Max Pope's house. It was across the street, on the corner, and there was a light on there—which had to have meant Max was home that night. I'm almost sure *he* drove Gabe to End Haven. And if Rebecca was screaming at me for help, I don't think she could've been at Max's. I remember later, the next day, Gabe told me I needed to keep it all a secret and tell the police—and anyone else—that he took a taxi. He made me say it ten times fast. *Taxi, taxi, taxi . . .*"

As Clovia's mind whirled, her heart sank. "Eloise, thanks so much for sharing all that. It really helps. Are you open to taking more calls if Alice Winterblume wants to do a follow-up interview? I'm guessing she will."

"No—please, no," Eloise replied. "I hated being on camera back in June. I don't want to do it again."

"Oh. Well, I'm sure we can—"

But Eloise's mounting breaths cut to silence. She had ended the call.

AND THEN CAME CHRISTMAS EVE. It was Clovia's first holiday with Jonathan Flite, and despite the possible gas-explosion lie that hung between them, they sat like old friends in the new Chelsea high-rise, next to a wall of tall windows separating them from the evening's forecasted snow. Outside was New York's jungle: the concrete, the honking cars, the movers and shakers and dreamers bustling about, even tonight, as if their very lives depended on it.

"Okay, here's the idea," she said to Jonathan, taking a sip from her pinot noir and vaguely glimpsing a life in which all her ambitions had come to fruition. "But first, full disclaimer: it would be piggybacking off of you. And us, whatever this is." She gestured back and forth between them. "Still, it came to me full force back in October, when you told me to use my money for 'something better.'"

Jonathan smiled. As always, it made her melt like a snowflake.

"I can't be some kept woman," she continued. "I can't just take handouts without doing something that could benefit both of us—like, as some sort of payback. I need to stand on my own two feet."

"Okay," Jonathan said, spreading some brie on a seed cracker from Zabar's. "Though, before you continue, I want to challenge you on that idea—standing on your own two feet. Does it mean wasting your money on living expenses when you don't need to, just to prove that you can? Or does it mean standing on the opportunities life is offering?"

"Honestly, it might be both."

"Fair enough."

"But this project idea is getting clearer and clearer, and I think I need to jump on it," Clovia said. "Watching Alice run around Europe these last two months, interviewing all those people about Victor Zobel and the Geneva bombing and weapons smuggling—it all made me realize very clearly that I can't just be on the sidelines. I want to *direct*. In this case, something I'm passionate about. A documentary."

Jonathan stared at her, his hazel eyes dark under the apartment's dim light. Then he looked out the window at the intensifying snow. Contrary to her expectations, however, his gaze shifted back to her over an even wider smile. "I'd love to see you make something."

"I want to explore why I had those feelings in Idle County—like, why it all felt so familiar."

"You mean outside Mrs. Grime's house?" Jonathan asked in a low voice.

"Yeah. I just can't shake that it meant something," Clovia replied.

"And who knows? Maybe it was just so I'd have the idea to make this documentary. But I think this new season of *WorldLine* could really create a market for it, especially if we make it about us—like, a truly honest and open-minded look at whether or not it's even possible to see if we actually had past lives together. We can shoot most of it for free, if I teach you how to use a camera. All the other necessary gear is cheap."

"And what if you don't get answers?"

"Then I don't get answers. But it's just a gut feeling—I need to do it."

Jonathan leaned farther backward on the couch, holding his tea close. "If *WorldLine* shakes people up as much as Alice hopes, I think a follow-up doc like this could have a huge audience."

With a surge of relief, Clovia leaned forward and put a hand on Jonathan's knee. Everything hung in the balance of the words she needed to say next.

"Okay, so, if you're serious about helping me, I need to know something. I've been trying to figure out how to ask this for almost three months, but I think I just need to be direct: Did you and Rebecca Sparks lie about the night of that gas explosion in 2007? Like, how it all played out?"

Jonathan's smile turned to glass. "Why do you ask?"

"Eloise Creed told me last month that she doesn't think her brother Gabriel took a taxi to End Haven that night. She thinks Max Pope drove him."

A gust of wind made the snowflakes outside dance. For the first time tonight, Clovia couldn't bring herself to look Jonathan in the eyes.

"I just need to know your version of the truth," she continued. "I'm going against the rules here—I'm not supposed to talk to you about the show. I haven't told Alice about this yet, in the chance it could somehow make your life worse. But if you're holding something back, I need to know. Especially if you're going to work with me on this documentary."

Distant car horns honked. Silence passed between them. And suddenly, Clovia saw the truth in Jonathan's eyes. He had indeed lied to *WorldLine* about the gas explosion.

Now she needed to find out why.

R EVIS ZOBEL SAT ONCE AGAIN in Prohibition Bar in Minneapolis, waiting for Natalie Pent. It was January 16, 2040, and he had paid to keep the establishment empty. As he nursed his second gin and tonic, three names ran in circles through his mind:

*Cassandra Pope.*

*Jillian Pope.*

*Max Pope.*

His mother, his half sister, and his half sister's biological father. All three had been connected to Revis's own father, Victor, before their deaths or disappearances, entangled in a web of college love, naive marriages, and one seemingly bitter divorce. Given what Jonathan Flite had said back in September about Jillian once overhearing Raphael Dumont talking about poisons, Revis now wondered: Had Raphael played a role in his mother and half sister's deaths? And perhaps in the 2010 disappearance of Jillian's dad, Max? And why on earth was the FBI forcing *WorldLine* not to speculate about these things publicly?

WHEN NATALIE PENT FINALLY ARRIVED at the bar and relieved his mind from its never-ending orbit, she wasted no time in ordering a whiskey and getting to the point. "I don't know why you wanted to meet in person again, other than the obvious fact that you're trying to seduce me."

"Me? Never," Revis said with a grin.

"I can read your eyes, Mr. Zobel."

Revis flicked his brows up and down quickly as he grazed over Natalie's strong, perfect body. Tonight, she was wearing all black, save for a necklace with a silver heart bordered by diamonds. The look suited her.

"Well, to *truly* answer your question," he continued, "I would never have a conversation like this on video or audio. People record things, and when you're in my family, recordings make it onto the news. I even made the bar employees here sign NDAs. Speaking of that, you're not wearing ActoLenses, are you?"

"Wouldn't you like it if I were?" Natalie asked, sipping her neat Glenfiddich and keeping her expression stoic. "But just so you know, this is the last time I'm going to humor you. You can't just text me weird shit about 'the FBI and *WorldLine* screwing us over with the Raphael Dumont story' and then go radio silent for three months."

"I'm sorry. I was nervous about breaking my agreements," Revis said. "But this is it. I've officially decided to say fuck it. Which is why we're here."

"Spit it out, Mr. Zobel."

Revis took a deep breath, then looked straight into Natalie's eyes. "Okay, here goes: the FBI isn't letting *WorldLine* say anything about Raphael Dumont. Which means a lot of the story you shared with them isn't going to reach the public."

Natalie, in the midst of raising her whiskey glass to take another sip, froze. The ice inside it wobbled like a stuck rubber duck, and her face slowly turned red.

"I'm obviously not supposed to be telling you this," Revis continued, "but quite frankly, I think it's bullshit. People need to know about Raph. My dad. The whole lot."

Over her own mounting breaths, Natalie said, "And how, pray tell, do you suppose we do that? *WorldLine* was our one chance at having a credible source behind us." She shook her head and looked toward the ceiling. Tears had formed in her eyes.

"Hey, don't give up so fast," Revis retorted. "I got you somebody at the *New York Times*. A friend of a friend. She wants your Raphael Dumont story. Probably as an op-ed, contingent on whether *WorldLine* actually does leave the narrative out of their show. You couldn't mention the FBI angle or that I was working with them, but you could definitely name Raphael Dumont and stir up some questions."

Natalie blinked twice, then moved her neck backward with an incredulous expression. "Jesus. The *New York Times*? You're serious?"

"Someone needs to tell that part of the story," Revis said, sipping his last gin-and-tonic drop.

"'Someone' meaning me."

"Yes. You."

"And why not *you*?"

"Because I told those FBI agents at my *WorldLine* interview that I wouldn't bring Raph up to any other outlets," Revis whispered. "And *you* were the one who saw him in Idle County. *You* saw him the day of that gas explosion and during the Moon Woods searches. *You* found the Thai candy wrapper in that ravine. It all matters."

"But none of it is actual proof."

"It's not about proof. It's about putting a name to a face. If Raph knows what really happened to my mom, there's a chance other people might have shit on *him*—especially since he flashes that goddamned snake tattoo wherever he goes. That thing is memorable."

"And what about the FBI?"

"Who cares about the FBI? They've told me jack shit about what they're actually investigating. If they really suspect Raph of being some criminal but aren't arresting him, then fuck it. Events are up for grabs."

"You sound like an entitled famous person," Natalie said, finally with a hint of flirtation.

Revis wondered just how aware she was of her own superiority over him—that shrewd confidence, that certainty, that oh-so-perfect way she strutted into a room as if she already owned it.

He turned to hail down the waiter, who (like most Midwesterners) was enamored with Revis's fame and trying not to make a fuss about it. Revis ordered two more drinks, then turned back to Natalie. "My dad and Raph have a bunch of crazy history—and like I said, Jonathan Flite says my sister Jillian heard Raph talking about my dad using aconite on people. This was right around the time my mom started getting sick."

"And you think she was poisoned?"

"I don't know. Maybe."

Now, in a moment of vulnerability, Natalie caught Revis's eye, held the gaze, and said, "There's something I didn't tell you last time we met. Even though I wanted to."

"About Raph?"

Natalie nodded. Revis waited.

"Basically, it's that Lindsay Thorsen's dad and I went to France together in 2012," Natalie continued. "We talked to Raphael face-to-face. I even got it on video. When I first told Alice Winterblume, she promised to put it in the show."

Shock glazed Revis's face. "You're kidding me."

For the second time tonight, Natalie smiled. It was crisp, reminiscent. As the waiter brought them their new drinks, she watched—not quite politely—as he set them on the table. When he was gone, she continued. "It was the fucking craziest thing I ever did. I told *WorldLine* about it, and so did David Thorsen, apparently. I guess he and his wife did their part of the shoot in Colorado."

"And you actually went to France *together*?"

"Yeah, that October. On David's dime. We met up randomly that year and . . . yeah. Our lives were both falling apart, and we got to talking about all this stuff. We did some Googling and tracked Raphael down to Saint-Paul de Vence, the town your dad partially grew up in." Natalie scoffed and shook her head. "We first saw him at church—which by the way *was* Jean-Claude Apostol's parish before he became Mr. Nuclear Terrorist. We took photos and video of them both before following Raphael home. That's when he finally saw us. We told him who we were, and I could tell he recognized us from the candlelight vigil in Idle County—or at least me, because he had a particular look when he made eye contact."

Natalie's bravery—no, her *dominance*—was like an assault on Revis's senses. He basked in it.

"And?"

"And he didn't say a word. We told him our concerns and asked our questions, but all he did was *smile*. Like, the whole fucking time. I got it all on video."

Revis raised his eyebrow, sat back, and sipped his gin and tonic. "How old were you then?"

Natalie chuckled as nostalgia lightened her eyes. "I was only twenty. My parents had no idea what to think."

"Are they still alive, your parents?"

Somehow, Natalie's humored expression remained intact. "No. My mom died two years ago, and my dad a year before that. They were always so worried about me—if I would ever make it in life and all that. Even after I started working for your sister a few years ago, they were still asking me what my backup plan was." She shrugged. "I'm sure you'll notice in my brother's *WorldLine* interview how 'wealthy East

Coast' he's become. I think my parents always compared me to him in that light. Like, wishing I had become more 'upper crust.'"

"And what would they say now?"

"You mean now that I'm sitting here with you, or now that *WorldLine* is dumping my story?" Natalie asked with a glower. For a second, her attention was a million miles away. When she didn't answer the question, Revis dug into his coat pocket and slid a written note in front of her. She glanced down at it.

*Georgia Rogers*
*grogers@nytimes.com*
*212-553-6632*

"Here. Make your parents proud," Revis said with his best shit-eating grin.

When Natalie grinned back—not at the situation, not at his desperation, but at *him*—Revis felt tremors in his soul. She took the note, pulled up her purse from the floor, and stuck the note inside. When she looked back at him a second later, resolve filled her eyes. "People need to know about Raphael Dumont. And to see that video of him in France, laughing at our questions."

Leaning forward, Revis held her gaze. "Then let's share it with the world. Burn my dad and his friends to the fucking ground."

In that moment—suddenly and finally—he and Natalie Pent became allies. Perhaps even friends.

On January 31, 2040, deep-seated worry crept back into Winifred Flite's mind for the first time since her near-death experience. It started first behind her brain, in the fathoms of energy behind her nerves. She hadn't felt such a thing since before Weston Carrow's suicide bomb a year and a half ago, and while life had since brightened in the wake of those events, even in the face of cripplety, she now wondered: Was the glow of that heavenly in-between escapade finally wearing off?

After her coma, she had actively chosen to return to her life. To heal. To try again with a new approach. But this unwelcome, unsanctioned worry felt like a decline back into her old self, the one she had hoped was gone.


It gained a secure foothold when Jonathan and his new *WorldLine* girlfriend, Clovia Bell, visited her on February 12. Upon walking into her room, their expressions were lighter than Winifred would've thought possible, considering it was just four short months until *WorldLine's* premiere date—May 30, 2040, Jonathan's twentieth birthday.

"To whaaat do I owe the honooor?" Winifred asked as they both exchanged whimsical expressions. She struggled to pull herself up from her chair, which of course caused the impossibly likeable Clovia to rush to her side and offer a supporting hand.

"Well, since you like it when I'm direct, we kind of need to talk," Jonathan said. "We're wondering if you could put us in touch with Uncle Michael. I need to ask him something, but he didn't give me his phone number last year. I think he was nervous around me."

A chill touched the back of Winifred's neck, as if Jonathan's very mention of her brother were secretly sending the afternoon on a downward track. She glanced at his bodyguard, Sounder, who was talking quietly in the hallway with Roger, Clovia's brawny bodyguard from Global Protection Group. Nothing seemed particularly unusual, so she looked back at Jonathan with narrow eyes. "Michael's a goddamned hermit. He liiiikes it that way."

Jonathan's bouncy demeanor deflated just enough to reveal his ever-present edge. "That's fine. But this is a security issue for you, your parents, Dr. Lumen, my dad, his family—everyone. Given how removed Michael is from all the hoopla, though, I'm wondering if he'd risk talking to me."

"And I'm aaaasking: Why?"

Clovia's pixielike energy also now dissolved in the shadow of Winifred's skepticism. She took a seat on the bed and addressed Winifred gently. "I'm not sure if Jonathan told you, but the FBI thinks my dad and his girlfriend were killed by the same guy who threatened me at that ramen restaurant back in October. He was trying to use me to get to Alice Winterblume—basically to tell her she needed to cancel her show 'or else.'"

Winifred remained silent as the afternoon tilted past the point of no return.

"We don't quite know what 'else' he was talking about," Jonathan continued, "but we want to get off the grid before *WorldLine* hits. You told me once that Uncle Michael lives out in some yurt in Washington State. I'm hoping we can join him for a bit, or get his help finding a similar setup. I doubt we'll have Clovia's security team for much longer, considering she's—"

He looked at Clovia. Clovia looked at Winifred.

"I'm leaving *WorldLine* once my work on this season is done," the young woman said. "Jonathan and I have been talking, and we think it makes sense for us to leave sooner rather than later, before the media swarm gets even bigger."

"We can't be anywhere findable once people see the show," Jonathan added. "The plan is to drive to Washington with Sounder and Roger so people won't see us taking a flight to Seattle."

"Flite on a flight," Winifred replied. Except she couldn't even laugh at her old family joke, because Jonathan and Clovia were serious—more so than their jovial moods from moments ago had let on. And here she was, thinking they had just come for a friendly visit.

With a heavy sigh, Winifred looked out her bedroom window, at Newport's blustery harbor. Hell, she couldn't think of a safer place for Jonathan and Clovia than the yurt village her brother, Michael, owned. It was as far off the grid as one could get these days.

"I can't promiiise Mike will answerrr iiif you send him a message," she said.

"That's fine," Jonathan replied through gritted teeth. "But can you promise to keep this between us? No word to Dr. Lumen or my dad?"

Yes. Winifred could promise. She owed it to Jonathan after all those years of being the worst mother imaginable.

When she gave Jonathan her brother's phone number and email

address, however, she immediately sensed that her lack of pushback had just opened Pandora's box. It was a hunch. A new type of black intuition. As Jonathan and Clovia escorted Winifred to lunch in New Dawn's commons area, they excitedly discussed their plans to move west, saying nothing of the foreboding that now underscored every facet of their lives.

ON THE NIGHT OF MARCH 23, 2040, Dr. Thomas Lumen arrived from Minnesota for his first long-term visit since October. He had visited briefly in January to coincide with Dominic Bock's second trip to see Jonathan, but even then, Winifred's 'nightly' ActoVid chats with him had begun transitioning to weekly, biweekly, and sometimes even monthly. When the man walked into her room tonight, she could tell by the bags under his eyes, his sallow skin, and his ultra-pronounced limp that he had been drinking again—more than usual, and more than was healthy. Winifred herself hadn't touched alcohol during her entire tenure at New Dawn Recovery Center.

After pleasantries, when they were lying as spoons on her king-size bed and listening to the rain outside, she asked, "Whaaat's going on? You look ten years older that the last time I saaaaw you."

"Ha. Gee, thanks," the psychiatrist said, loosening his arm hold. Winifred picked up on a wave of his energy, feeling every layer of it like a shiver: humiliation, hesitation, melancholy. He was silent for almost a full minute before resuming. "It's hard for me to be out here. I guess partially because I've failed at everything I planned to do with my life."

Lying horizontally in his arms and staring out the window at the last of the day's dim light, Winifred cocked her head. "What do you mean 'failed'?"

"I don't know. It might be all those years I spent researching Idle

County, trying to get that book about it together. Alice Winterblume's people even set me up with that literary agent, but I didn't follow through. Maybe I just wasn't ready."

"They're highliiighting you in the show, though, riiight?" Winifred asked. "You're telling your story at least. That's something."

"True," Dr. Lumen said. "But when I told them about the Moon Woods cult and losing my sister, Mary, I just . . . I don't know. I think I realized I was giving up on the book *because* of the show. How it made me feel, I mean. Like, getting involved with all this again. I just . . . I feel like I'm sinking. I've also made some decisions lately that—"

He stopped, and Winifred could almost feel the gears of his mind turn away from whatever had just been on the tip of his lips. She shifted in his arms, and his voice grew brittle.

"I went back last week and looked at some old book material I probably shouldn't have," he continued. "Did I ever tell you about the diary my sister left in her backpack, before my dad and his cult friends made her kill herself?"

"I think I saaaw stuff about it in your reeesearch."

"Yeah. Probably. Anyway, my dad burned all her old diaries right after she died. I guess he knew she used to hide them under her mattress. But there was a new one left in her backpack, between a few library books. She only wrote one entry in it, and I keep going back to it lately. There's a paragraph in it that's been bugging me."

Dr. Lumen leaned out of their cuddle and grabbed his ActoPhone. After a few moments of fiddling with it, he placed the screen in front of Winifred.

"Here. The paragraph in the middle."

Winifred grabbed the phone with her cold fingers and squinted at its bright screen. She had no words to describe the mournful sensation that descended upon her as she read the words written by Dr. Lumen's sister so long ago—possibly mere hours before her cult-forced suicide.

*I see forward and backward. I see whatever is causing this. I see the subsequent upheaval. Proof before proof before proof, because that's how people are, and they're so afraid of acknowledging the obvious. But someday they will believe. I'm only one gear. I know that now.*

At first glance, it looked like the ravings of a mad girl on the brink. Except something about it also felt relatable to Winifred. Perhaps even prophetic.

*Proof before proof before proof.*

"Tell me why it's buuugging you," she whispered.

Dr. Lumen's head brushed the back of hers as he shook it. "I can't."

"What do you mean?"

"I just . . . I keep wondering if Mary somehow saw all this coming. Jonathan. Rebecca Sparks. *WorldLine.* Like, how she mentions 'proof before proof before proof' and how someday people will 'believe.'"

Winifred's spine stiffened, but the psychiatrist didn't even seem to notice.

"I guess I feel like no matter what I do, that damned cult . . . my abusive dad, my grandfather . . . it'll have a life of its own once *WorldLine* comes out. Like, maybe that thing in the Moon Woods drove them all crazy, and now it'll drive everyone else crazy. Maybe even me." For a moment, Dr. Lumen breathed through the pitter-patter of the raindrops outside. Then: "Did I ever tell you about the time I saw my sister's ghost?"

The chill returned to Winifred's neck. Though she had read about the supposed encounter in his book research, the way he mentioned it now—as if it were fact and not some figment of his imagination—brought on a sense of self-consciousness she couldn't explain. Was it fear that she had slowly chosen over these last two years to start loving a madman?

No. He was Thomas Lumen. He was good. He was *sane*. She shook her head and let him continue.

"It was the day after my old librarian friend, Elizabeth Grime, told me about her last encounter with my grandfather—that priest who killed all those people. It happened in 1947, right after the guy killed her husband, Joshua. Anyway, they saw each other in that old cemetery on the western edge of Idle County—the one Jonathan said he visited on his first shooting day there. It was the same 'place with no name' Molly Butler wrote about in her ghost hunting journal."

Winifred shifted uncomfortably in Dr. Lumen's arms. More dark images crept into her mind. On their backs rode feelings she couldn't name.

"Anyway, I went to this cemetery after Mrs. Grime told me about it—it was a small field at the top of a hill, with old headstones sticking out of the ground. I saw Mary standing at the far edge of it, just in front of the trees. Then she turned and started running into the woods. I followed her just in case I *wasn't* going crazy, and that's when I found—"

Dr. Lumen, now weeping, dabbed his tears against Winifred's shoulder. He hugged Winifred tighter as his ActoPhone's screen went black in her clutched hands.

"I think it was a coffin. Old and rotted. There was a scuffed-up wine bottle inside it, with an old letter preserved under the used cork. It sounds crazy, but I'm pretty sure my homicidal grandfather wrote it. And there was also this little rock next to the bottle, with one side polished. It had the same scratchy circle symbol on it that my grandfather drew all over his crazy diaries, which my dad and his cult friends hid in that Moon Woods chapel for all those decades. I guess I'm just looking at it now, and after all my years as a psychiatrist, treating patients with legitimate problems—and hell, even working in the godforsaken CIA—all this ghost stuff sounds so crazy. I feel like, on the surface, I've always projected to the world that I have this 'normal' life. But here I am, trying to tell you that I found a letter my murderer grandfather wrote after my dead sister led me to an old coffin in the woods—one that didn't even have a body in it. It's *crazy*. Except I objectively know it happened. I still have the letter from the wine bottle, and I also picked up that rock with the scratched circle symbol and threw it into the field with all the headstones. Molly Butler of all people found it a couple weeks later and kept it as a ghost-hunting trophy. How the hell did *that* work out so perfectly?"

There was panic in Dr. Lumen's voice now, as if his mind were approaching an existential brink.

"And then there was one last thing from my grandfather's diaries," he continued. "Something he apparently experienced over and over as a kid, way before he ever started killing people. He—"

The blood in Winifred's veins chilled as she waited for Dr. Lumen to finish his truncated statement. When he didn't, she shrank under the warm air from his nose. It wasn't just tickling her neck; it was also offering her an unpleasant reminder that the physical world around her, borne from her five senses, might simply be an illusion.

"I just want it all to go away," he finished. "I think whatever's in the Moon Woods—that 'anomaly' Jonathan keeps talking about—it could drive the world crazy if people aren't careful. Like, all the questions it'll make everyone ask. I don't think people are ready. They don't want to drop their daily routines and stop to think about why those routines exist at all. It's just not comfortable."

"Is that reeeally the only thing bugging you?" Winifred asked. "I feel liiike there's more."

Dr. Lumen took five deep breaths. Again, his warm exhale tickled her neck. "I just want you to know that whatever happens, I'm only trying to make this messed-up situation better. That's all I've ever wanted to do."

As Winifred took in the man's cryptic words, her sense of self, previously made whole by her near-death experience, bisected. Down one path, she found solace in the fact that there was more waiting for her after this life, no matter what happened and no matter what Dr. Lumen was talking about. Down the other, she found this heavier, more viscous world that all living beings were still trapped in—and the possibility that the man holding her now wasn't just hiding something but also choosing a path mired in grief.

2010

N ATALIE P ENT STARED AT HER BROTHER, Alec, as the truth about her mysterious whiteout in the Moon Woods hung silently between them. They were sitting in Alec's rusted Honda Civic at the top of Windsong Road, a block up from their house. The engine idled as the streetlight outside threw Alec's face into harsh relief against the night.

"Seriously, Nat. I need to know. What the hell happened out there?"

He'd been asking pointed questions since picking her up on Old Mill Road, but she wasn't ready to give thorough answers. Yes, she was fine. No, she didn't need to go to the hospital. Yes, the last thing she remembered was being in the middle of the Moon Woods.

Even so, she was crying, because she couldn't explain any of it.

Alec was crying, too, probably because they both knew he'd never understand. They would go their separate ways next fall, build their separate lives. He would succeed, and she would be stuck—where, she didn't know, but surely always wishing to get a glimpse of whatever mental sensation had enveloped her after she found that Thai candy wrapper in the ravine.

"Just take me home. I need to go to bed," she whispered.

Alec shook his head, then wiped his tears. "Mom and Dad were already freaking out when I left, but I covered for you. I told them you went for a walk. They don't know about the Find My iPhone app, so I told them you texted, and I was just going to pick you up. But your leg—Jesus, how did you . . . ?"

He winced as he looked down at the blood-soaked pants covering her shin. If any part of their relationship had survived since childhood, it was the fact that he hated to see her in pain.

"I fell on a rock," she said. "And then I . . ."

She felt in her pocket for the candy wrapper from Tickle Me Thai. She flashed back to her dream—to the sorrow man yelling after her in the Moon Woods, and then to the Idle County Seven standing around her bed—and wondered for the hundredth time: *How the hell did I get out of that forest?*

Alec was waiting. "Then you . . . ?"

But he would never accept the truth.

"I blacked out. I think I was hungry. I woke up in the Outer Ring."

Uncertainty shaded Alec's face. Natalie saw the gears of her story shifting in his mind: the six miles she'd somehow walked back in the dark, the impossibility of her knowing which way to go, the possibility that this might be the start of some type of mental illness.

She could never tell him the full truth, because he couldn't know she'd almost died playing detective and finding that goddamned candy wrapper. She would bring the shred of blue litter to the Idle County Sheriff's Department, for whatever it might be worth, and that would be it. From here on out, she would stop chasing clues. Wouldn't she?

"I just need to go home," she whispered. "Please take me home."

"Okay. Fine," Alec said. His expression grew stony.

Unspoken words about her mysterious psychological event in the Moon Woods hovered between them, and it would stay that way until May 30, 2040—the day *WorldLine*'s streaming exposé on Idle County finally premiered to the world.

PART 5
HELLO AGAIN

From an op-ed published in the *New York Times* on June 1, 2040:

### Victor Zobel: Foe, Not Friend
#### By Natalie Elena Pent

*By the time this piece hits the press, many will have seen WorldLine's new exposé on Jonathan Flite, Victor Zobel, and the long-lost Idle County Seven—some of whom were my childhood friends. I participated in the production of Alice Winterblume's documentary series last summer, and if you're reading this, it means part of my story wasn't included in the final cut, nor was a video I shot in 2012, which supports what I'm about to share. While I've lightly edited this piece since the show's premiere this past Tuesday, I wrote much of it four months ago, when I first learned that WorldLine intended to omit much of the story they had initially encouraged me to tell.*

*Please note that my story is meant only to add to what WorldLine has shared with the world, not take away. The documentary series Alice Winterblume has created is a game changer—not just for me and those who cared about the Idle County Seven but also for society as it comes to grips with a new understanding (or lack thereof) of what life and consciousness actually are—and the depths to which people threatened by these ideas might go in an effort to evade them.*

*If you've been following the news, you're probably aware that Jonathan Flite, the Rhode Island "nurse killer," is one of the main subjects of WorldLine's new exposé. I won't debate here the legitimacy of his "past-life-memory" claims about the Idle County Seven, but I will say that I believe they're real. I met Flite last summer, during WorldLine's Idle County shoot, and he knew things about my childhood he couldn't possibly have known—mostly mundane events I experienced alone with Pauline Gilbert, who was my close friend until we had a falling out in seventh grade. I don't know how or why, but Jonathan's mind, however one can truly define the mind, is somehow connected to my old friends.*

*As a second disclaimer, I must also share that I once met the now-famous "psychic" physicist Rebecca Sparks (a.k.a. Dorothy Garland). During the time we both lived in Idle County, I witnessed her mind-reading abilities firsthand at a small social gathering, and believe me or not: they are real. People can doubt this fact all they want, but I've witnessed it for myself. The reason it matters for this op-ed is because I'm convinced Victor Zobel also witnessed Rebecca's shocking abilities and saw them as a legitimate threat not just to his lucrative New Naturalism brand but also to his goal of ridding the world of spirituality once and for all.*

*So, why does this matter?*

*Because Zobel and his associates are the least common denominators linking together four seemingly isolated events:*

- *The gas explosion at Rebecca Sparks's childhood home in End Haven, Minnesota, in the early morning hours of November 13, 2007.*
- *The disappearances of the Idle County Seven in 2010.*
- *The nuclear terrorist attack in Geneva, Switzerland, on August 12, 2037.*
- *And the assassination attempt on Jonathan Flite later that same year, on November 30, 2037.*

*WorldLine did an outstanding job outlining many of the hidden threads connecting these events—particularly showing the threat that Jonathan Flite's memories have not just on Victor Zobel's antispiritualist, money-making New Naturalism ideology but also on the celebrity billionaire's fragile ego. Perhaps the show's most compelling element, though, was its grand introduction of the reclusive and controversial physicist Rebecca Sparks. Not only did Sparks grow up in Idle County, but her family was killed in the gas explosion mentioned above (she was just eighteen at the time, but luckily out of the house).*

*Even more captivating, perhaps, is the fact that she was also scheduled to lead a conference regarding her new (and potentially testable) Theory of Everything at CERN in Geneva, Switzerland, on August 12, 2037—the same day Jean-Claude Apostol detonated a nuclear bomb just half a kilometer from CERN's main cluster of buildings.*

*It doesn't take much to envision a scenario where both of these tragedies—the gas explosion in 2007 and the bombing of Geneva in 2037—were masqueraded attempts on Rebecca Sparks's life. Given the mysterious attack on Jonathan Flite shortly after the bombing (which some have since attributed to Victor Zobel), along with Revis Zobel's suspicions about his physicist mother's death in 2006, it's easy to see a pattern emerge: people who threaten Victor Zobel's highly lucrative New Naturalism ideology keep dying.*

*But why?*

*In her documentary, Alice Winterblume included parts of an interview I gave last summer, in which I discussed an "out-of-body" experience (or something similar to it) I had near the center of Idle County's famed and fabled Moon Woods in 2010, shortly before Victor Zobel purchased the land. As outlined in the docuseries, this "whiteout" event happened near a rocky ravine Victor Zobel asked people to avoid during searches for the Idle County Seven following their disappearance. It was where I also found, mere moments before my "whiteout" occurred, a wrapper from one of Lindsay Thorsen's favorite Thai candies. The wrapper was lodged between two rocks.*

*WorldLine also showed that I wasn't the only person*

*to have strange experiences in the Moon Woods. The docuseries showed candid video of Shelly Bryce, mother of the missing Elijah Bryce, having a similar experience during an unexpected visit to the Zobel compound on August 3, 2038, less than two years ago.*

*Given what I experienced (and despite having visited the premises many times since without having as intense of "whiteouts"), I fully support Alice Winterblume's thesis that the Moon Woods is ground zero for a massive criminal cover-up and perhaps even the underlying reason for Rebecca Sparks's astonishing psychic abilities. What people should know, however, are the following ten facts that WorldLine omitted from its exposé:*

**1.** *On November 12, 2007, the day before the gas explosion that killed Rebecca Sparks's family, I saw Jillian Pope (Victor Zobel's stepdaughter, who later went missing) arguing heatedly with Victor Zobel's assistant, a Frenchman named Raphael Dumont.*

**2.** *On November 13, following the early morning gas explosion, I unexpectedly walked in on Jillian Pope and Lindsay Thorsen (both of whom went missing in 2010) in the school bathroom. Jillian was sobbing to Lindsay, saying (and I quote), "Victor wanted her gone, and this is how he tries to do it?" During my recorded meeting with Jonathan Flite last summer, I asked him to confirm details of this conversation both to prove his validity and to satisfy my own curiosity. He accurately recounted Jillian and Lindsay's conversation in detail and their memories of seeing me walk in. He also told me that Jillian had* *indeed been talking about Victor Zobel and that she had suspected he'd sent Raphael Dumont to the Sparks house to create the gas leak that caused the explosion. While* WorldLine *did sufficiently discuss how Rebecca Sparks's mind-reading abilities frightened Victor Zobel when he met her—enough, possibly, to try to kill her—it left out this particular circumstantial detail relating to Raphael Dumont.*

**3.** *The next time Raphael Dumont was present in Idle County with Victor Zobel (along with one other member of Zobel's posse) was on July 4, 2010. That very night, Victor's stepdaughter, Jillian Pope—along with her six friends—went missing. Two unidentified men were later seen on gas-station-security footage driving separate cars down I-35, toward Dallas, Texas. The two cars, which belonged to Jillian Pope and Clayton Graf, were later found outside Dallas, abandoned. Was Raphael Dumont one of these men? Given his presence in Idle County that day, I suspect yes.*

**4.** *During the Moon Woods searches in the days following the Idle County Seven's disappearances, Raphael Dumont helped Victor Zobel keep people clear of a "dangerous" rocky ravine that ran through the forest's center. (As discussed on* WorldLine, *Lindsay Thorsen's father, David, was part of this search group.) This was the same ravine where I later had my strange "out-of-body" experience and found the wrapper from Lindsay Thorsen's favorite Thai candy.*

**5.** *On September 10, 2010, there was a candlelight vigil* *for the Idle County Seven that Victor Zobel, Raphael Dumont, and four bodyguards attended. I was able to confront both Victor and Raphael with my questions about the events listed above, but they completely deflected me. They also shut down the conversation entirely when my friend asked whether they knew anything about an "old journal" Jillian Pope, Clayton Graf, and Pauline Gilbert came to possess in the weeks before they disappeared. According to Jonathan, they used directions written in this journal to find a cave underneath Idle County's legendary Moon Woods, believing that a "natural anomaly" there might help "save" their friend Molly Butler from her brain tumor.*

**6.** *In 2012, after sharing all of the above information with Lindsay Thorsen's father, David, I accompanied him on a trip to Saint-Paul de Vence, France, where we tracked down Raphael Dumont. Near the end of that trip, we saw him interact with a priest after Mass at Collégiale de la Conversion-de-Saint-Paul, a Catholic church. This priest, we learned decades later, was none other than Jean-Claude Apostol, the nuclear terrorist who bombed Geneva.*

**7.** *After observing Raphael Dumont as he spoke with Jean-Claude Apostol, David Thorsen and I followed him home. In a video I recorded of this encounter, you'll notice that instead of shutting us out when we started to ask our questions, Dumont listened, smiling the whole time. When we were finished, he asked, "Are you done?" We confirmed yes, and he slammed the door in our faces.*

**8.** *In the twenty-eight years since, I've built a fitness training business in Idle County. In terms of finances and reputation, I've done well. I eventually signed a contract to train Victoria Zobel at the Zobel family's compound at the center of Idle County's Moon Woods. (As mentioned above, I've experienced mild forms of that peculiar "whiteout" sensation there over the years, but I've been able to keep it under control.) Last April, in 2039, I witnessed a conversation between Victoria and her brother, Revis, during which Revis confronted her about Raphael Dumont and the man's possible knowledge about the 2006 death of their mother, Cassandra Pope. Victoria Zobel, in a great imitation of her father, deflected all of Revis's concerns. It's important to note that Cassandra Pope's death was the reason Jillian Pope moved to Idle County to begin with, to live with her real father, Maximilian Pope.*

**9.** *You won't be able to tell from the final cut of WorldLine's new season, but in the show's original recorded conversation between Jonathan Flite and Revis Zobel, Jonathan confirmed that Jillian Pope had once overheard Raphael Dumont mention Victor Zobel's affinity for poisons, particularly one called aconite. According to Jonathan, Jillian overheard Dumont telling a colleague that Victor would "aconite people's asses" if they crossed him. I've relayed this story here, with Revis Zobel's permission, because . . .*

**10.** *. . . late last year, I learned from a private source that WorldLine was asked by law enforcement to remove any* *mention of Raphael Dumont from their eight-part series, lest they interrupt an ongoing investigation.*

*While WorldLine achieved much with its series—namely, to unveil the many alarming connections between Victor Zobel, the 2037 Geneva bombing, and the existential challenges posed by Jonathan Flite and Rebecca Sparks—I spent thirty years waiting to tell my story. I was told by Alice Winterblume that I could, and that the circumstantial trail left by Raphael Dumont was integral to WorldLine's original narrative. Alice Winterblume should have included this testimony in her show, because it's an important part of the history preceding it. Sharing it could have opened doors to further witness testimony from people who might remember this mysterious Frenchman.*

*So, here is my truth. Raphael Dumont's involvement with the dramas of Idle County and his links to Jean-Claude Apostol matter. They may not be hard proof of anything, but they're enough to fill in some key blanks—and make a person like me speak up.*

L YDIA CLARK'S HEART pounded as she stared at the news and navigated the caustic burn of humiliation. *WorldLine* had premiered just three days ago, and if it weren't enough that Alice Winterblume had just told Jonathan Flite's story better than she ever could have, now came this: a rancid lie from Timothée Boucher.

Because his name wasn't Timothée Boucher at all. According to this Natalie Pent woman in the *New York Times*, it was Raphael Dumont. And—*Christ*—there had even been photos and videos of him from 2012, shot by Natalie in his hometown of Saint-Paul de Vence, France. The pictures and video footage were now included in the *New York Times* piece, and they didn't just show him laughing off Natalie's attempt at questioning him; they showed him interacting with the terrorist Jean-Claude Apostol under the door of an ancient stone church.

Now the whole world would recognize him. Not just his nightmarish snake tattoo but also his links to the nuclear travesty in Geneva.

*I have to ask him if it's true*, Lydia thought.

But no. She couldn't. Regardless of the accusations made in that op-ed, Timothée was already a criminal. He'd given her illegally acquired information from Jimmy Barber's hacked ActoPhone, which meant it wasn't a stretch to assume he might have helped Victor Zobel cover up even worse crimes. Furthermore, they'd been in touch only a handful of times (and never sexually) in the year since Lydia dragged Dominic Bock's name into the limelight.

And yet.

*Yet.*

This was a real story. One Lydia had direct access to. If law enforcement was somehow monitoring the man, as Natalie Pent claimed, perhaps they were doing so under his name Raphael Dumont. Maybe they didn't know about his Timothée Boucher identity. And even if they did, they would likely already have copies of his emails, text messages, and call history with Lydia. They would be aware of her connection to him.

Still, she couldn't let him have the last word.

Could she?

Two DAYS LATER, they were face-to-face. Timothée had been in Florida, he said, and he had driven north just to see her, despite a bout of terrible weather lining the East Coast. They now sat in the Red Pear café in Barrington, Rhode Island, just southeast of Providence, and Lydia was recording the encounter with her ActoLenses. She stared at Timothée while cupping a warm mug of coffee in her hands.

*And stop calling him Timothée*, she thought. *His name is Raphael. If you call him by the name you're more comfortable with, he'll think you're weak.*

"Why did you use me?" she finally asked, once it became clear he was waiting for her to lead the conversation. Yet her voice was pathetic. Quivering.

"Why does a person use anyone?" Raphael asked in response. "I had a desire."

"But you're not just talking about sex."

The man chuckled, causing his snake tattoo to ripple. "No—but the sex was mighty fine. Truly. Suffice it to say, I have my reasons. Do you realize how many police agencies around the world are likely waiting for me to lead them to a smoking gun, Miss Lydia?"

"A smoking gun for what?"

"What do you think? I'm a small fish in all this. They're going after the big fish."

"Victor Zobel?"

Raphael smiled. "See? You do have the mind of a reporter. And you should know that these law agencies and I seemingly want the same thing."

"Which is?"

"Access to Victor."

"Why?"

"Quite the curious little bird." Raphael flashed her a smile—the same one that sometimes overtook his face after sex, and the same one he'd been wearing in Natalie Pent's video from 2012. When he continued, however, his expression grew dim. "Five years ago, Victor Zobel framed me for a crime after I threatened to expose him," he said. "You can put this on the record, once I get what I want. You're recording me, yes?"

Self-consciousness stained Lydia's face as Raphael scanned her eyes for ActoLenses. She blinked to distract his gaze, then resettled in her seat. "That still doesn't explain any of this. Why you'd come after *me* of all people and lead me on for two goddamned years."

"Well, first, because I heard you telling that swooshy boy Jimmy Barber in the hospital that you were desperate to make progress in your career. Contrary to popular belief, I understand desperation, and I wanted to help you. Second, I've been—what is it they say?—*grooming* you for a job. One I should have pulled the trigger on long before *WorldLine* premiered."

"Bullshit," Lydia said.

"No, not bullshit. If anyone has access to Victor now, it's Jonathan Flite. Not even Victor's children see much of him these days—not with any regularity, at least. But one thing I do know is that Victor has been watching Jonathan since he started making news back in 2034. If he can't murder this nurse killer, he'll want to meet him. Mark my words. Victor Zobel is a desperate man."

"Why?"

"Because he's more fascinated by the unknown than he lets on—if only so he can get ahead of it and explain it away to his lowly followers, before they get smart enough to question him. I just want to talk to Jonathan before Victor sets a trap for him."

"Sounds like you're making an awful lot of presumptions," Lydia said. "Unless of course you have information I don't."

Raphael Dumont sipped his coffee. "Are you aware that Jonathan Flite hasn't been seen in over three weeks?"

Lydia shrugged. "What's it to you?"

"You read his text messages with Jimmy Barber. He wanted to disappear—to 'get off the grid' before Alice Winterblume's little show hit the internet. Do you remember the idea he mentioned in those messages last summer?"

"Yeah. Something about his uncle."

Raphael nodded.

"Is that the job you have for me?" Lydia continued. "To find Jonathan Flite?"

Raphael's grin, even under its original name, still melted that lonely, demoralized corner of Lydia's heart. "I can't exactly show my face around society without drawing undue attention now," he said.

"And since I no longer have friends, I'm offering you this: a million US dollars if you can find Jonathan Flite for me. His uncle's name is Michael—that might be a good starting place. Once you find Jonathan, though, I need to give him something. When that's done, I want *you* to share my story with the world—which I'll email to you when the time comes."

*A million dollars.*

The price was fierce. Sudden. It rattled Lydia's skull.

Yet everything in her heart told her to run right now. To call the police. To turn this man, this *Raphael Dumont*, in to the authorities.

*But for what?*

"When you had me drag his dad into the press spotlight, it didn't turn out so well," she said with a resentful sniff. "I didn't get any recognition. Or credibility. Or even a fucking *job* offer."

"See? You need the money I'm offering. Don't think I didn't listen to you during all those bedtime conversations. Contrary to what you may presume, I don't like wearing facades."

Lydia was shaking. She couldn't help it. This man had once been so sweltering sexy to her. So mysterious. And now?

*Christ.*

Now she was *this fucking close* to being part of the Jonathan Flite story. *This fucking close* to making her big splash.

"That's the only job?" she asked. "Lead you to Jonathan Flite and then publish your story?"

Raphael Dumont's smile crinkled like paper. "It could open many doors for you."

"Yeah, easy as fucking pie," Lydia said. "And how come you haven't already found this 'Uncle Michael'? Everyone's findable these days."

"Not him. Last address I found was in Washington State, on Bainbridge Island. But he doesn't live there anymore."

"How do you know?"

"Because I *visited* the person who lived there. But now that this Natalie Pent bitch has smeared my face all over the internet, it's hard for me to travel without drawing attention."

"Why don't you just have one of your criminal friends find Jonathan?" Lydia pushed. "Seems like you must know quite a few."

"Well, for one, even if any of them *were* willing to help, they might snitch to Victor Zobel. Plus I'm a lone wolf now. I no longer have access to Victor or his friends."

Lydia looked him in the eyes. He appeared to be telling the truth, but how could anyone trust a man who lied about something as simple as his name?

"Are you trying to kill Jonathan Flite?" she finally asked.

Raphael leaned his neck across the table, wearing the most serious expression Lydia had ever seen on him. "Far from it," he said. "I'm trying to help him. And the world. It's why I started tracking Jimmy Barber after Weston Carrow's bomb two years ago. Except I couldn't get close to him without having the police breathing down my neck. But then I found *you.*"

Anger surged through Lydia's body—a defense against the humiliation flushing her face. Yet this user, this *hoodwinker*, was offering her a million dollars to . . .

To what? To *find* somebody.

"I'll do it on one condition," she said, sensing an opportunity to use Raphael Dumont in return.

"And what would that be?" he asked.

"You give me half the money up front. Right now. You do that, and I'll do everything I can to find Jonathan Flite."

Raphael smiled and grabbed his phone. He made a few clicks, and within moments, Lydia saw a payment notification slide into the upper right corner of her ActoLenses' display.

*Five hundred thousand dollars.*

"You've got work to do," he said.

Then he stood up, turned toward the door, and walked casually out of the café, leaving Lydia wondering whether the money that had just hit her account was too good to be true. She half expected her phone to start ringing immediately with calls from ActoPay or the bank or government snoops, asking why she'd just received such a large sum.

Her entire chest was on fire. Suddenly, it seemed that everyone in the café was watching her.

*I'm not doing anything illegal,* Lydia thought at them. She stood up and left her half-empty cup of coffee on the table. As she swung out the café door, the acne-ridden barista boy behind the counter called out "Have a nice day!" and she didn't reply.

Revis Zobel, wearing only pajama bottoms after a day of lounging at his house in Salerno, Italy, had just poured himself another drink to celebrate the weeklong fallout of *WorldLine*'s audacious premiere—and Natalie Pent's *New York Times* op-ed—when his ActoLenses' display blew up with message alerts from friends whose names he barely recognized.

*Holy shit, did you know your dad was going to do this?*

*Dude, call your lawyers. Looks like your dad is FUCKED.*

*You watching the US news? Your sister is probably freaking out right now.*

It was 12:01 a.m. on June 5, 2040. As Revis sipped his gin and tonic, he spoke to his television wall. "TV. ABC. *World News Tonight*."

Skye Blythe, his favorite American anchor, was midreport, looking extra perky in her bright blue dress.

"... yet another development tonight regarding the celebrity atheist Victor Zobel," Skye was saying, "who's currently under fire from Alice Winterblume at *WorldLine* for allegedly covering up crimes relating to the Geneva bombing three years ago and the unsolved disappearances of Minnesota's famed Idle County Seven in 2010."

The stream in Salerno must have been on some sort of delay, because Revis's ActoPhone was now sustaining constant vibration, as if his friends had just seen Skye Blythe unveil something even bigger.

"Zobel is currently at the front and center of a firestorm relating to the so-called past-life-memory claims of Jonathan Flite, Rhode Island's infamous nurse killer. Flite's alleged memories, asserted by *WorldLine* to be valid, have deep ties not only to Victor Zobel but also to the physicist Rebecca Sparks, who says she hid from Zobel in 2008 after the man allegedly tried to kill her after learning about her supposed psychic abilities. More recently, Sparks's groundbreaking work in theoretical physics has offered the scientific community a potentially testable explanation for what Jonathan Flite and *WorldLine* have called 'the Moon Woods anomaly,' a strange, mind-altering point in space located in a cave underneath Zobel's secretive Minnesota compound. This anomaly, Sparks says, is one that Zobel will—and I quote—'stop at nothing to keep quiet.'"

Revis wet his lips with the gin and tonic as Skye Blythe cleared her throat.

"A public ActoVid from Zobel posted just forty-five minutes ago shows him inside what appears to be Star Island, his famous orbiting space hotel. He's speaking into the camera, appearing to address Jonathan Flite directly."

The news cut to a video of Revis's father, who had clearly been down to Earth's surface recently. Revis could tell, because whenever the man spent more than three weeks in orbit, it was visible in his eyes: not just the gauntness but also the mood shift from the isolation. Tonight, however, he was sitting in his Star Island study, in front of his sparsely stocked bookcase. He looked bright and healthy, the way he always did before stepping in front of any camera.

Finally, Victor Zobel spoke.

"In light of Alice Winterblume's recent *WorldLine* documentary, I want to address Jonathan Flite directly," he began. "Jonathan, while facts can't change in the eye of the beholder, understanding of them can. I'll neither confirm nor deny the allegations made in *WorldLine*— or by you personally—because that would simply feed into our current media frenzy, which needlessly perpetuates a type of drama I'd just as soon do away with."

Victor showed no signs of discomfort. He sat tall and stared into the camera.

"I believe human beings should spend their energy pursuing their passions and the things they care about, not focusing on trivial hearsays they have nothing to do with. But given your nature, Mr. Flite, I suppose it's impossible for you to forget about my stepdaughter and her six friends. That's why I want to extend to you directly an invitation to visit me up here on Star Island. No matter what you think you remember, I would presume you have many questions."

As Revis watched his father speak, he felt it all begin to crumble: the man's empire, the house of cards he had built on lies, his very family.

"As a token of my sincerity," Victor continued, "and in gratitude for your taking the time to visit with me, I would also offer you a prize directly related to the 2010 events you so faithfully remember. I think we would benefit from a meeting, seeing as both of our supposed cats are out of the bag. Otherwise, the final word won't belong to us but to the masses, who might otherwise treat *WorldLine*'s report as their source of truth. I will message you directly with further instructions for a possible visit, assuming your ActoHub privacy settings allow it. For the sake of both my integrity and my general aim for transparency, however, I wanted the world to see this invitation."

Revis waited for his lying, cheating, homicidal father to say more, but—

The video cut to black abruptly. As always, the Zobel patriarch's guise of false calm was the last thing people saw.

*"I would also offer you a prize directly related to the 2010 events you so faithfully remember."*

Had that been some sort of veiled admission?

Just then, a video call alert hit the display on Revis's ActoLenses.

*Victoria.*

"Answer," Revis said, firming his stance.

The view on his television wall suddenly switched to that of the camera hidden above it: Revis, standing in his Salerno villa's living room, preparing for his sister's vitriol.

When the woman's video connected, it reduced Revis to a small video window in the bottom-right corner. This was the first time Victoria had deigned to speak with him since April of last year—the day he first met Natalie Pent. But there were no FBI agents listening in today, to his knowledge. Just Revis, Victoria, and their secure quantum key VPN connection.

"I was hoping you'd call in a rage the day *WorldLine* premiered," he said, feeling light as a fucking feather.

"You little *shit*, Revis! You fucking little *shit!*" She was pacing back and forth in the Minnesota compound's glass-decorated living room with the buzzing energy of a fly, just as their father did whenever he was trapped in a corner.

Oh, the Victoria apple had not fallen far from the tree. But Revis was safe in Salerno. Removed from her. His damage had been swift and cutting.

"Your little *WorldLine* stunt was a low fucking blow, even for you,"

Victoria continued. "And Jesus, Revis. The fucking *New York Times* piece from Natalie Pent, and now this thing with Dad—"

"You mean how he basically just admitted that Jonathan Flite 'faithfully remembers' what happened to our sister?"

"*Half* sister!" Victoria spat.

Revis reveled in his smugness. Fuck Victoria. Fuck their father. He had spent his entire life bowing to them. Now in *WorldLine*'s afterglow, he reveled in the fact that he had helped Alice Winterblume bring his family down. It was finally his throne, and he would enjoy every minute of relaxation on it. In some ways, it was the first relaxation he'd ever felt in his life.

"Are you scared?" Revis asked Victoria.

Words itched to escape Victoria's lips—he could tell—but instead of answering, she simply roared and stormed back and forth across their father's living room.

Revis laughed in her face. "How does it feel? Seriously, I'm curious. To know you've aligned yourself with our crazy-ass dad all these years, knowing full fucking well he was an obsessive psychopath. Do you wish you did things differently? Maybe treated *me* differently?"

"Fuck off, Revis! Fuck the fuck off!"

"You called *me*," he said. "Don't pretend you're not looking for some kind of comfort. Or an escape hatch. I know you. This is what you do."

Victoria spun around to face her camera, then walked toward it to get in Revis's face. "Don't you *dare* say you know me. Don't you fucking dare. You don't know what Dad put me through or how it feels to know I've been betrayed by the few people—the *few* people—I thought I could trust."

"Are you including Natalie Pent in that?" Revis asked, still smiling. "You know she was planning to rat you out all along, right?"

Victoria kept pacing as she processed the tone of familiarity in the way he said Natalie's name. "What the fuck are you talking about?"

"As I'm sure you figured out from that *New York Times* piece, Natalie Pent and I have—shall we say—struck up a friendship. And if you try to sue her for talking to *WorldLine* or the *New York Times* or for breaching her NDA, I'll be funding her legal team. So, don't even bother."

Victoria roared again.

"Maybe it's time for you to realize that you never did anything to gain people's trust," Revis continued. "Not *anything*. And maybe now you can face what's coming to our family. I'd say it's not a moment too soon."

Before Victoria could respond, Revis said, "End call." His television jumped back to the streaming American news report, which had now transitioned to a commentary from some male physicist on the potential testability of certain thermodynamic abnormalities posed by Rebecca Sparks's new Theory of Everything—particularly as they related to the so-called Moon Woods anomaly in Minnesota.

It was all over Revis's head, so he walked outside to the patio overlooking the dots of light in Salerno's main harbor—the boats, packed in for the night. A wave of glowing houses beflecked the hillside above them.

*You finally made a difference*, came a voice from deep inside his chest—from the spot where his strongest self-doubt had always taken bites at him from within. *You finally stepped up to fight Dad and Victoria, and you knocked them out of the fucking ring.*

Alone in his villa—now drunk on his gin and tonic and feeling light as air—Revis realized that his inner monologue was no longer a negative one he needed to stop. So he began to dance. From his mind came the music.

From a news commentary in the *Daily Gossip* on June 8, 2040:

### *Cut and Run: Where Is Jonathan Flite?*
#### *by Anton Mitchell*

*Unless you've been living under a rock—and we realize some of you have—you now know the story of Jonathan Flite: that he was a troubled child, that he was just thirteen when he killed his nurse, and that his release from juvenile detention sparked not one but three attacks on him, seemingly from religious fanatics riled up about his claims of having detailed "past-life memories" of the Idle County Seven, a group of teens who famously vanished in Minnesota in 2010.*

*Now that twenty-year-old Flite has finally spoken publicly about these memories—and all but proven the validity of his flabbergasting nature—people are asking questions. Big questions. The kind that make the hairs on the backs of their necks stand on end. Perhaps the only question people are ready to discuss, however, is the most pertinent one:*

*Where is he?*

*Sources close to Flite say he's gone off the grid on his own volition with his girlfriend, Clovia Bell, to escape the public eye. Never mind the irony that Bell was also, until four weeks ago, a creative producer at WorldLine, the streaming newsmagazine that recently gave the world an intimate look at the young man's story.*

*Our sources have spun a different tale, however: that Flite and Bell have left in an effort to hide from attempts on their lives. But we're skeptical of this. Flite has everything at his disposal: money, bodyguards, and even friends at the FBI (if recent news reports about his participation in the Victor Zobel investigation are to be believed).*

*Thus, we speculate—and not just about the fact that witness protection would be impossible for someone like Flite, whose fame seems to be increasing by the day.*

*His recent public absence in the lead-up to the* WorldLine *premiere—and to Natalie Pent's follow-up bombshell op-ed in the* New York Times*—has now become all the more ill-timed in the wake of a shocking personal acknowledgment from Victor Zobel, whom Flite has now publicly accused of murdering the Idle County Seven in 2010. In Zobel's only public statement about the accusations since the show's premiere, he dangled in front of young Mr. Flite a personal invitation to Star Island, the billionaire's orbiting space hotel and* *semipermanent residence, offering a much-sought-after prize directly linked to the "2010 events [Flite] so faithfully remember[s]."*

*Whoa. Stop. "So faithfully remember[s]"? That sounds like a corroboration of WorldLine and Flite's murder accusations, does it not? Did Victor Zobel really just admit to killing those long-lost teenagers in a cave under Idle County's so-called Moon Woods? And if so, did his obsession with covering up that Minnesota event—perhaps combined with his meeting of mind-reader Rebecca Sparks there in 2007—truly inspire enough sociopathic reasoning for him to bomb the entire city of Geneva in 2037? Could there have been a deeper motive?*

*Furthermore, this much-sought-after "prize" he mentioned to Jonathan Flite has also given us pause. We know it isn't the flashlight from young Lindsay Thorsen's fascinating abduction case—and let's take a moment to remember the unsettling implications of that—so what could it be? Could it be facts about Victor Zobel's mysterious private-jet flight to Alaska right before the neurologist Maximilian Pope disappeared? Or perhaps the old journal Jonathan Flite claims the Idle County Seven used to find that cave in the forest? If so, was there information in the journal that the young man didn't tell us about?*

*Whatever the case, one thing seems certain: No matter what WorldLine just introduced to the world, it seems Lindsay Thorsen's flashlight was just a bit too bright for this story to disappear quietly into the night.*

## 2006

JANUARY. 2006. It came and went swiftly for Lindsay Thorsen, without a single hint of progress in her brother Drew's case. Between school, kickboxing, and meetings with Molly Butler and Elijah Bryce at the Lemon Avenue Library, she hid away in her bedroom, chatting with Alan Sparks on her new laptop. Yet ever since she'd chased Drew's ghost in circles around Lowell Grendel's house, life had started to feel like a facade for something else. But *what*?

AS IF TO ANSWER THAT VERY QUESTION, the ghost symposium at Benedict Wise University crept up on her like a ship in the night. As Lindsay sat on her bed on January 29, the Sunday before the big event, she pondered her well-procrastinated English assignment to find three arguments that did *not* support her end-of-year essay argument to legalize the death penalty in Minnesota. On the surface, her position was as solid as a good day's kickboxing stance: that criminals should pay the highest price for horrible, unthinkable crimes. But something about that opinion now crawled like bugs beneath her skin.

*Drew's dead, but he's still laughing.*

Her new belief in ghosts clouded an argument that should have held up in her head: that Lowell Grendel, who was living peacefully at the end of Elijah Bryce's street, deserved to die for killing her brother. Yet wouldn't that simply give him an easy escape from life's trials?

Even so, Ms. Olson had requested their essay topics and positions be set in stone two days ago. Lindsay had chosen this argument, and she was now stuck with it.

THE FOLLOWING EVENING, Coach Martinez handed out a sheet detailing the upcoming kickboxing tournament's initial fighting pairs. He had grouped students according to his own assessment of their fighting level, and just as Lindsay had feared, she was paired with Jeremy Brown, the weakest boy in class. It stung to know Coach Martinez considered Jeremy a fair match for her, but her only option was to suck it up and fight. Each of the ten pairs would fight best-of-three matches, refereed by the coach. Different hits and blocks would be worth different numbers of points, and the fighter with the most points at the end of ten minutes would win the match and, in subsequent weeks, move on to fight those remaining.

Molly and Elijah, who had again joined Lindsay at the community center tonight, vowed to practice kickboxing moves with her and Alan on the sidelines once the tournament started on March 1—just one month away.

BUT FIRST CAME the ghost symposium.

On Friday, February 3, David Thorsen drove Lindsay, Molly,

and Elijah to Benedict Wise University in Wind Prairie, a waterfront town one hour southeast of End Haven. It was a trip of whispers so that David could take a conference call on his BlackBerry, but soon, they passed a long stretch of rolling hills that flattened into a seemingly endless stretch of winterized cornfields. Moments later, Wind Prairie welcomed them.

It was Lindsay's first visit to the town, and she was surprised to find it larger and slightly more developed than any of the towns in Idle County. Despite it being winter, the streets looked cleaner, the stores looked better kept, and the large frozen lakefront along the town's small city center sparkled in the sun, hinting at the coming summer days when it would be crowded with relaxed, frolicking people.

Then, four blocks past the city center, she saw a large sign in a calligraphy-like scroll:

### Benedict Wise University
*Home of the Saints*

Most of the campus's buildings were uniform in construction: red brick with roofs that looked almost colonial, like something out of a history book. Each building had four floors, and the farther one drove into the campus, the more there seemed to be.

"Man, college looks big," Elijah said.

Molly nodded, wide eyed. "I thought switching classrooms in fifth grade was a big deal, but this is, like, switching *buildings.*"

Lindsay, recalling the university dorm she had slept in during last summer's kickboxing camp in Washington, DC, simply watched as they rolled through the campus toward Cougher Hall, where the symposium was set to take place.

After parking in the nearest lot, they walked across a cobblestone courtyard that spanned a square block. Surrounding it were frozen-over gardens and trees that looked brittle enough to shatter. When they finally escaped the prairie's harsh February wind and entered Cougher Hall, they were immediately greeted by a long table with a banner reading, **"Welcome to Benedict Wise University's First Annual Ghost Symposium!"**

David ushered the three teenagers forward. "Go on. Looks like everyone gets a name tag and a welcome packet." No sooner had he said it than his phone rang. He sighed, glanced at all three kids, and gestured for them to check in without him.

Wondering what kind of looks they might get, Lindsay beckoned to Molly and Elijah. They approached the table together.

"Hi there!" a bubbly young woman with pink hair said. "You guys registered for the symposium?"

"Yes. Four spots reserved," Lindsay replied. "I made the reservation with my dad's credit card. He just went outside for a work call."

"And what's your name, hon?"

"Lindsay Thorsen?" she said, articulating it like a question because this pink-haired woman seemed so confident. So *independent*.

"Well, I must say, you three are definitely the youngest ones here, but super cool that you came!" She handed Lindsay, Molly, and Elijah their clip-on name tags. "So, how'd you hear about us?"

"Our English teacher, Ms. Olson," Molly chimed in. She turned to Lindsay, who nodded with a questioning shrug. "I was also—"

Molly tripped on her words. The pink-haired woman waited with a patient smile.

"I was also friends with Elizabeth Grime," Molly finally said. "Before she died, I mean. She owned the library we all like to hang out at."

The young woman (whose name was Jennica, according to her name tag) beamed. "You knew Mrs. Grime? That's *amazing*! She used to do guest lectures for Dr. Dearborn's Spiritualism 1 course every year."

Jennica handed all three of them folders, each of which had a schedule in the right-side pocket. She also grabbed a fourth one as David Thorsen ended his conference call and finally approached the table.

"Anyway, we've got an opening keynote lecture today followed by a lunch social, where there'll be a bunch of different leaders in the field of paranormal research visiting with attendees. Intro to the keynote starts at 10:00 sharp—that's in ten minutes. It's being given by Thomas Lumen, one of our alumni. He graduated two years ago but was pretty much responsible for putting this whole event together." With a wide-eyed smile, Jennica added, "He recently got an article about this area's crazy history published in a *very* prestigious magazine called *The Renegade*. There's a copy of it in your welcome packet. He's definitely on to big things!"

*The Renegade.*

The magazine's name scratched at Lindsay's brain until she remembered: she had read Thomas Lumen's article online the night she first saw Drew in the showers at Fairfax Community Center.

It was Molly, however, who voiced her familiarity. "Wait—isn't Thomas Lumen the guy whose sister—" She tripped on her words again. Behind the table, Jennica grew somber.

"Yeah. His sister was the one who died in the Moon Woods in 2003, because of that cult. He was a senior here when it happened. It's kind of why he pushed for us to have this symposium. Like, to publicly ask the question of how his dad and the entire sheriff's department up there could have gotten sucked into thinking they were legitimately worshiping the ghost of his biological grandfather—that serial-killer priest." As if to shove the topic under a rug, albeit a bit grudgingly, Jennica adopted a lighter tone again and handed David Thorsen his welcome packet. "Now, Tom's keynote intro starts in ten minutes. Then comes the keynote itself, which is being given by a *very* special guest who's visiting from Laguna Beach, California—though he's actually moving back to Idle County soon to start a round of Alzheimer's drug research. His name is Max Pope."

Next to Lindsay, Molly took a sudden sharp breath. For some reason, the girl's eyes were blinking faster than usual, and something flickered in her gaze. Had she recognized the man's name?

Lindsay looked at Elijah, then at her father. Neither seemed to have noticed Molly's behavioral shift. Certain it was just a lark, Lindsay glanced down at the pamphlet in her hands, then at the title of the opening keynote.

### *Life, Death, and the Brain Between: Why We Are Fascinated with the Beyond*
*By Maximilian Pope*

The name.

*Maximilian Pope.*

She had seen it before—on the same night she read Thomas Lumen's article in *The Renegade*. Maximilian Pope had been the main point of contact for something called the Gateway Project. His research organization, perhaps?

It was Elijah who finally brought Lindsay and Molly back to the moment. "Want to go find our seats?" he asked, like someone at a movie who didn't like to miss the previews.

Molly nodded first, but when Lindsay, her father, and Elijah made their way toward the auditorium, the dark-eyed girl followed a few steps behind.

THEY TOOK THEIR SEATS in the auditorium—David first, followed by Elijah and Lindsay, and then Molly next to the aisle. As they waited for the lights to dim, Lindsay took out her copy of Thomas Lumen's *Renegade* article. Yes, it was indeed the one she had read online back in November.

Elijah, noticing Lindsay skimming the piece, began to browse it himself. After a few seconds, however, he nudged Lindsay and pointed at the copy in her hands, to the sixth paragraph. As Molly noticed and glanced at her own copy, Lindsay began reading.

*There are many ghostly legends around Idle County. One is about a white-eyed soldier haunting the long empty stretches of Old Mill Road, which circles the now-infamous Moon Woods. Then there's Taconite Rose, the "woman in the dress," who disappeared in Jackson Taconite Mine north of Idle County in 1959 while search-ing for her missing son; she's said to haunt towns as far south as Wind Prairie.*

Molly, now visibly clammy, glanced up suddenly with the same expression she'd worn the night they saw Drew standing with the rag-gedly dressed woman under the streetlight. Elijah looked at her with wide, nervous eyes, and then at Lindsay.

*Oh my God. We found her*, they all thought at one another. *Taconite Rose.*

Lindsay's father, David, reading the symposium brochure, re-mained none the wiser as the auditorium's lights finally dimmed. Then Thomas Lumen, the article's author, limped toward the podium, signal-ing the beginning of their journey into the world of the dead.

"I WANT YOU TO LIE BACK on the couch and find a comfortable position," Dr. Cora Crowe said in her Boulder office, from a chair that sat opposite the plush sofa Sandra Thorsen was resting on. "Feel the soft, cool texture of the couch under your back, and allow your body to sink into it. Allow your eyelids to loosen, and all the muscles of your face to soften."

Sandra followed the psychiatrist's directions as best she could, but as soon as she felt one of her face muscles loosen, another one tensed. She had used trance recordings as a form of self-care only a handful of times—always with mixed results—and at this step of the relaxation process, she usually lost it.

*I doubt I'll be able to get truly hypnotized.*

Yet Dr. Crowe's soothing voice directed Sandra to relax in her toes. Then up, past her ankles and into her legs and torso. The tranquility being dictated to her became real.

When her husband, David, shifted in his chair next to the sofa, however, self-consciousness crept in. Sandra adjusted her neck on the thick, malleable pillows.

*I'm not going to be able to calm down enough.*

"Now that you're feeling completely calm," Dr. Crowe pressed, "I want you to imagine yourself on a set of beautiful marble stairs, going down toward a bright sandy beach. You can hear the ocean surf running up and down the sand with the tide . . . up and down . . . up and down."

Sandra saw the surf in her mind, below the marble staircase.

She heard its peaceful, vague rush.

Up and down, up and down.

"Next, I want you to walk down the staircase leading to the beach, all twenty-five steps, counting downward. With each step lower, you'll sink deeper and deeper into relaxation. Count with me now: twenty-five . . . twenty-four . . . twenty-three . . ."

Sandra walked down the stairway, counting along with Dr. Crowe.

At the bottom of the steps, the psychiatrist's words sounded distant. "And now take a moment to listen to the ocean surf. Imagine yourself closing an inward set of eyes and letting the surf go. The ocean disappears, and all you can feel between your toes is the sand."

Suddenly, Sandra felt it. Her imagination was becoming real.

"Now let that go, too. The beach is gone, because it's only an illusion. You're finally in the real space that is your true existence."

Before Dr. Crowe could even say what came next, Sandra saw it.

"You're in a hallway of doors. Endless. Boundless. A circle. Each door represents both your entire existence and one individual life that has helped shaped it. You have lived many lives, and there are many doors."

Sandra could still hear the ocean surf in her ears, just past her closed eyes.

"Walk down the hallway and look at the doors. Let one stand out more than the others, one that will lead you toward the knowledge you seek regarding your relationship with—"

*Lindsay. Oh, Lindsay.*

"—your daughter, Lindsay. Realize that Lindsay had her own hallway, her own set of doors, and while you may have shared experiences, the doors here are *yours*. Allow yourself to walk . . . to take in the long, endless hallway . . . to notice the light coming from somewhere above, a light that's . . ."

*That's me. The light is me.*

"Now pick a door."

The door picked Sandra.

She didn't even have to think.


A GLOW SHONE FROM behind its frame, gleaming through the cracks even brighter than the hallway, which had grown dim. Dr. Crowe's voice was now both far away and inside Sandra's mind.

*"Get closer. Notice what the door is made of. Is it wood? Is it metal?"*

It was wood. Dark mahogany—different than the other doors in the hallway. In fact, they were all different.

*"Open the door and step through it."*

Sandra did as she was told.

*"Now what do you see?"*

Dead grass. A yard. And in the distance, tree-covered hills. Without looking, Sandra knew that somewhere behind her was a wooden one-room house.

*"Look down at your feet. What are you wearing?"*

Brown leather boots. Tall to the knee. Men's boots. The image came to Sandra's mind with no effort; imagination hadn't been necessary to conjure it. She allowed it in.

*"Notice what's happening around you. Are there buildings? Is there nature? Are you inside or outside?"*

She was chopping wood. She was a man, and she was splitting logs in an open yard, feeling the axe's power in her hands. It was a daily routine in the autumn through early spring—going out to find, gather, and prepare wood to keep the house warm. Without any prompting from Dr. Crowe, Sandra got a sense of this man's feelings at the current moment: he was dissatisfied with his circumstances and hadn't wanted to wake up a few hours before.

There had also been children in his life—three of them. They were all dead.

"Wow, I'm impressed," Thomas Lumen said as he began his introductory speech at Benedict Wise University's First Annual Ghost Symposium.

He peered out into the darkened crowd, which had grown larger since Lindsay and her party arrived.

"Gotta be, what, a hundred people in here? A hundred fifty? Totally cool. Anyway, my name is Thomas Lumen, and I'm here to welcome you to this university's first-ever ghost symposium. Contrary to what you might expect, I'm about to get really honest, really fast—but I promise I'll be brief."

Thomas took a deep breath.

"To be blunt, I'm a guy you probably don't want to be. Two years ago, I lost somebody very close to me: my twin sister, Mary. She was a casualty of the now-infamous Moon Woods cult up in Idle County, about an hour northwest of here. She died in late 2003 at the hands of the men involved in that group, shortly before it was discovered. Now,

I'm not going to dwell on darkness, grief, or my family's own biological connection to the priest who inspired the cult—you can read about that elsewhere—but I wanted to mention it all, because it's part of why *I'm* here. It's why I helped organize this symposium."

The young man looked down at the podium, then rebalanced himself.

"After my sister died, I got a bit lost. In those first few months after it happened, I became rather obsessed with questions relating to why we humans are so easily swayed to believe in things we can't see. Perhaps even more relevant, I began to wonder what, if anything, could ever drive me to do the same. At one of my lowest points, I had a late-night conversation with an old librarian named Elizabeth Anne Grime—the person who first and foremost inspired this symposium. She lived up in Idle County most of her life, and it was there that she first met Benedict Wise, the Capuchin friar who founded this university. She also was a student here before returning later to teach some very memorable English courses. In her older years, kids up in Idle County knew her as Mrs. Grime—everyone's favorite librarian. She was a fixture around town, always gracious and always kind, and upon her death a year and a half ago, she left this school a large sum of money. It is, in part, why you're sitting here today."

An unexpected gentleness—not quite enthusiasm and not quite pathos—touched Thomas's face.

"Still, this woman's life wasn't all sunshine and roses. She, too, had darkness in her past, some of which related to the cult activity responsible for my own sister's death. In that last conversation we had, we talked about life, death, and the things that might exist in between. I was a bit closed minded back then, so when she told me about an incident where she and her friend saw multiple apparitions at the same time, I initially didn't believe it. I probably still wouldn't were it not for the ghost I saw the very next day—that of my sister, Mary."

As if straddling the gulf between self-assuredness and mental instability, Thomas looked out at the audience and gave a melancholic laugh.

"For all the questions I still have about what I actually saw the day after talking with Mrs. Grime, I can say this: she comforted me at a time when I was still realizing that it was okay to wonder. She didn't just persuade me to look outside my own socially accepted box for answers; she also pushed me to acknowledge that the box was there to begin with—something I've now realized was key to letting myself truly wonder freely, with an open mind. So, if there's anything I hope for you this weekend, it's this: that you'll recognize the boundaries of your own limitations so that you can learn—or remember—how to contemplate the unknowable."

While Thomas's grin now grew warmer, the weight of his losses remained visible on his face. Perhaps even recognizable.

*He went through the same process you're going through*, Lindsay reminded herself. *Maybe you're more alike than you think.*

When Thomas continued, however, his grief finally flickered toward invisibility. "Now without further ado, I'd like to introduce our keynote speaker. He comes to us all the way from Laguna Beach, California, though soon he'll be returning to his hometown of Blue Hill, in Idle County, for his day job as a medical researcher. Ever since childhood, he's been fascinated by ghosts, and his status as one of Benedict Wise University's alumni is why we're lucky enough to have him here today. Now let's all give a warm welcome to Dr. Maximilian Pope!"

As everyone in the auditorium clapped, Lindsay noticed Molly grab the armrests of her chair. Even in the darkened room, the girl's knuckles looked white.

"Hey, you okay?" Lindsay whispered to her.

Molly's head shake was almost imperceptible, and her lips were tight. Lindsay saw beads of sweat on her forehead. "I don't think I can—" the girl started, but then she switched to an even quieter whisper. "I think I'm getting sick. I have to go to the bathroom."

She stood up from her seat, stepped into the auditorium's left aisle, and walked briskly toward the exit.

Lindsay turned back into her seat with furrowed eyebrows. Next to her, Elijah watched after Molly curiously. "Maybe it was something in her breakfast burrito?" he whispered with a shrug.

The words barely registered in Lindsay's ears, however, because walking toward the stage's podium was the most handsome man she had ever seen. As the audience applauded, a rush of attraction surged through her body. Was this how Natalie Pent felt when she saw Karly Lillefeld's dad in his biking shorts?

Even Elijah's eyes were transfixed. His mouth hung open slightly.

"My, my, my," were Maximilian Pope's first words to the audience. "I suppose I don't need to introduce myself further—Mr. Lumen here did *quite* a nice job of that, other than the fact that all of you here can call me *Max*. Suffice it to say, I couldn't be more excited to be back in my home state again after so many years away. One thing's for sure, though—California is a *lot* warmer than Minnesota!"

He flashed a movie-star smile as everyone in the audience laughed graciously.

"So, why am I really here, you might ask?" he continued. "Well, first, I'm a neurologist and medical researcher by day, and my research organization recently acquired an old nursing home in Idle County. We've retrofitted it to become an accredited research facility, and we're now just three months away from hosting our first double-blind study for a new Alzheimer's drug called Dasparta, created by a pharmaceutical company based in Laguna Beach, where I currently live. We hope the drug will make strides to prolong quality of life for people with Alzheimer's."

When Max paused for effect, a few people in the audience clapped. The rest of the audience, including Lindsay and Elijah, hesitantly followed suit.

"In any case, I'm here to talk about my moonlight career as a researcher into the paranormal—*and* why I think this university should claim its spot at the forefront of making such things a legitimate academic pursuit," Max went on. "It's no secret to those who are familiar with this school's namesake—the actual man Benedict Wise—that he was a rather mysterious person. He was born in 1851, and he was the first Capuchin friar to settle in this area. What you may not know is that he was a well-known 'mystic' who sparked a whole lot of strange stories, some of which people tell to this day. To start this lecture off, I'll tell you just how interesting the man was and why it's fitting that we're holding this particular symposium at his fine, thriving university."

To Lindsay and Elijah's right, David was sitting with his arms crossed, taking in every word. His expression didn't let on whether he was skeptical or intrigued.

"Mr. Lumen here already introduced you to Elizabeth Anne Grime, the late benefactor whose financial contributions helped fund this symposium. But did you know that when she was just sixteen years old, Benedict Wise saved her life?"

Silence from the audience.

"I first heard this story just a few weeks before the lovely old woman died, and it probably would have been too incredible for even me to believe were it not for two things: first, Elizabeth Grime was unimpeachably honest; and second, there were multiple recorded witnesses for what I'm about to tell you. When she was sixteen, Elizabeth Parker—that was her maiden name—almost died in a house fire that killed her parents and younger brother. She was stuck on the third floor of her family's house, screaming out her bedroom window as the room burned behind her. Right when she started getting dizzy from the smoke and praying for God to spare her life, she saw seventy-five-year-old Benedict Wise running down the street toward her house. When I spoke with Elizabeth about it during the last summer of her life, she claimed that 'old Father Ben' was moving with the agility of a healthy fifty-year-old. He told her to jump the thirty-foot drop into his arms, and do you know what?"

Max paused for effect once again.

"She *did* jump. And get this: she swore she floated gently down. A man of nearly eighty years caught her as if she were as light as a feather."

Lindsay and Elijah exchanged fascinated—if not a bit doubtful—glances.

"And that's not even the crazy part. The *crazy* part is that Father Benedict Wise, at that very hour, was in Stone Ridge, standing over the bed of a dying woman named Esther Morrison, along with ten of Esther's family members. He was there with them all night after Esther died—they all swore to it. Yet somehow, the man was also in End Haven to save Elizabeth Grime's life. Now, we know via actual science—quantum mechanical experiments in particular—that this type of 'bilocation' isn't just possible on a particle scale; it's also a *rule*. And while there's no solid evidence to suggest it can happen to larger conglomerates of matter—say, to you or me—the concept appears in everything from ancient Greek philosophy to all of the world's major religions. If you read up, you'll see it referenced in the Hindu *siddhis*, in Jewish mysticism, and in multiple stories about Christian saints and monks, Muslim Sufis, and others, all claiming some type of multi-location ability or another. To this day, Elizabeth Grime's story about Benedict Wise is one of the reasons locals around here still refer to him as 'the Saint.'"

Max began gesturing with his hands. "Now, I know this is supposed to be a ghost symposium, but really, aren't we all here to share our experiences, thoughts, and overall knowledge about things science dismissively calls 'the paranormal'? I thought it appropriate to let you all in on why the man who founded this university is as good a dead spokesperson for our event as any."

Chuckles escaped a few audience members.

"If you aren't yet aware, Benedict Wise wrote a series of journals before he died. All of them discussed the nature of life, the soul, and physical reality. Some people even say he was a medium and that the material was 'channeled' from some sort of higher spiritual source altogether—a skill he was rumored to talk about on occasion. What's been quite challenging in deciphering the content, however, is that the first journal is missing. From what we can infer, this journal set up much of what he wrote about in his subsequent journals—a key to the information, so to speak. His eleven other journals are here at the library, but nobody has yet tracked down the missing first one."

Lindsay and Elijah looked at each other again. For some reason, there was something electric in their shared glance, as if they were recognizing something forgotten in Max's words.

"It's funny, living in a world where the majority of people have some sort of spiritual outlook but outright dismiss anything they consider to be paranormal," Max continued. "It's a strange way to describe things, isn't it? *Paranormal.* Ghosts, spirits, psychic events—all those things relegated to an angle of supposed reality we can't objectively measure and that we can't say for certain exists. Our lack of measurement tools, then, often leads people to presuppose that they *can't* exist and *can't* be part of nature. After a few things I've seen, though, I'd have to disagree with that. How many of you out there have seen a ghost? And if so, who among you would swear on your life that what you saw was definitely there?"

This time, Lindsay and Elijah instinctively turned to look at the audience. At least fifty people raised their hands. Shrugging, both of them also raised theirs. Lindsay wished Molly hadn't run off to the restroom—she was the first of them to have seen a ghost, after all.

At the podium, Max appeared to take special notice of Lindsay and Elijah—because they were young, perhaps?

"Many of us can *say* we know this unknown side of nature exists,"

Max continued, "but why doesn't it get more attention? Life after death is a concept so many people cling to, whether it's out of fear that this life is all there is or hope that we'll someday see our loved ones again. Apart from certain fringe scientists who've made careers out of studying children who claim to have past-life memories, most scientists relegate such concepts to the realm of spiritual hokum—no questions asked. This, of course, makes it simple for people to say it isn't a subject supported by rational thought or conjecture."

Max sighed, shook his head, and once again adopted his dazzling smile.

"That, my friends, is nonsense. Some of the greatest discoveries in history have been a result of people wondering about the impossible, and I'm hoping today's symposium will pierce through that barrier, at least on some tiny scale. With its reputable programs in psychology, physics, and biology, Benedict Wise University can at least now say it has addressed these concepts with an open mind."

Suddenly, he looked again at Lindsay and Elijah.

"I see we have at least two young people in our audience today, which shows that people of all ages *do* indeed care about this subject. I'd be willing to bet that most living people, if presented with evidence of the so-called paranormal, would become genuinely curious about how—and *why*—it might exist."

In her mind's eye, Lindsay saw her brother, Drew, standing outside Elijah's house in the bitter cold with Taconite Rose, the woman in rags. Could there possibly be an explanation for it?

On the stage, Max Pope started pacing back and forth. Lindsay now noticed that he was wearing some sort of wireless microphone rather than using the one attached to the podium.

"You're going to meet a lot of spiritual researchers at this symposium, including Dr. Geraldine Sampras from Cambridge University, renown ghost hunter Stuart Redmond, and Benedict Wise University's own local historian, Emily Tarnish, who just started working on her PhD here. Apart from discussing and dissecting our local supernatural legends and their origins, we'll also take a look at what they have in common with stories from other cultures around the world. Before we do that, however, I'm going to do what an English professor might call 'refuting the con.' I'm going to tell you why much of the neuroscience community considers spiritual experiences nonsense and then tell you why I consider these viewpoints to be egregiously myopic."

As Max digressed into a surprisingly scientific discussion of the areas in the human brain often involved in so-called spiritual phenomena—and how triggering certain areas could recreate these sensations in research subjects' perceptions—Lindsay wondered: Could her visions of Drew and Taconite Rose all really be in her head?

Except Molly, Elijah, and possibly even Lowell Grendel had seen the exact same vision she had the night Drew led her in circles through the snow. Nobody then had been triggering particular areas of their brains at the same time, so what did that imply?

*That maybe, at the very least, it doesn't matter what other people think*, Lindsay thought.

With that, she finally decided she wasn't crazy for having seen Drew. Perhaps she simply had a new set of eyes.

Two years ago, Natalie Pent would have never anticipated that she'd someday be sharing her deepest secrets with Lindsay Thorsen's father, David—particularly the ones about her disturbing pilgrimage into the Moon Woods and the puzzling "whiteout" experience that had followed. She also would have never thought she'd be sitting with him in her car behind Saint Andrew's Church, navigating the nervous exhilaration that came with recently consummated sexual adventures.

Memories flashed before her: The bluff above the sparkling town of Blue Hill. The lights in the Moon Woods beyond. The distant sound of the construction trucks.

On that lonely ridge, they had touched hands. Then held them. Then turned and embraced each other.

*She* had led it all. *She* had taken action. *She* had been capable of that after her traumatizing experience in Minneapolis—that boat trip to the middle of Lake Minnetonka, where nobody heard her struggles and screams as Andy McCain violated her. Natalie had come out of that experience thinking she would never be able to have sex again, let alone enjoy it. As such, tonight's discovery wasn't just empowering. It was jubilant.

For the first time, she felt no shame about the attraction she'd always felt toward David Thorsen. Neither was she burdened by what had happened on Lake Minnetonka. That night—that *rape*—hadn't destroyed her. Couldn't she be proud of that? Of returning to Idle County and rebuilding her self-worth? Yes, this place had unhinged her mind over the years, but hadn't it also opened her perception, in some odd way?

"I'm—" David started to say from the passenger's seat. Then he looked out the windshield.

"You . . . ?"

"I just feel like I took advantage of you. I know you said I didn't, but I shouldn't have let it go as far as it did. I just—"

"Mr. Thorsen: Did it ever occur to you that I'm capable of making my own choices?"

Natalie let the question idle along with the car's engine, trying not to let her old emotional walls creep up: those domineering facades that covered her lack of self-worth, the fears about what other people might think of her, those beliefs that she would never be worthy of another person's respect. But she had to push them down tonight, because David was actually letting her talk openly. Letting her *feel*.

"Hell, maybe meeting you tonight taught me that I *could* make my own decisions," she said. "I think a lot of girls grow up being told they're fragile and incapable of that. But quite frankly, sex with you was the best I've ever had. I'd love to do it again."

"So would I," David said, flickering through his shame.

The truth of their unexpected union—fueled by the forbidden— rushed through Natalie's body again.

"Then maybe we should just be honest with ourselves and enjoy it," she said. "Not to mention we have a million things to talk about—Victor Zobel, Raphael Dumont, all that."

For a second, Natalie thought David might put a hand on her leg to assert his position as the older, wiser person present. Yet he didn't. He was allowing her to have this moment of dominion.

In his gaze, however, she saw deep chasms. Possibilities. Futures where they might somehow join together to extinguish their ever-present feelings of isolation.

"We'll definitely need to look into those details you remember," he said. "Hell, even if it means going to France and tracking this Raphael guy down, we'll—"

David cut himself off, seemingly on instinct. But it was too late; the moment his words were out, a tandem choice clicked into place between them. Natalie already saw it in her mind: the packing of bags against her parents' wishes, the fight to feel guiltless as she loaded them into David's car and accompanied him to the airport, the loathing and disgust her parents would feel for David in the years that followed. For a fleeting second, it seemed as if time and its events were things she might grab, examine, and decipher in both directions. She didn't even need David to confirm it. They would walk this investigative path together, even if it was fleeting.

"We'll talk soon," David finished. He opened the passenger-side door and stepped out of Natalie's car, then bent over and peered back in. "One more thing. I'm not running away from you right now. I want that to be clear. I just need to think. And I'll look into those jobs for you at Steelhead first thing tomorrow. Deal?"

Natalie smiled. "Deal. And wait—don't go yet."

David waited.

"Phone numbers." Natalie pulled out her iPhone. "I need yours, and I don't want to ask my parents for it."

A blush rose on David's face. "My number is 773-232-1908."

Natalie typed it into her phone and pressed Call. When she heard a phone buzz in his pocket, she hung up. "There, now you have mine. And Mr. Thorsen—"

"*David*," he said.

"David," Natalie repeated, thinking back to her first view of him earlier tonight, sitting on that cliff behind Saint Andrew's Grotto. "I just . . . thanks. I'm glad we didn't jump."

David's grin widened. "Maybe we actually did."

He leaned back out of her car and slammed the door shut.

Natalie watched him run to his BMW and look back at her one last time. As he crawled into his car, her heart rushed with excitement. It was her first-ever sense of true adult independence, and it was telling her *yes*. She could do anything she wanted in life. She didn't have to be broken.

A T THE GHOST SYMPOSIUM LUNCH BUFFET, Molly Butler looked
pale as she picked at her food. Lindsay and Elijah had followed
her to the far end of the hall's only long table, which, unlike
the circular tables dotting the space, had no white-rose centerpieces.
David Thorsen had stepped outside to take another work call, and the
only person seeming to take note of the three young people, at least pe-
ripherally, was Thomas Lumen. He was limping around the room with
a large camera strapped around his neck, taking photos of everyone.

"Maybe it's normal for people our age to be banished from all the
smart people," Molly said, glancing at a group of prattling middle-aged
academics sitting at the next table over. Thomas had just stopped to
snap their photo.

Hoping some optimism might negate Molly's sudden despondent
behavior, Lindsay gestured at the young man. "Do you think we should
ask him about Taconite Rose? Maybe he knows something about her
that we don't."

Thomas suddenly turned toward them, raised his camera, and said, "Hey, guys—smile!"

Lindsay barely had time to comply before the camera's flash momentarily blinded her. And then the young man rushed away.

"Seems like he knows just as much as we do," Elijah replied. "I mean, none of these people have any actual answers about the ghost thing, do they?"

"That Max Pope guy seems like he might," Lindsay said with a shrug.

Molly straightened her posture but kept her gaze glued to her sandwich. "I wouldn't be so sure. From what I heard, it sounded like he spent most of his speech saying that all the stuff people think is supernatural is actually just happening in our brains."

"No, he wasn't saying that at all," Lindsay retorted. "He was saying the brain might be more of a filter for consciousness that only lets us perceive certain things. His point was that even science tells us that there's more going on in the universe than our five senses can pick up on."

"You kind of missed most of it, because you were in the bathroom," Elijah added.

Molly picked at her Caesar salad. "Well, I'm sure the brain can do a lot of crazy things."

Just as Lindsay was about to respond, a wave of pink hair fell in front of her face. It was Jennica, the young woman who'd checked them in.

"Hello!" she said. "Mind if I join you guys? I actually brought one of our bigwig speakers with me, because he got curious when he noticed you all sitting way over here."

Lindsay, at the head of the table, looked at Molly and Elijah. Elijah waved lightly at the newcomers through a shy smile that contorted around his chewing. Molly, however, stopped chewing her sandwich altogether.

Behind Jennica was Max Pope, the keynote speaker. He looked even more like a movie star now that he had taken off his neck tie and undone the top button of his shirt. His rimless glasses glimmered in a shaft of sunlight as he extended his hand first to Lindsay, who was closest, and then to Molly and Elijah.

"Hey there, I'm Max," he said. "I was just talking to Jennica here, and she said you three were the youngest people in attendance today. I thought that was pretty damned cool. She also said one of you knew Mrs. Grime, the librarian?"

He looked directly at Molly when he said this.

Molly, seemingly struck by Max's incredible good looks, opened her mouth to reply just as Lindsay's father returned to the table, ending the call on his cell phone. "Sorry, kids—had to put out a fire at work." He looked up at Max. "Oh, hi there. Max, right? David Thorsen." He extended a hand. "Great lecture earlier. Gave me a lot to think about."

"My ex-wife tells me I'm nothing if not challenging," Max said with a wide grin. "Are you being the good dad tagging along today, or are you a ghost person, too?"

"I'm *this* one's dad," David replied, gently dodging Max's question and patting the top of Lindsay's pulled-back hair. "This here is Lindsay. These two are Elijah Bryce and Molly—" He stopped short, embarrassment rouging his face. "Oh jeez, Molly. I'm forgetting your last name. Actually, I don't think I ever learned it."

"Molly Butler," Molly said, smiling politely at David and extending her hand shyly to Max. Max shook it with a polite nod, then extended his own to Elijah.

"Nice to meet you," Elijah said, finishing their round of introductions.

"Do you mind if Miss Jennica and I join you?" Max asked.

David gestured toward the two empty chairs on Lindsay's right. "Go right ahead. I'm going to go grab some food before it's all gone."

Max and Jennica sat down.

"So, you're all from End Haven, then?" Jennica asked. "I figured you were, given that you knew Mrs. Grime and all."

"Yep. Lived there my whole life," Molly said. Elijah, who had a mouthful of macaroni and cheese, tried to answer in some sort of made-up sign language. With a sigh, Molly answered for him. "Elijah's pretty much been there forever, too."

"My family moved there about four years ago," Lindsay said in her best small-talk tone. Realizing she sounded exactly like her mother in social situations, her gaze flitted toward her father, who was now in the food line, dishing himself some salad. He glanced up at her, then nodded his approval.

*"Good practice for when you're meeting people in a business setting someday,"* he would likely tell her later.

"I'm actually from Idle County myself," Max said. "I grew up in Blue Hill for a bit, but then my dad died when I was eight. My mom and I moved down to her parents' farm in Iowa after that."

"And you met Mrs. Grime when you went to school here?" Elijah asked.

"I did," Max said with an almost-too-happy grin. "She was my English professor, in fact."

Just then, Lindsay's father returned with a full lunch plate. "You mentioned in your speech that you're doing drug research, right?" he said, taking a seat across from Max and next to Elijah.

"That I am," Max said. "I'm CEO and medical director of a small clinical research organization, primarily working with BioSave Pharmaceuticals out of Laguna Beach, California. It's a new venture, actually."

David smiled. "A startup! Fun. What's it called?"

"The Gateway Project," Max said with a hint of pride.

Now Lindsay was sure she'd seen the man's name before. "I think I saw your website once, actually," she said. "Isn't it white and black and kind of basic?" She turned to Molly and Elijah. "It was that night I was Googling about ghosts and Idle County—the same night I read Thomas Lumen's *Renegade* article." Lindsay gestured with her neck toward the young man with the camera.

Max's smile seemed touched by genuine chagrin. "Don't mind the website just yet! It's super bare-bones—I've been so busy getting this first research site in Blue Hill up and running that I've totally neglected it. But I'm glad you actually found it!"

"I think it was because I Googled 'Idle County' and 'ghosts,' and your address in Laguna Beach said something about 'Ghost Road.'"

"Dale Ghost Road—how funny is that? When I found an office on that street, I knew it was meant to be."

"And how come you're so interested in ghosts?" Molly cut in, her voice sounding unusually direct. "I didn't hear why in your speech." She looked back down at the scraps of her Caesar salad.

Lindsay, blushing over Molly's curtness, glanced quickly at Elijah. His eyes took on a confused look as he gave an almost imperceptible shrug. David, however, seemed unaware of Molly's behavioral change.

Max also seemed unfazed as he offered Molly a fair nod. "To be honest, it was something that happened when I was a kid, the day my dad died. My friends and I saw him when we were up on that bluff over-looking Blue Hill. We were out playing cops and robbers, and he was standing up there on a rock, looking like Jesus or something. He even talked to us. Then, when I got home, I found out he'd died three hours before, in a chainsaw accident."

Instead of softening, Molly suddenly looked pale, on the verge of being sick again. "I'm sorry to hear that," she said to Max. "And sorry again—I need to go to the restroom. I think I'm still not feeling well." She stood up from her lunch and walked straight toward the bathrooms on the far side of the lecture hall.

They all watched her for a moment before Lindsay glanced back at the others. "She got sick earlier, too. I thought she might be better enough to eat lunch."

"Easy to come down with a bug or two this time of year," Max said, taking a bite of his sandwich.

THE LUNCH BUFFET CLOSED BEFORE MOLLY came back. When she returned, it was just Lindsay and Elijah at their table; David had run off to the bathroom before the symposium's next lecture started.

"You okay?" Lindsay asked as Molly took her seat.

"I think I am, actually," she said. Then she chuckled in an odd way—almost dismissively. "I just talked with Max Pope for a tiny bit. He invited us to volunteer at his research place in Blue Hill. It's basically just a nursing home for Alzheimer's patients. He asked if we wanted to come visit them, especially the ones who don't have much family nearby."

Elijah's first reaction was to scrunch his face.

Lindsay herself, not 100 percent enthralled by the idea of spending her free time visiting old people, nonetheless saw a light of excitement—perhaps even some type of relief—in Molly's eyes. It cracked her heart's door open to the idea.

"Maybe we could start after the kickboxing tournament," Lindsay said.

"Oh—no, I didn't mean it like that," Molly replied. "I don't want to volunteer there. But something about it just made me realize that I don't really want anything to do with all this stuff. Ghosts, Max, any of it. I think after this symposium, I'd rather start talking about other stuff if that's okay."

Lindsay, whose only thing in common with her new friends was a belief in ghosts, simply sat there, shell-shocked.

Elijah, too, was subtly shaking his head. "Wait, what?"

"I just want to be normal," Molly answered. "I don't want to believe in ghosts anymore after this."

Lindsay dared to ask: "Does that mean no more library meetings?"

"It means whatever you want it to mean."

With that, Molly ate the rest of her salad and sandwich, drank the rest of her lemonade, and, as far as Lindsay was concerned, threw away the entire basis for their friendship.

L  YDIA CLARK DROVE in silence out of Seattle-Tacoma International Airport on June 10, 2040, veering southwest on I-5 before looping north on Highway 101, toward the Olympic Peninsula. Her destination? Hoodsport, Washington—the last publicly known location of Winifred Flite's brother, Michael.

To her left, towering in the distance, were the snowcapped Olympic Mountains, peeking out from thick ropes of fog. How very different this scenery was from Providence, Rhode Island, where Lydia had hopped a flight at 8:45 that morning on Raphael Dumont's dime. If the fickle man remained true to his word, he would follow her out here as soon as she had a hint of Michael Flite's whereabouts. Until then, however, she was alone: a pariah chasing a dream the piranhas didn't want her to have.

AFTER CHECKING INTO Sunset Inn, Hoodsport's newest and nicest motel, Lydia staked out the town's ramshackle post office to see if Michael

Flite might come to check his PO box. The mailman, dressed in the USPS's telltale blue outfit, came in at 3:00 p.m. Guessing he worked on a consistent afternoon schedule, Lydia decided to spend her next two mornings at a nearby café that also offered a view of Hood Canal Grocery, the only other local establishment residents would surely visit regularly. She found a seat and sat with her laptop for hours, watching both places while pretending to write.

For three days, she saw nothing, nothing, nothing, which signaled the obvious: that she needed to take her reporting strategy to the next level, and *now*.


"Oh, sure—I've seen that guy," a checkout clerk at Hood Canal Grocery told her when she held out an old picture of Michael Flite on her ActoPhone—the only one she'd been able to find online. "He comes in for food once a week. Sends his girlfriend on the off days. I think they live out by Lake Cushman."

As the young man bagged Lydia's few groceries, he gestured with his neck toward the towering snowcapped mountains at the center of the peninsula.

*Lake Cushman*, Lydia thought, making a note to look it up on ActoMaps.

She smiled at the young clerk and walked out carrying a grocery bag stocked with chips, carrots, and pesto chicken sandwiches—her breakfast, lunch, and dinner for the foreseeable future.


The road to Lake Cushman was walled in by fog-covered trees. Lydia drove as far around the lake as she could, knowing from her ActoMap that the road would eventually veer north, away from the lake and into the mountains. When she reached a small park along its shore, all she could see at the glassy water's far edge was a steep ascent of pine trees crawling upward into the clouds.

The road led her nowhere. She gained no new knowledge. Not even a hint of where Michael Flite might be.

On the night of June 14, Lydia called Raphael Dumont with a status update.

"My little bird," were his first words. "Syphon of my money."

Lydia scoffed. "Yeah, money Victor Zobel probably gave you." She waited for him to laugh, but he didn't. "Anyway, an update: I found Michael Flite. Almost."

She told him about the checkout clerk at Hood Canal Grocery.

With a flare of exhilaration, Raphael asked, "And this boy said Michael does actually live there somewhere?"

"Yes," Lydia confirmed. "And that he usually comes in for food once a week."

"Good. I'll start driving up from Texas tomorrow. We'll find him together. I hope you have room for me in that warm motel bed."

By the time Lydia scoffed again—she had indeed booked a room with a single king bed—Raphael had ended the call. But this was it: she was poised to make a million fucking dollars off this deal *and* dip her toes into the story of the century. The money would have to be taxed, yes, but that was nothing compared to the prospect of finally making her long-awaited, well-deserved career splash.

She went to bed thinking of Raphael Dumont. For a few harsh seconds, she even imagined his sinewy arms wrapped around her, holding her close, showing her that yes, yes, yes, he loved her, and he would have her back no matter what.

DOMINIC BOCK was from Texas. A place where love wasn't supposed to break. Where family values kept people together, and God and marriage and morals were guiding lights for people lucky or foolish enough not to question their bounds.

On the morning of June 17, 2040, however, he knew his life would never be so simple.

He was in the main bedroom of his family's Marriott Extended Stay suite in San Antonio, freshly back from his trip to visit Winifred Flite and Dr. Lumen on Cape Cod. Yet he was already packing his bag again.

His wife, Carolyn, sat silently in the suite's adjacent living room while their daughters, Anna, Edith, and Jessa, watched him from the nearest bed in stoic silence, seemingly processing the ramifications of his decision to pursue his famous son further. Did they have any context for how much danger Jonathan was in? Did they even care that a visit with Victor Zobel might mean the end of his life?

It was Edith, Dominic's middle and most analytical daughter, who broke the silence first. "I just don't get why you came back from Massachusetts at all if you're only running off again. And who the heck is this psychiatrist guy?"

Dominic, feigning a smile, gave Edith the lowdown on Dr. Lumen and his relationship to Jonathan. When his too-happy tone failed to penetrate the girl's perturbed expression, he stopped packing and looked directly at all three girls. "Look," he continued, "I came back because I wanted to talk this out with all three of you—and your mom—face-to-face, before heading out to Washington. I'm trying to be as open as possible, considering we're all in this mess together."

Edith glanced at her sisters—first at younger Jessa, who looked confused, and then at older Anna, whose expression was still unreadable.

It was Jessa who spoke next. "Aren't we in this mess because you *wanted* to meet your other kid?"

Anna whipped her head toward Jessa. "No, we're in it because that *stupid* reporter Lydia Clark outed Dad to the world. He didn't have any control over the situation!"

"Yeah, but he didn't have to, like, *start being a dad* to Jonathan Flite," Edith cut back in, flashing Dominic another grudging look.

The tension in Dominic's shoulders hit a crescendo when he turned to look Edith in the eyes. "Honey, I know it's not fair that you and Mom and your sisters were dragged into this or that you have to be afraid of dangerous people coming after you," he said. "I'm guessing this Raphael Dumont guy was trying to get to me, but do I know why? No. I can tell you this, though: if I had never met you, and I found out you were my daughter, I would want to know you. I would want to meet you and have a relationship with you, no matter where I was or what my life looked like. That's just who I am. It's why I chose to meet Jonathan last year, and it's why I'm trying to help him now. Just like you, he's facing some scary things that nobody his age should ever have to face."

In the next room, Carolyn let out a sardonic chuckle before getting off the couch and shuffling toward the suite's bedroom. "Maybe you should just go, Dom," she said upon reaching the door. Then she glanced at their daughters. "Come on, girls. Let's go get breakfast. Say bye to your dad."

But the girls stayed put.

"Are you getting a divorce?" Jessa whimpered.

Carolyn froze midstep. Then she turned around, absorbed her looming tears with a fake smile, and rushed to Jessa's side. "Honey, that's something your daddy and I have to worry about. No matter what happens to us, we'll love you, and you'll have a wonderful life."

Dominic's heart withered as he realized Carolyn hadn't denied the possibility of a divorce.

"Now come on—I read about a *really good* waffle place down the street," she continued. "We can sneak out the back of the hotel so the reporters don't see us!"

But all three girls were too old to fall for Carolyn's charlatanic attempts at levity. And yes, Dominic hated that he now thought of his wife this way. He also hated her closed mind, her reaction to the situation with Jonathan, and the eroded respect he now had for her.

He zipped up his bag as Edith eased off the bed and walked toward Carolyn.

"Bye, Dad," Jessa said without offering a hug. She followed Edith.

Carolyn, looking defiant, ushered the two girls toward the door. When she looked back at their oldest daughter, however, the girl was still sitting on the bed.

"Honestly, I don't see what the big deal is," Anna said. "Dad's just doing what any good dad would do."

Her mother stiffened. "Anna, I said *now*."

"No, not *now*. I'm just saying: Dad doesn't deserve to have you all treat him like garbage just because he's trying to do his best with all the crazy stuff that's happening. And if *WorldLine* was right about there being infinite versions of the universe so we can learn from all the choices we might make, doesn't it mean we have nothing to worry about? And maybe we should just let Dad do what he needs to do, since in some other version of things, he's staying with us?"

Blood flooded Carolyn's face. "Anna, that's science fiction nonsense. Now, if you don't come with us, you'll have to eat the hotel breakfast."

With a desperate look at Dominic, Anna groaned and stood up. "I'm just saying that we shouldn't freak out before we know the full context of the situation." She stopped next to him. "Are you going to be gone when we get back?"

"My flight is in ninety minutes," Dominic said, standing to give Anna a hug. She accepted it warmly.

"*I* care what happens to Jonathan," Anna said. "I hope you get to talk to him."

She held the hug. Tears welled in Dominic's eyes.

"Bye, honey," he whispered. "I love you."

"Love you, too."

When they parted, Anna offered Dominic a glimmering smile—his sole bit of familial support—before following Carolyn, Edith, and Jessa out of the room. The hotel suite's door clicked behind them, punctuating Dominic's solitude.

He checked his ActoPhone clock. It was almost 8:45 a.m—time to hire a car, get to the airport, and fly to meet Dr. Lumen in Seattle. Grabbing his luggage, he made for the door. On his way out, however, a small glittering object on the kitchen counter caught Dominic's eye. He let the door go and stepped back into the room for a closer look.

It was Carolyn's wedding ring.

She had taken it off.

Grief pummeled Dominic's chest. It tugged him in all directions like a wave until he remembered a quote Rebecca Sparks had told Alice

Winterblume via her neural chip in the final episode of *WorldLine*—likely the same quote that had just inspired his own daughter to cite the multiverse concept. Anna had watched Dominic type it into his ActoPhone notes so he would remember it.

> *Life is all about choice and exploring its ramifications. But the big secret—one that our physics has been hinting at for a while now—is that all things that can happen are happening, in one system of reality or another. Which means our souls, on a level above the physical reality we create, get to learn and grow not just from each choice we make but also from all their alternatives.*

If Dominic truly was in a multiverse, it would mean that somewhere, in another version of *now*, he was choosing to stay with his family. Yet his choice today—to leave—was one he'd have to live with.

After looking at Carolyn's lonely wedding ring one last time, he shut off the lights, left the suite, and didn't look back.

L OWELL GRENDEL WAS GLAD End Haven, Minnesota, was a small town. A small town meant a small police force, and since the Idle County Sheriff's Department had no solid evidence to implicate him in the murder of Drew Thorsen, they could neither arrest him nor spare the manpower to keep eyes on him at all times. He thought perhaps the FBI would have done things differently, but so far, they had also kept their distance.

His coast was clear.

Which was why, on February 8, 2006—a Wednesday—Lowell hired a cab to drive him down to Wind Prairie, where he rented a tan Toyota Corolla. It was the newest model, which would make him look modern, normal, and invisible.

THAT SAME DAY, he drove up to Minneapolis to buy five vials of ketamine and twenty syringes from a friend of a friend of a friend. As expected, it was a simple transaction. Fast and neat. When it was finished, he drove back south.

THAT NIGHT, IN END HAVEN, Lowell sat inside the parked tan Corolla under the shadows of Fairfax Avenue. Through the dark, he watched older kids and the few fitness-oriented folk of End Haven walk in and out of Fairfax Community Center. According to the facility's online calendar, its two-hour "Kickboxing - Boys/Girls" class had just ended.

Tonight, he watched Lindsay Thorsen and one of her friends—a muscular boy with dark hair—talk and laugh as they exited the building. It was snowing lightly around them, and as Lowell wondered what it would be like to have such strong connections with other people, he saw the two teenagers' orbs glowing among the snowflakes—faintly at first and then stronger.

He forced himself to sit silently in the car, in the dark, unseen, before driving back to Windsong Road. After parking the car on the street's north end, far enough from his dead-end house to keep it inconspicuous, he walked home.

ON FRIDAY, HE STOOD in his darkroom, which had been stripped bare by police, seemingly for good. He had yet to replace any of the equipment they'd taken—the film, the photo paper, the chemicals. What was the point, when they could burst through his door anytime and confiscate his life's work? And what if Taconite Rose, the woman screaming in his ear, were to appear in the photos? What if the police were to recognize her as the ghost who followed killers?

In the darkroom, under the red light, Lowell sat on his basement steps. Somewhere upstairs, daytime turned into night.

Time for a drive, perhaps?

A HALF HOUR LATER, he sat in the tan Corolla outside Lindsay Thorsen's house, on her cul-de-sac, waiting for something to happen. What, exactly, he didn't know. The house looked empty.

He imagined what it must be like for Lindsay these days, amid the weight of her broken family. Yes, he had done the breaking, and yes, he was ashamed. And with Taconite Rose still screaming in his ear, despite his attempts to block her out, each shred of guilt was like a shard of glass slicing into his soul.

He would prove himself. He would show Taconite Rose that he could control his urges. He would show everyone that he wasn't as awful a man as his actions might suggest. True, he had dumped a four-year-old boy's body into an underground chasm, where it had been washed by a waterfall to kingdom come, before the winter freeze. But no—at his deepest level, he wasn't horrible. He couldn't be, because he still felt guilt.

Once he got hold of the boy's sister, the very second he got the chance, he would not kill her. He would show her he was capable of the opposite. Because hadn't she chased her dead brother through the snow in December? Wasn't it true that she, too, could see ghosts?

Together, they would find Taconite Rose and set her free. Then, finally, Lowell himself would be free.

I T WAS ALMOST 6:00 P.M. on June 17, 2040, when Lydia Clark noticed two men unpacking the trunk of a white Ford Air parked in
front of Sunrise Motel's southernmost room, only six down from
the one she now shared with Raphael Dumont. She had just returned
from Hood Canal Grocery with a bag of wine, cheese, and crackers, and
upon seeing the newcomers, her first thought was that they might be a
gay couple on a romantic getaway.

When they walked toward separate rooms, however, she noticed
that one of them had gray hair, a beard, and a limp—just like Thomas
Lumen, the psychiatrist on *WorldLine* whose sister had been killed by
that cult in 2003. Lydia processed the sight for a full ten seconds before
the truth dawned on her.

*Holy Christ. It actually* is *him.*

She immediately turned left so the men wouldn't see her face,
then walked toward the motel's back patio, which faced the western-
most finger of Puget Sound. Before passing the building's northwest

edge, however, she dared a glance at the taller man laughing with Thomas Lumen. Her gaze lingered just long enough to confirm his identity.

It was Dominic Bock, Jonathan Flite's father.

*Shit. This is it.*

Lydia dawdled on the back patio sidewalk until both men had entered their respective rooms, and then she rushed back to her own.

"Jesus, get the hell out of bed," she said to Raphael, who was still lounging shirtless between the cheap sheets. Without waiting for a response, she rushed to put in her ActoLenses and check the battery on her ActoPhone, which would serve as a video transmitter. "Jonathan Flite's dad and that psychiatrist friend—they're outside. Don't fucking ask me why, but they just got here. We have to be ready to follow them the second they leave. It might be our one shot."

"Look at you, Miss Reporter."

"Shut up and send me the rest of my money. I found Jonathan Flite for you. Now it's time for you to follow the hell through."

"Ah-ah-ah," Raphael said as he rolled out of bed and ambled toward her. He leaned close, smelling her neck. "Good things come to those who wait."

She batted him away. "No. Fuck that. I've been out here for two goddamned weeks. I did what you wanted me to do. Now, either send me the rest of the money or your story. Because if this all goes south and I get nothing, I'll—"

"You'll what, little bird?"

Lydia rushed to the window and looked out. The white Ford was still parked six rooms away.

"I'll report you to the fucking police," she finished, checking her phone to confirm that her ActoVid settings were set to beam any footage she recorded both to her ActoPhone's hard drive and to her ActoCloud, assuming there was cell service. She'd start recording as soon as she knew Jonathan Flite was close.

As Raphael dressed, Lydia waited by the window, watching for any sign of movement by the white Ford. She barely noticed when he brought his duffel bag into the bathroom with him and closed the door.

AND THEN IT WAS TIME.

"Christ, there they go," Lydia said, rummaging through her small yellow purse to make sure she had her keys, wallet, and phone. "Are you ready? We need to get in the car right now."

Raphael surprisingly reached her side in less than five seconds. He was now dressed in running shoes, jeans, and a baggy jacket. "Yes. Let's go."

Lydia nodded, then looked back over the room, out of habit.

"What are you waiting for, little bird?"

With a roll of dissatisfaction, Lydia realized she was leaving nothing of value in the room. No expensive jewelry. No expensive clothes. No high-priced electronics. By everyone's standards, she was nothing, nothing, nothing.

*But that's about to change.*

"I'm *not* waiting," she said. "Let's go."

With a surge of adrenaline and dollar signs floating behind her eyes, she led Raphael out of the motel room. They walked briskly to her rental car and climbed in, all the while hiding their faces from Thomas Lumen and Dominic Bock. When the two men's white Ford Air left the parking lot, Lydia followed about ten seconds behind.

SHE FOUGHT TO KEEP HER DISTANCE while trailing the car up Highway

119's tree-lined passage, toward Lake Cushman. Every time the white Ford Air slowed down, she slowed with it. Every time it took a curve, she sped up to do the same, certain she'd lose it.

But no, she didn't. When the car finally did turn, it was off a long straightaway heading north, just past the point where the highway continued away from the lake. Lydia glanced at her ActoMap and saw that the side road they'd taken was a dead end; it looked as if it led to a trailhead or a parking lot. She slowed when she approached it but passed without turning.

"What the hell are you doing?" Raphael said. "We're going to lose them."

"Last I checked, you still owe me five hundred thousand dollars and your goddamned life story. We only have one bar of service out here, so either send it now, or I drive us back."

With an unusually prissy expression, Raphael took out his phone. As he fiddled with its screen, Lydia surged with the power she had just exerted; never before had she possessed the gumption to threaten someone. Fueled by the adrenaline pulsing through her, she found a random turnout amid the pine trees and made a U-turn. She drove slowly back toward the dead-end road Thomas Lumen and Dominic Bock had disappeared down.

As the turnoff came into view, she heard the telltale whooshing sound of an ActoMessage notification.

"There," Raphael said. "You have my story. I'll send the money after we're done here tonight."

"No, you'll send it *now*, or I pass this road again," Lydia said. Her gaze flitted between Raphael and the looming turnoff.

Then things happened quickly, and not in the order Lydia would have expected. Just as she remembered that the man sitting next to her was a criminal, she came to a humiliating understanding that greed, desperation, and self-deprecation had led her here today. As both truths settled with a deathly stillness in her mind and heart, Raphael pulled a silver handgun from his jacket pocket.

"Turn the fucking car," he said, pointing the weapon straight at Lydia's head.

I T WAS NEARING SUNDOWN when Dominic Bock and Dr. Lumen met Michael Flite a few miles west of Hoodsport, Washington, in a gravel parking lot that sat under a small opening in the Olympic Peninsula's towering evergreens. Beyond the clearing, a single trail led west toward a nearby mountainside that was just visible in the late afternoon sun.

Michael Flite, a stranger to Dominic, was surprisingly large compared to his ropy sister, Winifred. Standing at least six foot three, he had broad shoulders under a flannel shirt and was just soft enough around the edges to make it clear this remote wilderness refuge offered him a life of comfort and abundance.

After throwing a side-eye glance at Dominic, however, Michael greeted Dr. Lumen first. With a cautious handshake, he said to the psychiatrist, "Hey there. I hope it wasn't too hard to find the place."

"Thank heavens for ActoMaps," Dr. Lumen said, stepping back to allow Dominic the courtesy of a handshake.

Dominic and Michael shook. "Sure was a beautiful drive," Dominic said, despite the claustrophobic feeling such solitude inspired in him. "You've been here for how long now?"

"Going on ten years," Michael said with a hint of Winifred's famous curtness. "Figured if I had to exist at all, it might as well be somewhere away from the rat race."

Dominic, aware Michael had attempted suicide in high school, offered him an encouraging nod.

Dr. Lumen, however, seemed more than willing to commiserate. "Sometimes I dream of getting off the grid like this," he said. "I'm a bit envious of you, actually."

"Winifred said you had alcohol and marriage problems after you worked in the CIA," came Michael's blunt response.

The psychiatrist offered a transparent shrug. "Yeah. I put work and stress first for way too long, and the result was two kids who don't talk to me and an ex-wife who encourages it," he said. "With all those years overseas, I was never present. Even after I was back, it was hard for me to let go. Sometimes my life seems like a series of bad mistakes."

*Mistakes.*

In his mind's eye, Dominic saw his wife and daughters. A year ago, none of them would have expected he'd now be searching for his long-lost son in this remote mountain range at the edge of the country. Was he now following Dr. Lumen's footsteps on the same path toward loneliness?

"I suppose you told Jonathan and Clovia we're coming?" the psychiatrist continued.

"Yeah, they're aware." Michael gestured with his head toward the trail. "It's a bit of a walk—about a mile or so. They're using my girlfriend Gianna's yurt. If you're staying overnight, you might want to bring your bags now."

Dominic and Dr. Lumen had traveled light to the camp, upon

Michael's advice; they had each brought just an overnight backpack and a jacket. After grabbing them, they started out through the evergreens toward Jonathan and Clovia's yurt.

Nobody spoke for the first few minutes of the trek. Despite the fog and damp air, the path remained dry as dusk overtook the mountain ridge ahead of them. After ten minutes, they reached another clearing in the trees that wasn't quite a field. Patches of sky dotted the canopy in irregular shapes just above the camp's first darkened yurt, where they turned left on a trail that stretched another quarter mile. Soon, they came upon a second yurt that had bubbly rainbow-colored flowers painted on it.

"Here it is," Michael said with a grunt. "You'll notice that Gianna's a little bit hippie-dippie."

After glancing at three neighboring yurts in the distance, Dr. Lumen grinned. "They're living in this flowery one?"

"Yeah. And probably hearing you talk."

Dominic stood taller. The last time he'd seen Jonathan was four months ago at the new condo he and Clovia Bell shared in New York City. When the yurt door opened, Jonathan stood under its doorframe, casually wearing jeans and a fleece jacket (to say nothing of his unruly hair). A hesitant grin spread across his face. He was barefoot, and for a second, Dominic thought he might run down and offer hugs, like some long-lost puppy. But no. Always calm and collected, Jonathan simply stood there on the yurt's single wooden porch step.

"Hi there," he said, sounding amused as he looked at Dr. Lumen first. "Michael told me you were coming. I knew my mom would cave and tell you where we were, eventually."

Dr. Lumen returned Jonathan's grin. "We guilted her into it. I'm just glad we got here in time."

"You mean before I blast off into space?" Jonathan asked, tilting his eyes up toward the night's first few twinkling stars. "Victor Zobel aside, I've been wanting to visit Star Island ever since it opened."

"Then become a damned astronaut," Dominic said, taking a step forward through an immediate blush. No matter how hard he tried, he couldn't pretend to have the same humorous rapport with Jonathan that Dr. Lumen had.

But his son offered a warm smile. "Hey, Dad. I'm glad you came."

Dominic's constricting heart eased—just a little—as Clovia Bell appeared in the yurt's entryway, just behind Jonathan. Her close-cropped hair was growing out, and she was holding a small video camera. "Hi," she said in a strangely focused way. "Do you mind if I film this?"

Dominic had never seen either of them this relaxed, which immediately made him question the camera. "Didn't you come here to escape those things?"

"Sort of," Clovia answered. "But we're also working on something new. I didn't just up and leave *WorldLine*."

Dr. Lumen's body immediately tensed. "Another documentary?"

Even before Clovia answered, Dominic saw it in his mind's eye: the two young adults visiting Victor Zobel on Star Island together, filming the encounter not just for public transparency but also to "get the shots they needed."

"It is a documentary of sorts," Clovia said. "But we're keeping it under wraps for now."

Dr. Lumen looked squarely at the young woman. "Well, whatever you're doing, I hope you're keeping Jonathan in check."

"I'm not sure anyone can really do that," she replied with a laugh. "But yes, I'm trying."

Everyone's unspoken feelings about Victor Zobel's lure to Jonathan floated between them in the mountain dusk. From somewhere in the trees came the hoot of an owl.

"Well, come on in, I guess," Jonathan said. He glanced at his uncle. "Michael, you're welcome to join if you want. I just made some of that Mountain House rice and chicken stuff. We're making a campfire after."

"Sounds nice, but I'm gonna go make some real food, thanks," Michael replied, hovering just below a snicker. He turned to Dominic and Dr. Lumen. "Guys, if you need anything, I'm just back there in that first yurt we passed. These two dingbats don't drink coffee, so if you wake up tomorrow morning wanting to die, stop on by."

"I'm sure I'll see you bright and early, then," Dr. Lumen said, once again with a jolliness that didn't quite reach the shadows under his eyes.

Dominic, noticing an eerie similarity between the two men, only offered Michael a polite smile and nod. As the man walked back toward his own yurt, Clovia and Jonathan made room in their yurt's doorway.

"Food's getting cold," Clovia said, ushering Dominic and Dr. Lumen inside.

As the night grew dark, nobody heard the approaching crackle of sticks deep in the forest—footsteps that had followed the two men from the parking lot, straight to the camp.

*J*AB. *JAB. CROSS PUNCH. Hook. Side kick. Roundhouse. Half hook.*

It was Wednesday, February 15, and Lindsay Thorsen was alone at kickboxing for the second class in a row. Alan Sparks was on his family's annual winter-break vacation in Florida, and Molly Butler and Elijah Bryce had both pulled back socially since the ghost symposium, sending Lindsay into an isolating mind spiral. Despite her budding relationship with Alan, the last four months—a cyclone made of Drew's disappearance, friend shake-ups, and dead-end questions about Lowell Grendel—was a mental storm that only seemed to be getting worse. Tonight, all she wanted was to fight it to smithereens, but like the wind, it couldn't be wrangled.

Molly's sudden self-imposed distance since the ghost symposium—whether due to a temporary disinterest, a true change in outlook, or something else altogether—hadn't faded. As a result, Elijah had also followed suit. It seemed he wasn't up to the task of being the connective glue for their budding friend group.

*"Maybe she'll come back around,"* he had said to Lindsay on their way out of school last Friday. *"Either way, I think I might wait to go to kickboxing again until Molly wants to come."*

When they parted ways that afternoon, Lindsay had forced herself to wave, but her brittle parting smile made her feel green in the face.

And so came tonight. She was kicking Brady Jones's ass at kickboxing. He was huffing and puffing, and she was upset.

Lindsay went into a side kick. A back fist. A bolo punch. She dodged all of Brady's punches and kicks, and then—

"Five, four, three, two, one . . . and time!" Coach Martinez shouted. "Jones, you might have a problem in two weeks if Thorsen keeps kicking everyone's butt. Now, just a reminder: I've set all your sparring rotations for tournament time. It'll be like open gym for everyone who isn't competing, and it'll last three weeks, starting March 1. Get ready!"

For the first time, Lindsay felt complete ambivalence about the upcoming kickboxing tournament. No nerves. No excitement. No self-comparisons to all the boys.

She went through the motions for the rest of class. When it ended, she walked briskly to the locker room without saying goodbye to anyone.

IN THE SHOWER, there were no water burns. No voices. No ghosts.

WHEN SHE EXITED the community center to wait for her dad—still warm from her shower and thus welcoming the frigid February night—she let out a deep, relaxed sigh. Her condensed breath floated up under the community center's bright lights, while snowflakes floated lightly down from the sky like confetti.

As the boys from her class filtered out of the building, guffawing like idiots (the way they always did when Alan Sparks wasn't there to keep them in line), Lindsay purposefully turned away and wandered up the sidewalk. She walked toward the corner of Fairfax Avenue and Twelfth Street—just north of the community center's entrance.

Her footsteps crunched over brittle ice on the concrete as the facility's fluorescent illumination gave way to darkness. The streetlight up ahead at Fairfax and Twelfth became an island of light, and as she approached it, she checked the clock on her cell phone.

It was 8:12 p.m. Her dad was late, like he always used to be. Maybe things *were* finally getting back to normal.

Above her, snow flurries danced under the streetlight. The air was cold and crisp—her favorite.

*Is happiness just something grown-ups tell us is real?* she wondered.

An answer glimmered somewhere deep in her heart, and just as she was about to grasp it, someone's shoes crunched on a patch of sidewalk ice behind her.

And then—

Darkness suddenly muzzled her mouth and nose. The arm of a wool jacket. She was being pulled backward in a choke hold, toward a shadowy portion of Twelfth Street, where the snowbanks were a foot and a half tall.

*My neck. I can't breath—*

Lightheadedness overtook Lindsay as she tumbled to the ground. Under a pine tree in the corner-lot yard, the arm around her neck tightened. She looked up at the tree for a few seconds—that normal, regular tree—then glimpsed once again the dark edge of the person's coat, which was obstructing her view. She finally gave up and closed her eyes.

"Shhhhh, that's a good girl," the man clutching her said. "Yes, that's right. We're going to go find Rose. We're going to go set her free."

Lindsay didn't even need to identify the whisper. As the pressure around her neck loosened for the briefest second, she found her ability to gasp and open her eyes just long enough to see a mop of shaggy black hair interrupted by two strips of white.

As a needle pricked her leg and ushered her into oblivion, she heard the distant sound of a woman screaming in rage.

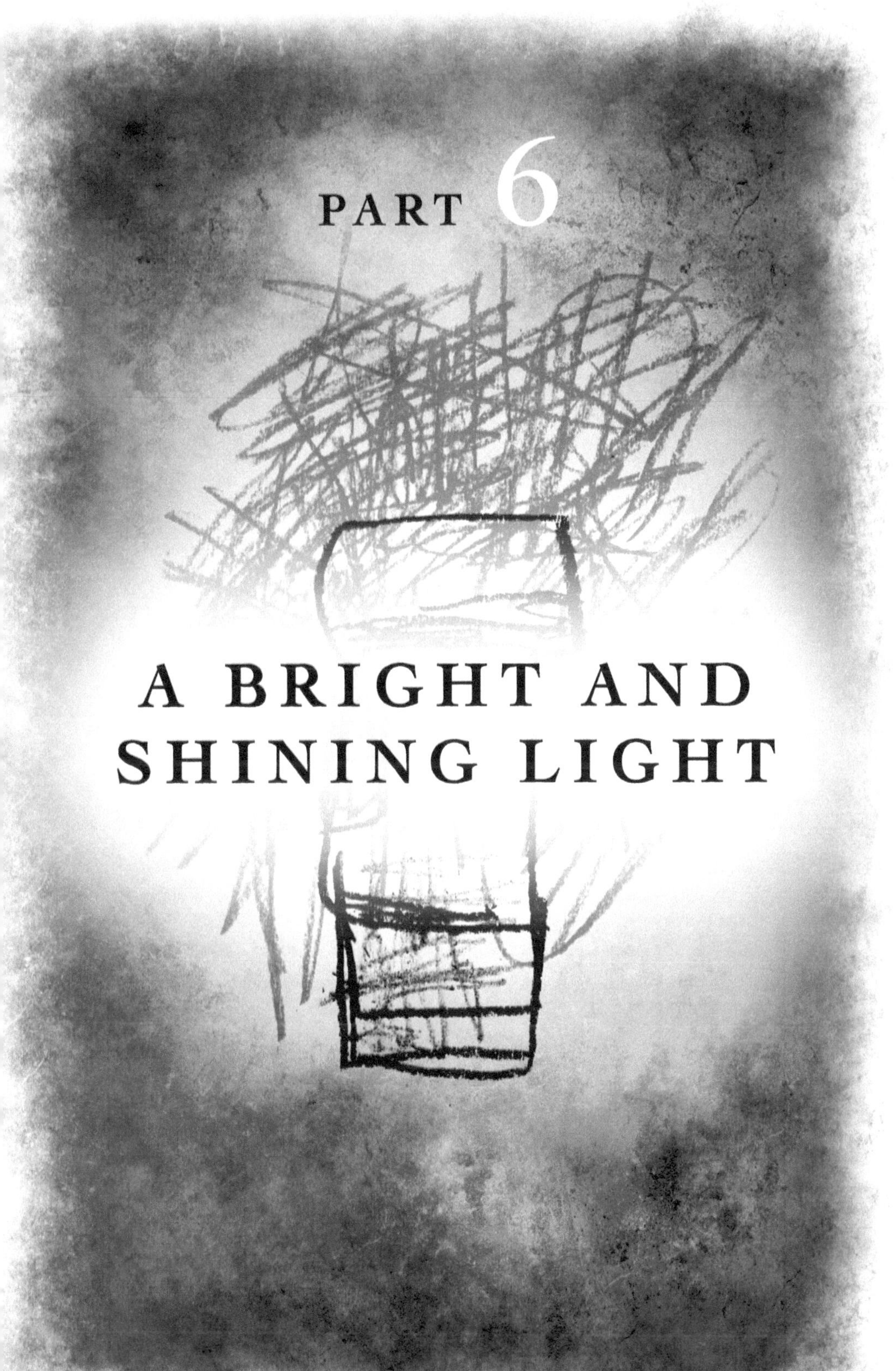


PART 6

A BRIGHT AND
SHINING LIGHT

"I NEED TO LOOK AT MY LIFE," Jonathan Flite said as he sat on the floor of the yurt he was sharing with Clovia Bell. The sun had set, and outside, his campfire was dwindling. The orange-tinted LED lamp lighting the circular living space reflected as dots in his hazel eyes.

Dominic, noticing a number of half-finished paintings around the yurt, shifted uncomfortably on the dwelling's small futon couch while Clovia, on the sidelines, recorded the visit with her camera.

"I know you want to protect me and make sure I don't do anything crazy," Jonathan continued, "but Victor Zobel won't kill me. He can't. The whole world is watching him now."

Dr. Lumen's gaze flitted toward Clovia's camera, then back to Jonathan. "And do you know what this 'prize' relating to the Idle County Seven is?"

"Possibly," Jonathan said. "In that video he recorded on Star Island, did you happen to notice a big leather book on the bookshelf behind him? There was gold foil on the spine in diamond shapes."

Neither Dominic nor Dr. Lumen nodded.

"Okay, well, I'm pretty sure it was the journal Clayton Graf and Elijah Bryce tracked down a few months before they died," Jonathan continued. "The one written by that old friar, Benedict Wise. It had directions to the Moon Woods cave written in it and a lot of other stuff about the supposed nature of reality."

Dominic leaned forward. "You and those other people talked about that on *WorldLine*, right? In the second episode, I think."

"Yeah. Me and Natalie Pent and David Thorsen."

"That was also the episode where you talked about Lindsay Thorsen grabbing the flashlight from outside her body. Does this have anything to do with that?"

He waited for Jonathan to reply, but Jonathan didn't.

"Okay, well, I need to know why going up to visit Victor Zobel would constitute needing to 'look' at your life," Dominic continued. "I'm trying to understand your motivation here."

Jonathan grimaced. "Not to sound like an asshole, but you haven't known me for that long. I wouldn't expect you to understand."

Dominic's chest tightened as his son's truth stung in all the appropriate places. As if to buffer the tension, Dr. Lumen cleared his throat. "Honestly, Jonathan, we just want to help you make the best decision. You haven't really had a normal life so far, and—"

"No, I haven't," Jonathan cut in, speaking with a level of firmness Dominic often noticed in himself—usually at WaveForm Electric, when he was sure of the facts and certain an engineering decision would benefit the company.

Jonathan glanced at Clovia and gave her a subtle nod. She stood up, tightened the camera tilt on her tripod, and walked toward the king-size bed and dresser near the back of the yurt. She dug into a file folder that sat atop the dresser, then pulled an envelope from it. It was robin's-egg blue.

"I'm guessing you've seen these?" she said to Dr. Lumen.

The psychiatrist stared at the blue envelope. He didn't have to nod; his expression confirmed his familiarity.

Clovia must have seen the confusion on Dominic's face, because she turned to him next and said, "Jonathan started getting these letters from Rebecca Sparks two years ago, when he was still at Crescent. Revis Zobel and his dad got them, too—some during the *WorldLine* production and some before."

Dominic took the crinkled robin's-egg-blue envelope from Clovia. Inside it was a single piece of folded paper. "I didn't see anything about these on the show," he said.

"That's because the FBI took all the other ones Jonathan got," Clovia replied. "Not to mention that we thought the letters might make Rebecca look too manipulative. She met Jonathan face-to-face the same day as we did, so Alice figured it wouldn't hurt to keep any previous communication under wraps."

"Either way, this one came two years ago, a few days before my first *WorldLine* interview," Jonathan said. "I never showed it to anyone—not even the FBI—and I didn't show Clovia until after the show was done."

Dominic took the typed letter out of its blue envelope, angling it so Dr. Lumen could also read.

*Dear Jonathan,*

*I believe our shared goals with* WorldLine *are finally about to put us on the same path. For that I am grateful.*

*Your guides, however, are telling me one thing that I urge you to consider: If you must mention Benedict Wise's journal during shooting, limit your story to what the journal said about the location of the cave in the Moon Woods. The world may not yet grasp the rest of what it contained.*

> *Also, for my sake, I'm wondering if we could stick with the police's version of events regarding the night my family died. It is a lid I wish to keep closed from the public sphere.*
>
> *Warm regards,*
> *R.S.*

Nobody spoke. From outside the yurt came the sound of sticks cracking under someone's feet—a person from the yurt camp, surely.

"The rest of what the journal contained—what does that mean?" Dr. Lumen asked.

"Honestly, I'm not a hundred percent sure," Jonathan replied. "The cave location was pretty close to the front of the journal—it was on a hand-drawn map that marked the path of big rocks that led from the End Haven side to the entrance. I remember Lindsay Thorsen and Clayton Graf wondering if the Indigenous people in Idle County were the ones who put the rocks there—like, maybe they knew about the cave, too."

More sticks crackled outside, punctuating Dominic's sense of isolation. Or maybe it was just the fact that he was stuck out here, miles from the nearest civilization.

"Anyway, from what I remember, a lot of the journal went over Clayton's head. He was dyslexic and had trouble reading. That's why the kids were mostly focused on the map and finding the cave."

"And how did they even know to look for it?" Dr. Lumen asked.

"Max Pope knew about it and told Molly Butler. After she told Clayton, he tried to track it down through Emily Tarnish, the daughter of one of Mrs. Grime's old friends. She was on *WorldLine*—the one with gray hair and a mole on her upper lip, talking about how the rest of Benedict Wise's journals read like the flip side of Rebecca's Theory of—"

A knock rapped on the yurt's door.

Jonathan and Clovia froze. After a second, they looked at each other.

"Michael, maybe?" Clovia whispered.

Jonathan shook his head. "He never comes out after dark."

For a second, Clovia stared at him, calculating. Then she got up and approached the door. "Who's there?" she asked.

"A friend," came a male voice from outside. His speech had a slight accent—possibly European.

Clovia flashed Jonathan a nervous expression, but Jonathan only shrugged. If it was someone who wanted him dead, he'd likely be dead already.

When Clovia slowly opened the door, her body blocked the person standing outside it. On the futon, Jonathan sat frozen like a bird, staring and waiting.

"Um—" Clovia started, but before she could continue, Jonathan jumped to his feet and rushed to the door.

"Who is it?" After settling next to Clovia and putting a hand on her shoulder, however, he said, "Oh Jesus. I—"

"Please listen to me," the European man interrupted, but Clovia was already shaking her head and stepping backward.

"Jon, get back. He's got a gun."

Dominic leapt to his feet just in time to see Jonathan pull Clovia away from the door and take her place under its arch. There was indeed a man with tight and wrinkled skin standing outside on the ground below the yurt's single front step. Coiled around his leathery neck, bouncing in the light of Jonathan's dying fire, was a tattoo of a writhing snake.

L INDSAY THORSEN AWOKE to the sound of her own heartbeat.

Or was it?

No. It was the muffled sound of a car interior.

Her body was cramped, contorted. She'd been having a nightmare about a man made of sorrow who was sitting on the bank of an underground river, amid a pile of human skeletons. Now the heartbeat thumps in her chest coincided with the road's bumpiness as she jounced back to reality.

*The trunk of a car. Lowell Grendel drugged you and took you somewhere.*

Her body, sweaty and unnaturally fatigued, rolled like a Raggedy Ann doll as the car turned off the pavement, onto gravel. Through the trunk's floor, the sudden loud crunching of rocks under rubber tires sounded like a crumbling freight train.

*Gravel means you're in the country, far away from anyone.*

Panic overtook Lindsay's mind. When her heartbeat met it in the darkness, they began a horrifying tandem dance. She suddenly sensed with only a modicum of doubt that this would be the last night of her life.

And there was somebody cuddled up next to her. A boy. He wriggled in her arms, somehow touching her even though he didn't have a solid, physical shape.

*"Linny, we're almost there,"* the boy said, cuddling her closer. *"We're almost safe!"*

It was Drew.

Upon realizing it, Lindsay began to scream.

2006

OWELL GRENDEL GRIPPED the steering wheel of his rented Toyota Corolla, thinking *go, go, go* over and over. Yet he needed to stop. To rethink this night. To undo everything that had led to it. Perhaps it was all in his mind—the orbs, the ghosts, the certainty that everything in the world was some sort of illusion. Perhaps this didn't have to be a dead end.

But he had kidnapped Lindsay Thorsen. *That* would never be forgiven. Not by the girl's family, not by the law, not by himself. He had started and stopped, started and stopped on his drive north, unaware even of time passing, despite watching the clock tick from 8:00 to 9:00 to 10:00 to 11:00.

He had stopped six times—or was it seven?—pulling over the tan Corolla on the country roads leading toward the ghost town of Arrowhead Hills. Four times, in his panic, he had sat under the hollow moonlight, wondering how on earth he would get out of this. Twice he had exited his car to reinject young Lindsay with ketamine.

*But she'll be coming down again soon, if she isn't already,* he thought. *Hopefully she won't be too scared when she realizes she's locked in the trunk.*

For the first time in his life, Lowell wondered—*truly* wondered—if he had lost his mind beyond recovery.

As he took the last turn toward Arrowhead Hills, relieved the old roads around it weren't covered with snow, his mind's eye showed him something he had been dreading for weeks: an ending, a curtain closing on his life in a way he could never be proud of. Whatever had caused him to stalk people, study their orbs, and eventually lose his mind and kill them—it was out of his control now. He had irrevocably lost everything.

*You have one chance to prove yourself,* he tried to remind himself. *One last opportunity.*

But did he really? Was his ability to reason truly still intact? Every way forward ended with him either dead or behind bars. There would be no escaping his transgressions.

The only way out, he knew, was *up.*

A N EXCERPT FROM THE AUDIO TRANSCRIPT of Sandra Jean Thorsen's first past-life regression with Dr. Cora Noreen Crowe on November 22, 2034:

**Dr. Cora Crowe:** *Okay, so, you're seeing yourself as a man chopping wood. And you're saying his children are dead?*

**Sandra Thorsen:** *Yes.*

**Dr. Cora Crowe:** *Clearly there's a lot of sadness in this life. Maybe we can use it as a kind of emotional anchor to help you settle into that life a bit. Can you do that for me?*

**Sandra Thorsen:** *I think so.*

**Dr. Cora Crowe:** *Great. Now let's dig in a bit deeper. I want you to remember three significant events from this life—hopefully ones you've taken into the life you're living now, as Sandra Thorsen. Maybe these lessons have helped you already, or maybe they're things you're still struggling with. Worst case, we can help you remember so you can get rid of any negative feelings holding you back now. Does that sound good?*

*[Pause.]*

**Sandra Thorsen:** *Yes.*

**Dr. Cora Crowe:** *Good. Now on the count of three, I want you to think of your life as this man who's chopping wood, and go to the first important event you think of. Whatever you remember is just fine—it'll be exactly what you need to see.*

*[Pause.]*

**Dr. Cora Crowe:** *I'll count now. One. Two. Three.*

*[Pause.]*

**Dr. Cora Crowe:** *Where are you?*

*[Pause.]*

**Sandra Thorsen:** *I'm younger. Still the same wood chopper, but . . . I'm a boy. It's during childhood.*

***Dr. Cora Crowe:*** *How young?*

***Sandra Thorsen:*** *I must be . . . oh, I'd say five or six years old. I'm standing on a hill with a big sky above me. There are other people next to me. One is my mother. She's staring at something swinging from a rope in front of us. It's—*

*[Pause.]*

***Sandra Thorsen:*** *Oh my God. It's a body. A woman who was killed for being a witch. We're watching her hanging at a place called . . . Gallows Hill, I think. It's early America—Connecticut, maybe? And my mother is frowning, because I think she disagrees with what's happening. She doesn't believe in witches, and she's—*

*[Pause.]*

***Sandra Thorsen:*** *Oh gosh. I—*

*[Pause.]*

***Dr. Cora Crowe:*** *What are you seeing?*

***Sandra Thorsen:*** *My mother. She's—*

*[Pause.]*

***Dr. Cora Crowe:*** *She's what? Or who?*

*[Pause.]*

**Sandra Thorsen:** *She's Lindsay. My mother in this life was Lindsay. And—my God. She's so incredibly sad. And I think I'm finally seeing why.*

Davɪᴅ Tʜᴏʀsᴇɴ ᴄᴏᴜʟᴅ sᴛɪʟʟ sᴍᴇʟʟ Natalie Pent's scent on his clothes when he shuffled with more urgency than usual toward his front door, which was closed against the gentle breeze sailing through the western hills of End Haven. He checked his iPhone and saw that it was almost 11:00 p.m.

There were lights still on in the house. His wife, Sandra, would be in there somewhere, either awake and drunk or already passed out.

David crossed the threshold, imagining the sounds of Lindsay's and Drew's feet entering the foyer.

*My children, lost.*

He thought back on his early days with Sandra—how she had unexpectedly gotten pregnant with Lindsay three months after they started dating and how he had jumped head-first into the pressures and joys of being a parent. He now saw it all through a lens of compassion; they themselves had practically been children when it happened. Maybe they still were, in some ways.

Tonight, however, a cyclone of images and thoughts—some about his evening rendezvous with Natalie and others about their speculation over Lindsay's disappearance—whirled in David's mind. It had taken all his willpower not to call Sheriff Kevin Applebee's cell phone on the drive home to ask whether he had made the connections about Victor Zobel and Raphael Dumont that Natalie had, and to see if the police had any further thoughts about the secrets Molly Butler—and possibly the others—had been keeping about Max Pope.

*Calm down. You're grasping at straws again. The police hate that.*

Yet the links Natalie had made buzzed in David's mind. On the surface, none of the young woman's stories had been particularly alarming, save perhaps for the one about her near-deadly trek into the Moon Woods. When juxtaposed with Zobel and Dumont's possible involvement with the gas explosion that killed the Sparks family, however, they mattered. And then there were Max Pope's mysterious "death tests" on his Alzheimer's patients, his peculiar discussion with Molly at the ghost symposium, and his eventual disappearance in Alaska mere months before Elijah Bryce's birth mother was accidentally killed there.

It all seemed too strange. Too connected. Too untouched by police.

"Sandy? Are you here?" David said in a louder voice than usual. He couldn't even remember the last time he'd called out like this upon arriving home; it had probably been shortly after Lindsay disappeared, when he and Sandra were still frantically allowing themselves to hope their daughter might come back unharmed.

Tonight, as he expected, there was no answer.

David moved through the front foyer, turned right, and walked down the hallway leading toward the kitchen and family room. The lights in the kitchen were still on, and the back patio's sliding glass door was open.

"Sandra? You out there?"

He approached the patio, and yes: there she was, sitting with a half-full gin and tonic at the new glass-topped table she had purchased in April. Her blond hair looked more unkempt than usual, indicating she hadn't gone out at all today. And—*God*. She was smoking again. Not pot, the odor of which David could handle, but a cigarette. He hoped the wind wouldn't blow it back through the open door, into the house.

"Please don't comment on the cigarette," Sandra said, rattling the ice in her glass. "You know I'm trying to quit."

"I wasn't going to comment."

"But you were thinking about it." Instead of looking at him, Sandra stared into the backyard, toward Drew's old swing set, which neither of them had yet posed getting rid of.

David shrugged and took a seat. "I think we're past the point of judging each other. Speaking of which, you're never going to guess who I randomly saw tonight."

"I give up," Sandra replied. Her gaze was still locked on the swing set.

"Natalie Pent," David said.

Now Sandra looked into his eyes, taking a long drag. She blew the smoke out through pursed lips, then gave him a sardonic smile. "Is she just as flirty as she used to be?"

"Yes and no," David said. "But that's not the point."

For a flash second, Sandra's expression betrayed a hint of genuine grief. About the state of their marriage? About the fact that they both no longer cared about the extramarital affairs?

Doing his best to channel the investigative flare he and Natalie had shared tonight, David continued. "The point is that Natalie had some pretty major thoughts about Lindsay's disappearance—ones I think we need to follow up on."

Sandra stiffened in her seat, took the last drag of her cigarette, and snuffed the butt out harshly on the table's bare glass. "Please stop talking."

"Sandra, wait—you need to hear this. There are some things the police haven't seriously looked into, and—"

"I said *stop!*" She stood up and spun away from her chair.

David knew he couldn't win over a drunk Sandra, but this was important. If she didn't let him share it tonight, it might mark the end of their relationship. He felt it in his bones.

"There's a man named Raphael Dumont who apparently lives in Saint-Paul de Vence, France—near Nice," he said. "He was one of Victor Zobel's friends who walked with us during the Moon Woods searches after the kids disappeared. I even talked to him at one point."

"And why the hell am I supposed to care?"

David took a deep breath. It rode the wave of anger building in his chest. "Apart from the fact that Victor Zobel is now apparently building something in the Moon Woods—which is fucking *weird*—it matters because Natalie Pent saw this Raphael guy in town the day before the gas explosion at Alan Sparks's house. And the *next fucking day*, she walked in on Jillian Pope telling Lindsay how she thought Victor made it all happen."

"And why the *hell* would Victor Goddamned Zobel have blown up that house?" Sandra hissed, despite herself.

In a quiet voice, David said, "Do you remember what I told you about Rebecca Sparks the winter after Drew was taken? How she told me that first New Year's Eve about your affair with the UPS driver?"

Sandra's agitation became icy silence. David didn't need to read her mind to see the storm within: whispers of ghosts, psychic activity, and other paranormal things she didn't believe in.

"Sandra, *please listen*," David said. "Rebecca Sparks was actual, living proof of everything Victor Zobel tried to argue against in his book *In God We're Dust*. Considering the platform he's built off it, don't you think he'd want to cover up anything that might invalidate it?"

"Maybe—but to *actually* think he and his stooges broke into Rebecca's house and caused a gas leak that killed her entire family? That's *crazy*, David."

"Is it, though? Rebecca disappeared to California right after it happened, and—"

"No, David. Stop. Even if Rebecca *was* psychic, wouldn't she have known what Victor was up to? Wouldn't she have tried to prevent it?" Sandra laughed bitterly as if their very conversation were straining her sense of credibility.

"I don't know!" David said, standing up to meet Sandra's words head-on. "Maybe the psychic thing doesn't work that way! I can't say. But if Jillian Pope thought her stepdad was capable of going after Rebecca like that, and if this Raphael guy was here in town *that day*, don't you think it's worth looking into?"

Sandra took a deep breath, then shook her head while fending off tears. Her words came out with a guttural intensity David rarely saw in her. "I don't *care* if it matters, David. I can't think about it anymore. I just . . ."

Now her entire body was shaking. With grief? With rage? In that moment, David both loved her and hated her.

"I can barely live life as it *is*," Sandra finally managed to say. She slurred the words more than she had a second ago—likely a result of the gin and tonic finally hitting her. Then, in a brittle voice, she said, "Did you sleep with Natalie Pent?"

No matter how confident David had felt in the fact that Sandra had broken their marriage vows first, humiliation now left him numb.

"Yes," he whispered.

What he wasn't prepared for was the look of utter dejection on his wife's face. Her tears came now like a sudden hemorrhage, followed closely by David's own realization that, tonight, their buried choices would finally come out to haunt them, like lost skeletons beckoned forth, into the light.

**2006**

W HEN THE CAR rolled to a halt, Lindsay Thorsen heard soft footsteps outside, approaching the trunk behind the crown of her tilted head. Drew's ghost had left her, but in her twisted panic, she now wanted him back, along with any comfort she could get if these were indeed the last moments of her life.

Lowell Grendel's footsteps stopped outside the trunk's hatch.

When he opened it, the strips of white in his hair glowed under the moonlight. It silenced Lindsay's racing heart like a promise of false peace.

"I'm not here to hurt you," were his first words.

"The fuck you aren't," Lindsay said, aiming her retort like a jab in his face. It was the first time she had ever outright sworn at somebody. But this wasn't some schoolyard attempt to impress her peers; this was life and death, the only real trophy fight in the world.

Lowell Grendel simply stood there. There was no anger in his expression. No derangement or murder. Only shame.

"I had to put you in the trunk. You'd have woken up and maybe tried to jump out otherwise. Mind you, it's cold tonight, and we're far out of any town. You might freeze to death if you try to run. I also gave you a few hits of ketamine, which might make you feel a little wobbly."

*Ketamine.* Lindsay had never heard of it. Might it explain the dreams she'd had while asleep? Those nightmares so vivid that she could have sworn she was awake?

"Here's the honest truth," Lowell continued. "I'm going to take you home after this—or at least drop you at a gas station—before I leave forever. I don't want you getting hurt. That's not why we're here."

*He's crazy. Don't forget it. He took you just like he took Drew, and now you're a witness to his crime.*

"Where are we?" Lindsay asked.

"We're in a town called Arrowhead Hills, about forty-five minutes north of End Haven. Here, come on out."

He extended a hand, and Lindsay immediately recoiled. Her elbows hit the back of the car trunk.

*Be smart,* a voice in her head said, ushering in a series of thoughts in sync with her heartbeats. *Think of all the ways you could escape. It'll be easier if you're on your feet. Maybe you can even try grabbing his car keys.*

Lindsay began to see the possibilities in her mind. Trembling, she half rolled, half crawled toward the front of the car trunk, then popped her head up into the cold as if it were the most normal thing in the world.

At first, she could see only the bright moon. Then the trees came into focus. And the overgrown dirt road. Even some old ruined mine carts poking up from the roadside underbrush. In a nightmare, they would have been monsters, crouching and waiting.

Lowell extended a hand again, and this time, Lindsay allowed him to pull her out of the trunk. The moment he touched her, however, a black rotting feeling ran through her entire body.

*These were the hands that killed Drew.*

But she had to focus. She couldn't turn her back on the man. If she did, it would give him the means to—

Her feet hit the ground at a bad angle, forcing her to face the car. Lowell immediately seized her arms and held them against her back. For a few seconds, she could hear only his heavy breathing as she peered through the dark, hoping to see something that might help her escape. But no. All she could see was the vague outline of a hillside.

When Lowell spoke, however, it became clear they were here for a reason. "There, up ahead," he said. "See?"

She looked through the dark. Again, nothing. "I don't know what you're looking at," she said. Instead of sounding strong, it came out as a whisper.

"Up ahead. We have to find her and help her."

"What? Find who?"

"The woman who was standing with your brother under the streetlight the night you ran through my yard. Don't think I didn't see them both, too."

*Taconite Rose. That's who he's talking about.*

Yet his next words weren't coherent. He rambled in a childlike way with starts and stops, referencing orbs, ghosts, and unfamiliar historical facts about Arrowhead Hills that Lindsay had no context for. All she could glean was that this woman, this *ghost*, had been tormenting him ever since he'd killed Drew. Apparently, she was now somewhere inside his mind, screaming at him constantly and driving him mad.

*Which means he's even more dangerous than he lets on*, Lindsay thought.

Seeming oblivious to her panic, Lowell pushed her forward, and the hillside came into better focus. There was something manmade built into it. A doorlike structure.

*A mine shaft.*

The instinct to survive beat through every corner of Lindsay's body. If she was going to escape, she had to play every moment just right. But how? Even if she were to get Lowell's car keys, she had never driven before. Yet neither had Elijah Bryce last summer at Spinner's Lake. Hadn't he driven a truck home with Damon Jacoby's body in the back?

Lowell Grendel's words, suddenly clear again, cut into Lindsay's thoughts. "Have you read the stories about Taconite Rose?" he asked.

"Some," she replied, vaguely remembering Thomas Lumen's *Renegade* article.

"The last person to see her alive said she was walking toward this old mine. Likely to look for the man who killed her son. Apparently, the police said these abandoned sections were too dangerous to search." Again Lowell leaned close to Lindsay's face from behind, and the heat of his breath warmed her ear. "But we need to show her we care, Lindsay. It's all we can do. Maybe then she'll leave us alone."

*Think, think, think*, Lindsay's mind raged. *Do anything to distract him.*

But her entire body was rolling with nerves. She was burning hot one second and cold the next, and her bladder, not even full, was threatening to give way.

And then—

There. In front of her. A ruined railroad tie.

Lindsay let her feet go limp. She tripped just long enough to slip from Lowell's grip and taste freedom, but a second later, he pulled her back up as if he were doing her a favor. He locked the girl's arms even tighter around her back and pushed her forward under the moonlight, toward the open mine shaft.

Then he leaned toward her, close enough for his lips to touch her ear. "Do you hear her screaming?" he whispered.

Lindsay's shoulders were now straining under his grasp. As she replied to Lowell—"Hear who?"—her own urine warmed the inside of her jeans. Because yes, she was indeed hearing something familiar: the screaming she had heard in Lowell's arms, as he'd injected her leg with ketamine under the tree.

"It's Rose," he said. "She's with us now. And she wants to be found. To be set *free*."

For a frightening moment, Dominic Bock couldn't place the man standing at the door of the yurt. Then came a recent and searing memory: Natalie Pent's op-ed about Raphael Dumont in the *New York Times*, followed by Anna, Edith, and Jessa's confrontation with the snake-tattooed man in their Texas hotel nine days ago.

"We're already calling the police!" Jonathan shouted. It was clearly a veiled cry for help, because there was no cellular service out here; Dominic had already checked. There was also no other way out of the circular yurt. Stalling was their only option.

"Please," the man said. "I don't mean you any—"

"What do you want?" Jonathan demanded. "Tell us now, or we'll raise fucking hell."

Dominic put a protective hand on Jonathan's shoulder as Dr. Lumen finally limped over to the door. Now all four of them—Jonathan Flite's makeshift family—were framed under its entryway. And Clovia had been right: there was indeed a gun in Raphael Dumont's hands. He looked older than he had in the social media pictures posted in the *New York Times*, and shadows of deep grief dimmed his eyes.

"Victor Zobel once said that if he couldn't kill you, the next best thing would be to meet you face-to-face," Raphael said. "But mark my words: he'll try to manipulate you into serving his purpose—it's what he does. And he won't stop. Geneva was just the beginning—a test. I'm almost positive."

It was Dr. Lumen who spoke next, over Jonathan's shoulder. "What do you mean 'just a test'?"

The tattooed stranger shrugged desperately and shook his head. "I only know that he was planning more attacks. More cities. Major religious sites. He's been hiding in plain sight in Idle County, doing studies on the human mind in that cave, and—"

"Was it him back in 2010?" Jonathan cut in. "Did he really shoot the Idle County Seven down there?"

Raphael shuddered under his answer. "We both did, along with one other."

A flash of movement outside the yurt caught Dominic's eye. It was another person—a woman—standing behind the nearest pine tree. Before Dominic could place her, however, Clovia leaned in toward Jonathan's ear. "Jon, that woman out there—" She furrowed her eyebrows in confusion. "Jesus. It looks like—"

Just then, the woman disappeared behind the large pine. She'd barely been visible in the dwindling fire's dim light, but there was something familiar about her. Dominic couldn't quite place it, but in the back of his mind, he knew it somehow connected to his wife, Carolyn.

Raphael extended his free hand toward Jonathan now. Between the tips of his thumb and pointer finger, he held a small, dark capsule. "Batrachotoxin," he said.

Dr. Lumen reached past Dominic to grab Jonathan's shirt. "Jesus—Jonathan, don't! That's a poison. It's—"

But Jonathan was already screaming into the night. "Michael! Anyone! If you heard me before, call the police! There's someone with a gun here at Gianna's—"

Raphael hissed through Jonathan's words, then stepped forward and raised his gun to his own head. He thrust his other hand, the one holding the dark capsule, forward.

"I've been trying to meet you face-to-face so I can give this to you—so you could take it with you if you go to meet Victor Zobel. Please. He needs to be taken down, or else there'll be—"

Suddenly, Michael Flite's voice, deep and angry, cut through the darkness. "You're surrounded on three sides! Put the gun down!"

From somewhere in the dark, near the tree Raphael's accomplice had just disappeared behind, Dominic heard a low-voiced woman—Michael Flite's girlfriend, Gianna?—say to someone: "*Don't you fucking move.*"

Raphael, still holding the gun to his own head, turned toward Dominic's left, in the direction of Michael's yurt. "Tell them to put the guns down!" he urged. He looked at Jonathan again and rushed toward the yurt's wooden front porch. "Please, I'm only here to—"

Before he could finish—and just as Dominic thought once again of his own wife and daughters—the night exploded in gunfire.

L owell Grendel rambled on about Taconite Rose as he led Lindsay Thorsen into the abandoned mine in Arrowhead Hills. Instead of listening to him, however, she was counting every numb step.

A *hundred four . . . a hundred five . . . a hundred six . . .*

Her legs were freezing from her urine-filled jeans. Each step felt like one more toward her own death, and something deep in her mind was telling her not to acquiesce to Lowell.

*Reason with him*, the voice said. *Treat him like a human being. It might remind him that you're a person, too.*

". . . but if she's a ghost, she needs release," Lowell was saying as he aimed a small yellow flashlight deeper into the mine shaft, lighting their way forward. "If we can find the place where she died, which I'm sure would be a mound of dirt now, assuming it was a collapse, maybe she'll—"

"The ground might be frozen," Lindsay said. "We probably won't be able to find her. Don't you think it might be better to—"

"Shhhh, Lindsay. Shhhh. This is sacred ground. And oh, you should see your orbs. They're positively dazzling tonight. Lighting up everything about you. They're your guides, you know. Your protectors."

*He's totally crazy,* Lindsay thought in the part of her mind closest to the surface.

Then she remembered what the police had said about the photos in Lowell's basement: that they had depicted figures made of light. And much of what he was saying now about ghosts and spirits sounded familiar. Some of it harkened back to her own visions of Drew and Taconite Rose; other bits gave shreds of rationale to her recent interactions with Rebecca Sparks. All of it seemed like pieces of a much bigger puzzle.

*Stop giving him credit,* her surface mind continued as the frigid, echoing mine shaft enveloped them. *He's a monster. That's all he is.*

In her meanderings, Lindsay had lost count of her footsteps.

Where had she been? A hundred eighty-six? A hundred eighty-seven?

Lowell was still yattering on about how important it was for humanity to start waking up to its own nature. "Think of what it would mean for society if people were to see what we see!" he said. "It would undo fear. It would undo war. It would help everyone realize they're a part of something so much bigger and that all this is just a mirage. That's why I study the orbs, Lindsay. And yes, I'm so terribly sorry about your brother. But his orbs were *racing* around him. Positively *racing*. It was like they were there to prove to me that life is just—"

"Life is meant to be *lived*," Lindsay said, relying fully on instinct now. "You *killed* him. An innocent kid! And now you're going to kill me."

"Oh, Lindsay, I won't be doing that. Not anymore. I hate it when the killing happens. Truly. It's like a monster that lives deep in my heart, and sometimes I just—"

"Just what? Kill four-year-olds?"

Lowell's breaths grew heavier.

"Nobody would understand why I had to study him," he continued. "Even the police—they saw my photos. But they don't understand why the photos *matter*. Like I said before, if people were to really see proof that life exists beyond death—that there's really never anything to be afraid of—it could fundamentally change how they look at the world."

Lindsay's heart twisted in a strange knot as she began not just to make sense of Lowell's words but also to agree with them. Yet he was tangled by beliefs—and by the need to prove their validity to the world.

Still, hadn't her attendance of the ghost symposium been a result of her own similar desire—that urge to question the unknown? Society was riddled with stories about ghosts, psychics, and life-altering near-death experiences, so why did people have such trouble acknowledging their validity?

*That doesn't need to be your fight*, Lindsay's combative voice piped up. *Your fight is to get out of here before he realizes he'll end up in prison if he doesn't kill you.*

Now, still pushing Lindsay from behind, Lowell slowed. "Oh, what have we here?" He let her go and shined his light forward onto a mound of dirt blocking their path.

Lindsay glanced ahead. The tunnel was indeed obstructed by a collapsed portion of the mine, which meant—

"Rose, are you here?" Lowell called out. "Was this where it happened?"

He looked and sounded insane, yet it was no different than when Lindsay had called out to Drew in the Fairfax Community Center showers.

*No. Don't believe it. You'll never be like Lowell Grendel, even if it means dying here in this—*

"We're here for you, Rose!" Lowell shouted. "We've both seen you, and we want to set you free so you can move on!"

He was now shining his flashlight frantically around the blocked mine shaft.

*Get his car keys*, Lindsay thought. *And his flashlight.*

But Lowell, still behind her and growing more agitated by the second, grabbed her arms again—this time with more force. The beam from his flashlight bounced around the tunnel as he found a solid one-handed grip on both of her wrists.

"I'm here!" he screamed, again to no one Lindsay could see. Anger mounted in his voice, and he started breathing faster. "I've done everything I possibly can to find you and help you!"

This is how it would start: his willingness to kill.

*Get out now!* her intuition screamed.

Lindsay, knowing the car keys were likely in Lowell's pocket, let her instincts take over. She watched the angle of his fluttering flashlight beam so she could judge where behind her he was standing.

*Okay. One . . . two . . . three!*

She ripped free from Lowell's grip, then swiftly turned and hit him with a push kick to the groin.

"No—!" he said through a grunt before lunging toward her.

Lindsay aimed another kick, but Lowell spun around and grabbed her again. She punched feverishly, then pushed backward off her legs with all her strength, slamming him into the mine wall. Lindsay couldn't see anything, so she had to trust that luck would be on her side and that his head would hit the tunnel's wooden frame— or better yet, a sharp rock or metal spike. If that happened, she'd be able to—

"Fuck!" Lowell screamed, colliding with the wall. Lindsay squirmed out of his arms, readying herself for another kick. But the man had grabbed her by the jacket and was now yanking her with one hand.

He brought the heavy flashlight down in a swift arc onto her skull. The bludgeon was immediately blinding, and she saw stars. Saw *light*.

*Oh fuck—*

Down his flashlight came again. Another blow to her head.

Lindsay's body was moving automatically now, and she was screaming, struggling with her brother's killer against the mine wall.

Then she heard it: the unmistakable sound of dirt falling from the ceiling. It didn't start with a rumble, the way it might in a movie; it started with a pebble here, a pebble there, and then pebbles everywhere—

"Get the fuck away from me!" Lindsay screamed, spinning with Lowell toward the opposite wall. She ducked forward, bulldozing him into it.

The collapse happened in slow motion: another bludgeon from Lowell's flashlight onto her head, dots of light in her eyes, and a heavier rain of dirt and rocks from the ceiling. Lindsay used her last ounce of strength to push Lowell—along with his car keys and flashlight—deeper into the mine, toward the blocked section.

And then the rumble came.

*Go, go, go!*

Lindsay ran ten feet in the inky darkness, toward the dull glow of moonlight shining into the tunnel's opening. It was far, far away—a small blip in the claustrophobic distance. No sooner had she registered its location than she tripped over an old mine cart track and went sailing face-first into the ground.

Above her, the mine shaft collapsed, and her world went black.

SCREAMS OUTSIDE THE YURT. Gunshots. The black of night, locking them in the wilderness. From what Dominic Bock could hear, there were at least two men and one woman from the yurt camp approaching and perhaps five more in the distance. As the next round of shots rang out, he spun in a half circle, away from the door, trying to glimpse something—anything—in the cornerless yurt to hide behind. Jonathan screamed for Clovia to get down, but the young woman instead ran toward her camera, which was still recording quietly on its low-standing tripod.

"Let it go!" Jonathan said. "Get down!"

Clovia shook her head. "Michael's not shooting at us! Neither is Raphael. And Jon, that woman out there, behind the tree—"

"Yeah, I saw her."

Clovia looked straight into his eyes. "It was Lydia Clark, the reporter from—"

"You guys, *get the hell down*!" Dr. Lumen screamed.

More gunshots rang out. In the fray, Dominic ran toward Clovia, grabbed her tripod with the camera still attached, and seized her by the shirt. "Behind the bed! Get as far back as you can! The canvas won't do anything to stop those bullets!"

"Shit-shit-shit-*shit*—" Dr. Lumen said on repeat until the guns outside suddenly went quiet.

From the forest, they heard Michael Flite scream, "Stand down!"

Four more gunshots rang out.

"I said *stand*—"

Then came a fifth shot from just outside the yurt's door, where Raphael was standing. A second later, Michael's yells turned into guttural screams—the worst and dirtiest ones Dominic had ever heard.

"He needs help!" Jonathan said, jumping up from behind the bed. Dominic and Dr. Lumen both lunged in one unified motion to pull him back. "No—let me go!" he screamed, pawing and kicking and trying to free himself from their grasp.

"Jonathan!" Clovia screamed. "Jon, no! Just wait until—"

The yurt door burst open. Dominic tried to duck behind the bed, but there was no room. All he could do was glance sideways to see Raphael Dumont standing in the open doorframe. Gaping from the right side of his chest, near his shoulder, was a bullet's bloody exit wound.

*Shot in the back by Michael or one of the neighbors*, Dominic thought. *If it hit his heart—*

Raphael's gun dangled from his dead right arm, but his left arm was still alive. Still raised.

*The poison capsule. He's still holding it.*

More shrieks from outside. The entire yurt village was now awake—neighbors in all directions.

Shouts, swear words, and rushing footsteps sailed into Dominic's ears as Raphael Dumont fell forward onto the yurt's wooden floor. The tiny capsule rolled after him, punctuating his horrific, intimate death wheezes.

"Jon, that reporter—she might have gotten away," Clovia whispered. "She could blow up this story. I need to go find her."

"No, you can't—"

"We need to control this!"

Without waiting for anyone's input, Clovia jumped up, hopped over the bed, and bolted toward the door. As she leapt over Raphael Dumont's fallen body, she pointed to the floor and said, "Somebody grab his gun! Film all this for the police!"

Then she ran out of the yurt, into the night, leaving their European intruder gasping and bleeding on the floor.

A N EXCERPT FROM THE AUDIO TRANSCRIPT of Sandra Jean Thorsen's first past-life regression with Dr. Cora Noreen Crowe on November 22, 2034:

**Dr. Cora Crowe:** *To confirm, the mother you're with in this Puritan life was your daughter, Lindsay, in your current life as Sandra Thorsen?*

**Sandra Thorsen:** *Yes. Same soul. Different body and life.*

*[Sandra chuckles.]*

**Sandra Thorsen:** *She's embarrassed about her weight. She thinks it makes her extra visible to the townspeople, who already don't like her. She eats all she can, because we live on the far edge of the settlement, and she knows* *we're surviving day by day. Food could run out anytime, so instead of rationing, she eats a lot. She doesn't really trust the New World—I think because my religious dad made her come here from England.*

**Dr. Cora Crowe:** *And how do you feel when you're with her?*

**Sandra Thorsen:** *Like I'm not good enough. I want her to love me, but she always tells me she was forced to get married and have children. That she was always just "playing the part." Now we're watching our closest neighbor get hanged. She was an old spinster who lived in the woods and was friends with the Indians.*

*[Pause.]*

**Sandra Thorsen:** *My mom always liked her, but now she's watching the lady die. I keep thinking to myself, "Gosh, she's playing the part again." I feel sour about it.*

**Dr. Cora Crowe:** *And what is the lesson here? Why are you seeing this memory?*

**Sandra Thorsen:** *Well, I . . . I kind of hate her for not wanting me or my siblings. I think to myself at least twice a week that she couldn't possibly be a good woman. That maybe she's a witch, because all women are supposed to want children.*

*[Sandra sighs deeply.]*

**Sandra Thorsen:** *But I guess I'm seeing now that the time and culture just didn't fit with who she was.*

*[Pause.]*

**Dr. Cora Crowe:** *Hmm. Interesting. Let's come back to that later. Now, though, on the count of three, I want you to go to the next event from this life that matters. Again, it should be one that's affecting you now, in your life as Sandra. Are you ready?*

*[Pause.]*

**Sandra Thorsen:** *Yes.*

*[Pause.]*

**Dr. Cora Crowe:** *Okay, here we go: One. Two. Three.*

*[Pause.]*

**Dr. Cora Crowe:** *Now tell me where you are.*

**Sandra Thorsen:** *I'm in a suit—a cheap one. My . . . my mother made it.*

**Dr. Cora Crowe:** *Your mother who was Lindsay in your current life as Sandra?*

*Sandra Thorsen: Yes. Her.*

**Dr. Cora Crowe:** *Why did she make you a suit? What's the occasion?*

**Sandra Thorsen:** *I'm getting married. To a woman I don't like. Men get married, so I'm doing it. I keep thinking that nobody's ever given me a choice about my life track. I hate things like hunting, but I do it anyway, because that's what men are supposed to do. This wedding is just like that.*

**Dr. Cora Crowe:** *What would you rather be doing?*

**Sandra Thorsen:** *Running a business in town. Maybe as a shoemaker. But I never pursued that dream, because I never had the means.*

*[Pause.]*

**Sandra Thorsen:** *I've also always been too embarrassed to admit what I wanted to do. Nobody would take me seriously since there are already two other shoemakers in town. So, I'm getting married, because it's . . . prescribed.*

**Dr. Cora Crowe:** *Does this new wife know you don't like her?*

**Sandra Thorsen:** *She doesn't care. She just wants children. And since I've always thought poorly of my mother for not wanting kids, I tell this wife I want them, too.*

*[Pause.]*

**Dr. Cora Crowe:** *Is there anything else you want to share about this experience?*

*[Pause.]*

**Sandra Thorsen:** *No. I'd like to move on.*

**Dr. Cora Crowe:** *Okay. Then on the count of three, we'll go to a third memory from this life. Are you ready?*

**Sandra Thorsen:** *Yes.*

**Dr. Cora Crowe:** *Great. Here we go: One. Two. Three. Can you tell me where you are?*

*[Sharp breath inward from Sandra Thorsen.]*

**Sandra Thorsen:** *Oh gosh, no.*

*[Whimpers from Sandra Thorsen.]*

**Dr. Cora Crowe:** *You're calm and safe in my office, and these are just memories from another life. Ones you've always had access to. Now take a moment to see and feel what's happening, then tell me what you're experiencing.*

**Sandra Thorsen:** *We're in the field behind our house. Me and my wife. We're burying our last child. My son. He was our third.*

**Dr. Cora Crowe:** *All your children are dead?*

**Sandra Thorsen:** *Yes. All three. They got terrible fevers, and we think my mother must have put a spell on them. She ran away with an Indian the week before the kids got sick, and we're sure she was taken in by his un-Christian ways.*

**Dr. Cora Crowe:** *Can you describe what you're feeling, watching this last child being lowered into the ground?*

**Sandra Thorsen:** *Guilt. Tremendous guilt. Because just like my mother, I never wanted kids. Now I'm getting my wish. All I have left is my wife, and we hate each other. I've made a mess of things. Such a mess.*

**Dr. Cora Crowe:** *And why is this memory relevant to your life as Sandra?*

**Sandra Thorsen:** *Because of my mother.*

**Dr. Cora Crowe:** *Tell me why.*

**Sandra Thorsen:** *Because even though I thought she might be a witch, I was secretly just like her as a parent. She was braver, though. She was honest about the life she wanted and eventually ran off to restart with that Indian. I've never been that honest, and now all I have is this distraught, angry wife. I loved my kids, but they were a bigger burden than I ever wanted to admit, especially when there wasn't much food. I've never let myself* *believe I didn't want them until now—probably because I didn't want to seem evil, like my mother. Now that I'm lowering my boy into the ground, though, I see the truth, and I hate myself for it.*

**Dr. Cora Crowe:** *What was different about your mother? How come she found it easier to be herself?*

**Sandra Thorsen:** *Because on whatever level she could get away with, she always accepted who she was in that life. In the end, she didn't care what people thought of her. That was her superpower.*

"Get up," somebody said to Lindsay. The words came as sensations in her mind—thoughts, but clearer than any sounds she had ever heard.

It was a woman. She was standing in a realm of light that Lindsay, even with her eyes closed, didn't feel ready to acknowledge.

*"I'm not sure I can,"* she thought back, slowly registering that the events occurring in the mine with Lowell Grendel were now both far away and in a completely different construct of space-time.

Lindsay opened her eyes—which were now mere echoes of her old body's eyes—and looked at the woman. Yes, it was indeed Taconite Rose. She wore a gentle expression on her pocked face, and her ragged dress hung like shimmers under an old-fashioned coat.

She was surrounded by the light. Perhaps even made of it.

*"You always have a choice,"* Rose said.

Thinking of Lowell Grendel, of the violence he'd been unable to contain, Lindsay said, *"My brother, Drew, didn't."*

Except that was an assumption, wasn't it? Could she really claim to understand the ways of the physical world she had just left?

"*There's more for you to do,*" Rose insisted. "*Find a way out. Do it for Drew.*"

Lindsay had no idea what Rose meant. She looked down, through this new world of light, and saw her own motionless body. Not even half-buried in the collapse, it was lying horizontally across the mine tunnel with the dirt mound's edge just touching her head and feet.

Yet the light behind Rose was so beautiful. So inviting. Whatever it signified—perhaps a gateway toward some level of existence Lindsay couldn't yet conceive of—it felt like the safest, easiest, and most welcoming option. Everyone died, didn't they?

Then she thought of the people she cared about most: her father, Alan Sparks, Elijah Bryce, Molly Butler, and even Natalie Pent.

*Go to them. Make one last effort. Tell them where you are.*

The impulse came from the depths of her soul. And the moment she perceived it, she realized that the dimension of reality her old body was trapped in—including that old abandoned taconite mine—was a balance of projection and perception, an ever-shifting reflection of her deeper self. It was all made of energy. *Her* energy.

The moment Lindsay surrendered to it, she was sailing not into the light but through it—back toward her friends and family.

"You think all our issues are my fault, but *you* dragged us to this god-awful town," Sandra Thorsen said to David Thorsen under the ambient lights of their back patio.

She extended an icy-cold finger from her gin-and-tonic glass, and David took a step back in reflex.

"*You're* the reason we lost Lindsay and Drew. And this"—Sandra gestured with her free hand toward their empty house—"is like a prison I can't escape. Even if I wanted to go somewhere, I couldn't, because I have no money. No job. No skills."

"Then why don't you do something about it?" David said. "You just sit around drinking and smoking and having affairs with *god* knows who instead of—"

"This isn't about the affairs!" Sandra hissed. "Jesus, David. You never fucking get it!"

Images writhed in David's mind: skin, bodies, his wife taking the flesh, energy, and life force of other men. Yet he had no right to feel jealous, let alone revolted. He had done the same with other women—first his assistant, Mia Waltrix, and as of tonight, Natalie Pent.

"Okay—if I'm not getting it, then tell me," he continued. "Is this about more than just Lindsay and Drew?"

The question seemed to hit Sandra's drunken brain like a hot knife, melting through her emotions like butter. "It's about *way* more than that, David. *Way* more."

"Our marriage, then?"

Sandra spread her arms wide in an extravagant shrug. "What even is marriage to you, David? Please. I want to know. Because you've always acted like it's supposed to *be* some particular thing, like some prescribed version of life that follows all those Western church vows step by step. But that isn't us, and we've both known it for years. So, my question is: What should we be doing here?"

"We should be *loving* each other!" David yelled, pushing the words through his grief. "You fall down, I pick you up. I fall down, you pick *me* up. Isn't that what marriage is? Unconditional love? 'Good medicine' for each other, as my dad's family would've said? Except you haven't been giving me that. Even before we lost the kids, you seemed completely detached. But I'm *falling* right now, Sandy. I'm fucking *falling*."

Tears gleamed on Sandra's face as the emotional cord connecting them twisted further and further into knots.

"I don't know how to catch you," she whispered.

Nameless emotions swelled in David's chest. He could only stare at Sandra, his broken wife, and remember the day of their wedding, when they had promised to care for each other in good times and in bad, in sickness and in health, till death did they part.

Those promises had been real to him then. They were *still* real.

"I've tried to give you a good life," he said through a rush of tears. "I know I haven't been perfect, but all I ever wanted was to make you happy. I was trying to—"

"You were trying to give me *your* version of a good life!" Sandra screamed. "You might have given me the houses and the cars and the family, but you weren't even *here*. You also never even asked me what I wanted!"

David's mouth hung open. The loaded momentum for his next verbal punch disappeared. He looked into Sandra's bloodshot eyes—*caves of despair*, he thought—and waited to hear her truth.

"When I was pregnant with Lindsay, you never even asked me if I wanted to keep her," she whispered. The words bled from her mouth.

Flashes of their past hit David's mind: their meeting at a Labor Day barbecue in Naperville, Illinois; their not-quite-defined first three months of dating; and then—oh so quickly—that walk along Chicago's Lakefront Trail, when Sandra unexpectedly told him she was pregnant. It had happened so fast, yet what had his reaction been? He had pulled her into a hug. Comforted her. Told her that yes, he would help her raise this baby—even marry her—and give her the best life his budding finance career could afford.

But now this: a truth he had never once suspected.

"You didn't want Lindsay and Drew?" he whispered.

Sandra stared at him, brittle-faced. Tears rushed down her cheeks, free of their prison. Then, shaking her head, she spoke ten words that shattered David's soul. "I just wanted to *live*, David. I wanted to *live*."

L INDSAY NEEDED ONLY TO IMAGINE herself standing in front of her father to make it so. He was in their living room, sitting on the couch, holding both his cell phone and their cordless land-line phone. His hands were shaking as if he were realizing that life would never again be as simple as he had once thought.

*"Dad!"* Lindsay screamed, remembering only after the words were out that she was merely an imprint of her old self; she no longer had a physical mouth. Even her tears were phantom. *"Dad, please! Help me! I'm in Arrowhead Hills! I'm trapped!"*

On the couch, David Thorsen cocked his head, seemingly trying to make sense of some impossible sensation. When he looked up, his eyes immediately focused on Lindsay as if he already knew where she would be standing.

"Lindsay?" he whispered. "Honey! Where were you? The police told me to wait here. God—I didn't even hear the door. I—"

*"I'm not there!"* Lindsay screamed. *"Please, listen to me! I'm in*

*Arrowhead Hills! In the mine where Taconite Rose died! Call Molly and Elijah—they'll tell you everything!"*

But the effort was futile. Her father was only shaking his head in confusion.

Through the silence of Lindsay's disembodied screams, realization dawned on his face. "Honey? Are you there?"

*"I love you, Daddy,"* Lindsay said, knowing she could do nothing more to reach him. Even though time was different here, she knew her physical body, still trapped in the mine, had very little of it left.

Shaping her intent a second time, she focused on Natalie Pent, her first friend in End Haven.

And suddenly—

—DAVID THORSEN TASTED THE TEARS falling from his own eyes. "I thought all this was enough for you," he whispered to his wife, Sandra. "I thought—"

"That's right: you *thought*," Sandra cut in through her own sobs. "But I hated this life, David. You were never home, and motherhood was *lonely*. My parents weren't around to help, and we all knew what your mother thought of me."

David shook his head furiously as if it might erase Sandra's truth. "My mom never hated you. She just had reservations about the fact that you never opened up about anything! She only ever heard you talk about surface stuff, and—"

"Because I was never happy!" Sandra screamed. Now she began pacing back and forth. "I loved you when I got pregnant with Lindsay, but I had *goals*! I wanted to do more with my life! Become a therapist, maybe. Help people. But then—"

"You can still have goals, Sandy! Hell, my dad told me I needed to have goals by age ten—it's why I always pressured myself to do well. I never expected you to just—"

"To just what? Raise your kids? You weren't about to get a nanny after all that talk about how 'thankful' you were your dad worked his ass off back in the day so your mom could raise you at home. Hell, I remember you even *praising* him for how successfully he dominated rich White culture after leaving his tribe as a kid—how you wanted to be just like him and make sure your wife didn't have to work. *You* said that."

Humiliation bloomed alongside the truth in David's chest. He wiped away a rush of tears.

"And maybe now I *could* have goals again if . . . if . . ." Sandra backed away from him, shaking her head. She let out another rasping sob, then glanced left and right, as though finally worried the neighbors might be listening. ". . . if we weren't *here*," she finally whispered. "If we weren't tied to this godforsaken place as the parents of two dead kids we'll never get back. The way people look at us . . . I can't even go out now. Not without wanting to bury myself alive somewhere. And now you're having sex with Natalie Goddamned Pent, and I'm just—"

"I'm sorry, Sandra. I'm so sorry. I was just—"

"I don't care about the sex, David!" She stopped pacing and looked David straight in the eyes. "I'm just saying: I need to let the Idle County Seven stuff go. I need to *leave*." She shook her head with a dire chuckle. "And I saw the email you sent to all the parents about Molly Butler and Max Pope. *None* of them responded, David. Not a single one. I honestly think it's because everyone just wants to move on. The cops aren't going to figure it out, and I can't keep theorizing. So, no. I don't care what Natalie Pent heard. I don't care about Victor Zobel and his friend with the snake tattoo. I don't care if they were both here the day Lindsay disappeared. I just need to escape it! I need to get out."

"Where do you want to go?" David whispered.

"Somewhere warm. Somewhere with color. Maybe California."

David sniffed back his tears, recalling their short (and very late) honeymoon in Sausalito, California. Sandra had already been four months pregnant when they got married, and they hadn't found time to celebrate until Lindsay was three.

"Are you saying you want to move out there on your own?" he asked.

Sandra shrugged, and her entire frame shuddered under her tears. "I just know I can't live like this and do nothing. I have to do something for myself, or I seriously think I might end up dead, like everyone else in this fucking town. I know you've thought it yourself."

They stared at each other for almost a minute. All their cards were on the table, and David knew in his soul that the future—the one he had promised Natalie Pent he'd live to see—hung in the balance.

"Then we move to California," he said. "We restart."

Sandra nodded. "I have to."

"And what about the affairs?"

"I don't care what you do, as long as you let me be me," Sandra said. "I need to have a life that *I* want to live. And I'll promise to do the same for you. Whatever that means."

Raphael Dumont's name hung in David's mind like a shadow.

"Then I need to do one more thing before letting Lindsay go," he said.

Sandra waited.

In his mind, David saw the trip to France he had started to discuss with Natalie Pent. Saw their investigation into Raphael Dumont. Saw their newly intertwined path open up as—

—LINDSAY WATCHED NATALIE wake up in her bed. The girl looked groggy, detached from her nighttime reality. The clock on her nightstand read 11:23 p.m.

Natalie's bedroom had changed in the four months since Lindsay had visited; she had torn down the girly collage of hot boys behind her pillow and replaced it with a generic poster of the ocean, as if she were trying to play the part of someone older.

Natalie's gaze locked on Lindsay, and she bolted upright in bed. "Jesus, Lindsay! What the fuck?"

*"Help me!"* Lindsay tried to scream, using all the mental power she could muster. *"If you can see me, call my dad or Molly Butler or Elijah Bryce or the police! Tell them I'm stuck in a mine in Arrowhead Hills! Please!"*

Somehow, despite being outside her body, Lindsay could still feel emotions. Could still cry. Could still miss her old world, where her body was now dying in a collapsed mine. Her words were still illusory, however, just like her sobs.

Natalie shook her head in wide-eyed shock, blinking multiple times, as if she were trying to decide whether Lindsay was actually there. In a surge of panic, she threw one of her bed's decorative pillows straight through Lindsay as—

—Lydia Clark ran in the dark, thinking *Fuck, fuck, fuck*.

Everything had gone wrong. So, so wrong. Her mother had been right. Her ex-boyfriends had been right. Hell, even the people of Providence, Rhode Island, had been right—at least through their blind eyes and lack of engagement with any of the independent news on her failing blog.

*You're a star, Lydia,* her grandmother had always said. *Don't you ever let anyone tell you what you can't do.*

Deep down, Lydia had always clung to this. Her grandmother had been the only encouraging person in her life, the only one pushing her to heed that rush of intuition in her heart telling her to *follow the dream.*

But fuck the dream. It had led her here, to the middle of nowhere in the smack-dab center of Washington's Olympic Goddamned Peninsula. Towering pine trees caved in all around her, and she suddenly remembered that this was true wilderness in pitch darkness. There were wild animals out here—nocturnal ones—and all she had to scare them off was the LED flashlight from her ActoPhone.

Questions swirled in her mind.

Why had there been guns?

Why had she trusted Raphael Dumont?

Why hadn't she realized that Victor Zobel, the man behind the fucking curtain, really was at the center of all this madness?

Lydia tripped over a branch and went flying to the ground. Her face hit first, scraping along the dirt and rocks hidden under the pine needles covering the forest floor.

Above her, clouds obstructed the stars. She imagined creatures skulking toward her in the dark.

Would this be the last night of her life?

*Up, up, up!*

Lydia's feet wobbled as she righted herself. She glanced backward. The light from Jonathan Flite's campfire and yurt was still visible—barely a glow. Had Raphael been identified? Had he even intended on walking out of this forest alive?

Maybe it wouldn't even matter. She'd be seen as an accomplice no matter what; she had led Raphael Dumont here, and now everything had gone to hell.

He had been edgy. He had been mysterious. He had promised to fulfill her life dream by sharing stories that might jump-start her career, hooking her even before he was famous, before that bitch from Idle County—Natalie Goddamned Pent—had so recklessly smeared his name in the *New York Times*.

For almost two years, Lydia had liked Raphael Dumont—even after finding out that all he'd really wanted was to exchange information. To get a piece of her pie and to give her a piece of his. Even if she were never to get her remaining $500,000, she could consider their relationship clean. Legal. A done deal.

But then he'd put a gun to her head in the car today.

Just so he could give something to Jonathan Flite.

*Bat Racko Toxin.*

Lydia hadn't understood the first two words—or syllables—Raphael had used, but she'd understood what the psychiatrist Thomas Lumen yelled out next: that it was a *poison.*

Even so, she hadn't been able to hear the rest of Raphael's exchange with Jonathan, because she'd been too focused on Michael Flite, who was approaching Raphael with a raised hunting rifle. Then had come someone else—a middle-aged woman also holding a rifle. Lydia hadn't even noticed her until a hard muzzle pressed into her back.

*"Don't you fucking move,"* the woman had said.

The rest was already a blur. Lydia had caught the first few seconds of the standoff on video with her ActoLenses, but then there had been gunfire, and she'd bolted into the night.

Yet she hadn't recorded Raphael's sudden turn on her earlier that evening or his forcing her into the woods at gunpoint. The true story would be muddled regardless of how she cut it.

There were shapes ahead now. Cars.

*The parking lot.*

When Lydia emerged from the forest, she finally slowed so she could catch her breath and listen.

Screams echoed in the distance.

Looking up, she expected still to see more clouds, but they had opened to reveal a diamond-shaped patch of dazzling night sky. It touched the edges of the trees.

It would take her less than thirty minutes to drive back to Hoodsport. From there, it would be another ninety to Seattle-Tacoma International Airport. If she could get out now—tonight, before the story broke and before Jonathan Flite's location made the news—she might escape any suspicion attached to her name. Unless—

A stick cracked behind her.

Then came the muffled patter of footsteps on pine needles.

*Someone running.*

Lydia reacted like a scared deer, immediately bracing herself to run, only to meet paralysis. When she heard the person's light pant—not Raphael's—she had to orient herself to remember where her rental car was parked.

*Far back. Left side, if you're facing the road.*

She moved. As her feet crunched over the dirt, she reached into her pocket, feeling for the key fob, and—thank God. It was still there. She pulled it out, pressed the touch screen, and unlocked her rental car.

"Wait!" the person behind her screamed. It was a woman.

Lydia turned, holding out her ActoPhone's flashlight to blind whoever it was.

"Lydia, wait!"

*Fuck.*

The panting figure waved her arms.

It was Clovia Bell, the creative producer from *WorldLine*.

"Stay back!" Lydia screamed. "I'm getting out of here!"

Clovia started toward her. "Please, wait! We need to talk!"

Lydia had no reason to be afraid of Clovia Bell, yet she found herself retreating just the same. "You stay back," she said. "I didn't do anything wrong! I didn't know what Raphael was going to do. He forced me to come here, and—"

"I don't care! Just—please hear me out." Clovia stopped and stood there, gasping and watching Lydia as her breaths slowed. "I know you're going to break this story. I'm just hoping you can do it right. I want to help."

"Bullshit. You're just—"

"Jonathan's friend Jimmy Barber told us about you. He said he visited you in the hospital after Weston Carrow's bomb went off in Newport. That you were trying to start your own news site last year."

Lydia shuddered as her ego cracked, threatening to become dust.

"I can help," Clovia said. "I can get you on CBS. As soon as we get cell service, I can give you a voice. But please—I don't know how much you heard, but if people get the wrong idea about what happened here tonight, it could have serious ramifications."

*Oh, fuck off,* Lydia thought. If all this girl cared about was bad PR, then she could go straight to—

"I'm just asking you to wait until we can get the police and medics out here," Clovia pressed. "We need to give our statements."

The young woman was serious. Sincere. A fucking *Goody Two-shoes.*

"I don't need you," Lydia said, fully aware that she was throwing away the opportunity of her lifetime. But fuck CBS. Fuck Clovia Bell. The world was itching for news of Jonathan Flite, and come hell or high water, Lydia was going to give it to them *her* way.

"Could you drive us to where we have cell reception?" Clovia continued. "We need to call 911 and get the—"

"I'll call 911 as soon as I get the hell out of these goddamned woods. But I'm not going anywhere with the girlfriend of a murderer. You take your own fucking car."

Clovia stood her ground. "The police are going to wonder why you left. Why you didn't stay to answer questions."

"Then I'll figure out a fucking answer!" Lydia said through gritted teeth. "But this—whatever it was, I didn't mean for it to happen. I had no idea what Raphael wanted."

"Then you should know the FBI's going to get involved," Clovia said, taking another step forward. "They're going to know you were here. There's a reason we didn't mention Raphael Dumont in the *WorldLine* documentary."

Crushed under the weight of her mistakes, Lydia shuddered. "What reason?"

"I can't say," was Clovia's only reply.

In its vagueness, the statement allowed Lydia to find her footing. She locked eyes with Clovia for a second, then turned and ran for her rental car, leaving the young woman standing alone in the dark, in front of—

—MOLLY BUTLER. If anyone would be able to hear Lindsay, it was Molly, the one who no longer wanted to talk about ghosts. Who no longer wanted to believe in them. Who no longer wanted to be touched by her peculiar gift to see the dead.

The black-haired girl was awake in her bed and wearing a stony expression when Lindsay appeared in front of her. Light from her dim bed lamp bloomed on the room's salmon-pink walls, illuminating her hands as she held what looked like a pink notebook. On its cover page were twelve letters written in big blocky penmanship.

**THE GHOST HUNT**

At the exact moment Lindsay read the words, Molly looked up and saw her.

First, her expression was one of confusion. Then it shifted to belief. Finally, it became fear.

When Lindsay spoke, it was like a conversation. She could already feel a connection emanating from Molly's mind, stronger than it had been with her father or Natalie Pent. Lindsay knew she wouldn't have to work to reach Molly.

"Lindsay?" Molly said, speaking first.

*"I need your help!"* Lindsay screamed. *"He took me! Lowell Grendel! He took me outside the community center after kickboxing. I'm in that mine up north, in Arrowhead Hills, where Taconite Rose died. I'm trapped, and I need help to get out!"*

Tears formed in Molly's eyes, and she shook her head frantically. "Arrowhead Hills? Did I actually hear that? I don't know if you're real or just in my head!"

*"Yes! Yes, Arrowhead Hills!"* Lindsay screamed, nodding her head. *"Call the police! Call my dad!"*

Molly's head shaking became a vigorous nod, and suddenly Lindsay was flying again, knowing there was another unexpected friend who had brightened her life during the last few months, one who had given her reason to—

"—GO TO FRANCE. There's something about the case I have to check on there, and then I promise I'll let it go," David Thorsen said to his wife, Sandra.

Balance suspended itself between them as she waited for him to continue.

"I need to talk to this Raphael Dumont guy if I can. All the stuff Natalie Pent was saying—it raised too many questions for me not to follow up. Everything about Rebecca Sparks, Victor Zobel, and, hell, even that damned flashlight the police still have locked in evidence from the night Lowell Grendel took Lindsay. She grabbed that thing from outside her body, Sandy. She really, truly did. If Victor Zobel is somehow covering up answers about how or why that might've been possible, I need to know. But if I don't get answers, I'll let it all go. This time for good."

The night's breeze had grown chilly—autumn, hinting at winter. Sandra shivered under it as she contemplated David's words.

"You go to France, and I'll get our house on the market," she finally said. "Then we restart. Or I swear to God, I'll walk out and do it myself."

David finally closed the five-step gap that separated him from Sandra and wrapped her in a hug. She hung in his embrace, and for a long time, neither of them spoke. As his emptiness found hers in the dark, David thought back on his lost children: Drew, who had disappeared, and Lindsay, who had become interested in ghosts the winter after. It was all a tangled web. Lowell Grendel had started it, but hadn't Max Pope been the one to continue it? Hadn't he been the one who targeted Lindsay, Molly, and—

"*E*LIJAH.*"

Unlike Molly Butler, Elijah Bryce wasn't awake when Lindsay appeared at the foot of his bed.

"*Elijah!*"

As he stirred under his covers, Lindsay realized she could walk. Or was she floating? It didn't matter, because in the next instant, she found herself leaning over Elijah's left ear, which faced the ceiling. She was close enough to touch his mind.

"*Thank you for being my friend,*" Lindsay whispered.

Elijah's hand flew up to his ear as if he were swatting a fly. Then it floated gently down to rest on his cheek.

In the same moment, something glinted on his dresser, next to a red lava lamp. Lindsay immediately knew the glint was significant, as if reality itself were directing her to it.

Simply by thinking it, she was floating next to the dresser, looking down at a shiny metallic object.

It was cylindrical but tall. The shaft of a handle? It had a switch near the middle, like—

*Like a flashlight.*

The device was standing on its face, handle facing up.

Lindsay hovered close enough to sense the particles making up the metal. Knowledge that she was one with them felt innate on this side; they were like masks at a masquerade ball—camouflage for a deeper reality. The truth of it slinked into her mind with perfect grace.

There was something etched in the flashlight's metal—a delicate engraving:

*E.C.B.*

*Elijah Christopher Bryce.*

He stirred in his bed again.

Lindsay forced her mind to take its old shape, to echo the energetic imprint of her old body. The more she focused, the more solid she felt. She could feel her energy swirling as if it were excited to reengage with the thicker, more viscous world that had, until tonight, so thoroughly weighed her down.

*Grab the flashlight!* all her instincts cried in unison. *Do it while you still can!*

Suddenly, it was in her hand. She could feel it, but instead of being cold, its metal handle was warm—almost alive—as if the particles creating it were pulling up their own masks. In that moment, Lindsay knew they themselves were somehow conscious and connected to her very essence.

She'd been planning to visit Alan Sparks next, but now with the flashlight in her hand, she knew it wasn't necessary. She didn't need to say goodbye.

Because she would live to see another day.

She would survive to see Alan again. And her friends.

She would celebrate every day of life she had left with them, because they had shone bright, like beacons of hope, during this dark and most challenging year.

With a burst of joy she would never again feel until the moment of her death, she disappeared from Elijah's bedroom, along with his flashlight.

AN EXCERPT FROM THE AUDIO TRANSCRIPT of Sandra Jean Thorsen's first past-life regression with Dr. Cora Noreen Crowe on November 22, 2034:

**Sandra Thorsen:** *I'm outside my body now. Going toward a light, like everybody always describes. But I already know it's just my consciousness shedding that body's physical brain. This is what it looks like to die.*

**Dr. Cora Crowe:** *I do hear that often. But right now I want you to look back on your life as this Puritan man. Look back on how you didn't embrace your passions or take the paths you wanted to take. How does all that feel now that this life has passed?*

**Sandra Thorsen:** *I'm relieved. And all of this feels familiar* *again. It's lighter than air here, after death. And so color-ful! But—gosh. I really wasn't happy with that life.*

**Dr. Cora Crowe:** *That's okay. We all have lives that teach us how we might have done better.*

**Sandra Thorsen:** *Yes, I suppose.*

**Dr. Cora Crowe:** *What do you see next?*

*[Pause.]*

**Sandra Thorsen:** *Rest, finally. My guides are taking me to rest, and then to discuss the life I just lived.*

*[Pause.]*

**Sandra Thorsen:** *I know I'll be going through all the choices I made and all their alternatives. I've done this before.*

**Dr. Cora Crowe:** *Can you tell me more about what hap-pens now that you're dead?*

**Sandra Thorsen:** *Well, it's immediately more peaceful on this side. More universal. I'm not just the miserable Puritan man who lost his mother and children. I'm also Sandra Thorsen. And every other person I've lived as, be-cause there's no time here. There's only a sense of my full self—and how it's part of something much greater. I'm always aware of that here.*

**Dr. Cora Crowe:** *Is there anything else you can take back into your life as Sandra Thorsen? Any special knowledge?*

**Sandra Thorsen:** *My guides are saying yes. They're telling me I'm perfect the way I am. That my not wanting Lindsay and Drew was okay. And that the biggest thing holding me back right now is the guilt I still feel about it.*

**Dr. Cora Crowe:** *Can you explain that in more detail?*

**Sandra Thorsen:** *It's just that . . . I've always inwardly beaten myself up for feeling relieved that I got a chance to pursue the life I actually wanted. But they're saying . . .*

*[Pause.]*

**Dr. Cora Crowe:** *Saying . . .?*

**Sandra Thorsen:** *That I still loved them. Lindsay and Drew. Even though I never wanted kids, I loved them just the same.*

*[Pause from Sandra Thorsen as she begins to cry.]*

**Sandra Thorsen:** *It was always a contradiction. But my guides are saying I can let that go. They're saying that Lindsay and Drew chose me as a mother before coming into life. Not just to explore their own paths of development but also so they could teach me how to be myself. To be proud of who I am.*

**Dr. Cora Crowe:** *And does that lesson satisfy the missed opportunity in your life as the Puritan man? Or is it just in your life as Sandra?*

**Sandra Thorsen:** *It's both. Because both are me. All my lives are me.*

L INDSAY OPENED HER EYES to blackness. It was freezing cold, and the heaviest weight she had ever felt pressed against the back side of her body. Somewhere behind her, close but buried, were the muffled sounds of Lowell Grendel screaming and suffocating.

In her hands was something cylindrical. A handle. It was ribbed and warm but growing cooler by the second.

*You're alive.*

*You're back in your body, in the taconite mine.*

Lindsay realized she was still breathing. Her mouth and face were free to gasp in the frigid air, but there was dirt in her throat. In the distance, however—at least three hundred feet ahead—was a bluish dot of brightness in her vision.

*The moon. It's glowing on the trees outside the mine's opening.*

It was light. A beacon of hope.

Next to her, invisible but present, was Taconite Rose.

*"You need to crawl out, Lindsay!"* she screamed.

Because something was tickling Lindsay's spine through the dirt. At first it was subtle, like a worm. Then it grew fingertips and started grabbing her by the shirt.

*"Get out right now!"* Rose yelled.

The muffled cries from the dirt mound grew louder just as it became clear that the person—*Lowell Grendel, it's Lowell Fucking Grendel!*—was trying to survive being suffocated by the collapse.

"No!" Lindsay screamed as she rolled out from under the mound. She fought a wave of nausea as more dirt fell around her. Her limbs were too heavy to move.

*No—you're not giving up that easily,* her intuition commanded. *Get up and run.*

*"Right now!"* Taconite Rose shrieked.

Another section of the ceiling fell as Lindsay turned onto all fours and began crawling toward the light. Her knuckles, wrapped around Elijah Bryce's flashlight, split open as they dug into the ground. As the skin covering them scraped away, her own hot blood picked up every ice-cold rock and frozen bit of dirt in her path. Yet this was it: her last chance to survive.

*Push, push, push.*

The mine's opening inched closer.

When Lindsay was finally clear enough from the collapse to stand up, her vision blurred. A gaping pain shot through the back of her head, and it grew more and more severe every second. She touched it with her free hand and felt a warm mess of dirt, hair, and blood.

*It doesn't matter. Go!*

Lindsay reached the mouth of the mine shaft and switched Elijah's flashlight on. As she struggled to stay upright, Molly Butler's shocked face rose in her fading mind.

Had her out-of-body visits to her father, Natalie, Molly, and Elijah been real? Had any of them heard her?

And even more important, was there any chance she might escape this abandoned town alive?

*Alan. Survive for him, because you didn't get to say goodbye.*

Lindsay nodded to herself in the silent darkness.

On the road up ahead was Lowell's car—a sedan, different than the Jeep searched by police back in December. Maybe it would still be unlocked. Perhaps even warm.

Lindsay made a final charge toward it. Ten feet from the road, however, her legs gave out. She collapsed into the hard, shallow snow at just the right angle to aim the blinding beam of Elijah's flashlight into the sky. She lay there for nearly thirty minutes, forcing herself to breathe, to stay awake, to hope. And yes, the fight was worth it, because the last thing she heard before losing consciousness was the chopping whir of an approaching helicopter.

PART 7

NOW YOU'VE
DONE IT

<br>

A N EXCERPT FROM the *Providence Journal* on June 20, 2040:

### *Providence "Reporter" Outs*
### *Jonathan Flite, Hits It Big Before Arrest*
#### *By Carl Harvey*

*PROVIDENCE — Lydia Clark, the amateur news blogger from Providence who leaked nurse killer Jonathan Flite's location in Washington this past Tuesday, has been arrested and charged with aiding and abetting suspected criminal Raphael Dumont in an attempted conspiracy to murder scorned celebrity atheist Victor Zobel and in the murder of Michael Flite, Jonathan Flite's uncle. Clark, according to sources, has spent the last six years pursuing her dream of being an independent news reporter, but that dream came crashing down on Tuesday, when the FBI raided her apartment in Elmwood.*

*On June 17, Clark published a "tell-all" text allegedly written by Dumont to her news blog,* Providence Today. *The confession documented Dumont's years in Victor Zobel's inner circle—and his purported involvement in the murders of the Idle County Seven, a group of Minnesota teens who famously went missing in 2010. The unsolved cold case, along with Jonathan Flite's claims of having "past-life memories" of the missing teens, was recently investigated by celebrity journalist Alice Winterblume in her hit docuseries,* WorldLine. *The show also went on to outline the first substantive links between Victor Zobel and the 2037 nuclear terrorist attack in Geneva, Switzerland.*

*Clark's single blog post containing Dumont's confession, which has since been removed from her site, accompanied a self-recorded ActoLens video (also removed) of her Tuesday trek with Dumont to a yurt camp on Washington's Olympic Peninsula. The camp was privately owned by the deceased Michael Flite, who was helping his nephew hide from the public eye following the young man's recent featured appearance on* WorldLine. *Dumont, who allegedly forced Clark to the camp at gunpoint, later died from wounds suffered during an unexpected shootout.*

*Dumont recently made headlines after Idle County resident Natalie Pent publicly accused Alice Winterblume of omitting damning circumstantial evidence against him from the latest season of* WorldLine. *Pent's* New York Times *op-ed, which presented her suspicions of Dumont's involvement in multiple murders in Minnesota between 2007 and 2010, aligned almost fully with Dumont's supposed written confession briefly posted to* Providence Today *on Tuesday. Further aligning with Pent's suspicions are Dumont's claims of having known Geneva bomber Jean-Claude Apostol while both men lived in Saint-Paul de Vence, France. According to the text, Victor Zobel paid Dumont to build and maintain a relationship with Apostol through the years, going as far as renting lavish homes for Dumont in every Roman Catholic ecclesiastical province where Apostol served during his ascendancy to the rank of cardinal. Dumont claimed Zobel took regular "private meetings" with Apostol and "egged the cardinal on about how big a threat science was to both Christianity and the concept of God."*

*Dumont's putative confession further accused Zobel of other underhanded activities, including the monitoring of his stepdaughter, Jillian Pope, in Minnesota from late 2008 to mid-2010 and illegally trafficking high-tech weapons—including multiple portable weapons of mass destruction—out of Ukraine and into multiple locations throughout Europe, Asia, and the Middle East.*

*Despite the removal of Clark's post yesterday, multiple news sources obtained copies of the confession and published snippets of it after she alerted them to its existence. Clark's accompanying ActoVid, also copied by multiple sources, depicted not only her collusion with Dumont in tracking down Jonathan Flite on his uncle's private property but also Dumont's attempt to give the young man and his girlfriend a small unidentified object.*

*Clark's heavy breathing obscured any audio explaining what this object might have been. The video, which may have been truncated, stopped shortly after she retreated from the gunfight.*

*Also present in the skirmish were the psychiatrist Thomas Lumen, who briefly appeared in WorldLine's recent docuseries, and Dominic Bock, Jonathan Flite's biological father. Neither could be reached for comment.*

*Despite online reactions to the video speculating that Clark seemed unaware of Dumont's intent in seeking out Jonathan Flite, she remains in police custody as of Thursday evening. She could not be reached for comment.*

O N SUNDAY, FEBRUARY 19, 2006, Lindsay Thorsen sat opposite her parents, David and Sandra, in their mostly unused decorative living room. It was a mirror image of her discussion with Agent Forester and Detective Rhymes last November 1, when the two law enforcement officials questioned her following Drew's disappearance.

Yesterday morning, before she left Saint Mary's Hospital in End Haven, her parents had scheduled this talk. The doctors had kept her under watch for three days after the incident with Lowell Grendel, to monitor both her head injury and her reaction to his ketamine injection. Now here she was: both lost *and* found. While she hated the heavy bandages on the back of her head, she was present. Alive. Back in reality, but also questioning its very nature.

"Honey—" David started, but he stopped when he noticed Lindsay's unfazed eye contact.

She allowed him to collect his thoughts.

"We just want to talk about what happened," David finally said before glancing at Lindsay's mother.

But Sandra was staring at Lindsay as if she were some sort of inexplicable aberration.

"Sandy, do you have anything to add here?" David pressed.

Lindsay's mother, cold as ice, said, "I want to know how in the hell you really got that flashlight. The police said Shelly Bryce saw it on Elijah's dresser the same day you took it."

"Sandy—"

"*No.* I want to know right now how the *fuck* you got it. It had to have been in your gym bag, because you didn't go to Elijah's at all that day."

"It *wasn't* in my gym bag," Lindsay replied, determined not to cave to her mother's disbelief. "Not to mention that I didn't have the bag when Lowell took me into that mine. It was locked in the trunk of his rental car. You can ask the police."

When Sandra only sneered in response, Lindsay came to a troubling realization: that her mother was simply another person and that their biological bond was just that—biological. They might never see eye to eye; they might never even like each other. Since her father would always be caught in the middle, it seemed clear enough that Lindsay was now *here*, and her parents were *there*. In her heart, she knew this gap would never be bridged. Not while she was alive, at least.

"Sandy, you already heard what Lindsay told Detective Rhymes," David said, injecting a bit of sharpness. "Not to mention that we wouldn't have even found her if Molly Butler hadn't called our landline—*regardless* of how she found out where Lindsay was. But I'm telling you: I *saw* Lindsay that night, just like Molly did."

"Oh yeah? Then how come *you* didn't hear her screaming? How come this freaky little Molly girl—"

"Sandy—"

But Sandra's face was like molten stone. "No. I won't believe *nonsense*, David! Our daughter didn't leave her body and become a ghost. That was just the ketamine. And if you're actually going to sit there and believe that, then . . ." She collapsed into her own anger and looked out the window.

David looked to Lindsay for support, but Lindsay could only shrug.

"I told the police the truth," she said. "A ghost helped me. She was following Lowell Grendel around because he took Drew. She's always in a raggedy old dress, and people call her Taconite Rose."

When Sandra rolled her eyes again, Lindsay adopted an even firmer tone.

"If the police don't want people to know the truth—or if *you* guys don't—that's fine. But I'm not dealing with these sorts of questions after today. I'd say it all might have been the ketamine if it weren't for the flashlight—*and* for Molly hearing me and telling Dad where I was. Those things prove I left my body. I *did* visit Dad and Molly and Natalie and Elijah. I was about to visit Alan Sparks, but then—"

"Why *them*?" Sandra hissed. "Why didn't you visit *me*?"

Lindsay studied her mother's face. The anger in it pulsed with many shades, some so grief-stricken that it was impossible for Lindsay to find a good answer. "You weren't the first person I thought of," she finally said, settling for the truth.

Sandra recoiled as if the words had slapped her face. Both Lindsay and her father watched the woman stand up and stomp out of the living room, her silk bathrobe drifting behind her like a ghost's floating white shroud.

2034

S ANDRA THORSEN STEPPED OUT of Dr. Cora Crowe's plush therapy room in Boulder, Colorado, feeling light as air. Her husband, David, had run ahead to fetch their rental car, so the only other person in the office besides Dr. Crowe was Taisha, the psychiatrist's ravishing daughter, who had checked Sandra in earlier that afternoon.

As if reading Sandra's mind, Dr. Crowe, who was following a few steps behind, walked around the desk and put a hand on the young woman's shoulder. "Sandra, I take it you met my daughter Taisha earlier?"

Sandra, now realizing Taisha's mesmerizing blue eyes were the same as her mother's, smiled politely. Taisha smiled back.

"Honey, I told Sandra here I'd give her copies of my other books—she already has *Our Many Lives*. Do you still have the others in that box back here?"

"Just the first three," Taisha said. "I gave away the last new one a few days ago."

She handed her mother two books—one called *Love Between Lives* and another called *Live in Your Light*. The psychiatrist presented them to Sandra. "Here, as promised. Partially."

"I'll buy the new one online," Sandra replied.

Taisha watched the book handoff closely. "Was the session everything you expected? You sounded nervous earlier."

"I honestly don't have an answer for that yet," Sandra said. "But God, was it ever vivid. It definitely made me think."

"We get that a lot," the young woman replied.

Sandra recognized something in her smile: a pasted-on look, as if she weren't altogether happy to be sitting behind her mother's front desk.

"Taisha here just graduated from CU," Dr. Crowe said. "She's actually thinking of moving to California. I keep telling her I couldn't bear to lose her, but she keeps saying she needs to get the hell out of Colorado."

"Everything happens for a reason, right?" Sandra said. Without a second thought, she unshouldered her purse, pulled out a business card, and handed it to Taisha. "If you ever make it to San Francisco, let me know. I'm sure David and I could help you land on your feet."

The dissatisfaction underscoring Taisha's demeanor flickered. "You're serious?"

"Of course." Sandra now felt even lighter. For the first time ever, the idea of helping someone else pursue a dream—unweighted, guilt-free, wings spread wide—was actually appealing. She glanced back at Dr. Crowe. "Not to mention that I'll probably be in touch anyway if Alice Winterblume really does make this Jonathan Flite documentary. Though, from what she told my husband, it might not be for a few years yet."

Intrigue glimmered in Dr. Crowe's eyes. "Please keep me posted on that. I'd love to participate, if she'd ever be interested. And that physicist you mentioned—I'll definitely Google her. I'm so curious if she's gone public with any of her theories yet. I wonder if they'll corroborate any of the stuff this Jonathan Flite kid is talking about."

Taisha cocked her head and looked between both women. "As in Jonathan Flite, that Rhode Island nurse killer?"

Sandra nodded. "My daughter, Lindsay, was one of the kids he claims to remember."

Taisha's eyes widened.

"And I'm serious about calling me if you want to move to California," Sandra continued, extending a hand to the young woman for a friendly goodbye shake. "Let me know if I can help."

"I . . . thanks," Taisha stuttered under Sandra's firm grip.

Dr. Crowe shook Sandra's hand next—slowly, seemingly to gauge the sincerity of her new patient's sudden warmth. "It was a pleasure meeting you today. I'm glad you gave this a shot. Oh, and I'll send the recordings of your session this afternoon. Thanks so much for coming all this way."

"Thank *you* for prying open my rigid mind," Sandra replied, flashing a hesitant, fledgling grin.

She waved, then stepped through the office door. When it clicked behind her, she stood alone in the office building's hallway, wondering what on earth she had just done here, and why oh why it had hit her like a million bullets of light. Sandra's joy rushed so potently through her body that, for a moment, she had to lean against the hallway wall. In her mind, all she saw were images of that life as the Puritan man in Connecticut. Had she made it all up? Did it even matter?

Maybe it didn't. Because right here in this office hallway in Boulder, for the first time since Sandra could remember, her guilt was gone. She was proud of who she was—of moving on after losing her children and reveling in the experiences that loss had unwittingly afforded her.

First it had been the move to California. Then the late-blooming career as a psychotherapist. And finally the three-book deal and house on the San Francisco Fucking Bay. Because this life was hers. It was *hers*.

O N Friday, February 24, under a strict directive from her parents, Lindsay Thorsen went to see her first psychotherapist, a middle-aged woman named Katerina Prewett, who practiced in Wind Prairie. Most adult family friends Lindsay remembered from Chicago had spoken positively about their experiences with therapy, so Lindsay had no qualms about it. The icy silent drive with her mother was by far the worst part.

In southern Minnesota, however, therapy still seemed to be a hush-hush sort of thing people didn't admit to needing. When Lindsay told Molly and Elijah about it during lunch the following Monday, they blushed as if she were letting them in on some deeply personal secret they had no right knowing.

"What kinds of things did you talk about?" Elijah asked, fiddling with his empty lunch bag.

Lindsay glanced over both her shoulders. The only person nearby was the more stringent of the two regular lunch ladies; as always, she was watching with hawklike eyes over the popular kids crowding the center of the cafeteria.

"We talked about a lot, I guess, considering it was just the first session," Lindsay said. "Most of it was about my English essay and how I don't really believe in the death penalty anymore. Some was about my parents, though—basically how we're living in totally different worlds now."

Next to Elijah, Molly watched Lindsay with a perplexing expression—almost one of longing, as if talking to a therapist were just outside her own reach. "Do you think your mom is just freaked out because of what I saw?" she asked, tiptoeing around a full admission of her nighttime vision of Lindsay.

They had already discussed how the ketamine injection from Lowell Grendel couldn't explain Lindsay's out-of-body experience in the collapsed mine shaft—not to mention the fact that Molly had saved Lindsay's life by trusting that her vision of Lindsay was real. Had she not alerted David Thorsen to it, the police would not have sent out search helicopters. Yet the truth of it all dovetailed closely with the subject of ghosts, a topic Molly was still hesitant to discuss.

Wanting to respect the girl's wishes, Lindsay simply shrugged before glancing at Elijah. "It's the flashlight," she said. "My mom still doesn't believe I took it. She thinks I was just high on ketamine."

"I'm still confused about how you *did* take it," Elijah said.

Lindsay acknowledged his confusion with a nod. Whatever had allowed her to command physical reality from that in-between realm— like a ghost moving objects around someone's house—she couldn't label it with a how or a why. It had just *happened*.

The three friends, now bonded by the unknown, ate their lunches in delicate silence for nearly two minutes. Lindsay was just about to fold up her paper lunch bag in tandem with Elijah (she had joined in their peculiar, still-to-be-explained custom) when Molly sat up straighter, turned to her, and asked, "Did you talk to Alan Sparks's sister Rebecca about what happened?"

Lindsay shook her head. "Alan's come over to my house a few times since that night, but I haven't been over there. Why?"

"Oh, nothing," Molly said. "I'm just curious about what she'd say."

Elijah was the one to shrug before raising a humored eyebrow. "I'm guessing she'd say that Lindsay's spirit guides are shining extra bright right now."

But he didn't follow up the comment with a full-on laugh. None of them did.

ON OCTOBER 6, 2012, Natalie Pent stood on the curb outside her parents' house under an overcast morning sky, waiting for David Thorsen's BMW to drive around the north curve of Windsong Road. She was facing the street, because her parents were likely looking out their living room's large bay window, waiting to see her drive off with David to Minneapolis-Saint Paul International Airport—the first stop on the way to Raphael Dumont's hometown of Saint-Paul de Vence, France.

Natalie had told her parents nothing of this recent affair with David, but she guessed they suspected their own version of the truth: that a fit middle-aged man who had lost both his daughter and his decency was pursuing a beautiful younger woman in an attempt to mend his paternal scars in some twisted sexual way. Wasn't that how it always was to people looking in on such romances from the outside?

But Natalie was twenty. Her feet were steady now. She had never even been out of the Midwest, let alone the country, and she needed to make this trip with David Thorsen, if only as an exercise in independence, a step toward being the strong, independent woman she knew she could be. If it were to result in some sort of vindication for the Idle County Seven—and herself, considering how poorly she had treated those kids over the years—that would be icing on the goddamned cake. If she and David were to uncover nothing, no hint of Raphael Dumont's questionable activities with Victor Zobel, at least she'd know they'd tried.

Natalie glanced south, past Elijah Bryce's old house, toward Windsong Road's dead end. Sitting on the lonely, detached plot was the house that had once belonged to the murderer Lowell Grendel. It had been empty since February 15, 2006—the night he took Lindsay Thorsen to that abandoned mine up north. The house's white paint was still chipped, like a fading memory.

Across the dead murderer's backyard was the trail leading to the Moon Woods—now Victor Zobel's property. Natalie thought of the Tickle Me Thai candy wrapper she'd found in that ravine two years ago, how it had become just another dead end amid all the other nebulous hints and false starts. If this trip to investigate Raphael Dumont in France would become the last of them, what then? Would she really be able to let the Idle County Seven mystery go?

*No. Not a chance.*

A car veered south onto Windsong Road. Natalie heard it before she glanced left and saw it.

Yes, it was David's BMW.

Upon stopping, he exited the car and greeted her with a warm "Good morning," then placed her childishly pink luggage in the BMW's trunk, next to his own black roller. He caught her gaze and smiled. "You ready?"

She grinned. "Yeah. I definitely am."

Just like that, very simply, they climbed into the car and pulled away. Neither of them looked back at Natalie's house or at her parents, who were indeed standing at the living room window, tattered with concern.

THE ACTUAL TOWN of Saint-Paul de Vence, France, was a tiny gated medieval village made of stone. Roughly thirty minutes by car from the sparkling city of Nice, it sat perched along the French Riviera, overlooking the house-speckled countryside to the north and the Mediterranean Sea to the south.

The first thing David Thorsen realized upon his arrival at La Colombe d'Or hotel—an old but renovated charmer just outside the village's front stone gates—was that Raphael Dumont, based on his Instagram account, likely lived outside the gates as well, in one of the large villas dotting the surrounding hills. He wouldn't exactly be a needle in a haystack, but given that the ramparted main village was less than three square miles in area and filled with off-season tourists, finding the man was going to take some luck.

"Or we can just be strategic about it and look at the location tags in his Instagram photos," Natalie said. Her hair glowed in the afternoon light, which in turn glowed gold on the distant hills. "I saw tags at certain cafés. There's also a church he's tagged multiple times. I took screenshots of them on Google Maps since I knew I wasn't bringing a SIM card. Look."

She pulled the map images up on her phone and showed them to David.

*Café Frei.*

*Café de Paul.*

*La Brouette.*

*Collegiale de la Conversion de Saint Paul.*

"That last one—the church—is a huge tourist spot, and the only Mass schedule I could find was for Saturday nights at 5:00 p.m.," Natalie continued. "So, we missed it yesterday. But it's still decently warm out. Maybe we can sit at these cafés and keep an eye out for him. Or use the Wi-Fi to check his Instagram."

"You're quite the sleuth," David said with a grin.

"He posted a picture at that first café three days ago, so I'm hoping he's at least still in town." Natalie's skin sparkled with the perspiration of travel—they hadn't yet showered since the plane ride to Nice—but her energy, contrary to what it was the night they had met at Saint Andrew's Grotto, dazzled with exhilaration.

OVER THE NEXT WEEK, between sexual rendezvous, they staked out Saint-Paul de Vence, both inside the fortress and out. Within its walls, they walked the ornately decorated cobblestone streets and alleys, enjoyed the cafés and restaurants, and visited what seemed like endless art galleries. They also stood outside Collegiale de la Conversion de Saint Paul every day and held out photos of Victor Zobel and Raphael Dumont to anyone who looked local, hoping someone might know one or both of the men. While everyone knew Victor Zobel's face, nobody would share the location of his family's old house. Most locals shook their heads with uncertainty, suggesting that David and Natalie weren't the first fans to search out the controversial celebrity who had spent much of his childhood in their hills.

One woman, however—a gallery owner and artist named Sylvie— frowned when she saw Raphael Dumont's face on Natalie's phone.

"Ah, this man," she said in heavily accented English. "He breaks hearts." She tapped the photo with her pointer finger and scoffed. "And yes, he walks by on Saturdays, when he goes to church."

She gestured with her head toward Collegiale de la Conversion de Saint Paul, which was less than two hundred feet away.

"Do you have any idea where he lives?" Natalie asked.

Sylvie nodded. "Yes, a few blocks outside the gates. But I don't know the address." She sighed and turned back to her painting. "But he will be back. He goes to church every Saturday." She pointed again. Then, still looking at her canvas, she cocked her head. "Oh, and you know, that man Victor Zobel—his mother once threw a fit just there, outside the church. My mother used to talk about it when I was a girl."

"Oh really?" David said. "What about?"

Sylvie shrugged. "I don't know. Mother never said."

*Yet another bread crumb*, David thought. But he had to reserve judgment. Even bread crumbs sometimes led to those who left them.


On Saturday night, David and Natalie attended Mass at Collegiale de la Conversion de Saint Paul. Since neither of them was Catholic, they sat in the back pew and simply observed. While the church itself was small, solemn, and quiet, the priest at the front—a beady-eyed bearded Frenchman of perhaps forty—spoke with a level of religious conviction David almost envied.

For the first few minutes of the Mass, it verged on relaxing to simply let go of life's ills and listen to the prayers. But then came an interruption: a younger man arriving five minutes late, walking almost antagonistically to the front pew while someone gave Bible readings in French from the pulpit. The newcomer walked with a swagger, his tied-back ponytail failing to cover the snake tattoo coiled around his neck.

It was him. Raphael Dumont.

David tapped Natalie's leg.

"I know, I know," she whispered, subtly holding up her iPhone to record the man on video.

Their hearts raced in tandem until Mass ended. As people filed out of the church, they lingered near the door outside, where Raphael was talking with an overt type of friendliness to the beady-eyed priest. Natalie surreptitiously snapped photos as the priest seemingly tried to get away, but Raphael continued to engage him, as though purposefully trying to make the older man uncomfortable.

When the priest finally managed to break free, Raphael smiled, then strolled away from the church, down the narrow cobblestone street leading back toward the village gates. David and Natalie followed.


Once the enclosed village center was behind them, David and Natalie followed Raphael up a street called Route de Vence, then left on another called Chemin Notre Dame. Midway up the latter, the man stopped at the gate of a large villa and looked directly at them.

"*Puis-je vous aider*?" he said.

David was the one to hesitate. Natalie, however, wasted no time. Holding her iPhone stealthily in her left hand, she took five steps toward Raphael and said, "Mr. Dumont? My name is Natalie Pent. We met in End Haven, Minnesota, two years ago."

Raphael suddenly stood taller. Stiffer.

Natalie grabbed David's hand, and they continued toward him.

"We're here to ask you some questions, if you don't mind," she continued. "Could we talk for a second?"

Raphael, unmoving, let them approach. He glanced only fleetingly at the oddly angled phone in Natalie's left hand.

THE YOUNG WOMAN did most of the interrogating. She asked Raphael about everything: the conversation he'd had with Jillian Pope the day of the Sparks-house gas explosion; his presence in Idle County the day Lindsay and the others disappeared; Victor Zobel's possible misdirection away from the rocky ravine in the Moon Woods during the searches that followed; and—finally—any knowledge he might have about what Victor Zobel was now building in that forest.

When Natalie finished, Raphael smiled for an uncomfortably long moment. Then he asked, "Are you finished?"

Natalie, breathing hard, didn't grace him with a response.

And that's when Raphael began laughing in their faces. When he seemed good and satisfied with the absurdity of their visit—and this final Hail Mary of a confrontation—he flashed his eyebrows up and down in what seemed like good humor, then walked through the villa's gate.

David and Natalie never saw him again.

On September 23, 2040, Dominic Bock sat alone in his new month-to-month apartment in Corpus Christi, Texas, playing this past summer's events over and over in his head, trying to make sense of everything that had happened. All he had for company now were his generic art prints, cheap furniture, and ActoPhone. If his wife, Carolyn, had her way—and if this wasn't simply a major bump in their sixteen-year marriage—this empty apartment would be his home for the foreseeable future.

On Dominic's phone screen now was an article from *Scientific American* about the psychic physicist Rebecca Sparks. Its title and subheading, dated yesterday, seemed to articulate the reason for his life's sudden emptiness.

### Will Inward "Science" Ever Be Science?

*Rebecca Sparks's (a.k.a. Dorothy Garland's) outing as a*

*supposed "psychic" would place her in the crackpot pile if her proposed "Theory of Everything" didn't offer enticing possibilities for testability. But will its blatant incorporation of consciousness mark the end of science as we know it?*

As the article dug into the increasingly intriguing details of Rebecca Sparks's Theory of Everything—particularly the idea that every conscious entity created its own multiverse—Dominic sensed that it marked a fundamental shift in the way humanity would soon be looking at existence. While he was only just beginning to grasp the concept of higher-dimensional physics creating the rules for this hologram-like reality, he wanted to learn more. To *know* more.

Carolyn, of course, wanted nothing to do with speculative metaphysical questions. Somehow, for her, a simplistic belief in Jesus was enough, and curiosity about the unknown—not to mention acknowledgment of it—had no place in her cognitively dissonant bubble.

Earlier today, Dominic had driven north to visit his girls at Comfort Café in San Antonio. While saying goodbye to his oldest daughter, Anna, he had leaned in for a hug, only to hear her whisper, *"I don't hate you. I just want you to know."*

Now this: the result of his choices. His family had left him, and Jonathan Flite, the son he had chosen to love, was on his own trajectory, intending to find impossible answers to the nature of his own existence.

Dominic glanced at his ActoPhone, which sat next to an untouched Rob Roy on the cheap end table alongside his new couch. For almost a full minute, he stared at the phone as if it were his only portal to the outside world.

Suddenly, the phone buzzed. Winifred Flite's name lit up the caller ID.

He picked up on the second ring, but before he could even say hello, Winifred said, in mildly slurred words, "Well, Jonathan's going to Staaar Island."

Dominic's heart sank. "Jesus. After all that."

"Yes, after all that."

"Is he going alone?"

"No. Tom Luuumen and two FBI agents are going with him. Victor Zobel said Jonathan and the agents can liiive stream the entire thinggg to assure everyone feels safe."

"Live stream to what? His ActoChannel?"

"I'm guessssing so. I'm sure Clovia Bell will also waaant the footage for this little documentary she's making."

"Part two of *WorldLine*," Dominic said, almost growling.

"Did you heeear anything more from the FBI about the Olyyympic Peninsula? Did theyyy find that poison vial?"

The question triggered terrible memories in Dominic's mind: the gunshots and screams in that secluded forest; Raphael Dumont's bloody, gaping exit wound; and the man's face-first collapse onto the yurt's floor, which was the last moment Dominic had seen the tiny vial.

"No—it wasn't in Gianna's yurt," he finally said, remembering how the police had been unable to find the pill-sized container. "I'm almost a hundred percent sure Raphael dropped it on the floor, though. Why do you ask?"

As always, he could almost hear Winifred purse her lips. After all these years, it was still obvious when she was feeling uncertain.

"No reason—just curious," the woman finally said with a freshness that immediately betrayed the fact that she was lying. As if to deflect his confusion over why she would still be worrying about the missing poison, she added, "And how are youuu?"

The question echoed through Dominic's heart. From outside, he heard the sound of traffic, seagulls, and boats. The world, moving on around him.

"I'm alone," he told Winifred. "I feel like I pulled my own rug out from under me by welcoming Jonathan into my life."

When she laughed in response, Dominic knew better than to take offense. While hints of Winifred's old sharpness had slowly made a comeback in the year since their reunion, she still seemed lighter than she was twenty years ago. More free.

"Did I ever tell you whaaat I learned durrring my coma?" she asked.

Light slowly filled the hollowness in Dominic's chest. "No, you didn't."

"Well, it was thiiis: that none of us are ever alone. Not ever. Don't youuu forget that."

With that, and since idle chatter was difficult for Winifred Flite even on a good day, she ended the call, leaving Dominic to find the meaning in his Saturday morning—and in the choices that might light his path forward.

On October 26, 2040, Clovia Bell arrived on Dr. Cora Crowe's doorstep with her small video camera, a mini tripod, and a weekend's worth of luggage. It had been almost a year and a half since *WorldLine*'s shoot here in Boulder, and today, snow dusted the city's famous Flatirons, which lay just west of Dr. Crowe's gated community.

It was a relief to be back here without the *WorldLine* crew—no eight-part documentary to worry about, no psyche-permeating concerns about how people might receive it. Because, yes, they already had their answer. Over the past four months, people of all types—curious spiritualists, religious devotees, and even some secular scientists—had begun descending upon Idle County in larger numbers than ever before. It seemed to be a pilgrimage destination nobody yet knew how to describe. Clovia wondered what, if anything, this new interest in reincarnation, the Moon Woods anomaly, and Rebecca Sparks's correlating Theory of Everything would amount to.

She glanced again at Boulder's jagged Flatirons. They had seen it all: humanity's rise, its tumbles, its evolution. What might they see now, going forward, as society opened its doors—and minds—to new ways of thinking?

When Clovia rang Dr. Crowe's doorbell, the sound of church bells echoed through the house beyond. The chiming, while pleasant, inspired a burst of nervousness. If there was one thing Clovia was hoping to get answers about here, it was the recurring dream that had been plaguing her for the past two years: the burning bedroom, her screams, and the person standing below the open third-floor window, telling her to jump. In the dream, she knew her parents and siblings were dead and that she was an orphan. The only way to survive was to take the leap.

*And maybe I'm doing just that*, she thought. *Maybe those dreams led me here to prepare for whatever comes next.*

When Dr. Crowe answered the door, her bright blue eyes sparkled as if Clovia were an old friend. "Clovia Bell! How lovely to see your face again!" She immediately extended her arms and took Clovia into a hug. "Sorry it took me a second to get to the door—I was putting in a load of laundry. How are you doing? How's our dear boy Jonathan?"

"We're both okay," Clovia said. "Except Jonathan finally decided to take Victor Zobel's bait. He leaves for the Star Island training program in two weeks."

With a raised eyebrow, Dr. Crowe ushered Clovia inside. "He's going up alone?"

"No. He'll be with two FBI agents and Dr. Lumen, that psychiatrist friend from Minnesota. He's worried about causing more deaths, but we all insisted he needed at least some protection."

"And how do you feel about it?"

"Oh, I'm hiding in work, as usual," Clovia said with a melancholic shrug. "And I love him. I know that now. But it's just . . . I feel like he's being reckless. Like maybe he's seeing his life as a source of pain for other people and doesn't care about his own safety anymore. I'm trying to keep him busy with this new documentary we decided to make, but of course he wants his visit with Victor Zobel to be part of it."

"And you're wanting to film your regressions here as part of this new project?" Dr. Crowe asked, eyeing Clovia's camera bag.

Clovia fought the self-conscious flutters in her heart. "That's the plan. Except this time, we don't quite know what the final product will be. But there was something Rebecca Sparks said to me last year, a few weeks after the *WorldLine* office bombing. It got me thinking."

"Oh? What about?"

"She said Jonathan and I were task companions. That we made certain agreements with each other 'before coming into this life.' I'm curious what that could mean, even though I still don't a hundred percent believe in reincarnation."

Dr. Crowe grinned. "Well, I've said it before, and I'll say it again: belief doesn't matter with what I do. Like Rebecca Sparks said to Alice Winterblume on *WorldLine*, 'reincarnation' is just a word that describes a concept. It may or may not apply to what we're doing, and it may or may not be real. The thing that matters with regressions is whether or not they help you. And don't worry—if you're embarrassed to be here, you're not the first. Just try to keep an open mind, and don't beat yourself up about it. The people who do that are usually the ones who don't see any progress."

Clovia nodded politely, but she wasn't yet comfortable enough to tell Dr. Crowe about the other things bothering her: Rebecca Sparks's motive for asking Jonathan to lie about the 2007 gas explosion; what Jonathan's loyalty to the woman might mean, longer term; and how she, Clovia, was supposed to navigate the flood of direct messages now inundating her ActoHub inbox. Would she ever be equipped to handle not just the fame that had accompanied Jonathan into her life but also the pleas for help from people trying to navigate this new, slowly dawning existential crisis?

Dr. Crowe, appearing to sense Clovia's twirl of emotions, raised her eyebrows. "You can be real with me, honey. What else are you looking to uncover here?"

Self-consciousness rose from Clovia's chest and rouged her face. "I guess I just want to see if Jonathan and I might have been together before, in some other life. There are a few feelings I haven't been able to shake."

She thought back to that second day in Idle County, when *WorldLine*'s cameras captured her reaction to the tan house on Lemon Avenue—the one that had once belonged to Mrs. Grime, the revered librarian. In Clovia's mind, the house had been the wrong color. It should have been blue, with yellow roses out front. Yes, *yellow*—the kind that had always reminded Clovia of angels. She had envisioned the house like this even before Jonathan described on camera Molly Butler's memories of it from the day Mrs. Grime died, when Max Pope had cornered the young girl in its dilapidated basement.

"Make yourself at home, then," Dr. Crowe said, reaching for Clovia's bags. "Let me take these up to the guest room."

As Clovia took off her shoes and jacket in the psychiatrist's front foyer, the shell shock of the last two years dissipated—the violence, the deaths, and the controversies surrounding her boyfriend, Jonathan Flite. Right here and now, she was content. This was the beginning of her next step, the very place she needed to be.

W HEN LINDSAY THORSEN WALKED into the Fairfax Community Center on March 1 flanked by Molly Butler, Elijah Bryce, and Alan Sparks, she was happy. True, she couldn't participate in Coach Martinez's tournament due to her recent head injuries, but she was excited to be here, supporting her friends and feeling safe.

Her therapist, Katerina, had now asked twice whether she was having any nightmares, flashbacks, or panic attacks relating to the incident with Lowell Grendel in the mine ("Nope, nope, nope") or perhaps general anxiety and trouble focusing in school (again, "Nope" and "Nope"). Lindsay knew the woman was merely looking for signs of post-traumatic stress. Still, by all measures—and despite the fact that Drew's absence in her family had now become its own type of ghost—she felt oddly equipped to tackle each new day.

Two nights ago, however, while Googling PTSD on her own time,

Lindsay had found one symptom that gave her pause, which Katerina hadn't mentioned.

*Emotional numbness.*

Was that why she wasn't more disturbed from almost being killed by Lowell Grendel? Because she could no longer feel?

Lindsay didn't know. What she did know was that life now felt like a facade, a curtain she so badly wanted to peek behind once more. She had traveled outside her own body and seen proof that her own existence continued past this experience of physical life and perception. In light of this, how could she be afraid? How, too, could she ever fully engage with life again?

One thing she did know was that the past year's traumas wouldn't define her, because they had illuminated the single most important bit of knowledge she would ever have: that nothing on this planet could end her.

And so she laughed as Elijah and Molly bickered on their way into kickboxing. She clung to Alan's hand while cheekily lamenting the fact that she wouldn't get to beat him in Coach Martinez's tournament. She decided that life with friends—with people who truly understood her— was very, very worth living, at least for now.

Still, Lindsay could feel herself waiting, longing, and preparing for that moment when she would earn another glimpse beyond the veil.

N OT EVEN ROSE MARGARET LAYTON heard the gunshots underneath the Moon Woods on the night of July 4, 2010. Like those caught in the fray, she was too mesmerized by the mysterious anomaly on the far side of the cave's underground river to do much good. From her vantage point, the aberration looked like the brightest light she had ever seen, and it felt like a warm bath—a stronger-than-ever pull toward a state of mind she still, even after all these years of bodily death, couldn't embrace.

The teenagers bursting under the gunshots had all dropped their flashlights, which now lit the cave from seven disconcerting angles. Among the dying was Lindsay Thorsen, the boy Drew's sister, whom Rose had once helped escape that fateful abandoned mine in Arrowhead Hills. Had the girl any idea that one of the small skeletons now lodged against the rocks lining the pooled river water belonged to her long-lost brother? That the waterfall chasm he had been tossed down near Idle County's notable Old Mill had washed him here, to this very cavern? The water had lain his body gently on the rocky shore of a small pool separating the cave's main floor from the spot where this aberration—this *gateway*—hovered. Here still were Drew's remains, now just one set of bones among many, a harbinger of what his dying sister and her friends would soon become.

And there was someone else in the cave tonight besides the seven teenagers and the three gun-toting men—an emaciated figure sitting on the closer side of the underground river, right inside the fray of bullets. This man's mind had long since been pulled toward the light, and now his body was finally seeing the promise of letting go.

Rose knew the aberration in this cave was like a sieve for the minds of the living, a pulled-back curtain that forced people to acclimate to the truth or succumb to it. Rose herself was on the verge, but she couldn't yet succumb. She still had more to do, because these men—the ones shooting their guns—couldn't simply continue their lives unpunished.

But oh, how easily these dying teenagers were embracing the light! As blood soaked their bullet wounds, Rose could feel their resolve. Perhaps even their relief.

She turned away from them so she could identify the tall blond man screaming orders from the ancient stone steps leading down into the cave from the world above. And yes, he might have been handsome were it not for his overly tan skin and the derangement in his eyes. For no reason Rose could ascertain, his two henchmen—one who was bald, muscled, and pockmarked and another who had oily black hair and a snake tattoo coiled around his neck—listened to him without question. They inched down the steps, toward the cave's main floor, which preceded the underground river.

"Shoot them all in the fucking heads!" the blond leader screamed as he watched the teenagers—including the fighters among them—fall one by one.

He was the one who shot the last of them—a teenage girl with flowing red hair named Jillian. Whether he also saw the girl's spirit detach from her body, Rose knew not; but the girl was now standing *here*, on *this* side of life, looking not just relieved but also joyful. She walked as if on air toward the emaciated male figure sitting by the river, putting a ghostly hand on his shoulder just as bullets ripped through his cadaverous chest.

*They're at peace with each other and with death,* Rose thought. *Just like I should be.*

But no.

Rose couldn't join these people in the light. Not yet. She was here because of the men with guns. She had a job to do.

Her raging screams blended with chaos as the blond-haired leader—Victor, his name was—fell to his knees and grabbed his temples. He pressed his eyes shut and gritted his teeth together like rocks as the aberration on the far side of the underground river drilled open his mind.

The tattooed man, whose name was Raphael, wasn't as affected. He knelt next to Victor in an effort to help, but the older man only batted him away and spit out an order to get the kids' car keys and cell phones, along with an old leather book one of the dying boys was carrying. "Get them, get them, get them!" the vicious man screamed. His voice echoed through the cavern.

But his more muscular henchman, the pockmarked one named Theo, was closest to the seven teenagers. He was young—perhaps in his early twenties—yet he inched across the cave's stone floor like a terrified child. Rose didn't know if he could actually see the mysterious, powerful light on the far side of the underground river, but it was clear he could feel it, because he suddenly grew still. Then he collapsed.

Panic.

Pandemonium.

Victor shrieked as he sent Raphael down the stone steps to fetch the car keys, cell phones, and leather book. Upon reaching the teenagers, Raphael staggered, held his head for a moment, and then found his footing once again before snatching up the items he came for. On his way back to the stairs, he stopped next to Theo, slapped him awake, and pulled him up.

They stumbled together toward Victor, then followed him up the cave's ancient passageway, away from the aberration that was pulling back the mental filters separating them from death.

Rose, too, pried herself away from the aberration, then set out after the murderers, screaming curse after furious curse.

THE MEN WERE LUCKY ENOUGH to escape the forest cave without blood on their clothes—including Raphael, who had managed to pocket the teenagers' car keys and phones after giving Victor the leather book, which looked brittle enough to disintegrate under the raindrops now falling one by one from the sky.

But they weren't free of trouble yet. Victor the monster was already spewing more orders to Theo and Raphael.

"Cover up any footprints!"

"Close the cave opening with rocks, but mark it so we can find it again!"

"Take their cars south! Wear hats, and make sure no street cameras catch you on your way out of town!"

"*Now, now, now!*"

The men got to work.

IT WAS THUNDERING AND WILDLY POURING RAIN when Victor staggered out of the woods alone, holding the old leather book and whispering rage-filled nothings to himself. He was panting. Panicking.

Finally worrying that the house of cards he had built around his life was about to crumble. He had killed before, yes—but this? This would be his greatest test.

The very fact that he viewed tonight's murders in such a cold, clinical light only fueled Rose's rage. She screamed at him louder and louder with each step, willing him to perceive her.

Victor's rental car was parked on the road that circled the vast forest. Soaking wet, he climbed into the vehicle and forced himself to breathe.

Rose, ever enraged, drove herself into his space—into his breath, his lungs, his mind.

*"You terrible man!"* she screamed. *"You killed those children in cold blood, just so you could hide what's in that cave! The shame you must feel!"*

Victor twitched in the driver's seat.

Had he heard her?

No. He pressed the car's Start button, drove south on Old Mill Road, and took the back roads out of Idle County.

At sunrise, he reached a small airport in Iowa, where a white airplane—sleeker and more modern than any Rose had seen during life—waited for him on a quiet runway. His clothes were still damp from the rain, and his hair was disheveled.

He tried to straighten himself out.

To fix the imperfections.

To paste on a smile.

After placing the rental car's key atop its front right tire, he left the vehicle in the airport's small parking lot and boarded the plane. Rose followed.

The plane's engines roared to life as Victor sat back in one of the comfortable leather seats. Now that it was just them together, Rose could read his thoughts, and they were chaos: all focused on himself, on whether he would be able to hide what he had just done in the cave beneath the forest. Yet he was also fascinated by the aberration there—that break in the illusion of space-time. He wanted to study it. He *needed* to.

As Victor closed his eyes and tried to find a comfortable position in his seat, Rose lost herself once again in her usual mess of hatred, frustration, and broken concentration. Her energy flickered through time and circumstances, projecting over and over into the events from the cave and even into those that had come before: the murderers' joint trek into the Moon Woods after the seven teenagers; their discovery of the ancient stone stairway carved into the earth; their failure to notice a blue Thai candy wrapper accidentally dropped by the girl Lindsay Thorsen, who now lay among the dead.

For what seemed like both an instant and a thousand more years, Rose fumbled through this ever-shifting angle of reality, seeking hints of anything that might bring justice to the dead teenagers. She walked and rewalked into the cursed forest over and over, vaguely aware of her own timelessness—and of those still living who would eventually come and go over the years, tangled by similar emotions.

Conversely (and as always), she sensed the shadow of a long-ignored truth amid her endless circles: that she needed to escape her own rage. Because that was the reason she was stuck in this perpetual in-between place, was it not? If she could never let go of Earth's toils, how could she ever expect to move on?

Knowing her very soul was at stake, Rose harnessed all her energy, scattered as it was, and refocused on the murderer sitting in the airplane.

Victor twitched in his seat a second time.

*"It's people like you who've kept me here!"* she wailed. *"I need to let go, but I don't know how to stop caring!"*

The man twitched a third time.

And then it happened suddenly. As Victor Zobel's plane lifted into the air, his eyes burst open and made contact with Rose, who was floating right in front of his contorted tan face. His acknowledgment of her was immediate, and in the hair-raising moments it took for his belief system about life and death to shift, the spectrum of his humanity—and of his *soul*—became perceptible to Rose.

This man had his own pains. His own hurts and wounds. They ran very deep indeed, to the part of his essence that was most fragile and most human. Rose now saw what had happened to make him this way, and, oh, it unveiled the truest, deepest, and most difficult meaning of compassion she had ever perceived.

Thus, at the very same moment Victor's mind shattered irrevocably, Rose's heart burst open. In that rush of forgiveness and eternal relief, she remembered what she should have recalled all along: that life on Earth was all a game, and everyone playing it was part of a mystery far grander and more beautiful than she had ever dared to imagine.

Finally, Rose turned to acknowledge the light.

Impossibly patient, it had always been waiting.

# ACKNOWLEDGMENTS

This book would not have been possible without the patience of everyone around me, particularly my partner, Benjamin Kimelman, who stuck by my side during all the ups and downs, the doubts, and the adjacent venture into San Francisco's tech industry. I also owe a debt of gratitude to everyone at that tech job, particularly Laura Moon, who supported my swerve back toward freelancing so I could pursue my writing goals.

As always, I must also thank my sister Mara, the reader I write for and my best friend/soulmate. The scariest parts of this book were my own attempts to mentally process her near kidnapping as a child. I'm so incredibly thankful that, out of pure luck, the probabilities *didn't* settle on that outcome. Mara, I don't know what I'd do without you.

Thank you to my other beta readers: Ana Beier and Amy Meyer, each of whom provided different and invaluable types of feedback.

Next, I'd like to thank my amazing new proofreader, Angie Wiechmann, along with Christine Zuchora-Walske for the referral. Thanks also to Troy Holland and Tim Henry, who helped me with challenging wording here and there.

Thanks also to all the real people who inspired characters in this book. First comes the real Lindsay Thorsen, who (almost fifteen years ago now!) lent me both her name and her love of kickboxing to use in this book. Lindsay, I know we haven't seen each other since then, but you've been in my mind tangentially this entire time! Next comes the person who inspired the character Rebecca Sparks. This series wouldn't exist without her. Finally comes Ms. Olson, my seventh grade English teacher, who didn't just teach me how to write essays. She also taught me what it looked like to be a proud member of the LGBTQ+ community before I was brave enough to embrace my place in it openly.

Also deserving major thanks is Dr. Brian Weiss, author of *Many Lives, Many Masters* and multiple other books that discuss the concepts that play into this story. Both he and my Heart Mom friend, Marina Baer, inspired the character Dr. Cora Crowe.

Thank you to my friends, new and old, who brought me varying types of joy or inspiration over the last four years, particularly Stabe (my life rock, as always), Allison DeLise, Nina Rush, Mel Alexander, Frank Gelat, Becca Schall, Katy Hooks, Leah Gift, Crystal Yescas, Anna Sederberg, Jim Provines, Michael Alexin, Jordan Wiklund, Philip Maret, Matt Russell, Madison Sackett, Liz Dolan Dix, Joe Gardner, Elysia Yeary, Jenn Matsunaga, Danny Nguyen, and Justin Grey (via Instagram, and whose Taylor Swift reaction videos I cannot get enough of).

Finally, I'd like to thank all the artists who inspired me during this "JF3" phase of my life. First has to come Taylor Swift, whose music, talent, writing ability, bottled feelings, and song-stories I finally discovered back in 2014, around the time I started writing the second draft of this book. I listened to her albums countless times during the process! Then come the other usual life inspirations: Stephen King, J.K. Rowling (but yes, I'm ready for a nuanced discussion), Kazuo Ishiguro, Michael Crichton, Audrey Niffenegger, Suzanne Collins, Philip Pullman, George Lucas, Steven Spielberg, David Yates, Peter Jackson, Fran Walsh, Philippa Boyens, Alan Ball, P!nk, Lady Gaga, Jonathan Van Ness, Sia, Kelly Clarkson, James Newton Howard, and all the other brilliant composers and musicians whose music I listened to while writing, editing, and designing.

Hopefully, that does it for the thank-yous—except to whoever is still reading this. Thank *you* for joining me on this step of my journey.

# ABOUT THE AUTHOR

Matthew J. Beier is a novelist, screenwriter, video producer, and visual artist based in the San Francisco Bay Area. In 2012, Matthew published his first novel, *The Breeders*, and in 2014, he began publishing his seven-book Jonathan Flite series, which thus far includes *The Confessions of Jonathan Flite*, *The Release of Jonathan Flite*, and *The Rise of Jonathan Flite*. In 2003, he attended film school at Chapman University, where he studied screenwriting, film production, and English before spending a final semester abroad at Victoria University in Wellington, New Zealand. When Matthew isn't working, he enjoys drinking tea, exercising, watching films and streaming television shows, and spending time with his friends and family. He's currently hard at work on the last four books of the Jonathan Flite series, along with multiple TV and film scripts. He would love to hear from you via email at info@matthewjbeier.com, on his Facebook author page, on Twitter @MatthewBeier, or on Instagram @matthewjbeier. You can also join Matthew's exclusive Patreon fan community at www.patreon.com/matthewjbeier.